Secrets Between Friends

By Sheila O'Flanagan

Suddenly Single
Far From Over
My Favourite Goodbye
He's Got to Go
Isobel's Wedding
Caroline's Sister
Too Good to be True
Dreaming of a Stranger
The Moment We Meet
Anyone But Him
How Will I Know?
The Season of Change
Yours, Faithfully
Bad Behaviour
Someone Special
The Perfect Man
Stand By Me
Christmas With You
All For You
Better Together
Things We Never Say
If You Were Me
My Mother's Secret
The Missing Wife
What Happened That Night
The Hideaway
Her Husband's Mistake
The Women Who Ran Away
Three Weddings and a Proposal
What Eden Did Next
The Woman on the Bridge
The Honeymoon Affair
Secrets Between Friends

SHEILA O'FLANAGAN

THE NO.1 BESTSELLING AUTHOR

Secrets Between Friends

REVIEW

Copyright © 2026 Sheila O'Flanagan

The right of Sheila O'Flanagan to be identified as the Author of
the Work has been asserted by her in accordance with the
Copyright, Designs and Patents Act 1988.

First published in 2026 by Headline Review
An imprint of Headline Publishing Group Limited

1

Apart from any use permitted under UK copyright law, this publication may
only be reproduced, stored, or transmitted, in any form, or by any means,
with prior permission in writing of the publishers or, in the case
of reprographic production, in accordance with the terms of
licences issued by the Copyright Licensing Agency.

All characters in this publication are fictitious and any resemblance
to real persons, living or dead, is purely coincidental.

Cataloguing in Publication Data is available from the British Library

Hardback ISBN 978 1 0354 3235 6
Trade Paperback ISBN 978 1 0354 3231 8

Typeset in ITC Galliard Std by Palimpsest Book Production Ltd, Falkirk, Stirlingshire

Printed and bound in Great Britain by Clays Ltd, Elcograf S.p.A.

Headline's policy is to use papers that are natural, renewable and recyclable products
and made from wood grown in sustainable forests. The logging and manufacturing
processes are expected to conform to the environmental regulations
of the country of origin.

Headline Publishing Group Limited
An Hachette UK Company
Carmelite House
50 Victoria Embankment
London EC4Y 0DZ

The authorised representative in the EEA is Hachette Ireland,
8 Castlecourt Centre, Dublin 15, D15 XTP3, Ireland
(email: info@hbgi.ie)

www.headline.co.uk
www.hachette.co.uk

To Jean

Chapter 1

It was the unexpected splash of pink among the sombre blacks and greys that caught Ailie's attention. An umbrella, she realised, carried by a tall, angular woman in a dark green raincoat, a matching leather bag over her shoulder. The woman's silver-white hair was short and well cut, and she wore a pair of stylish tortoiseshell glasses that added to her aura of quiet determination. She walked with purpose, the umbrella shielding her from the persistent drizzle that had been falling since early morning. Ailie wondered if she was an ex-colleague of Giorgio's, one of the few she hadn't yet met.

Despite the misery of the day, she was unexpectedly cheered by the brightness of the pink umbrella and the subtle elegance of the confident woman. Her gaze remained fixed on her even as she walked past the group of mourners standing on the steps of the crematorium and followed the narrow path that led to the older part of the cemetery, where family plots were located beneath tall trees. It was a serene and peaceful setting, although some of the older graves were so neglected that the headstones were cracked and mossy, the people in them now forgotten.

Not a colleague, thought Ailie, as the woman disappeared out of sight. Nothing at all to do with today's funeral. She closed her eyes and swallowed the lump in her throat.

'I'm sorry for your loss.'

The man who'd walked up to her while she'd been following the progress of the woman with the pink umbrella reached out his hands and clasped hers within them. Ailie smiled and thanked him for coming. She recognised his face, although she couldn't remember his name.

'He was one of the good guys,' the man said as he released his hold on her. 'A real gent. It was a privilege to know him.'

'That's kind of you,' she said, and thanked him again.

So many thank-yous. So many people telling her how great Giorgio was. What a shock his death had been. How much they'd miss him. But for how long would they miss him? she asked herself, thinking of the forgotten graves beneath the trees. A week? A month? A year? She doubted it would be that long. She was pretty sure his desk had already been reallocated. His card key deprogrammed. His work divided out between his colleagues. That was what happened in big business, after all. It would be his family who would never forget him: Marco and Flavia and Ailie herself. And those from Italy, who would hold him close in their hearts while happily wiping all memories of his marriage to her and pretending it had never happened.

Let them try, she thought.

'Would you like to get in the car now?' The undertaker asked the question, his tone professionally sympathetic.

Ailie nodded, and signalled to Marco and Flavia, who were standing side by side. They came over to her.

'We're leaving,' she said.

Secrets Between Friends

Flavia nodded and got into the black Mercedes. Marco followed her. Ailie joined them. The car slowly pulled away, leaving behind the woman with the pink umbrella, and everyone else visiting their loved ones' resting places on All Souls' Day.

Ailie had reserved a space in Giorgio's favourite gastropub for refreshments after his cremation. Those mourners who had arrived before her had already clustered into groups: Giorgio's friends and colleagues, friends of Marco and Flavia, Ailie's own friends and family. Although the Marchettis had arrived in the car behind her, they walked in ahead: his sisters, Sara and Mia, and his brother, Antonio. Not his mother, who was elderly and too infirm to travel. And not Chiara, the youngest of the siblings, who'd stayed behind to take care of Signora Marchetti at this time of sorrow. None of the husbands had come either, while Sophia, Giorgio's glamorous ex-wife, had remained in Italy too, for which Ailie was profoundly relieved. She'd been very afraid that Sophia might turn up with Marco, and that would have been too much to bear.

She sighed at the complications of extended, blended families. She supposed hers was no more complicated than many others, but it always seemed to be on a knife edge of possible conflict. Mainly because of Sophia, still beloved by the Italians. And also because of Signora Marchetti, the ninety-year-old matriarch who ruled them all with a rod of iron. It was because Giorgio hadn't wanted to be ruled that he'd left, even though, as he told her afterwards, it had been the hardest thing he'd ever done. And even though he constantly had to balance the life he'd made in Dublin with his family commitments in Trieste.

It was almost impossible to believe that their first meeting had been over twenty years ago. Ailie remembered how often she'd rolled her eyes and shrugged her shoulders as a teenager when her mother had said things like 'it seems like only yesterday' when talking about her own childhood. To Ailie, back then, it had been the Dark Ages. But now things that had happened years ago truly did seem as though they'd taken place in the recent past, no matter how crazy that was. Flavia, at eighteen, was living proof of how the years had flown by.

The memory of Giorgio's first visit to the dental clinic where Ailie worked as an administrator was clear. He'd come to the desk and pointed to his broken front tooth – smashed, he said, when he was bundled into a goalpost during a five-a-side football match. He told her he was hoping for an appointment right away, because he had meetings with clients later in the week and he couldn't possibly call on them looking the way he was now. Despite the broken tooth, he was a handsome man who carried himself with an innate sense of assurance and style. Ailie was surprised at the Italian name, given that his hair was a reddish-blonde that could have been pure Irish, and his eyes a luminous hazel, more green than grey. She told him that he was lucky, because the dentist had a cancellation and would be able to see him shortly, although it would take time to have a crown made for the tooth, so there was no chance of him having a perfect smile by the end of the week.

He was still sitting in the waiting room when she went for lunch at the café across the plaza. She was tucking into peach pie when she saw him walk in and order a cold drink and a sandwich. He saw her too and smiled as he approached her table. He thanked her for getting him the appointment, while acknowledging that he'd been foolish in hoping that a new crown would be available in a couple of days. But the dentist had been able to fit a temporary one so at first glance his teeth appeared fine.

Even now she didn't know what had made her say yes when he asked if he could join her. She liked being alone at lunchtime. But Giorgio was charming, and soon they were chatting like old friends He told her that he was a management consultant and had come to Ireland a few months earlier, having been offered an excellent opportunity with a global company based in Dublin.

'What exactly does a management consultant do?' she asked.

'Basically help businesses to do better,' he said. 'Advise them, work out strategies, that sort of thing.'

'You did that in Italy before coming here?'

'Yes. At first I worked in our small family business, then with a company in Rome, but it became complicated and I needed to move on.'

Ailie was about to ask about the complications, but then realised that she had exactly two minutes of her lunch hour left. She apologised to him for rushing away and said she might see him again when he returned for his permanent crown. Back at her desk, she checked when it was scheduled for, at the same time noting that he was forty-two, five years older than her, living in Blackrock, an upmarket coastal town outside the city, and, like her, divorced.

Then Marissa Lange arrived for her root canal treatment and Ailie forgot about Giorgio Marchetti, because Marissa was a nervous patient and had to be treated with calm understanding and lots of support.

She didn't think about him again until the day he showed up to have the crown fitted. When he came out of the dentist's room, he turned the full power of his repaired smile in her direction.

'I feel normal again,' he said as she took payment from him. 'The last few weeks have been horrible. I was embarrassed every time I opened my mouth.'

'But you had the temporary crown,' Ailie said. 'You looked fine.'

'I was very self-conscious,' said Giorgio. 'I disliked meeting clients face to face. I did as much of my work on the phone as I could, but that's not how it should be.'

'Well, you look great now,' she assured him. 'You can be confident about meeting anyone.'

'I am.' He smiled again. 'And I wondered . . . would you like to have dinner with me?'

'Dinner?' She looked at him in surprise.

'Or a drink,' he said. 'In Italy I would be more used to saying dinner, but I know in Ireland there is the pub, so if you'd prefer that . . .'

Ailie was torn between wanting to go to dinner with someone as easy-going and attractive as him, and not wanting to get emotionally involved with anyone, given that the two relationships she'd had since her divorce had ended badly.

'But if not, don't worry,' he said when she remained silent. 'I liked talking to you in the café before. And I thought you liked talking to me. I don't have any girlfriends in Dublin. Not girlfriends,' he amended quickly. 'Friends who are women. It would be nice to talk to a woman. Most of my colleagues are men. Most of my clients too, which is not a good thing really.'

She laughed then, and said OK, and they arranged to meet in an Italian restaurant in Blackrock that he assured her was authentic, the owners coming from a town not far from his own.

Giorgio was good company, and when he told her he'd grown up in a family of three girls and two boys with his widowed mother being the lynchpin that held it all together, she understood why he was so at ease talking with women.

'To be honest,' he said, as they enjoyed a nightcap in the pub next door after their meal, 'I was very tired of all the women in my life when I left Italy. But I miss them now.'

'Were they part of the complications?' she asked.

'A little,' he replied. 'It's hard to be businesslike with family sometimes.'

'How often do you go back?' she asked.

'Not at all yet.' His words were cautious. 'I needed some time away. But I miss my country.'

'I've never been to Italy,' she said. 'I keep saying I'll go to Rome some day, but . . . well, life gets in the way.'

'Hopefully you'll visit us,' he said. 'Naturally I'm biased towards my part of Italy. Trieste is closer to Slovenia than Rome, but it's very beautiful. My family home is a few kilometres outside the city, with views over the Adriatic.'

'Sounds nearly as nice as Blackrock,' she said, and he laughed.

The next time they went out together, she asked about his ex-wife.

'Do you mind if we talk about her another time?' he asked. 'I'm not sure I'm able to speak about the divorce in a good way yet.'

'Was it messy?' Ailie looked at him quizzically.

'Unfortunately, yes.'

'In that case, I won't mention it again,' she assured him. 'I was lucky with mine. There was no bitterness. We both realised we'd married too young and wanted different things. Josh has a new wife now and a couple of kids, and he's happy out.'

'Do you keep in touch?'

'No, but for a while he lived close by me and I bumped into him from time to time. Not any more, though; they've moved to Carlow.'

'And you're happy?' he asked.

'Marrying him was a mistake. Divorcing him wasn't. I'm very happy.' She was going to add that today was the happiest she'd been since then, but decided that made her sound overenthusiastic, so she said nothing.

But she knew she was falling for Giorgio Marchetti.

He was a very easy man to fall for.

She felt a tap on her shoulder and returned from the past to the present. Her brother's wife, Maggie, was standing beside her.

'Are you all right?' she asked.

Ailie nodded.

'You should have some soup,' said Maggie.

Ailie nodded again. The other mourners were now finding seats at the round tables, dividing themselves into the factions they'd been in before. All of the Marchettis were together, along with Marco and Flavia. It wasn't entirely unexpected to see Flavia sitting with them. Ailie's daughter with Giorgio and Giorgio's son with Sophia were close, and she knew Marco would keep an eye on his half-sister; he was unfailingly kind towards her. But the rest of the family were less so, although somehow this seemed not to bother Flavia in the slightest. She was smiling now, Ailie saw, and finding a seat beside Chiara's daughter, Beatrice, who'd come to the funeral in place of her mother. Beatrice was a few years younger than Marco and the two had always got along. It looked like she was getting along with Flavia too, for which Ailie was very grateful.

As she studied the occupants of the table, she caught the gaze of the oldest of the Marchetti sisters. At sixty-two, Sara was very much like photos of old Signora Marchetti at the same age, with her almost oblong face and her eyes, hazel like Giorgio's, impeccably made up. But while Signora Marchetti had looked like an elderly woman in the photos, Sara's skin was smooth and barely lined. Her dark blonde hair was shoulder length, without any traces of grey, and she was wearing a black suit trimmed with cream fur. She was as effortlessly stylish as her brother had always been.

Sara had spoken very briefly to Ailie at the service, saying that Giorgio's death was a family tragedy and that they were all broken-hearted it had happened so far from home. Then she'd swept to her seat, leaving Ailie standing alone in the aisle, the riposte that Giorgio *had* been at home coming too late to her to be of any use.

'Soup?' repeated Maggie.

Ailie dragged her gaze away from Sara Marchetti and allowed Maggie to steer her towards her own family. The Taylors took up four tables because her brothers and sisters, their wives and husbands plus their children had all come to the funeral. As some had to travel from her home county of Donegal in the north of the country, and others from the west and the south, it was a show of support that Ailie appreciated.

She slid into her seat, Maggie on one side of her and Deirdre, her younger sister, on the other.

'You doing OK?' asked Deirdre.

'I'm fine. A bit of a headache.'

'Here's some heavy-duty paracetamol.' Deirdre took a blister pack from her bag and handed her a tablet. 'That'll sort you.'

'Thanks.' Ailie swallowed it with some water, although she doubted it would have much effect as the noise level in the room continued to rise from the chatter of the mourners. There were occasional bursts of laughter too, and then some loud shushing when Antonio Marchetti stood up and began to speak in a mixture of English and Italian.

He thanked everyone for coming, and then said what a first-rate man his brother had been and how sad it was that he'd died in a foreign country, and how they'd miss him for the rest of their lives. Ailie felt herself tense at the proprietorial way he was taking control of things, as though he'd been the one who'd organised the funeral and was paying for the refreshments, when the truth was that he'd flown in from Trieste the night before and hadn't spoken to her either prior to his arrival or since.

There was applause after he finished speaking, and a hushed silence as he launched into what he called Giorgio's favourite song, 'Vesti la giubba', a mournful operatic number that Ailie had never heard before. She sat rigidly upright as he sang, conceding that while the song was sad, it was beautiful, and that Antonio had a wonderfully rich voice.

There was more applause afterwards. She worried that

someone else would start to sing because her head couldn't take any more, but fortunately nobody stood up.

'I think I'll go now,' she told Deirdre. 'I'm exhausted.'

'I'll see you home,' Deirdre said.

'There's no need.'

'You need someone with you,' she insisted. 'I'll tell Marco and Flavia it's time to leave.'

'If they want to stay, that's fine,' said Ailie. 'I think Flavia needs the comfort of having him close for a bit.'

Deirdre nodded, then went over to the Marchetti table while Ailie put on her black coat.

'Flavia is going to stay with Marco and Beatrice,' Deirdre told her when she returned. 'Sara says she'll call you in the morning. When are they going back to Italy?'

'Tomorrow afternoon, I think,' said Ailie.

'Good riddance,' said Deirdre.

'Ah, not really,' lied Ailie. 'They're all grieving too.'

She didn't look back as she followed her sister out of the pub.

Chapter 2

Sybil shook the rain from her pink umbrella and placed it in the brass holder in the private hallway outside her apartment. Then she unlocked the apartment door, removed her raincoat and hung it between the tweed jacket and the red anorak already on the coat stand. Despite its undoubted quality, the umbrella hadn't been completely effective against the misty rain that had swirled in all directions while she visited the cemetery. Her hair was slightly damp and had lost some of its shape. But unlike the days when she'd had long, dark tresses, and with a nod to the quality of the products she used on it now, it no longer frizzed manically because of a little bit of rain.

She walked into the kitchen and placed her bag neatly on the alcove shelf above the table. Then she made herself a mug of Earl Grey tea. She took an orange Club Milk biscuit from the jar on the countertop and sat at the table, where she unloaded her iPad, took off her distance specs and zoomed in so that she could read the news headlines without having to bother changing to the reading glasses she knew would be at the bottom of her bag. Not that she was truly interested in what wars were currently being waged, what politician was shamelessly riding out a scandal that would have sunk him in her youth, or what infrastructure project had run catastrophically over budget. In Sybil's sixty-eight years, she had seen all these things before, more than once. Although, she reflected as she bit into the chocolate edge of the Club Milk, not with hourly updates. That was the problem with digital media. Being fed constant information on crises you could do nothing about, and feeling vaguely guilty that you weren't doing anything to solve them. It was exhausting.

Even as she snorted at the updates, a notification arrived from a travel company she'd accidentally subscribed to a few weeks earlier who seemed to think she needed hourly prompts to book a holiday. As she deleted it with a swipe of her finger, it was replaced by a text message. Seeing the name of the sender, she heaved a sigh and reached for her bag. She took out her mobile, and grimaced as she realised she'd missed three calls.

She dug into the bag again and this time retrieved her dark-rimmed reading glasses, which, as she'd suspected, were right at the bottom. She didn't bother putting them on, but held them in front of her nose as she looked at the missed calls as well as the text.

'Oh, for feck's sake,' she muttered as she saw Tansy's name repeated over and over. 'What now?'

Though she knew her sister would have spotted that she'd seen the text, Sybil didn't bother getting back to her straight away. Instead, she finished her biscuit and sipped from her mug of tea, gazing unseeingly from the kitchen to the living room with its expansive views of Dublin Bay. Her thoughts returned to her visit to the cemetery earlier. Theo would have approved. He wasn't buried there (she'd done as he'd asked and scattered his ashes in the bay), but visiting old cemeteries was something they'd enjoyed doing together. Given that they both worked in forward-looking industries, they felt it worthwhile to respect the connection to the past that old cemeteries held. She knew some people might consider it odd that she liked to wander around graveyards, but these days she didn't care what other people thought. As a post-menopausal, childless and now single woman, she'd gone through the being-judged stage of her life and had emerged the other side with no more fucks to give. Besides, visiting the cemetery made her feel connected to Theo in the same way that looking out over the water from the comfort of her apartment did, and she was fine with that no matter what anyone else might think.

She'd almost finished her tea when her phone vibrated on the countertop in front of her. She was debating whether to answer when she noticed that the caller ID showed Claire and not Tansy.

'Hi, honey,' she said.

'Whew, you're alive,' said Claire.

'Why shouldn't I be?'

'Mum rang you earlier and you didn't answer. She texted too. No reply.'

'I was out and somehow managed to put my phone on silent,' said Sybil. 'I only saw her calls a few minutes ago. Did she get you to ring me in the hopes I'd answer you even if I was dead?'

'You *did* answer.' Claire laughed. 'So you're very much alive. Obviously.'

'Obviously,' repeated Sybil.

'Will you call her back?'

'What does she want?'

'I dunno,' said Claire, though her tone wasn't convincing.

'I'll call,' said Sybil. 'But not right now. I'm having tea and biscuits and drying off after being caught in the rain.'

'Oh no! Where were you?' asked Claire.

'Out stretching my legs. Maybe I should get a dog,' Sybil mused. 'Then every time I went out people could think I was walking it. It's more acceptable to be a dog walker than someone on a solitary stroll. And if you caught me talking to myself, I could say I was talking to the dog.'

'Stop it.' Claire laughed again.

'It might keep your mother out of my hair.'

'Probably not, knowing Mum,' said Claire. 'Could you please call her and put her mind at rest.'

'I might do it more often if she stopped treating me like a child who needs a tracking device.'

'You live on your own,' Claire reminded her. 'All she wants is to make sure—'

'That I haven't fallen down the stairs and broken my neck?' interrupted Sybil. 'There are no stairs in my apartment to fall down.'

'I know. But she worries about you.'

'I'm neither elderly nor infirm,' said Sybil. 'At any rate, she's not that much younger than me herself, so I don't know why she needs to fuss so much.'

'Fussing over people is Mum's thing.' Claire's voice was wheedling. 'Come on, Auntie Sybil. Give her a break.'

'Less of your auntie,' retorted her aunt. 'It's been Sybil to you since you were fourteen. I guess you'll text her and say you've spoken to me.'

'Um, yes.'

'Tansy worries far too much about far too little,' said Sybil. 'You can tell her I'll call in shortly.'

'Thanks,' said Claire. 'Love you.'

'Love you too.'

Sybil waited exactly ten minutes before contacting Tansy, who answered immediately.

'So you've finally surfaced.'

'I was out,' said Sybil.

'Anywhere nice?'

She hesitated before telling her sister that she'd been at the cemetery. She might not care about being judged by most people, but Tansy's ability to unsettle her was altogether different.

There was an equally long pause before Tansy spoke.

'Has somebody died?' she asked. 'You didn't say.'

'I didn't go for any specific reason,' replied Sybil.

'It's cold and damp out. Why would you go to a cemetery in the rain for no reason? It's weird. People your age need to guard against becoming weird.'

'I went for a walk, and believe it or not, it's a very calming place to walk through.' Sybil ignored the crack about her age. 'Not at all weird. Also, for context, it was an anniversary visit.'

'You mean because it's All Souls' Day? I didn't think religious feast days meant anything to you.'

'They don't. It's the anniversary of when Theo sold Echo.'

'Oh.' Tansy paused. 'I won't say weird, but it's an odd way of marking a happy occasion.'

'I accept that strolling through a cemetery mightn't be everyone's idea of a good time,' acknowledged Sybil. 'But we both liked to walk there and it seemed the right thing to do today.'

'Are you OK?' asked Tansy. 'Really?'

'I'm fine,' Sybil assured her. 'Anyhow, why were you looking for me?'

'It's my birthday next week.' Tansy's tone was more upbeat. 'I wanted to invite you to dinner.'

'Oh, fab. Where?'

'At mine,' said Tansy. 'I'm doing it myself.'

'Gosh. That's a lot of work for your birthday,' said Sybil. 'Who'll be there?'

'The whole family. James is back for a week, so it'll be nice to have us all together. Nothing flashy, very casual.'

Sybil mentally counted the family members. Between herself, Tansy and her husband, Colin, along with their children and grandchildren, there would be nine people.

'Shouldn't we be treating you to an extravagant meal out instead?'

'Which would mean Claire having to organise a babysitter,' said Tansy. 'This way, she and Larry and the kids can stay over. Saves them a lot of hassle. You can too, if you like. There's plenty of room.'

'That's very kind of you,' said Sybil. 'I can't help feeling it's putting you to a lot of bother. I don't mind treating—'

'I've told you what I want,' Tansy interrupted her. 'And it's not a case of throwing money at a problem like you invariably do. It's a case of me being with the people who matter to me on my birthday.'

'I appreciate that.' Sybil ignored the barb about money in the same way as the crack about her age.

'I'm not so sure,' remarked Tansy.

Sybil took a deep breath. How was it, she wondered, that conversations with her sister so often ended up like this, with her having to defend herself against vague accusations she didn't quite understand? Although she understood the 'throwing money at a problem' jibe. Tansy always said that she bought her way out of trouble, or indeed out of anything she didn't want to do. She'd first levelled the accusation over forty years earlier, when she discovered Sybil had a cleaner. Having a cleaner back then meant you were the kind of person who had notions about themselves. And Sybil knew that Tansy very much felt she and Theo had notions.

This had been triggered by the change in their relative wealth when Theo sold Echo, his first company. He'd made enough from it to allow them to move from the tiny starter home they'd bought in Swords, a commuter town near the airport, to the upmarket costal suburb of Sutton, overlooking Dublin Bay. And because he'd set up another company straight away, and because both Theo and Sybil were working long hours (him on his own projects, her in the bank where they'd first met), they paid someone to clean the house once a week. It was the cleaner more than the move that had rattled Tansy's cage.

But even Sybil's mother had used the word 'notions' when she'd heard.

Nobody apart from Theo and Sybil themselves had expected Echo to be a commercial success. After all, Theo came from a farming background and his family had no interest in technology. Sybil's father worked in the civil service and her mother, like most mothers of the time, stayed home to care for her children. In both cases, the only people they knew with their own businesses were shopkeepers, electricians or plumbers, and none of them were particularly well off. Even before Sybil and Theo married, there had been plenty of discussions between her parents about their freeloading prospective son-in-law.

'When will she be able to have a baby?' Dolly regularly asked her husband. 'How can she even think about a family of her own when she's working day and night to support his faffing around on that computer thingy?'

Dolly was longing for a grandchild, but on the rare occasions she tried to speak to Sybil about it, her daughter merely shrugged and said there was plenty of time for babies, if that was what she and Theo decided. Meanwhile, Sybil's father remained horrified that Theo had left a safe and secure job at IBM to work for himself. The day before their marriage, he asked Sybil if she was one hundred per cent sure about it, reminding her that she was already three years older than Theo and therefore more mature and responsible, and that her maturity and responsibility would only increase while she was the one with a decent job in the bank and he played games on a screen in the back bedroom.

Theo wasn't playing games. He knew exactly what he was doing. And Sybil, who'd first met him when he'd come to install the bank's brand-new mainframe computer that had an entire room of its own, knew that he was exceptional. Which meant she was totally prepared to support his brilliance until it was rewarded.

Sybil knew that Tansy also considered Theo, with his long hair and frayed jeans, to be a waster in comparison with her own husband, Colin, who wore a blue suit, white shirt and polished shoes to the office every day. Tansy occasionally voiced the opinion that one day Theo would have to get a proper job, especially when children came along. At those times Sybil would tell her that Theo did have a proper job. She didn't bother talking about her desire to have children or not.

Then Theo sold the company he ran out of the back bedroom for what was at the time an extraordinary amount of money, and things were never quite the same between Sybil and her sister again.

Which was utterly daft, Sybil thought now, as she listened to Tansy outline her plans for the birthday dinner that she was going to cook herself. Over the years, Tansy and Colin had done well too. He'd moved into property management and was now a senior partner in the company. He and Tansy lived in a large house on the south side of the city. Their children, Claire, James and Darragh, were as well adjusted as thirty-something adults could be in the modern world. Claire was happily married with two children. James was a political adviser for an MEP and spent a lot of his time in Brussels, and although Darragh still lived with his parents, it was in what he laughingly referred to as his man cave, which took up the enormous converted attic space of the house and was practically a self-contained apartment.

'It sounds delightful.' Sybil concentrated her attention on Tansy's birthday plans. 'I'd love to come, thank you. But I won't stay over. I know you've plenty of space, but you'll have the grandchildren, and—'

'And God forbid you'd have to deal with little ones,' said Tansy.

'I get on fine with Claire's kids,' said Sybil. 'In the same way I got on fine with Claire, remember?'

Almost immediately, she wished she hadn't said anything; she really didn't want to go back to the time when Claire and Tansy's own relationship was fraught and her niece had spent a couple of months living with her and Theo until things had calmed down again.

'You're such a saint.'

'Ah, lookit, Tansy, you know we're all trying our best.' Sybil's tone was conciliatory. 'Sometimes we don't get it right, that's all.'

'Please answer your phone in future,' said Tansy. 'It worries me when you don't.'

'I answer it when I hear it,' Sybil told her. 'There's times I forget it's on silent. Or I forget I've left it in the bedroom while I'm somewhere else. Maybe I should get a hearing test,' she added. 'See if I'm a deaf old coot.'

'I wonder if I'm going deaf myself from time to time,' Tansy confessed, her voice suddenly warmer. 'I'm forever turning up the TV volume and shouting at it for all the mumbling that goes on. And other times it's so loud I have to turn it to mute.'

'That's not deaf,' Sybil assured her. 'That's a real phenomenon. It's to do with bandwidth or something. Theo told me about it once.'

'Are you sure you're OK today?'

'I'm fine,' said Sybil. 'It's been five years, Tansy. I've learned to cope.'

'Well, look, you'll be at my dinner, won't you?'

'Wouldn't miss it for the world,' lied Sybil.

She heaved a sigh as she put her phone away. At times like this, she missed Theo more than ever. He used to tease her when Tansy got under her skin, always lifting her out of the mood she allowed herself to get into. 'Five years,' she said aloud. 'Five years. And I've managed to get on with my life. Yet sometimes I still think you'll simply open the door and walk in.'

Chapter 3

Rua looked at the spreadsheet in front of her as she thought about the calculation she needed to do. She picked up the pencil lying beside her laptop and scribbled a formula on a sheet of paper. She'd always found it easier to write things down before inputting them. Writing helped the thought that was forming in her brain become real in a way that using a keyboard didn't. She'd never told anyone at work that she did this. She was quite sure they'd think her antiquated if she had. Although they probably considered her antiquated already. At forty, she was the oldest person working in the division. She was also the most efficient.

She inputted the formula and watched as the onscreen numbers updated. Then she looked at the resultant graph and smiled. The computer agreed with the mental calculation she'd made before she'd even started. 'I am invincible,' she said out loud.

'Are you indeed?'

She whirled around in her chair and sent her plastic container of coloured pens tumbling to the floor.

'Bloody hell,' she said as she picked them up and replaced them. 'I didn't hear you come in.'

'No.' Brontë, her twenty-year-old daughter, smiled at her. 'You were engrossed.'

'Sorry.'

'No need to be sorry. You're working. I just wanted to let you know it's nearly eight and I'm going out.'

'Eight?' Rua's expression was shocked. 'Why didn't you dig me out of here sooner?'

'Because you hate being disturbed when you're working,' replied Brontë. 'Anyway, I was studying. I'm not responsible for you, you know,' she added.

'I know, I know,' said Rua. 'All the same, I don't like locking myself away when you're home too. I wanted to have coffee with you before you head off. Where are you going?' she asked. 'And . . . um . . . is that what you're wearing?'

'Mum!' Brontë's voice held an edge. 'I'm an adult. I'm at college. You shouldn't be asking me where I'm going and if that's what I'm wearing as though I was fifteen again.'

Rua couldn't help smiling at the outrage in Brontë's voice.

'You're right. Sorry. You look lovely,' she said.

Which was the truth. Her daughter, petite and slender, was wearing a cherry-red jacket over a purple bouclé mini skirt, black opaque tights and plum ankle boots. Her hair, flame red like Rua's own, fell in a cloud of curls past her shoulders, and was topped by a jauntily placed pink beret.

'Although,' Rua added tentatively, 'maybe a coat? It's freezing outside.'

'I've ordered an Uber,' Brontë told her. 'Going straight to Jack's. It's his birthday, in case you'd forgotten.'

Jack was a study companion of Brontë's. Not a boyfriend, though he may once have been. As far as Rua knew, her daughter didn't currently have a boyfriend. She didn't have a girlfriend either. Rua wasn't sure that young people were exclusive to each other these days, no matter what sort of relationship they were in. Times had changed. She didn't know if it was for the better or not. Everyone said that relationships were more complicated now. They'd been complicated when she was Brontë's age too. But parents tended to forget those complications.

'Do you have time for that coffee first?' she asked as she backed up her work and stood up from her desk.

'Not really.' Brontë glanced at her phone. 'The Uber will be here in five minutes.'

Even so, she followed Rua to the kitchen and accepted an espresso from her at the same moment her phone pinged.

'Sorry, Mum, gotta go.' She downed the coffee in a single gulp, then leaned forward and kissed Rua on the cheek. 'See you tomorrow.'

'Are you staying over at Jack's?'

'No. But we'll probably get pizzas, watch a movie, chill . . . you know.' Brontë picked up her bag. 'I dunno what time I'll be home. Don't wait up.'

'I stopped doing that when you turned eighteen,' her mother told her.

Although, thought Rua, as she watched Brontë close the front door behind her, she hadn't stopped waiting to hear her come in before being able to go to sleep.

Alone in the house, she was tempted to go back to the laptop, but her concentration was broken, and besides, she didn't want to spend the rest of the night peering at the screen. Instead she went to the fridge and, ignoring the unopened bottle of Sauvignon Blanc, selected sparkling water, which she poured into a long glass and topped with a slice of lemon. She would've liked a glass of wine, but she had a rule about not drinking alcohol when she was home and Brontë was out. She didn't want to be in a situation where her daughter might phone for a lift and she'd be over the limit and unable to collect her. In an emergency, she wanted to have a clear head. Not that Brontë had ever called her for a lift, and not that there had ever been an emergency, but she wanted to be ready just in case. Brontë herself was unaware of her mother's no-alcohol rule, and Rua had no intention of ever telling her. Nor did Brontë know that Rua didn't sleep until she heard her key in the lock. Rua wanted Brontë to think that she was a hands-off, chillaxed mother when her daughter was out socialising, not a neurotic wreck. She hoped that she was succeeding in keeping up the facade.

She sat down in front of the TV but didn't turn it on. She was thinking of her own mother, and how she'd quizzed her every single time she'd left the house. In Mary's case it was because she hoped Rua wasn't doing anything to let the family down, rather than out of concern for her safety. After all, she didn't truly believe there was a reason to fear for Rua in the small town where they lived.

Her mother had been wrong about that, as she'd been wrong about so many things. There was always a good reason to fear for a young woman's safety. Even in country towns like Loughmore, drinks got spiked and rows broke out and saying no, as far as some people were concerned, didn't always mean no.

Rua shook her head to dislodge the memories of Loughmore. It was a long time since she'd visited, even though her brother, Stan, regularly invited her to the home he'd built a couple of kilometres outside the town. She'd gone to the housewarming but had been happy to leave as soon as she could. She was pretty sure that the last time she'd been back had been for his daughter's christening, over a year ago. She hadn't hung around then either. She didn't miss Loughmore. She never would. The only place she ever thought of fondly was Les Hauts Champs, where she'd lived for a time after moving to France. Leaving Paris for an isolated village an hour and a half away hadn't been part of the original living-abroad plan. She had wanted to lose herself in the anonymity of a big city. But things had changed unexpectedly, and it had worked out better than she'd dreamed of. Nonetheless, Les Hauts Champs was another place she'd left abruptly and with no plan to return. Perhaps one day that would change, but not yet.

She finished her water and went into the kitchen for a refill. As she added the lemon, a sudden thought occurred to her, and she returned to the distraction of the complicated program to see if her idea was a good one. That led her down another path of calculations, and it was almost midnight when she finished. Her eyes were gritty, but she was happy with the results. She logged out of the computer and went to bed.

It was a little past 2.30 when she heard Brontë's key in the lock and her footsteps on the stairs. Rua heaved a sigh of relief and closed the cover of her iPad. She knew that being on the iPad in bed wasn't good for her sleep patterns, but she reckoned it didn't matter if she was going to be awake anyhow. She rolled over on her side and listened as her daughter clattered around in the bathroom, then hung up her clothes in the bedroom. The house, built in the early nineties, didn't have the greatest of soundproofing, but that suited Rua. She liked being able to hear Brontë. After all, it was a privilege to have her living here. During Brontë's gap year, when she'd travelled through Europe with her friends, the silence had weighed heavily. It had been even harder to sleep, and Rua worried about where Brontë was every night too. She'd asked her to send her a text when she was going to bed, but unsurprisingly, her daughter had told her not to be ridiculous. However, she did agree to a daily text, and somewhat surprisingly, she FaceTimed far more than Rua had expected. So although she'd been on edge as Brontë made her way through Germany and Austria and Switzerland and Italy before spending a few months on the Greek islands, she'd also been able to share her joy in the places she was seeing.

Brontë hadn't bothered with Paris, but she'd spent a couple of months waitressing in La Rochelle. *Very different*, she'd told Rua. *I liked it. It's somewhere I'd go back to.*

Maybe she herself would feel able to return to Les Hauts Champs eventually, Rua thought, as she turned over in the bed. Or she could get in touch with Alize or Valery, although she had no idea where either of them lived now, nor who they might be living with, and she was pretty sure they'd both forgotten her.

She thumped her pillow. She didn't want to be thinking of Les Hauts Champs. That was why she'd come back to Ireland. So that she could forget. Not everything. Not everyone. But so that she wasn't reminded all the time of how much she'd lost. Of how life always seemed to take what was most precious to her and leave her floundering.

It had happened in Loughmore and it had happened in Les Hauts Champs, and that was why she was terrified of it happening again in Dublin. It was why she worried silently about Brontë, and why she couldn't sleep at night, and why she liked to stay home when she'd once been the sort of person who was never in.

But she wasn't that Rua any more.

Being honest with herself, she couldn't remember what it had been like before.

And perhaps, she thought, as she willed sleep to come, perhaps it was better that way.

Chapter 4

Sybil arrived at Tansy's house exactly on time. She was punctual by nature, and although she usually tried to be a polite couple of minutes late, she never quite succeeded. Claire answered the door, wearing a mid-length red velvet dress and glittering shoes, her chestnut hair tied up on top of her head and held in place by a couple of diamanté clips.

'Goodness,' said Sybil as she stepped over the threshold. 'You look stunning. Tansy said very casual. I didn't dress up at all.' She removed her purple-flecked winter coat to reveal a pale blue cashmere top and slim-fitting navy trousers.

'Don't worry, you look great.' Claire hung the coat on a free wall peg. 'I like any excuse to get out of leggings and a T-shirt. Besides, you've accessorised beautifully.'

Sybil's fingers touched the elegant diamond and sapphire pendant Theo had bought her for her fiftieth birthday. He'd given her the matching earrings she was wearing too. They were part of the iconic Bluebell collection from Warrens, the jewellers. Over the years Theo had gifted her various pieces from Warrens, but the Bluebells were her favourites.

'All the same,' she said as she followed Claire along the

hallway, 'if I'd realised how much you were glamming it up, I would've tried to be more party friendly myself.'

'You're always stylish,' Claire assured her. 'You were my sartorial role model growing up.'

'I wore mostly jeans and jumpers. I still do.'

'You carry them off so well.' Claire grinned.

Sybil smiled in return. She'd pretty much lived all her life in jeans, even if the styles had changed over the years. Bell-bottoms with decorative inserts to make them flare even wider when she was a young teen; straight-cut when she was older, followed by skinny, low-rise, boyfriend and skinnies again, until her metabolism slowed down and suddenly it was mom jeans and comfort waistbands. She didn't have the inner strength to suffer for her fashion any more.

'Hi, Sybil.' Colin, Tansy's husband, got up from the armchair where he'd been sitting and gave her a welcoming hug. 'We're delighted you came.'

'Of course I came,' said Sybil. 'Where's the birthday girl?'

'In the kitchen,' replied Colin. 'I offered to help, but she shooed me out.'

'I'll go and check everything's running smoothly,' said Claire. 'You sit down, Sybil, and Dad will get you a drink. Sorcha, Tadgh, put down those consoles and say hello to Auntie Sybil.'

The two children, who were nestled together on the sofa, glanced up from their screens and chorused hello before turning back to the game they were playing.

'What'll it be?' asked Colin.

Sybil asked for a gin and tonic.

As she took the first sip, noting with satisfaction that Colin had given her a generous measure of gin, her nephew

Darragh walked into the room. He was wearing shorts and a navy polo shirt, which in Sybil's experience seemed to be the smart-casual look that many young men of his age preferred, no matter what the season and no matter how dressed up any female partner might be.

'Hi, Sybil.' He kissed her on the cheek. 'We haven't seen you in ages. How have you been keeping?'

'Good, thanks. Gadding about a bit. I went to London earlier this month to check out the latest V&A exhibition, and I used my free travel pass to visit my friend Juliette last weekend. Got the train to Galway and back.'

'Living your best life.' Darragh gave her a thumbs-up. 'I thought Juliette lived near you. Did she move?'

'She's divorced now,' said Sybil. 'For the last while she's been living in a granny flat attached to her daughter's home in Salthill. It's a temporary move,' she added. 'Her daughter, Saoirse, had a baby recently and her husband is a fisherman, so it's nice for her to have the company when he's away on the boat. Meantime Juliette's renting out her house in Raheny. Though I have to say, she seemed very settled in the granny flat when I visited.'

Too settled, Sybil thought. Unlikely to come back. She didn't want to think that. She and Juliette had been good friends, even closer after Theo's death and Juliette's divorce. They'd supported each other, meeting regularly for lunch or coffee and occasionally going to dinner or the cinema together. Sybil had assumed they'd continue with that easy friendship into the future. But when Saoirse asked her mother to come to Galway, Juliette hadn't hesitated, and her move had left a big gap in Sybil's life.

One thing that being older taught you, she acknowledged

to herself, was that nothing ever remained the same. And much as you'd like people to stay in your life, you couldn't depend on them forever.

'I must take a trip to the west again,' said Darragh. 'It's such a beautiful part of the country. Maybe get James to come along with me for some brotherly bonding.'

'How long is he back in Dublin for?' asked Sybil.

'You never know with James.' It was Colin who answered. 'Even when he's here, he always seems to be working. We hardly ever see him. You know he's bought an apartment near the airport?'

'James is a hard worker,' agreed Sybil, who was very fond of her nephew. Despite the fact that his role was as an adviser to an MEP and not a local politician, he'd helped to deal with a street-light problem outside her apartment block a few months previously. As a member of the block's board of management, Sybil had approached the council numerous times about the issue, with no success. She'd mentioned it in passing to James one day, and a fortnight later it was resolved. Despite James insisting it was nothing to do with him, Sybil felt it was far too much of a coincidence that it was sorted after she'd talked to him. On the one hand, she disliked the idea that if you knew someone who knew someone you got things done. On the other . . . well, it was good to have the new lighting.

The doorbell rang.

But instead of seeing her nephew as she'd expected, it was Tansy who entered the living room, followed by a man Sybil didn't recognise. He was, she guessed, around the same age as her, bald on top, with otherwise neatly cut grey hair that curled slightly over the collar of his check shirt.

He wore somewhat dated steel-rimmed glasses, and an enormous watch with multiple dials on his left wrist.

'You all know Burt,' said Tansy as she smiled at them. 'Except you, Sybil. He's our dear neighbour from a few doors up.'

'Pleased to meet you.' Sybil hid her surprise. She'd no idea anyone other than family would be at Tansy's birthday dinner.

'Burt's been a good neighbour over the years,' said Tansy. 'Sadly, he lost his wife eighteen months ago. I thought it would be nice for him to join us.'

Sybil gave him a half-smile. He returned it with a megawatt one of his own that showed off a mouth full of perfect teeth, their brightness worthy of a Hollywood film star.

'Good to see you, Burt,' said Colin. 'What's your poison?'

'I'll have a beer, thanks.'

While Colin poured the beer, Tansy gave a potted history of her neighbour – a factory supervisor, three children; his late wife, Maeve, had been a good friend.

'Oh, yes, Maeve.' Sybil nodded. 'I remember you mentioning her before.'

'An incredible woman,' said Burt. 'I didn't know how I'd cope without her, but people have been very kind, and Tansy in particular has looked after me really well.'

Sybil nodded again, then asked Tansy if she needed any help in the kitchen.

'Not from you.' But Tansy smiled as she spoke, and added that dinner would be served in twenty minutes whether James was here or not. A moment later the bell rang again, and James arrived carrying a couple of bottles of red wine. Soon afterwards, they took their places around the oval dining room table, which had been extended to its full length to accommodate them all.

Tansy had decorated it beautifully with flowers and scattered mottos, while birthday-girl balloons had been placed in the corner of the room. Sybil, who only ever celebrated birthdays with a zero at the end (and even those reluctantly), admired the effort her sister had gone to, although she couldn't help thinking it would have been simpler to hire a room in a restaurant. But that was her throwing money at the problem again, she thought. And if this was what Tansy wanted, well, why not.

Burt, who was sitting beside her, was very appreciative of her sister's efforts, praising the food and asking Sybil if she was as good a cook herself.

'Not a bit,' she replied cheerfully. 'Omelette and oven chips is my highlight; that's why Tansy has no time for me in her kitchen.'

'I had to learn after Maeve passed,' he said. 'I'm improving all the time.'

'Well done,' she said, while internally grimacing at his use of the word 'passed'. Sybil didn't like euphemisms for death. She and Theo had preferred to be direct about it. She never said he'd passed, always that he'd died. She knew he'd have said the same about her.

'You've got to get on with it, haven't you?' Burt went on. 'I was always good at firing up the barbecue, but I'm a dab hand with the air fryer now. It's such a boon in the kitchen. Do you have one? I have some recipes I could share with you.'

'I do indeed have an air fryer,' said Sybil. 'It's the biz for the oven chips. Oh, yes, thanks, Colin, I'd love a top-up.'

She used the moment while her brother-in-law filled her glass to turn to Claire, who was sitting on her other side, and ask about a recent Netflix series they were both watching. She didn't want to have a conversation with Burt that would inevitably veer into their post-bereavement lives. She knew that plenty of people who'd lost spouses often wanted to talk about them, and she understood the desire to keep their memory alive. But she found it difficult to listen to stories about other people's late partners, and didn't particularly want to talk about Theo with someone she didn't know. So she tried to avoid those conversations, something she knew made Tansy think she was either cold and unfeeling or suffering with repressed emotions.

However, after dinner she found herself beside Burt again, and this time she couldn't change the subject. She listened as he spoke of his late wife, saying that since their retirement they'd spent more time travelling and enjoying life together. He gave her a rundown of all the places they'd visited, stressing that they liked to see the 'real' country and not the tourist traps, although he conceded that they always tried to treat themselves to nice hotels. Despite herself (and the fact that she couldn't get a word in edgeways), Sybil acknowledged that Burt was a good storyteller. He spoke affectionately about Maeve, and made her laugh with his accounts of travel triumphs and disasters and language mix-ups, especially over ordering food.

'Of course now you can use Google Translate and it saves so much trouble,' he said. 'I totally recommend it.'

'Burt loves his tech, Sybil,' said Tansy. 'You have that in

common. Actually, the pair of you have quite a lot in common.'

And then, in a blinding flash, Sybil realised that Tansy had invited Burt along with the express intention of introducing the two of them. How stupid was she not to have copped it before, she thought, aware that her sister saw herself in the role of matchmaker, finding a suitable widower for her so that she wouldn't have to live on her own any more. About a year after Theo's death, Tansy had suggested that Sybil might want to register on a dating site, to 'find love again'. Sybil's response had been more cutting than she intended, and Tansy had initially backed off, although more recently she'd begun to regularly ask if Sybil had found anyone she might like to share her life with. Sybil always replied that she was happy how she was, but somehow Tansy never seemed to believe her.

Now she felt a surge of rage flood her body and had to hold herself back from snapping at her sister in front of Burt. Instead she said that she'd enjoyed the evening immensely but it was time for her to leave.

'Don't be daft, Sybil, it's only ten o'clock,' said Tansy.

'These days I need my beauty sleep, and it'll take a while to get across town.'

'You look great to me.' Burt beamed at her, showing his brilliant veneers to full effect. 'Very elegant and attractive.'

'That's kind of you, but I do like my early nights,' said Sybil.

'I thought you were a night bird, Sybil.' James raised an eyebrow.

'I've a meeting in the morning,' she told him. 'These days I like to make sure I get my full eight hours.'

'Are you meeting anyone nice?' asked Burt.

'The board of my late husband's company,' she replied. 'I'm a non-executive director.'

'Oh.' He looked surprised.

'Keeps me busy and off the streets,' said Sybil. As she got to her feet, she said that she'd had a great time and complimented Tansy on a wonderful evening.

'Thanks for your gift,' said Tansy. 'Though the best present of all was you turning up.'

'I wouldn't have missed it for the world,' Sybil assured her. 'Let's you and me do coffee together soon. Or maybe afternoon tea at the Shelbourne, with you too, Claire.'

'I'd love that!' exclaimed Claire. 'Afternoon tea is my favourite treat.'

'Superb idea,' Tansy agreed.

'My cab is here.' Sybil, who'd ordered it on an app, put her phone back in her bag. 'I'll love you and leave you. Great to meet you, Burt.'

'Maybe we could meet up again,' he suggested. 'Nothing too fancy. Perhaps a drink? A nice meal somewhere?'

'Um, let's . . .'

'. . . exchange numbers,' he said.

'Well . . .'

But he already had his phone in his hand, so she shrugged and recited her number. He rang it, and they heard the buzz from her bag.

'Excellent,' he said. 'I'll be in touch.'

She took her coat from the rack, said goodbye to them all, embraced Tansy and wished her a happy birthday again, then hurried to the waiting cab.

* * *

As soon as she got home, Sybil put the kettle on and made herself a cup of tea. She sipped it curled up in an armchair while she looked at the text message Burt had already sent:

> It was a treat to meet such an interesting and attractive woman as yourself. I look forward to having a bite to eat or a drink with you very soon. How does next week sound?

She exhaled slowly. Clearly Burt had taken the exchange of numbers as encouragement. She was perfectly aware that she didn't have to have coffee with a man if she didn't want to, yet the words her mother had spoken to her nearly fifty years before were echoing in her head: If a boy asks you to dance, accept. If he asks you out, accept. He's had to pluck up the courage to do it. Don't make him feel bad. There had been no question of how Sybil herself might feel.

Things were different now, she knew. And in most areas of her life, being older allowed her to do more of what she liked and less of what she didn't. Yet a nagging sense of responsibility towards Burt wouldn't go away. She supposed that at least it wouldn't be like the old days and the nervousness of going on a date with someone she hardly knew. Not that she was considering meeting Burt Kennelly as a date. And she wasn't young and naïve any more. But she was still susceptible to pressure. It surprised her to realise it. She'd thought she'd got to the point where she was able to say no whenever she wanted.

Maybe she could find an excuse, she thought as she drained her cup. Surely she could think of something. But the best she could come up with was a delaying tactic, messaging him that she was half asleep now and would check her calendar in the morning.

He sent back a thumbs-up and a string of smiley-face emojis.

She put the phone on the charger and went to bed.

She wasn't thinking about Burt or Tansy the following morning when she walked into the offices of Ambitec, the company that Theo had formed twenty-five years earlier when he acquired a smaller competitor. One of the things she most enjoyed was going to the quarterly meetings, because even if she didn't have a lot of input, it made her feel that she was contributing something useful to the business. Despite being a tech nerd, Theo had also been extremely savvy about the parts of the industry he'd become involved in. Ambitec was what had enabled them to live well during his life and during his illness, and it was what allowed Sybil to be stress-free about money now and have no qualms about splurging on the purple Louise Kennedy trouser suit and cream silk blouse she was wearing to the meeting. She always dressed well for business meetings. There was a time when she would have worn killer heels too, but these days she was concerned that if she stumbled in them, they really might kill her, and instead contented herself with elegant black ballet pumps.

The board meeting took a couple of hours, but there were no contentious issues to discuss and she was pleased that the company was being well managed. Afterwards, the CEO, Mike, asked her if she'd be coming to the Christmas party. Sybil shook her head and said that the party was for the staff and not for the likes of her, but that she hoped they'd have a great time.

'We miss Theo,' said Mike. 'It's not the same without him.'

'I miss him too,' she admitted. 'But he'd be happy to know that the company is continuing to do well and that you're looking after the employees. You said at the meeting that many are opting to work from home, although you insist on them coming in on a regular basis too. I know the charts you showed us said that productivity was good, but is it as good as always? Not that I mind them working from home,' she added. 'It's just that you hear so much about companies ordering their employees back to the office and the problems that come with remote working.'

'It's going well for us because a lot of our people like to work in the middle of the night.' Mike grinned. 'If they're on a solo project, that's fine. If they're collaborating, we get them in. It's allowed us to retain people who would've left otherwise.'

'I'm sure you know what you're doing,' said Sybil. 'Theo thought very highly of you.'

'And I of him.' Mike nodded. 'Don't worry, Sybil. I care as much about the future of Ambitec as Theo ever did.'

She was reassured by his words, and reassured too as she walked through the office and saw plenty of desks occupied by people busily tapping at their computers. In the staff canteen (breakout area, she reminded herself; nobody called it a canteen any more), people were sitting around tables and chatting animatedly as they drank coffee and ate sandwiches.

You did all this, she said silently to Theo. You. A man

my father thought would never come to any good. You did it all and you were brilliant.

I miss you.

She was home and sliding her feet into her slippers when Tansy FaceTimed her.

'So,' she said. 'What did you think?'

'Of what?' asked Sybil, whose mind was still on Ambitec.

'Burt Kennelly, you eejit.'

'He seemed like a nice man.' Sybil's tone was cautious. 'Amazing teeth.'

'He had them done after Maeve died. He felt he had to look younger to attract women. It proves he's making an effort and isn't just expecting someone to fall into his lap.'

Sybil shuddered at the mental image this conjured up but simply said that it was good to see a man taking care of his appearance.

'All men should invest in personal grooming,' said Tansy.

There was an awkward silence as both of them thought of Theo, a man who had never bothered about appearances. It was only because Sybil bought all his clothes and supervised his wardrobe any time he had to go to an important meeting or function that he ever wore anything other than a T-shirt and jeans. *In all the time I've known you, you haven't changed a bit*, she once told him in amusement. And he'd retorted that all the tech bros wore sweatshirts and jeans now, that it had come full circle and he was totally fashionable.

He'd had a point.

'Are you going to see him again?'

For a brief moment Sybil thought Tansy was talking about

Theo, and she looked at the phone screen in bewilderment before dragging her mind back to her sister's reason for calling.

'Burt?' she said. 'Oh, I doubt it.'

'You exchanged phone numbers.'

'I was being polite.'

'For heaven's sake, Sybil, *he* wasn't simply being polite. He was being interested in you. And it's long past the time you took an interest in other people too. You need to get out more. Visiting cemeteries and going to dreary board meetings aren't social events.'

'I'm perfectly fine the way I am,' said Sybil. 'I *do* meet people and I like my life as it is, thanks very much.'

'Forgive me for trying to help you,' retorted Tansy. 'I don't want you ending up old and alone.'

'Age is a mindset,' said Sybil. 'After this morning's meeting – which was very interesting and not at all dreary, by the way – I walked around an office full of people a lot younger than me, and I didn't feel old.'

'They probably thought you were,' said Tansy.

Sybil tilted the phone towards the ceiling while she made a face, at the same time conceding that her sister was undoubtedly right. In fact, it was more likely that the young men and women in the breakout area and gazing at their computer screens hadn't noticed her at all. Women were meant to be invisible after a certain age. She wasn't exactly sure what that age was, but she knew that she'd long since passed it.

'Look, I'm sure Burt is perfectly nice and I appreciate you looking out for me,' she said, facing the screen again. 'But honestly, Tansy, I'm not searching for . . . well, whatever Burt has in mind.'

'Listen to me.' Tansy gave her a steely look. 'You probably have another fifteen good years or so in you at least. Do you really want to spend them on your own?'

'Rather on my own than with a man whose teeth will outlive him,' retorted Sybil.

'If he asks you out, say yes.'

You sound exactly like Mum. The thought rushed into Sybil's head. *Why should I say yes if I don't want to?*

'Promise me you will,' said Tansy. 'If you don't like him, that's fine, but at least give him a chance.'

'All right, all right.' Sybil couldn't believe she was giving in to her sister, but she wanted the conversation to end.

'Good woman,' said Tansy. 'I can't wait to hear how you get on.'

Sybil said nothing. She was hoping that Burt wouldn't message her again.

She was fine the way she was.

Chapter 5

Ailie was alone in the kitchen, scrolling through her phone, when Marco walked in. He put a gift-wrapped box on the table in front of her.

'For me?' she asked.

'Christmas present,' he replied. 'It's early, I know, but I'm going home at the end of the week, so I wanted to give it to you now.'

She put her arms around him and held him tightly. 'Thank you for this. And for staying on for some extra days. It's been good for Flavia to have you here.'

'I should have come back before something like this made me. I've missed you, Ailie. Flavia too. And Dad. I know we were in touch a lot this last while,' Marco cleared his throat, 'but I should've been here for him.' He sat down opposite her, and she saw that a tear was rolling slowly down his cheek. She felt herself choke up too, but she made a big effort not to cry.

'Nobody expected it,' she told him. 'He was a strong, fit man.'

'Not so strong and not so fit after all,' said Marco.

'For most of his life he was,' she said. 'And that was a good thing, because he lived it well.'

'Thanks to being with you.'

'I think your dad was the kind of man who'd always live life well,' she said. 'He believed in happiness.'

'Sometimes at the expense of others.'

'Ah, no.' Ailie shook her head. 'He wanted all of us to be happy. Including your *mamma*.' She picked up the box and then put it down again. 'I was going to make coffee,' she said. 'Would you like a cup before I unwrap this?'

'A ristretto would be perfect.'

'No problem.'

She got up from her chair and went to the cupboard, taking out the tin of premium roast beans that Giorgio had always insisted on buying. She loaded them into the grinder and placed cups on the tray of the machine. The familiar routine, one that had always been his, ignited her grief all over again, and she kept her back to Marco as she blinked away the tears.

As she watched the coffee brew, her mind drifted back to the day her stepson had first walked into her kitchen and into her life. Not this kitchen – back then, she and Giorgio were living in an apartment in Sandyford at the foothills of the Dublin mountains. They'd bought it just as the financial crisis hit, leaving them in negative equity and very stressed, not only because of the mortgage but also because Ailie was pregnant, something they hadn't planned for. Meanwhile, the dental clinic had opened a new centre in the city centre and had asked her to transfer there. She hadn't felt able to say no, particularly as Giorgio had taken a cut in salary and was facing the prospect of another, and they needed her job. It had been a time when she'd wanted to hunker down and see nobody.

Yet Marco's visit, his first since his father had come to live in Ireland, couldn't be put off. It had taken months of careful negotiation for Giorgio to be allowed to bring his nine-year-old son to stay. Financial disasters and unplanned pregnancies weren't going to be allowed to stop it. Of course, Ailie recalled as the aromatic coffee began to flow into the cups, Marco didn't know she was pregnant then. It was a secret she and Giorgio were keeping. There would have been no chance of his son staying with them if anyone knew about the baby. As it was, the instructions were very clear. Ailie was never to be alone with Marco. And Giorgio wasn't to allow him out of his sight.

If she hadn't felt like an outcast from his family before, the sometimes heated discussions over the visit certainly made her feel unwanted then, especially as her not being alone with the boy had been negotiated down from her having to move out of the apartment while he stayed. Giorgio had read the message, his voice shaking with rage as he told her that his ex-wife would only let her son leave Italy if there was no chance at all he would set eyes on the woman she termed Giorgio's mistress.

'She can't order you around like that,' fumed Ailie. 'And how dare she call me your mistress. You're divorced, for crying out loud! The settlement allows you visitation rights.'

'Yes, but it doesn't say anything about Marco coming here and staying with another woman,' said Giorgio.

'I'm not some random woman!' cried Ailie. 'I'm your . . . your . . . I'm going to be the mother of your child!'

Which was when he said that the baby had to be a secret,

because there was no way Marco was coming if Sophia thought he'd be meeting the mother of another baby.

'He's a child himself,' Ailie said. 'He won't care.'

'It doesn't matter,' said Giorgio. 'You don't know Sophia. You don't know my family.'

Which was true. She and Giorgio had visited Italy the year before, but they hadn't even attempted to meet the Marchettis. Giorgio had said that it wasn't the right time. In any event, he'd added, they were enjoying themselves so much in Rome and Naples that it would be a real downer to have to travel north to face his troublesome family. Ailie had wanted to argue with him, but she'd given in.

Sometimes she wished she hadn't.

Giorgio had been a handsome man, but Marco was Michelangelo's *David* come to life, with luminous dark eyes in a perfectly smooth face, thick curly hair, and a firm mouth with baby-soft lips. When she first saw him, Ailie felt her stomach clench at the thought that his mother must be equally breathtaking. She'd never seen a photo of Sophia. She'd never wanted to. Now, she did.

He followed his father into the apartment and looked around, a slight frown marring that smooth forehead.

'*È piccolo*,' he said.

Ailie, whose Italian at that time was serviceable if not fluent, knew that he was saying that it was small. He wasn't wrong. Although the apartment had two bedrooms, the one allocated to Marco was scarcely big enough for a single bed. The rest of the apartment consisted of a living room, a galley kitchen and a compact bathroom. There was no other interior space. But it was south-facing and light-filled, and the early-evening sun flooded the surprisingly wide balcony, enhancing the colours of the large collection of potted plants that Ailie had amassed since they'd moved in.

'*Benvenuto, Marco,*' she said brightly. 'It's a pleasure to have you here. I hope you'll have a great stay with us.'

She knew his English was good enough to understand her.

'Where am I sleeping?' he asked Giorgio.

His father showed him into the tiny bedroom. Ailie had decorated it in blue and white, the colours of the Italian national football team, which she knew he supported.

Although Ailie's standby dish was garlic rigatoni, she didn't have the nerve to cook pasta for Marco, so they went out to dinner, where he elected to have chicken nuggets and chips. In fact, his favourite meals throughout his stay were burgers or nuggets, and she couldn't help feeling that he'd go back home and tell them that the food was dreadful. Yet he seemed to enjoy it, and she made the decision not to criticise a single one of his choices.

He stayed with them for four nights and nothing terrible happened, so she chalked it up as a success, even though she didn't feel that she'd got to know him at all.

Baby steps, she told herself as she waved him goodbye. Baby steps.

He came the following year too, a few months after Flavia was born. That had necessitated even greater levels of diplomatic skill, and the relaxing of the rule that Marco should never be alone with Ailie, but somehow Giorgio had managed it. Ailie had worried that he would resent his baby sister, but he adored her, and loved carrying her around the apartment, patting her on the back and humming 'Stella Stellina' to her, a lullaby that nearly always succeeded in sending her to sleep.

He didn't come to Giorgio and Ailie's wedding the year after that (Giorgio had already resigned himself to the fact that there was no way Sophia would allow it), but he did stay a couple of months later and once again was caring and loving towards Flavia, who smiled broadly every time she saw him and called him *fratello*. Marco only spoke in Italian to her, and it was a constant source of amazement to Ailie how her baby daughter switched between the two languages, even though she was only beginning to talk.

In subsequent years, things improved financially for Giorgio and Ailie. The economy began to grow again, and he was headhunted at a much-increased salary, while she moved back to her original location at the dental clinic, making her commute much easier. They sold the apartment and bought a house in the same area. Marco was allocated one of the three bedrooms for himself. He came for a month every summer and Flavia always looked forward to his arrival.

When he was eighteen, he told Giorgio that he'd applied to University College Dublin to study business.

'What does your *mamma* think of this?' Giorgio was delighted that his son wanted to study in Ireland but was doubtful that Sophia would be pleased.

'You know her. She's not happy unless I'm at Villa Farfalla tied to her apron strings.' Marco snorted. 'However, there is only so much time I can spend with Mamma and Nonna before they drive me crazy, and I told them that this was the perfect opportunity to improve my English.'

'I felt the same,' Giorgio agreed. 'It wasn't easy to disentangle myself from them. I would like nothing more than to have you live with us while you're at college, if that's what you want.'

'And Ailie?'

'She'll love it too,' Giorgio assured him.

Ailie enjoyed having Marco around, but it wasn't always easy. He liked to stay out late with his college friends, and he had a constant stream of girlfriends, each more besotted with him than the last. He'd grown out of his childhood beauty into an extremely handsome young man. Ailie worried about him and the girls he went out with, but Marco seemed to handle them with a casual ease that was mesmerising.

'You have to be kind to them,' she said one evening when he finished talking to one girl on his mobile only to move straight on to another. 'You can't string them along.'

'We are friends, nothing more,' he said.

Nevertheless, she hoped that there'd be no relationship dramas while he stayed with them.

Her wish was granted. His college years were mercifully drama-free, and she missed him when he returned to Italy after his graduation. She'd grown used to having him around the house, to tripping over his rugby boots, to the ever-changing aroma of his aftershave and the constant tapping of his fingers on the keypad of his mobile.

Flavia missed him too. She loved Marco, and having a handsome stepbrother had enhanced her reputation at school; even if her own friends were too young to care much about him, their older sisters absolutely did. She would tease him about the hearts he was breaking and he'd tell her that he never promised more than he could give. 'But if anyone breaks *your* heart, *sorella mia*,' he said, 'you must tell me and I promise I will deal with him.'

Eleven years old at the time of this conversation, Flavia didn't have a boyfriend and had no interest in having one either. But she told Marco that she'd learned a lot from him, and that when the time came that she *was* interested in boys (because right now they were all idiots as far as she was concerned), she would remember both how well and how badly he treated girls.

'I never treat them badly.' He looked at her in indignation.

She laughed and threw a cushion at him.

It was Ailie, walking into the living room, who caught it.

That memory came to her now as she handed him the ristretto and then carefully unwrapped his early Christmas present.

The gift box was pale green, imprinted with a line drawing of a butterfly on a blade of grass and the words *La Bonta della Villa Farfalla* in elegant script.

'Thank you,' she said, lifting the lid and revealing two bottles of scented oil carefully placed inside. 'I didn't realise you were making body oil now.'

'We're trying it out,' he told her. 'It was something Dad was very keen on developing. We talked about it a lot over the last year. One is for your face, the other for your body. It's infused with lavender. Very good for the skin and relaxation.'

'I need something for my skin.' She smiled at him. 'Too many wrinkles.'

'Not at all.' He spoke very seriously. 'You have good skin, Ailie. You always have had. But I think you probably need to relax. This has been a hard time for you.'

'For all of us.' She swallowed hard. 'You know your dad was very proud of you.'

'I wanted him to see my success.' Marco's face crumpled, and suddenly he was the young boy of his first visit again.

Secrets Between Friends

'I wanted him to come to the villa, to see how things were developing and what we could do for the future. We spoke about it often and he was very supportive, but he never came. And then this.' He shook his head. 'It's so hard to believe. There was no warning?'

'Nothing,' said Ailie. 'He seemed perfectly fine. Occasionally more tired than usual, but I thought it was because of work and his renewed interest in the Villa Farfalla. And then he collapsed and, well, that was that.'

'I should have come sooner.' Marco repeated the words he'd said before.

'It's not your fault this happened,' said Ailie.

'All the same . . .' He twisted the green ribbon from the gift box around his fingers. 'He was my father and I wasn't there for him.'

'You're here for me,' Ailie said. 'And I appreciate it.' She cleared her throat. 'How are things with your aunts and, um, your mother?'

'They were also very shocked,' he said. 'Nonna is heartbroken to lose her eldest son. Mamma is in denial. I don't think anyone has quite accepted it yet.'

'Understandable.' Ailie nodded.

'There will be things to sort out with the company too.' Marco frowned. 'Has anyone been in touch with you?'

'Anyone like who?' asked Ailie.

'Dad's *avvocato*. His solicitor in Italy. He's the one looking after his affairs there.'

'I don't suppose there's much to look after,' said Ailie. 'At least not as far as I'm concerned. Your dad's life was here.'

'His personal life,' agreed Marco. 'But he had an interest in the company and there will have to be changes. He and

I talked about the future, but it was a future we thought would take a long time to arrive, so I don't know exactly how he will have arranged things. The *avvocato* says he will arrange a meeting once he has drawn up a complete list of all the assets. A pity that he cannot tell us everything immediately, but the family is too distraught to think about business right now, so we carry on as usual.'

'I'm glad you're the one looking after things,' Ailie said. 'Giorgio had great faith in you. And I'm sure the solicitor will be in touch with me soon enough if there's anything I need to know.'

'Unfortunately it takes forever.' Marco grimaced. 'Which is hard emotionally and annoying when it comes to all the businesses.'

'What business is there apart from the hotel?'

'This, for one thing.' He indicated the box of oils. 'It used to be only the hotel, but the wellness side is becoming more important.'

'I didn't realise that.'

'I will speak to the *avvocato* as soon as I can,' Marco said. 'It is important for all of us to have things settled.'

'If I hear from him I'll let you know,' promised Ailie. 'All the same, I don't think there's anything in Italy I need to be involved with. My time will be taken up with things here, and those should be relatively straightforward. The house belonged to both of us. We had a joint account. Makes it simple, I hope.'

'Hopefully Italy will be simple too.' This time Marco gave her a wide smile. 'I'm sure Dad will have left things as organised as possible.'

'It'll all be fine,' Ailie assured him. 'I know he was very

happy having you involved in the hotel and he wouldn't have wanted to put you under any stress.'

Marco's eyes filled with tears again, and Ailie put her arm around his shoulders.

'He knew you loved him,' she said. 'It meant a lot to him that you came to us when you were at college.'

'I was nothing but trouble then,' he said.

'Ah, no, you weren't.' Ailie smiled as she released her hold on him. 'You were great.'

'You're such a liar,' said Marco. 'And I love you for it.'

He rarely told her that he loved her, even in a qualified way. But she'd loved him from his very first visit. And she'd never stopped.

Chapter 6

Sybil was feeling guilty as she sat in one of the most expensive seats for the candlelight concert in St Ann's Church, Dawson Street. In the middle of the first row, she was excellently placed to both see and hear the string quartet that would be performing Christmas music. On her right-hand side was a couple around the same age as her, who she assumed were husband and wife because of their easy familiarity with each other. On her left was an empty seat that should have been occupied by Burt Kennelly. He was the one who'd bought the tickets after all, and she'd accepted his invitation because on the two previous occasions he'd asked her out she'd been busy; the first having a massage, courtesy of a voucher she'd been given as a present the previous Christmas and which was about to expire, and the second for a scheduled DEXA scan at the hospital to check her bone density. She'd been suitably apologetic and joked about the amount of maintenance her body needed these days. He'd told her that she was very well preserved (which made her wince), then invited her to the concert. As she'd tried to book tickets for the same concert a couple of weeks earlier and it had been sold out, she'd been pleased to accept, thinking that listening to music would be sociable without having to do too much heavy lifting in terms of chat.

Now she felt sorry for Burt, who'd texted early that morning to say he'd woken up with a touch of the flu and a sore throat, and that he didn't think it would be fair to inflict it on her by coming to the concert. He'd added that the tickets were available for collection and if she wanted to go with a friend he'd be more than delighted. She responded by commiserating on his flu (in her head she amended it to 'a slight cold') and saying she hoped he'd feel better soon. And then she said that she'd definitely go to the concert and would let him know all about it.

Unfortunately she hadn't been able to find anyone to use the spare ticket. If Juliette hadn't deserted her for Galway, she'd undoubtedly have accompanied her and they'd have had an enjoyable night out together. Instead, she texted one of the casual friends she occasionally met for lunch, but Martina replied to say that she was in the airport on her way to the Christmas markets in Germany and suggested that perhaps they could get together in the new year. Sybil responded with a thumbs-up, somewhat horrified to realise that it was over six months since their last lunch together. She then scrolled to a WhatsApp group of ex-colleagues with whom she kept in touch but rarely met. She'd planned to post the invitation and see who answered first, but realised she'd muted the group months earlier and hadn't replied to other invitations herself. She decided against issuing an invitation out of the blue, reckoning that they'd think it odd, but considered unmuting the group. Then she remembered that its constant stream of jokey messages and inspirational quotes was what had caused her to silence it in the first place and decided not to bother. A last-minute call to Claire was met with the response that she would have loved a Christmas concert, but that she and Larry were going to Sorcha's nativity play that evening.

'I'd have asked you along, but the children are only allowed to bring two adults,' she added.

'No worries,' Sybil told her. 'I'm quite happy to go to the concert on my own.'

And she was. But as she took her seat, she had to admit to herself that maybe Tansy had a point about her not being sociable enough. Despite missing Juliette, she was happy with her own company, but she wondered if perhaps she did too many things alone, if she'd cut herself off without meaning to. It was chastening not to find at least one person able to come to the concert with her, and even more chastening to know that the list of people she could ask was so short. Maybe Tansy was also right about her meeting new people. Though not a man in need of a wife! Sybil had absolutely no intention of getting married again. The idea of having to compromise the way she lived to accommodate someone else was unbearable. But right now, she was having the best of both worlds, availing herself of Burt's hospitality without having to be with him at all, and she couldn't help feeling guilty about it.

The eighteenth-century church was elegant and inviting in the light of the candles around the apse where the quartet would perform. The rest of the church was subtly lit, and despite Sybil's somewhat loose relationship with religion, she allowed the spirit of Christmas to wrap itself around her, along with the warm Avoca shawl she wore over her flecked wool coat.

She took a photo of the church and sent it to Burt with a message that said she hoped once again that he was feeling better.

Much better. Perhaps I should have come after all.

Probably best that you recover properly.

Maybe lunch next week?

That might be nice.

It's a date.

He followed his message with a string of emojis, not all of which made any sense to Sybil.

There was movement at the front of the church and the quartet of two men and two women took their seats. The hum of chatter among the audience faded, and Sybil closed her eyes as the notes of 'It Came Upon The Midnight Clear' filled the space around her. The pieces were all traditionally festive, and by the time the quartet finished up with her own personal favourite, 'O Come, All Ye Faithful', she had completely embraced the holiday season. In fact she was regretful now that Burt wasn't with her, as she would have liked to talk about the music and the beautiful setting to someone. As it was, she filed out of the church along with the rest of the concertgoers and waited at the edge of the pavement to cross the road so that she could walk to the taxi rank.

The street was crowded with late-evening shoppers and people out for the night, and mindful of how easy it was to have a bag snatched in the bustle, she kept a firm hold of the small green satchel she carried crossed over her shoulder. But it wasn't someone trying to grab her bag that ultimately caused her to stagger; it was the young man coming down the street on an e-scooter, who caught a wheel in the tram tracks laid into the cobbled road and was catapulted in her direction. Although she tried hard to keep her balance, she suddenly found herself on her back, the man almost on top of her and a crowd of people surrounding them both.

'Are you all right?' A woman wearing a blue beanie over blazing red hair hunkered down beside her as the man rolled to one side. 'Take a minute. Don't move.'

'I'm fine,' gasped Sybil. 'A bit winded, that's all. And I've lost my glasses.' She looked around short-sightedly.

'Here they are.' Another woman handed them to her. Dark-haired, and wearing a white puffa jacket, she had an air of professional competence that reassured Sybil. 'Lucky they're not cracked. Stay still. I'm qualified in first aid. Let me check you out.'

'Better check him first.' Sybil nodded towards the young man. 'He sailed through the air and might be more injured than me.'

But he was already beginning to get to his feet and was asking what had happened to his scooter.

There was a general chorus of people telling him that he should be more concerned about the woman he'd nearly killed and insisting that those damn scooters were a menace and he should have been more careful. He dusted himself down, then looked at Sybil, who was now sitting up, supported by the woman in the puffa jacket.

'Sorry,' he said. 'It's those bloody tramlines.'

'They're for trams,' said Sybil. 'Not scooters.'

'Yeah, yeah.' He straightened up. 'Look, I'm sorry, honestly. Are you OK?'

She nodded, and he walked away, pushing the scooter, to a few jeers from the crowd, which was starting to melt away now it was clear the drama was over.

'Can you stand up?' asked the woman with the red hair. 'You took a terrible tumble there.'

'I think it was more shock than anything,' said Sybil. 'I feel fine. Nothing's broken.'

'Nonetheless,' the first-aider placed her hand on Sybil's shoulder, 'you should . . .' She paused. 'I know you,' she said.

'I really don't think so,' said Sybil.

'I do,' said the woman. 'From somewhere.'

The redhead looked from one to the other, then addressed Puffa Jacket. 'If you do know her, perhaps you should take her for a cup of tea. Or something stronger. For the shock.'

'We're perfect strangers,' said Sybil.

'I saw you,' the woman said, recognition dawning. 'A few weeks ago. At the cemetery.'

'Oh?'

'I'm Ailie Taylor. It was my husband's funeral. You were walking by. I noticed your umbrella. We don't properly know each other at all. I simply . . . knew you were familiar. I'm sorry, you must think I'm demented.'

'Not at all.' Sybil adjusted the shawl around her coat. 'I'm Sybil Hansen. I remember the funeral. I'm sorry for your loss.'

The younger woman remarked on the coincidence of them meeting like this, then suggested again that Sybil should have something to settle herself before going home. Because, she said, she might have a delayed reaction to her tumble and it would be better for her to relax for a while.

'The only reaction I have is that I'd like to ban those damn e-scooters.' Sybil flexed her wrists and ankles gingerly. 'But I do think a restorative drink is in order. Why don't you two Good Samaritans join me?'

'I . . .' Ailie hesitated. 'I wasn't planning on anything other than the concert.'

'I understand,' said Sybil. 'It's hard in the aftermath of your husband's death. Passing,' she amended so that the woman didn't think her heartless. 'All the same, if you feel up to it, I'd like to get you something to say thanks.'

'There's really no need,' Ailie said. 'I haven't been in a pub since the funeral. I haven't wanted to go out.' She hesitated. 'It might be nice to have a drink, but it seems . . .'

'Disrespectful?' Sybil's smile was sympathetic. 'It took me ages to go out after my husband died. I'm impressed you went to the concert; I wouldn't have been able for that so soon. If you want to go home, you should. But I'm going to follow advice for once in my life and have something restorative myself. It'd be nice to have the company of you both if you'd like.'

'I don't usually . . .' The younger woman looked doubtful. 'But if the two of you are having a drink, I'll join you.'

'We might be able to get a seat at Kehoe's,' suggested Sybil. 'It was a haunt of mine in my younger days and I doubt it's the first choice for concertgoers.'

Checking carefully for oncoming scooters and trams, the three women crossed the road together.

Unsurprisingly for a Thursday in Dublin, especially one in December, the bar was busy, but they were in luck and managed to nab a table that was being vacated by a young couple laden with shopping bags. Ailie found an extra chair and dragged it across.

'What would you like?' she asked Sybil.

'You two sit down, this is my treat,' Sybil replied. 'And I'm sorry, I know your name, Ailie, but I didn't get yours?' She turned to the redhead.

'Rua,' she replied. 'Rua Lehane.'

'How appropriate.' Sybil eyed her glorious red hair and smiled.

'I was christened Ruby after my grandmother,' Rua said. 'I guess that was pretty appropriate too. But my brother kept calling me Rua and it seemed to stick. I was Redzer in school,' she added.

'Rua is much prettier than Redzer,' declared Sybil. 'And it suits you. So, what'll it be, ladies?'

Both of them asked for dry white wine, and Sybil walked up to the bar, leaving them sitting at the table.

'This is a bit strange,' Rua said to Ailie. 'I don't generally go to pubs with random women.'

Ailie smiled and said that she didn't normally go for drinks with random women either. In fact, she was surprised at herself for agreeing to come at all when until today it had been an effort to even leave the house.

'Were you at the concert on your own?' asked Rua.

'My daughter came with me, but she went off to meet

some friends afterwards,' replied Ailie. 'I wasn't sure about coming to it, but I was gifted the tickets by a colleague of my late husband, and I felt Giorgio would've wanted me to use them. Plus I wanted Flavia to come into town, meet her friends and feel a little Christmassy. It's been tough for her.'

'Christmas is especially difficult when you've lost someone,' said Rua.

'Every single day is difficult, to be honest. Mostly I want to sit in a dark room by myself and cry. Whenever I go out, no matter where to, I dread coming back to an empty house.'

'Oh gosh, yes,' said Rua. 'When there's no one there, the atmosphere is totally different.'

'Exactly.' Ailie wiped a sudden tear from her eye. 'Sorry. I keep turning on the waterworks at the most inappropriate moments.'

'That's all right,' said Rua. 'I'm sure you miss your husband dreadfully.'

'It's the little things,' said Ailie. 'The smoke alarm battery needed to be changed the other day. That was one of Giorgio's jobs. He used to complain it was difficult to get the cover off the unit. I was afraid I wouldn't be able to do it myself and I'd be stuck listening to that bloody chirping all night. But even though it was a struggle, I managed it. Then I found the spare batteries and replaced them, and afterwards I cried for ages.'

'Fair play to you for managing to unscrew that cover,' said Rua. 'It's always a nightmare.'

Ailie smiled and dabbed at her eyes as Sybil returned to the table.

'They'll bring the drinks over,' she said. 'Gosh, having a

drink with women I don't know is a kind of unusual thing for me to be doing. I hope you don't feel I strong-armed you into it.'

'Not at all,' said Rua. 'We were just saying the same thing ourselves.'

'Perhaps it's the festive season,' Sybil said. 'It makes us all more . . . oh, I don't know . . . open with each other? I have to tell you, I'm not usually an open sort of person.'

'And yet you seem to be,' said Ailie. 'You came to the concert on your own, you organised us into having drinks, found us a table, and you look like the sort of woman who can take care of herself.'

'Actually, I'm a bit of a Billy No-Mates this evening,' said Sybil, who went on to explain about Burt and the tickets and the lack of people she could have invited. 'It's partly my own fault,' she conceded. 'After my husband died, I kept myself to myself a lot. I didn't mind. I've always been happy with my own company, so it suited me. It was only tonight that made me realise I've been a bit . . . well, not reclusive – that sounds like Miss Havisham mouldering away alone in a wedding dress – but perhaps a little antisocial. Maybe that's what made me act against type and force you to have a drink with me.'

'I'm quite glad you did,' said Rua. 'It's nice to be out.'

'I feel a bit odd about it,' confessed Ailie. 'But I suppose I have to do normal things again. How long are you widowed?' She turned to Sybil.

'Five years,' she replied.

'Does it get any easier?'

'You learn to live with it, which isn't the same thing.' Sybil spoke kindly to the younger woman. 'There's an emptiness that never completely goes away, and certain times of the year, like now, can often be overwhelming. But eventually you adapt, and the pain eases. Theo and I were together a long time, so it was a lot of adjusting for me. Thank you.' She spoke the final words to the young bartender, who placed glasses of wine in front of Ailie and Rua and a whiskey in front of Sybil herself.

'Cheers.' She raised her glass. 'Christmas wishes to you both, and thanks again for looking after me earlier.'

Ailie and Rua clinked their glasses against hers.

'So you're dipping your toe back in the dating scene with this guy Burt?' Rua looked at her enquiringly.

'Not really,' replied Sybil. 'This would've been the first time we'd gone out together.' She went on to tell them about meeting Burt at Tansy's, and her sister's role in trying to bring them together thanks to her belief that Sybil should have someone new in her life.

'And you don't agree?' asked Ailie. 'Because you prefer your own company? Or because nobody can replace your husband?'

'Nobody could replace Theo, that's for sure,' Sybil told her. 'As for the rest, I don't mind the idea of going out with a male companion from time to time. It would make a nice change. But in all honesty, I'm not prepared to invest my emotional energy in another man. It's taken me time to get my life exactly how I want it now, and I don't want anyone messing it up. Tansy thinks it's selfish.'

'It sounds blissful to me,' said Ailie. 'There was a lot of emotion in my marriage even at the end.' She took a large sip from her wine glass. 'I can't even imagine being with anyone else, now or in the future.'

'You might change your mind in time,' said Sybil. 'You're younger than me, after all. But I don't want to have to conform to someone else's ideals. Not at this stage in my life.'

'I doubt very much I'll change my mind,' said Ailie. 'I was divorced before meeting Giorgio. I'm shattered at being left alone, but I couldn't go through it all again.'

'That's completely understandable,' Sybil assured her. 'Being alone is hard. Adapting to someone new in your life is equally hard.'

'Do you have children, Sybil?' Rua asked her.

'No, I don't,' replied Sybil, then wondered as she often did if she should mention that she had nieces and nephews, and a grand-niece and grand-nephew too, and got on well with all of them. But she stayed silent.

'My daughter wasn't planned,' said Rua. 'Both of us are independent spirits, but I'm dreading the day she moves out. Like your girl, she was at the concert with me,' she added, turning to Ailie.

'Tonight wouldn't normally have been Flavia's thing, but like I said, I wanted her to come and she didn't want me to be on my own either,' said Ailie. 'She's only eighteen, but chivvying around me like a mother hen. I'm trying to take her grief into account and not pressurise her or make her feel like I depend on her for anything, yet she seems to think she needs to look after me. It'd be funny if we weren't both broken-hearted.'

'Brontë is twenty. She's into classical music, so this was a treat for her,' said Rua. 'She played the clarinet when she was in school. Though you've got a point, Ailie, about not wanting to depend on your daughter too much. I feel the same. I was . . . am . . . a single parent and I don't want to load too much onto her either.'

'Have you always been a single parent?' asked Ailie.

'I was when Brontë was born,' said Rua. 'And then I was married. Now . . . well, now I'm a widow too.'

'How bizarre is this?' Ailie looked at Rua and Sybil in surprise. 'What are the chances of three widows meeting out of the blue?'

'I suppose it's not entirely unimaginable given the circumstances,' said Sybil. 'The age profile at the concert was at the upper end. Stands to reason some of us would be widowed, although both of you are very young to have lost your husbands. I'm so sorry about that.'

'Giorgio had a heart attack.' Ailie cleared her throat and swallowed hard before continuing. 'That one they call the Widowmaker. Turns out it was.'

'Theo had cancer. He was ill for three years,' said Sybil. 'The last few months were very difficult. I hate saying it was a release for him when he died, but the truth is it was a release for both of us in the end.'

It took a moment for Rua to speak.

'Lilou was killed in an accident,' she said finally. 'We were married six months before it happened.'

'Oh, Rua. I'm sorry I made an assumption about your partner being a man.' Sybil was embarrassed. 'At least you *did* get married, even if for a short time. Not that it's the most important thing, but perhaps for you it was?'

'For Lilou more than me at the time,' said Rua. 'But when she died, it was a huge comfort to me that we were married.'

'It's a pretty name,' said Ailie.

'She was French,' said Rua. 'I met her when I worked there.'

'How long since the accident?' asked Ailie.

'A little over two years.'

'You poor thing,' said Sybil. 'Were you living in France at the time? Or did you move here before that?'

'France,' said Rua. 'Brontë and I came back to Ireland afterwards.'

'I can imagine having your family around you was important,' said Ailie.

Rua gave her a tight smile, and Sybil, noticing the strain behind it, looked at her sympathetically, although she was still feeling embarrassed about her earlier assumption. Now, though, she was racked with curiosity about Rua's story. But she held back from asking questions and instead said they should toast the memories of their spouses and happier times ahead.

'Happier times,' echoed Rua and Ailie, although Ailie's voice cracked on the words. 'Happier times.'

Chapter 7

It was almost 10.30 by the time Sybil got home, light-headed from the couple of whiskeys she'd had with Ailie and Rua, but also light-hearted because she'd enjoyed their company. She hadn't realised how much she'd missed socialising with people outside her family circle, and it had been good to be able to talk with women who were in the same situation as herself. She usually felt uncomfortable speaking about Theo, but these women, who'd also lost their partners, understood the crushing sense of abandonment that it brought, and the sense that the future you'd expected had been ripped away from you.

She was slightly worried that they'd think her harsh and unfeeling about not wanting new relationships, but she'd worked hard to rebuild her life since Theo's death and she regularly reminded herself that despite being alone, she was no longer lonely. Yet it had been surprisingly cathartic to talk about him to women who understood, and who themselves were learning to adjust to their new lives.

Regardless of their different backgrounds, their shared losses were the same, and although they hadn't gone into any great depth about their personal histories, they'd found comfort even in the things that were left unsaid. Nonetheless, and perhaps due to the whiskeys, Sybil had found herself talking more than usual, and certainly more than she'd intended about Tansy's desire for her to find someone new and her sister's selection of Burt as a potential partner.

Both Ailie and Rua had cackled with laughter at her description of him, although Rua told her that she shouldn't entirely close the door on finding love even if Burt wasn't her ideal candidate.

'Not that I can talk,' she'd added. 'I'm not looking for someone new myself. But you're further along the path, Sybil, and who knows what the future might bring.'

While Sybil conceded that nobody could foretell the future, she was pretty certain that romance wasn't on the horizon for her. She said as much to Tansy whenever her sister brought up the subject of dating again, pointing out that there were a limited number of available men for women in their sixties.

'Which is why you've got to get moving,' Tansy had told her the last time she'd raised the possibility of Sybil finding someone. She'd added that the years were rushing by and that Sybil couldn't hang around for ever. Exasperated by her sister's continued efforts to meddle in her life, Sybil had retorted that she was perfectly happy by herself. Yet when she mentally replayed the conversation afterwards, she was surprised to realise how long she'd been alone.

At least she'd had time to get used to the idea of Theo's illness and the inevitable consequence, not that any of that had been easy. But perhaps better than how Giorgio Marchetti had died so suddenly, leaving Ailie shocked and struggling with how quickly it had happened.

'One day he was perfectly fine,' she told them. 'The next he was gone. And I still think he's going to walk in the door every evening.'

'I was the same with Lilou,' said Rua. 'It took me a long time to learn to live with it. To be honest, I'm not sure I ever will.'

Yet you do, thought Sybil now, as she made herself a cup of Earl Grey; you have to. You learn to accept that the life you'd built with someone, and the person you were with that someone, was gone forever. She was grateful that she'd had the opportunity for a gradual goodbye with Theo, no matter how hard those last few weeks had been. It must have been immensely difficult for Ailie to have had no chance at all, and even though Rua and Brontë had had time to say their farewells to Lilou, whose injuries following the accident were catastrophic, it had also been a sudden, horrific blow.

At least Sybil had been able to tell Theo over and over again how much she loved him. How he was, and always would be, the love of her life. How fortunate she was to have found him.

'I'm the lucky one,' he said one day, opening his eyes and looking straight at her. 'You are my one and only wife. My forever love.'

His words had reduced her to tears.

It had been a comfort to share those memories with people who fully understood the complex emotions behind the loss of a loved one.

When they finally got up to leave, they'd talked about keeping in touch and had exchanged phone numbers. Sybil wondered if they really would contact each other again, or if the sharing of numbers had been nothing more than a consequence of having a few drinks and the undoubted festive atmosphere in the pub.

And yet, she thought, a friendship with Ailie and Rua would be welcome. Their talk hadn't only been about their late partners; the chat between them had been easy and wide-ranging, covering shared interests in concerts and eating out, bingeing on TV series and reading. They all had some complications in their family relationships. Most importantly, they were relaxed in each other's company and the conversation had flowed.

Sybil recalled how, after the overwhelming business of dealing with Theo's estate had finally come to a conclusion, her days had stretched out with unaccustomed empty time. She'd felt awkward around her casual acquaintances and felt that they were equally awkward around her. Many of those she'd known through Theo's work, or others she'd considered as joint friends, had stopped inviting her to events, as though without him she no longer existed. On the one hand, she was hurt by the fact that they were ignoring her. On the other, she knew that she wasn't ready to socialise again either.

Meanwhile, Tansy was obsessed with Sybil's 'grief process', as she called it, and was constantly badgering her about joining bereavement groups both physical and online, and 'working through it'.

Though undoubtedly adrift, Sybil considered herself perfectly capable of working her way through it herself, and until Juliette had moved to Galway, she'd been able to count on her for coffee or lunch and a good chat a couple of times a week.

However, after Juliette's move, and as much to shut her

sister up as anything else, she'd begun cramming her days with a wide range of new activities, flitting from one to the other so that she could say she was busy, even though few of them truly interested her. After a while, she decided that quality was more important than quantity, and she culled the bell therapy, the crafting and the dancercise, along with the hill-walking and the yoga. She kept up with Pilates and Irish language classes, but began to settle into a quieter, less frantic lifestyle, although she happily used her travel card to journey outside Dublin, and would overnight in good hotels, treating herself to any spa facilities they offered and to room service for her evening meal. She also went on occasional weekends to European capitals for concerts or cultural events. She was thankful that she was happy with her own company, although she conceded that it might occasionally be nice to have someone to share the concerts or dinners or simply the evenings with.

Her phone buzzed. It was Burt, texting to ask how the concert had gone. She hesitated briefly, then called him.

'It was excellent,' she said. 'My seat was perfect, thank you so much. I'm sorry you missed it.'

'So am I.' Burt's voice was hoarse, and Sybil mentally chastised herself for assuming he had man flu. 'I'd been looking forward to it for ages, and when you said you'd come, I was delighted. But hopefully another time?'

'Of course,' said Sybil. 'Get well soon.'

'I'm off to bed now,' said Burt. 'I've been dosing myself with hot whiskey, honey and lemon. I reckon a good night's sleep will sort me.'

Sybil didn't say that she'd also been drinking whiskey. She wished him a good night and pleasant dreams. Then she went into the bedroom, changed into her fleecy pyjamas and removed her make-up. Climbing into bed, she turned on the TV. Theo would've gone berserk if he knew there was a TV in the bedroom. He had always insisted it should be a tech-free zone. Mobile phones had been allowed only if they were in do-not-disturb mode.

There was no need for Sybil to put hers into do-not-disturb any more. As for the TV, it automatically shut itself off after two hours, so she usually turned it to a news channel and let it drone on in the background when she closed her eyes. She chose the news channel because it didn't keep her awake – quite the opposite; the voices of the presenters were soothing and made her feel less alone. Bedtime was the time she missed him most. Not for the sex, though that was part of it, but for the knowledge that he was beside her and the comfort of his arm around her. However, being in the apartment made his absence easier, because there was nowhere in it she'd shared with him. She didn't feel her loss as keenly as she had at Burrow Bay, their last home together.

It had been a double-fronted period house, stately in its proportions, with panoramic views across the sea. It had two big reception rooms, a dining room and a kick-ass kitchen that was wasted on her. Theo had told her to sell it when he was gone, that it would be a burden and difficult to maintain. Much as she'd loved living there, he was right; it was far too big to cope with on her own. Although Tansy told her not to rush into anything, Sybil sold it as soon as she could and moved to the top-floor apartment in a modern block less than a kilometre away. It was exceptionally spacious for an apartment and, crucially, came with the wide sea views that were so important to her.

She was happy here. She filled her days as much as possible with things she knew Theo would have wanted her to do – like her weekends away and her spa pampering, as well as retaining her non-executive-director role in the company. And even if every day was a challenge, she no longer felt the subtle judgement of people who assumed that by now she was perfectly fine.

But there'd been no judgement among the women tonight. Ailie and Rua had made her laugh. She'd made them laugh too. Most importantly of all, they were post-Theo people who didn't see her as the leftover part of a relationship. Nor did she see them in relation to their late spouses either.

She took her phone from the charging stand on the bedside table and set up a group for the three of them, then composed a message.

> Thank you for your kindness and your company this evening. It would be nice to meet up in the future like we said. I'm terrible for saying but not doing, so perhaps we could get together again in January? In the meantime, I wish you both the peace of Christmas.

It doesn't sound like me at all, she thought, as she read it back. None of it is the sort of thing I say.

But she pressed send anyway.

When Rua got home, she was surprised to find Brontë curled up in front of the TV, a mug of hot chocolate in her hand.

'I thought you'd still be out,' she remarked as she unwound her scarf from her neck.

'And I thought you'd be home long before me,' returned Brontë. 'Where were you?'

'I went for a drink.'

'A drink! With who?' Brontë was surprised.

'I met some people,' said Rua. 'Although I'm perfectly capable of going for a drink on my own if I want to. In fact, I'd kinda planned to.'

She didn't say that her original idea had been to go to the pub that she and Lilou used to frequent when they visited Ireland. Nor did she say that she'd planned to sit there and scroll through photographs of her late wife.

'What people? There wasn't anyone around when I left you. Not anyone you know, anyhow.'

'I bumped into some women,' said Rua.

'But who were they?' demanded Brontë.

'For heaven's sake, what's with the third degree?'

'It's only . . . well, you don't have any friends,' said Brontë.

'What are you talking about?' asked Rua. 'What about Merry and Suranne and Bella?'

'They're your online gym bunny friends. Not real friends. You don't have any friends in real life.'

'Not close friends,' agreed Rua. 'But I do have friends. Some of the people I work with are friends. I'm not some sad old sack living alone.'

'No, because you have me.' Brontë didn't point out that Rua rarely socialised with her colleagues. 'But what if I go away again?'

'Are you planning to?' Rua felt her heart tighten.

'Not straight away. All the same, I'd like to work abroad when I finish college. At least for a while.'

'In France?' asked Rua.

Brontë shrugged. 'I don't know. I haven't decided yet.'
'OK.'
'And I'd like to think that you weren't withering away on your own if I do,' she added.
'For heaven's sake, I'm not withering away.'
'You're not exactly setting the town on fire either.'
'I've no desire to be setting anything on fire,' Rua said. 'All the same, doesn't going for a drink with some new friends after the concert prove I have a life of my own?'
'I'm not sure.' Brontë frowned. 'It's all very odd.'
'You sound like my mother.' Rua looked at her in amusement. 'I'm the parent here, remember?'
'I know you are. All the same, I worry about you.'
'Oh, Brontë, you don't have to worry about me.' Rua sat on the edge of the sofa and put her arms around her daughter. 'I'm fine, honestly.'
'But you miss Lilou so much.'
'That's normal,' said Rua.
'Will you miss her forever?'
'Yes, I will. But it doesn't mean I'm miserable all the time. It means there's a place in my heart that will always be hers. Same as there's a place in my heart that will always be yours.'
'I want you to be all right,' said Brontë.
'I am. I promise.'
'What about Christmas then?' She made an abrupt change in the conversation.
'Christmas?'
'Are we going to Loughmore?'
'Do you want to go?'
'Well, it's not as if Alize and Valery will ever ask us, is it?'
'No,' agreed Rua.

'And even if they spoke to each other, never mind me, they're Lilou's parents, not my grandparents,' continued Brontë.

'That's true.'

'So the only grandparents I know are Granny and Gramps Lehane.'

'Yes.'

'And it's a bit . . . well . . . odd that we hardly ever see them.'

'I'm not fond of going back to Loughmore,' said Rua.

'You've made that clear many times.'

'There's nothing stopping *you* from visiting as much as you like,' she pointed out.

'I'm not going without you for Christmas.'

'We could visit this Sunday if you want.'

'What I want is for both of us to stay with them for Christmas Day like Granny suggested. Like she suggested last year too.'

They'd spent the previous Christmas in Dublin together. Rua thought it had turned out well. Christmas Day itself was quiet, but the small cul-de-sac where they lived had organised carol singing with mulled wine on Christmas Eve, and a group of Brontë's student friends had called around on St Stephen's Day. But perhaps it wouldn't work for two years in a row.

'OK,' she said after considering it. 'If that's what you want, that's what we'll do.'

'But it's not what you want?'

'*Ma chérie*, I want whatever is best for you,' said Rua. 'I mean it, I'm not just saying it. So if that means going to Loughmore, I'm perfectly happy to do it.'

'You won't sit around like a wet blanket?'

'Have I ever?'

'No. But that's only because normally you go your own sweet way about things,' said Brontë.

Rua laughed.

Her daughter was wrong about that.

Rua had lived a lot of her life doing what other people wanted.

Her phone pinged. She looked at Sybil's message and considered it carefully, before replying:

January's ideal. Count me in.

Ailie absorbed the empty feeling of the house without Giorgio. Flavia had texted to say that she and her friends had gone for something to eat, and although Ailie would have loved her company, she was glad that her daughter was having a good time. She changed out of her trousers and blouse into a pair of leggings and a fleece that had once belonged to Giorgio. The slightly woody scent of his Acqua di Parma Zafferano cologne lingered in the soft fabric, and she inhaled deeply, wondering if this was something Rua and Sybil had also done.

It had been good to meet them tonight. Had she gone to the concert with Giorgio, he would have booked a restaurant for afterwards. They'd have shared a bottle of wine and a drink and she would have felt relaxed in his company. She hadn't felt relaxed in anyone's company – not even Flavia's – in weeks. She was far too concerned about being strong for her daughter to be able to relax with her. And too concerned about their future to relax on her own.

And yet tonight, for a short time, she'd felt the stress ease.

Her phone beeped with Sybil's message about meeting up in January. She wondered if the feeling of being adrift would have lessened by then. Or the crushing guilt. Not guilt about suddenly enjoying herself, although that had been there. But guilt about the hours leading up to Giorgio's death. She rather suspected those feelings might be worse. And she didn't know if she'd be able to face socialising with the two women she'd met tonight either. Yet she couldn't sit at home brooding forever.

She stared at the message for an age and then replied.

Sounds nice. Let's keep in touch. Happy Christmas to you both too.

She added a smiley face, even though in real life she'd forgotten how to smile.

Chapter 8

Rua and Brontë arrived at Loughmore on Christmas Eve, their last couple of kilometres brightened by the trees of the town decked out in festive lights that twinkled in the falling dusk. Brontë had wanted to leave Dublin the day before, but Rua had to go into the office for a while, and by the time she got home again, it was too late to set off. She knew Brontë was irked by the delay, but she decided to ignore her daughter's ill-humour as well the text message from her mother asking what time they were arriving. (She didn't ignore Mary's text entirely, but she left it for a couple of hours before replying that they wouldn't make it until the following day.)

'Here at last.' Brontë was still grumpy as she got out of the car.

The door to the house opened and Mary stepped outside before either Rua or Brontë rang the bell. At seventy, Mary Lehane could have passed for someone a decade younger. Her hair, ash blonde since her fifties, was short and well styled. Her blue eyes were bright in a face that was remarkably unlined and without a visible scrap of make-up. She wore a dark green jumper over well-cut black trousers and flat indoor shoes.

'Granny!' Brontë let go of her wheelie case, which toppled over onto the gravel driveway. She flung her arms around her grandmother. 'I thought we'd never get here.'

'Sure, I thought the same,' said Mary. 'I've been waiting for you all day. Hello, Rua.'

Rua, who was now holding on to both her case and Brontë's, nodded in acknowledgement and followed her mother and daughter into the house, already feeling the perspiration break out on her forehead thanks to Mary's insistence on always having the heat on high.

'We get the north wind,' her mother would say whenever Rua complained that it was sweltering indoors. 'We need to keep warm.'

Rua removed her scarf and draped it over the free hook on the wall. She added her knitted hat and thermal jacket. Brontë, her grumpiness forgotten, didn't wait to take off her own jacket but followed Mary into the living room. Rua heard the exclamation of welcome from her father. She took a deep breath and stepped inside.

'Rua! It's lovely to see you too, sweetheart,' Conal said, releasing his hold on Brontë. 'It's been such a long time.'

'Sorry, Dad,' she said. 'I've been busy.'

'She buries herself in her office and spends all day on the computer,' Brontë told him. 'I bet she's looking at cute kittens on the internet and not working at all.'

'And here was I thinking that's something you young ones would be doing,' said Mary. 'Aren't you all supposed to walk around with your heads in your mobile phones?'

'Sometimes I do.' Brontë grinned.

'I'll put on the kettle,' said Mary. 'Tea or coffee?'

'Ooh, Granny, can I give you your Christmas present

now?' Brontë looked between Mary and Rua. 'It's OK for her to open it ahead of time, isn't it?'

'Of course. It's in the car,' said Rua.

'I'll get it.' Brontë hurried outside.

'It's a proper present having you both here,' said Conal.

'Brontë really wanted to come,' said Rua.

'You should visit us more often,' said Mary. 'After all, this is your home . . .' She broke off as Brontë walked into the living room carrying a large gift-wrapped box.

'It's for both of you,' she said. 'Go on, open it.'

Mary smiled at her and began to unwrap it, carefully folding the paper so that it could be reused.

'Oh,' she said when she saw the picture on the front of the box. 'A coffee machine. We do already have one, you know.'

'Yes, but yours is very basic,' Brontë reminded her. 'You're going to love this, Granny. I picked it out. It makes fabulous coffee *and* it produces boiling water so you can make a single cup of tea without having to boil a kettle.'

'It's very nice,' said Conal.

Brontë beamed at her grandfather. 'It grinds coffee beans and everything. We've brought some. And Mum added a pack of Barry's tea. I wanted to get you a fancy blend, Granny, but she insisted this was your favourite.'

'She's right about that,' agreed Mary. 'I'll make us a pot. You can help me set up the machine, Brontë.'

'Cool.'

The two of them went into the kitchen while Rua sat in the easy chair opposite her father.

'You have to make more of an effort with your mother,' said Conal abruptly. 'Visit more often. Be nicer when you do. I know you've always thought she's old-fashioned and behind the times, but she loves you. She knows it's been hard for you since Lilou died. She only wants to help.'

'I'm doing fine,' Rua told him. 'Brontë's doing fine too. I appreciate that Mam is concerned about us, but I don't need any help.'

'We all need help from time to time,' said Conal. 'Didn't she help you by arranging for you to go to France after you dropped out of college? And didn't that work out for you?'

'Yes.' Rua exhaled slowly. 'Mam and I are grand. We're different, that's all.'

'She always has your best interests at heart.'

Rua wasn't going to argue. It was Christmas after all.

'Are Stan and Millie coming tomorrow with Savannah?' she asked in an attempt to move the conversation to more comfortable matters.

'Of course they are,' said her father. 'Sure it wouldn't be Christmas if they didn't come.'

'I thought Millie might want to go to her own folks,' said Rua.

'Ah, well, she prefers it here,' said her dad. 'And why wouldn't she? Doesn't your mother always do a proper traditional Christmas.'

Rua nodded. Mary had always been relentless in her desire to make Christmas perfect. As long as everything seemed that way, she was happy. Whether anyone else was, thought Rua, was entirely irrelevant.

Rua's brother and his wife arrived with Savannah at two o'clock on Christmas Day. The family sat in the living room with glasses of Prosecco, and non-alcoholic sparkling wine in the case of Mary, who didn't drink, and Millie, who'd given it up when she was pregnant and no longer liked the taste.

'Which is perfect for me,' joked Stan as he poured it for her. 'I always have a designated driver.'

'That could change yet.' Millie made a face at him and then lunged at her daughter, who was tugging at the damask tablecloth to help herself stand up.

'I don't drink as much alcohol as I used to,' said Rua, 'but I do like a glass of Prosecco.'

'So do I,' said Brontë.

'You need to be careful,' Mary told her. 'I've read terrible things about what people add to drinks these days. Pills and whatnot. It can make you careless, or that you don't know what you're doing.'

'You don't need to worry about me, Gran,' said Brontë. 'I'm super careful whenever I go out. I never leave a drink out of my hand.'

'Good girl,' said Mary.

'Not that young women should have to worry about anything being put in their drinks.' Rua's voice was taut. 'Instead of telling girls to be careful all the time, we should be telling men not to act like—'

'You're right,' Stan interrupted her. 'There's definitely a lot more of that going on now. Lots of talk in schools about respect and consent and all that sort of stuff.'

'Probably not enough to counter all that misogynistic garbage that's pumped onto social media,' said Rua. 'When you look at it, you'd despair for men.'

'I think a lot of young men are confused about their place in the world,' said Stan.

'Yeah, though when women are confused or when we're treated badly, nobody excuses our behaviour,' Rua told him. 'The narrative is always "a woman was attacked". Never "a man attacked a woman". The language is all wrong, yet men always try to forgive themselves.'

'Could we not have some kind of political debate today?' pleaded her father. 'It's Christmas.'

'Gender violence is hardly political,' said Rua. Then she shrugged. 'But you're right, Dad. Let's stick to warm and fuzzy.'

So they began talking about how well Savannah was progressing and her rapidly expanding vocabulary, as well as some good news from Stan's business, and whether Millie would go back to her job as a primary school teacher in a few months' time. The conversation ebbed and flowed and Rua let most of it go over her head. She didn't want to spoil Christmas for anyone, and yet she found it hard to stay quiet when both Mary and Conal urged Millie to stay at home and look after Savannah because being a mother was the most important job in the world. Why did nobody ever say being a father was the most important job in the world?

As the thought struck her, she glanced at Mary who was getting up to clear the plates from the smoked salmon, their traditional Christmas dinner starter. She wondered if her mother really believed everything she said, or if she simply found it easier to believe it than to deal with the more horrible things that happened in life. And she wondered how happy her mother had been in her marriage of nearly fifty years. Because it couldn't always have been perfect.

She got up and helped with clearing the plates. Mary looked at her in surprise.

'I can manage,' she said.

'I'm sure you can, but I'll give you a hand all the same.'

She carried the crockery into the kitchen and stacked it in the dishwasher.

'Will I bring in the veg?' she asked.

'Yes, while I cut the ham. Your dad will carve the turkey.'

As he always did. With a flourish. As though he'd killed it and cooked it himself.

When Rua returned after placing the serving dishes on the dining room table, her mother had already put slices of ham on the plates.

'It's nice to have you here again,' said Mary. 'We've missed you.'

Rua knew she was supposed to say that she'd missed them too.

But she couldn't.

After dinner, when she and Mary had cleared everything away and her dad was snoozing in his armchair, Rua went upstairs. Mary had allocated Rua's old room to Brontë and given Stan's slightly larger bedroom to Rua herself. Both rooms had long since been redecorated and turned into guest rooms, so they didn't bring back any particular memories.

However, looking out of the window and across the fields at the neighbouring farm did.

When he'd bought the house and lands, the current owner, Pearse Mullery, had immediately demolished the original traditional farmhouse and replaced it with a six-bedroom Palladian-style statement home. Somewhat inappropriately, given the usual direction of the weather, he then changed the name of the farm from Gosheen Fields to Southwinds.

The locals, however, continued to call it Gosheen, or, occasionally, Southfork, after the sprawling ranch in a popular TV series of the time. In the intervening years, both his sons had built similar houses on the farmland too.

Rua had never been in the Palladian Southwinds, but she remembered being in the kitchen of the original Gosheen as a small child. It had been a warm, comforting place, heated by an enormous Aga, where Annie Kivlehan baked bread and pies that were occasionally sold in the local supermarket. Rua had loved Annie and had been sorry when she decided the farm was too much for her and went to live with her son in the city. Pearse Mullery, who'd had his eye on the land for years, was delighted to buy it. Rua didn't realise then that this would set the scene for her life to change irrevocably.

Her jaw clenched as she recalled the moment she'd said hello to Davey Mullery, Pearse's son and a year ahead of her in school, on the Cork Road. Over twenty years ago, the memory was as clear as if it had happened yesterday.

She hadn't noticed him at first because the rain was pelting down, driven at an angle by the wind so that it battered against the umbrella she was struggling to keep up. The orange lights of the street lamps reflected off the pavement where her eyes were focused, trying to make sure that she kept her balance on the uneven surface, regretting the impulse that had made her wear high-heeled shoes instead of sturdy boots. (Their local TD had contested the last election on a promise to improve the pavement on the road to Loughmore, but his party had been in government for three years and so far nothing had happened.)

The rain was beating down so heavily and she was concentrating so hard on staying upright that she didn't hear the footsteps behind her. And then he was beside her and saying hello and she was so startled that she nearly dropped her umbrella.

'Can I share it?' he asked as he bent his head to join her beneath the shelter.

'Davey Mullery, you put the heart crossways in me. What are you doing out?'

'I could ask you the same.'

'I was up at Charlene's. The rain wasn't quite so awful when I left.'

Charlene was one of Rua's closest friends and had been since their first day at school. They were now at college in Cork together, but home for the mid-term break.

'Same here,' said Davey. 'The rain wasn't as bad when I left. You're lucky I met you. I'm heading to Connolly's to pick up my car. I'll give you a lift home.'

Connolly's was the local garage, and a little out of Rua's way. But the offer of a lift home meant that a slight walking detour would be worth it.

'Great, thanks,' she said.

'How's college?' asked Davey. 'Computer science, wasn't it?'

'You've a good memory.'

'Sure, weren't we at the same school. I remember you talking about it.'

'Gosh. I don't remember that at all.'

'You were too good for the likes of me,' said Davey. 'The brainy one.'

'The nerdy one,' Rua reminded him. 'Nobody took any notice of me or Charlene. Or Breda or Kate,' she added, mentioning two of her other friends. 'We weren't enough fun.'

'Ye were a right little stuck-up clique,' remarked Davey.

'Not a bit of it,' said Rua. 'We were shy, that's all. How are things for you?' she continued. 'Didn't you go to Dublin to study politics?'

'I did. It's the family business after all.'

Rua bit back a remark about the 'family business' not dealing with the uneven pavement. Davey's dad was the politician who'd promised to fix it. It wasn't Davey's fault his dad broke his promises.

'Here, let me hold that.' He took the umbrella from her and held it more steadily over them. 'Good to know that men have their uses.'

The wind whipped up some more, and Davey struggled to keep the umbrella in place for the five minutes it took to reach the garage. Rua released a sigh of relief at being in from the rain at last.

Davey went to talk to the mechanic while she strolled around the showroom. Her interest in cars was minimal, but she liked the new smell of them. She was sitting in the passenger seat of a top-of-the-range model, fantasising about being able to buy it, when Davey called to her that his own car was ready and it was time to go. He drove a Mercedes that had belonged to his father. Unlike her own dad, who changed cars reluctantly, Davey's father bought a new one every three years and passed the previous models to his sons once they were old enough to drive.

'Nice,' she said as she pulled the seat belt across her chest.

'I like it too.' He eased the car out of the garage and turned left.

'Have you forgotten where I live?' she asked. 'It's the other way.'

'I have to drop off a package first,' said Davey.

'Where?'

'Killaden.'

'Davey! That's five kilometres in the opposite direction,' protested Rua. 'I'm only a couple from here. It's quicker to drop me off first.'

'Too late now,' said Davey. 'I can't do a U-turn on this road.'

She was irritated with him but said nothing. She would've been home by now if she'd walked. She slid her feet out of her shoes and allowed them to dry beneath the warmth of the heater. A couple of kilometres along the road, Davey turned onto a small track leading to a painted wooden hut. He stopped in front of the hut and turned off the engine.

'Here? You're dropping a package off here?' asked Rua.

'I wanted to show you the place,' he said.

'Why?'

'You'll see. Come on.'

'Davey . . .'

But he'd already got out of the car and come around to open the passenger door.

'Put on your shoes,' he said.

'Davey, don't be daft, I'm not getting out and going into some ramshackle hut with you. Leave the package and let's go.'

'You're the package,' he said.

'What?'

'Well . . . bringing you here is a gift to myself,' he told her.

'Now you're scaring me,' she said.

'No need to be scared, Redzer.' His voice was cheerful. 'Honestly. It's fine. Come on.' He pulled her arm, and, still barefoot, she half fell and was half dragged out of the car. 'You'll like it, you'll see,' he added.

He unlocked the door of the hut and gave her a gentle push inside. She blinked as he turned on the light. It was furnished like a studio apartment, with a table and chairs, a sofa and a bed. There was a TV on the wall facing the sofa. The other walls were covered with posters of classic cars and nude women.

'This is your man cave,' said Rua. She shivered slightly.

'It's a bit cold.' Davey noticed the shiver. 'But it warms up quickly.' He turned on a couple of infrared heaters. 'So what d'you think?'

'I think I should be getting home.'

'Not a bit of it,' said Davey. 'Sure, the evening's just getting started.'

'Davey, I told them I'd be back. They'll be worried about me.'

'Aren't you a grown-up girl now living in Cork?' demanded Davey. 'Why would they worry about you?'

'Mum is expecting me,' said Rua.

'We'd better be quick so.' Davey took off his jacket. 'C'mere to me now.'

'Are you crazy!' cried Rua as he put his arms around her. 'For crying out loud, Davey. Stop.'

'You said you weren't too good for the likes of me. Seems to me you think you are.'

'Ah, lookit, Davey, it's you who are too good for the likes of me.' She tried to sound light-hearted. 'Your dad's the local TD.'

'So he is,' said Davey. 'He's done well for himself. And sure I'm doing well for myself too. I'm working with him now. I'll be somebody one day. You're lucky I'm taking an interest in you.'

'I don't want you to take an interest in me,' she said. 'I need to get home.'

'You know, we always wondered about you,' Davey continued, holding her tight around the wrist. 'You and your little coven. We wondered why you didn't like boys.'

'Davey—'

'You do like boys, don't you? And if you're not certain, this'll be a little treat for you. Help you sort yourself out.'

'Let me go.' She struggled to free herself from his hold, but he was a lot stronger than he looked.

'I don't think so,' he said. 'You'll thank me for it afterwards. You can boast about it to your friends.'

'What would I boast about?' she demanded. 'That you forced yourself on me?'

'It's not forcing,' he said.

'No means no,' she told him. 'I'm saying no. You really don't want to do this, Davey.'

'Oh, but I do.'

'Why?'

'You walk around Loughmore like you're better than the rest of us. You're not.'

'I don't think I'm better than anyone.' She tried to keep the panic out of her voice as he pulled at the zip of her parka. 'Please, Davey. You're my friend. Please stop.'

She struggled to push him away, but he suddenly slapped her across the face, and when she gasped in pain, he managed to drag the zip downwards, revealing a cream top and the full red skirt that matched the shoes she'd left behind in the car.

'It's about time a real man gave you a right seeing-to.' He pushed her onto the bed, keeping his hand on her chest to hold her down.

'It's not too late to stop this, Davey.' She tried to get up again but he held her firmly in place. 'Let me go now and I won't say anything to anybody.'

'It doesn't matter if you do or you don't.' He slid his free hand beneath her skirt. 'Nobody's going to believe you. Rua Lehane, daughter of nobody, versus Davey Mullery, son of Pearse.'

'You've slapped me. There are marks. There'll be evidence. For feck's sake, Davey, think about this. Let me go. I'll walk home. I'll say I fell. There'll be no repercussions.'

'Oh, shut the fuck up,' he said, and slapped her again.

Everything after that was a blur. She remembered the weight of him on top of her, and the warmth of his breath and the scent of his aftershave. But she couldn't remember it happening. And she couldn't remember afterwards. The next cogent memory she had was him pushing her out of the car about half a kilometre from her house and telling her that the story of falling in the rain was as good as any. And then she remembered her hand shaking as she tried to put her key in the lock of the front door, and stumbling over the threshold when it finally opened, and then her mother standing over her and asking her where on earth she'd been.

Chapter 9

Sybil met Burt a few days after Christmas. As had become usual over the last five years, she'd spent Christmas Day itself at Tansy's and had been slightly concerned at first that her sister might invite Burt too. But he texted her to say that he'd be at his daughter's for a few days and that he was looking forward to seeing her in the new year. He suggested driving across town to collect her and bring her to lunch somewhere on the coast, but she replied that it was a lot of effort for him and meeting in the city would be more convenient for both of them.

Being picked up by him would have saved her a blustery walk to Sutton Dart station and an equally blustery one to the National Gallery, where they'd arranged to meet, but she preferred to have options of her own for getting home. She'd been the one to suggest the gallery, saying that it was a favourite haunt of hers and that they could have a wander through it before lunch. She added that she wasn't very good at simply meeting up for something to eat; that she liked to have something to do.

To be fair to Burt, she thought as she entered the gallery, he'd fallen in easily with the plan, saying that he was happy to avail himself of his free travel into town and that it would allow them to have a glass of wine together after the gallery tour. It was a long time since he'd been to the exhibitions, he told her, and it would be good for him to take in a bit of culture.

She looked around for him now, hoping that the image she had of him in her head from dinner at Tansy's was accurate. She wasn't good at faces. She hadn't recognised Ailie Taylor from the cemetery, although she'd been aware of the funeral as she walked by and had specifically observed the woman who was clearly the chief mourner. But Ailie had been dressed in black that day, not the white puffa jacket she'd been wearing when she'd come to Sybil's aid after the concert. So it wasn't entirely surprising she hadn't recognised her.

After Christmas, she'd followed up on her initial WhatsApp message to Ailie and Rua, and all three had agreed a date to meet later in the month, although they hadn't yet decided where. Sybil knew that she was looking forward to that much more than meeting Burt. It was extraordinary, she thought, that a few weeks ago she'd visited the cemetery alone and without any significant social activities in her diary. And now, partly as a result of Tansy's birthday dinner (dammit, maybe she should thank her sister for that!), she had some prospective new female friends, and a lunch with a man to deal with.

Lunch, that was, if Burt turned up. He was almost ten minutes late, and Sybil frowned as she checked her watch. But then she heard him call her name and she turned around.

'I'm sorry,' he said, his smile even brighter than she remembered. 'I used the other entrance and I was waiting for you there. Then I remembered you were coming in by train and this made more sense.'

'My fault,' said Sybil. 'I should have been clearer.'

'No problem.' He slid his arm through hers. 'OK. You're the expert. Lead me around.'

Sybil told him that she wasn't an expert at all, but had favourite paintings, which included *A Convent Garden in Brittany* by William Leech, one of the gallery's most-loved artworks.

'It's the light,' she said as they stood in front of it. 'And the simplicity of the colours. The model for the novice is his wife, which makes me smile given that she looks so virginal.'

'It's pretty,' agreed Burt.

Sybil thought the painting was beautiful rather than pretty, but said nothing. She then steered him to one of her other favourites, Vermeer's *Woman Writing a Letter, with her Maid*.

'I miss letter-writing,' she said. 'I had pen friends when I was younger and it was always exciting when the envelopes dropped on the doormat.'

'Are you in touch with any of them now?' asked Burt.

'No.' Sybil shook her head. 'All the letter-writing took place in my early teens. It petered out after that.'

'Have you ever tried to find them on Facebook?'

'That never even occurred to me.' Sybil looked at him in surprise. 'Social media isn't really my thing. Those girls are a part of my life that's over. All the same, I do wish people still wrote letters. It's depressing that the only post that ever arrives now is bills or junk mail.'

They continued their stroll around the gallery, with Burt making comments about various paintings before looking at his huge watch and saying they'd better go or they'd be late for lunch.

'I thought we were eating here,' said Sybil. 'The food in the café is quite good.'

'Are you joking?' Burt was horrified. 'I asked you to lunch, not a café sandwich. I booked the Ivy.'

'That's way too . . . too . . .'

'It's one of my favourite places,' said Burt.

Sybil was surprised. She'd only ever been there once, but she'd got the impression it was more of a venue to be seen in rather than a culinary hot spot for men of a certain age.

'Let's go,' said Burt, steering her towards the exit.

When they arrived at the restaurant, she could see it was busy, but Burt had reserved a window table with proper chairs rather than one in the centre of the room where diners sat on banquettes. Sybil was relieved. She hated banquettes.

'A bottle of red, I think,' he said. 'Given that it's cold outside.'

'I only ever drink a single glass of wine during the day,' Sybil told him. 'But red is fine.'

'Don't worry about getting home or anything,' said Burt. 'I'll make sure you're OK.'

'I'm not worried about that,' Sybil said. 'Anything more than a glass knocks me for six. I'd probably fall asleep at the table.'

'You were fine at Tansy's,' he objected.

'That was the evening,' she reminded him.

'I'll order a bottle anyway. You can stick with a glass if you want.'

'Whatever you like,' said Sybil.

Burt questioned the sommelier about the wine list while

Sybil remained engrossed in the menu, not getting involved as he asked about different vintages. Finally he made his choice and then they selected food. Burt opted for steak, while Sybil chose cod.

'Not ideal with the red wine,' said Burt. 'You should have a meat dish.'

'I like cod.'

'I'm a fan of fish and chips myself,' he said. 'But I do like a steak when I'm out.'

Sybil had to admit that the wine he'd selected was excellent, and the cod, when it arrived, was equally good. But she was beginning to feel the strain of Burt's company. It wasn't that he was boring – quite the contrary, he was an absolute treasure trove of information and anecdotes; it was that she felt he was talking at her rather than with her. There seemed to be no subject on which he wasn't an expert and didn't have a firm opinion. She was prepared to accept that he might be over-chatty because he was a little nervous at being out with her (although that didn't exactly fit with what she'd gleaned about his personality), but listening to him was exhausting. He was at it again now, talking about some restaurant he'd been to on one of his holidays, and giving a blow-by-blow description of the decor, the food and even the waiter who'd served him, followed by a tale about a mix-up over the main courses that was resolved amicably despite it having been the waiter's fault.

Sybil's mind drifted to the first time she'd gone out with Theo. They'd popped into McDonald's after seeing a movie at the Savoy Cinema. Back then, a movie followed by a burger and chips was the height of sophistication, and

McDonald's, not long open in Dublin, was regarded as a treat. As far as she could remember, the movie had been a Star Wars one. Theo was into sci-fi and they'd gone to every single Star Wars release, even the more recent ones that were heavy on CGI and light on plot.

Although she couldn't remember the details of the date with any clarity, she did recall how much she'd enjoyed Theo's company. There'd been an immediate attraction at the bank when she'd met him there, but socially they were on the same wavelength too. She wasn't as clued up on computers as him, but she liked talking to him about them. And unlike Burt, he didn't speak to her as if he was the expert and she knew nothing, although that was very definitely the case as far as the new technology was concerned. She was fascinated by how programs were developed and how, within a few years, so many of the office jobs that had once needed pen and paper and calculators, were transferred to the computers. It was an exciting time and she loved being part of it.

'You're away with the fairies there,' said Burt, who'd finished whatever story he was telling and was now looking accusingly at her.

'Sorry,' she said. 'A random memory popped into my head.'

'Oh, I know.' He nodded. 'There are times I remember an event in my twenties clearer than something I did yesterday. But you're as young as you feel, Sybil, and although I felt ancient when Maeve was ill, I'm good now. I want to get out there and live life to the full. When I saw you, looking so stylish and vibrant at Tansy's, I knew you were a woman after my own heart.'

'I—'

'The thing is . . .' He refilled both their wine glasses, even though she'd already told him she'd had enough. 'The thing is, at our stage in life there's no point in hanging around, is there? Nothing to wait for.'

'And what do you not want to hang around for?' she asked.

'Cards on the table,' he said. 'I'm looking for a lady to share my life with. I think she could be you.'

'This is only the second time we've met,' she reminded him.

'My point exactly,' he said. 'We're not kids. We don't need to go on half a dozen dates to know what we want.'

'Are you talking about sleeping with me?'

'Not just that, although I'm sure it would be fantastic,' said Burt. 'Marrying you.'

Despite her rule about only having one glass of wine, Sybil took a large mouthful of the red.

'That's moving a bit fast for me,' she said as she put the glass back on the table.

'You said it's been five years since your husband died,' Burt reminded her. 'You can't still be mourning him.'

'I still miss him,' said Sybil. 'Which is not quite the same thing, I admit. Regardless, Burt, I'm not ready to marry a man I hardly know.'

'You *do* know me,' said Burt. 'We're the same generation. We can talk about the same things. We remember the same pop groups. The same TV shows. The same Dirty Old Dublin of the seventies and eighties. You understand me and I understand you.'

'Perhaps,' conceded Sybil. 'But I'm not marrying someone

based on understanding. I wasn't planning on getting married at all.'

'Everyone needs someone,' said Burt. 'You don't want to eke out the rest of your days alone.'

'I'm not eking things out,' she objected. 'I'm living quite well, to be honest.'

'I didn't get that impression from Tansy. She said—'

'Oh, for feck's sake!' Sybil tossed her napkin onto the table. 'Tansy needs to butt out of my life. She doesn't know me like she thinks she does. I'm perfectly happy living in my apartment and doing my own thing. And if I *were* to marry again, I'd want to marry someone I know properly, not someone who thinks getting to know me is all about food and wine.' She paused. 'Look, you seem like a nice guy, Burt, but I'm not going to pretend that I want to marry you on the basis of one shared meal.'

'Two,' said Burt. 'There was a meal at Tansy's, don't forget.'

Sybil said nothing.

'OK, OK. Maybe I'm being a bit premature.' He shook his head. 'I wanted to let you know at the outset how I was thinking. So there were no misunderstandings. That's all.'

'Well, how *I'm* thinking is that we should pay the bill and go our separate ways.' Sybil opened her bag and took out her phone. She signalled the waiter to bring the bill.

'Maybe a quick drink in the Bailey first,' suggested Burt.

'Honestly, no,' said Sybil.

The waiter came over with the bill, and when Burt took out his card, she told him to split it.

'No,' said Burt. 'I asked you to lunch. I'm paying.'

'Split it,' she repeated.

The waiter looked uncertainly between them.

'Seriously,' she said. 'The lunch was excellent, Burt. But I'd feel better if I paid for myself.'

'I'll pay now, and next time you can pay for both of us,' said Burt.

Sybil doubted very much there'd be a next time.

'I came on a bit strong,' he said. 'I overwhelmed you. I'm sorry. Please let me pay.'

She didn't want to, but in the end she gave in.

Chapter 10

Ailie took Giorgio's suits from the wardrobe and laid them carefully on the bed. She hadn't been able to contemplate this task sooner, but with Christmas and the New Year behind her, she finally felt it was time. She'd texted Sybil and Rua the night before asking how long they'd left it before letting go of their late spouse's clothes. The three women had been in touch a couple of times about their upcoming lunch date, and she felt comfortable about asking the question.

Sybil's reply came quickly.

Does it feel right for you?

Ailie considered the question carefully before replying.

Yes. It's difficult to see his stuff hanging up every day. But it's only been 2 months. Am I heartless? Is it too soon?

If it feels right for you, go ahead. You might want someone with you. I did it alone, but that suited me. You may feel differently.

What did you do with them?

Gave them to a local charity. In fairness, Theo didn't have a lot of good stuff. He was a jeans and sweatshirt guy his whole life, and even those were chain store most of the time. I got the impression your Giorgio was a bit more stylish!

Ailie smiled at that. Her husband had possessed an Italian love of fine fabrics and expensive shoes, and his clothing collection represented a significant investment.
Then her phone pinged with Rua's reply.

I kept some of Lilou's jumpers for myself then gave the rest to a charity that supports young women who can't afford business or smart casual looks for interviews. Brontë took her jewellery. I felt better afterwards to be honest.

Thank you. You've both been hugely helpful. I'll let you know how I get on when we meet up.

Buoyed by the support from Sybil and Rua, Ailie felt able to make a start. It was difficult. Every suit and tie, every jumper or polo shirt triggered their own memories. It was hard to believe he'd never wear them again. Getting rid of Giorgio's clothes felt like a betrayal, and yet keeping them was becoming more and more of an emotional burden. Ailie couldn't help thinking that the practicality of dealing with his wardrobe was far more crushing than dealing with his estate, something that had so far been fairly straightforward.

With all the suits on the bed, she turned her attention to his selection of fitted shirts. Like the fleece she so often wore, they smelled of his cologne, and it brought memories back to her even more forcefully than carefully smoothing out his suits had done. Memories of him walking into the house and putting his arms around her, kissing her on the lips with a passion that had never left him. Memories of him stretched out on the sofa, his legs dangling over the arm, watching Italian football. Memories of him getting dressed for a formal occasion, taking far more care about his appearance than she ever did, making sure that his shirt and jacket sat exactly right on his broad shoulders and that his trousers skimmed his shoes. She remembered their wedding day, and how devastatingly handsome he'd looked. She'd wondered then what he'd seen in her, and he told her that he loved her with all his heart. She knew their relationship was very different to her short-lived marriage to Josh, and even more different to his marriage with Sophia, no matter that his family thought they had been a better match. For a long time she'd worried that marrying him would be a mistake, but despite the ups and downs, she knew she'd found the man she wanted to be with for the rest of her life.

It was unfortunate that his Italian family thought he should have been spending the rest of his life with them.

He'd explained his difficulties to her, but what she hadn't properly appreciated back then was that old Signora Marchetti continued to believe that despite his divorce, he was still married to Sophia. Nor had she known that his mother had threatened and cajoled and bullied him about his relationship with Ailie herself. All she'd known at the time was that none of Giorgio's family were coming to the wedding, and so the ceremony had only been attended by the Taylors and some close friends. To be fair, she'd said to Giorgio at the time, they made up a pretty decent number. The main star of the show had been baby Flavia, adorable in a white dress embroidered with tiny strawberries, a matching headband around her already luxuriant dark hair. There'd been a reception afterwards in a local restaurant, where they'd had a private room, and Giorgio's specially compiled music playlist accompanied their meal and dancing afterwards.

It had been one of the happiest, most memorable days of her life.

And then the last words she'd spoken to him came back to her, as they had every single day since he'd died.

'Oh, sod off then! Don't listen to me. Keep your silly secrets. Chatter away to people in Italy. I always knew one day it would be them or me, and it looks like you're choosing them.'

'*Sei una stupida.*'

He'd walked out of the room, slamming the door behind him. She'd stayed where she was, quietly seething.

And then, an hour later, he'd walked in again and said her name.

He was already falling to the floor before she looked up.

She'd called the emergency services before beginning CPR. But she'd known it was too late. On one level she was aware that her argument with him earlier hadn't been the cause of his cardiac arrest. But no matter how many times she told herself this, she still felt responsible.

'*Ti amo. L'ho sempre fatto. E lo farò sempre.*' She held one of the white shirts to her face, inhaling the scent of him more deeply. 'I'll always love you.'

'What are you doing?'

Ailie turned around and saw Flavia standing in the doorway.

'Tidying your dad's things,' she replied as she placed the shirt on the bed.

'You're not tidying them,' objected Flavia. 'You're . . . you've taken them all out. You're going to throw them away.' Her voice broke. 'How could you?'

'Sweetheart, his clothes can't stay here forever.' Ailie spoke gently.

'You were holding his shirt to your face. It's too soon for you.'

'It'll always be too soon,' she said.

'It's too soon for me.' Tears brimmed in Flavia's eyes, then spilled over onto her cheeks. 'You should have told me and we could have done this together. There are things I might want.'

'What would you like?'

'I could wear his white shirts.' She sniffed and wiped the tears away. 'So could you.'

'Can you imagine what he'd say if he saw me in one of his shirts?' asked Ailie. 'He didn't even like me ironing them. He preferred to do that himself.'

'He wouldn't mind *me* wearing them.' Flavia's tone was mutinous.

'OK,' said Ailie. 'Pick one.'

'More than one,' said Flavia.

'Whatever you want.'

Flavia looked at the piles both on the bed and in the chest of drawers, and eventually selected a couple of slim-fitting white linen Canali shirts as well as a casual Ralph Lauren in pale blue, along with a dusky-pink cashmere jumper that Ailie herself had bought for Giorgio the previous year.

'Do you want something more memorable?' asked Ailie. 'Marco asked for his watch, and I gave him that and his cufflinks before he went back to Italy, but you could have his ring if you like.'

'His wedding ring?' Flavia looked shocked.

'No, the silver one he used to wear. It was his grandfather's.'

'Oh, yes. I'd like that. I'll get it sized to fit me. What about you?' she asked.

'I'll be getting his wedding ring sized for myself,' said Ailie, although she'd only thought of it that very second. 'I'll wear mine and his together as a pair.'

'Great idea.' Flavia threw her arms around her mother. 'I miss him so much, Mum.'

'I know you do.'

'Sometimes you seem very matter-of-fact about everything. You don't even cry any more.'

'I cry plenty,' said Ailie. 'But I also have to be practical. Life goes on around us and we have to deal with all of the messy stuff that has been left behind.'

'Dad wouldn't have left anything messy,' said Flavia. 'He was always careful.'

'There are always things that need looking after when someone dies.' Ailie folded a charcoal-grey polo-neck jumper and put it on top of a neat pile.

'What sort of things?'

'Well . . .' She shrugged. 'His will. Or rather, his wills. He had to make two. One here and one in Italy.'

'Do you need to go to Italy?' asked Flavia.

'I'll talk to the Italian solicitor about it. Marco says that things move slowly there. Not that they're quick here either.'

'I was thinking . . .' Flavia's words were casual. 'Maybe I could do the rest of my gap year there.'

'In Italy?'

'Yes,' said Flavia. 'At the Villa Farfalla.'

'What?' Ailie couldn't keep the surprise out of her voice.

'Why not? After all, I haven't done anything since school except that short time in Australia before Dad . . .' Her voice faltered, then she cleared her throat and spoke again. 'I don't want to go back to the other side of the world, but I could work at the Villa Farfalla. Marco thinks it's a great idea.'

'When did you and Marco even talk about this?' Ailie couldn't quite get her head around what Flavia was saying. She found it hard to believe that her daughter had been discussing a move to Italy with her half-brother. Even more, that they'd talked about her working in the Marchetti hotel, unlikely though that might be. And that neither of them had said a word to her about it.

'At the funeral,' replied Flavia. 'He thinks I'd like Trieste.'

'Darling, you've only been to Italy twice,' Ailie reminded her. 'And you've never even set foot in the villa.'

'That's hardly my fault.' Flavia gave her a dark look. 'You and Dad never wanted to visit. But I have a spiritual connection to it. Dad used to talk with me about growing up there. And Marco sends me photos, same as he did with Dad. I feel like I know it already. It's so beautiful, with those big rooms and high ceilings. The marble floors. The fountains. The gardens.'

'Marco used to send your dad photos of the villa?'

'Yes. To keep him up to speed on how it looked. He always thought Dad would return for a visit.'

'But he didn't,' Ailie reminded her.

'He didn't have time,' conceded Flavia. 'But it's part of his heritage and I want to honour that.'

'I'm not sure how well it would work out,' said Ailie. 'After all, it's the Marchetti home as well as a business, and you know how they are about it. I don't want to be negative, but I'm not sure how they'd feel about giving you a job.'

'Marco says it will be fine,' Flavia told her. 'And it's a good opportunity for me to learn.'

'They—'

'*I'm* a Marchetti.' Flavia interrupted her. 'I *am* they.'

'I see that.' Ailie spoke slowly. 'But they've never exactly been family to you.'

'Whose fault is that?' Flavia demanded.

'Not mine.' Ailie knew she sounded defensive. 'I know Dad had issues with Nonna and . . . well, all that stuff about Sophia. It's so bloody childish. Why can't grown-ups be grown up? But it doesn't mean anything to me and it doesn't mean I'm not related to them either.'

'I know.'

'I'm as much Nonna's grandchild as Marco is.'

'You are.'

'And they talk all the time about him and what role he's going to have in the future.'

'Do they indeed?'

'They were yammering on about it at Dad's funeral,' said Flavia. 'I don't think they realise I speak Italian.'

'What were they saying?' Ailie sat on the bed and looked at her.

'That Sophia is getting legal advice.'

'On what?'

'Her position as Dad's ex-wife. She's calling herself his widow too, you know. She wants to know about her role in the business and what Dad might have left her.'

'Flavia!'

'I was going to tell you, but Marco said to wait. That you needed time to process everything.'

'I see.'

'He's not on their side, if that's what you're thinking.'

'I'm not thinking of there being sides at all,' said Ailie. 'So despite this possible complication with Sophia, you want to work there? If they even allow it.'

'I'm sure there's no real problem with Sophia. And Marco will fix up the job for me.' Flavia spoke with confidence. 'I told him it was about . . . well, honouring Dad's heritage.'

'That's truly how you feel?' Ailie looked at her thoughtfully.

'Yes. I want to . . . There's a whole side of me that I don't know anything about. Dad never talked about it. Neither did you. I want to experience it.'

'Among people who may not exactly be warm and welcoming.'

'Marco's there,' Flavia said. 'He'll be warm and welcoming.'

'I should hope so,' said Ailie.

But she wasn't at all sure about the rest of the Marchettis.

Chapter 11

Sybil lifted the box containing the sandwiches along with the brownies and soup containers from the boot of her car and carried them to the lift in the basement car park. She struggled to wave her pass card at the sensor that allowed access to the penthouse floor, but eventually she succeeded and the lift glided into motion. The doors opened onto the square hallway outside the apartment, and after letting herself in (another struggle while holding the box in her now aching arms), she walked rapidly to the kitchen and dropped rather than placed her purchases on the counter.

Once she'd got her breath back, she started to take the food out of the box and plate it. She'd bought a variety of sandwiches and a selection of brownies, as well as the containers of leek and potato soup. She emptied the soup into a pot, which she put on the hob, although it was too early to heat it yet. Then she took knives and spoons from the cutlery drawer and wrapped them in some pretty paper napkins before placing everything on the table. She lit a couple of scented candles and told Siri to start playing relaxing music.

She realised she was anxious. She told herself it was silly to be anxious, but this was the first time she'd entertained people in the apartment other than Tansy and her family. And they didn't really count as people who needed to be entertained. She'd invited them over shortly after she'd moved in, ordering pizza from the local Italian restaurant. Everyone had congratulated her on the move and enthused at her panoramic views over the bay. Only Tansy had homed in on the negatives, like being on the fifth floor and it not being half as homely as Burrow Bay.

'Burrow Bay was my home with Theo,' Sybil told her. 'This is my home for me.'

'But all your furniture – you've nothing but new things. There's not a screed of your other stuff left.'

'It was too big for here,' she replied. 'And the family buying Burrow Bay were quite happy to have some furniture included. Isn't that right?' She turned to Colin, who'd handled the sale for her. In an ideal world she wouldn't have had her brother-in-law as her estate agent, but he'd done a good job even if she was sure he'd given Tansy forensic detail about the various offers on the house.

Her sister and her family hadn't been to the apartment as a group in quite some time, although Sybil had invited them on more than one occasion. Tansy always insisted she come to visit them instead. After all, as she pointed out, there was only one of Sybil but a gang of Baskins, and Sybil lacked the necessary skills to cook a meal for all of them. Recalling Tansy's face when she'd been presented with the pizza slices, Sybil found it easier to agree.

She hoped that Rua and Ailie, who were coming for lunch, would approve of the food she'd ordered for today. Their original intention had been to meet in town, but as more and more messages with different prospective venues had pinged between them, Sybil had suggested they come to her apartment instead. There was plenty of parking, she told them. And the train station was nearby if they wanted to take public transport. Plus the bus stopped right outside too.

Both Rua and Ailie were enthusiastic, saying that it was a lot less stress than booking somewhere when, despite it being the end of January, all the restaurants seemed to be full at lunchtime. But nothing fancy, Ailie warned her. A few sandwiches would do them fine. She wasn't to go to any trouble.

Phoning the deli and ordering off their catering menu hadn't been any trouble at all. In fact, thought Sybil, it was a lot more convenient than making sandwiches herself. As for the brownies, she wouldn't even have known where to start. She conceded that she'd made soup in the past, particularly in Theo's last months, but she'd sworn she was never going to do it again. All that chopping and dicing and blending didn't do anything for her. However, the biting cold of the winter's day, along with the delicious aroma in the deli, had made her enthusiastic about their soup offering.

So no, she hadn't done anything to be stressed about, yet as she surveyed the room in front of her, she realised that she *was* stressed. She was stressed because she wanted everything to be just right for her new friends. She wanted them to feel relaxed and comfortable in her home.

She was surprised at how badly she wanted to cement their friendship.

She'd suggested one o'clock for lunch, and it was a couple of minutes past when the buzzer sounded. She checked the monitor and saw Rua and Ailie at the door to the apartment building.

'Did you come together or was your timing impeccable?' she asked as she buzzed them in.

'I ordered a taxi and picked up Rua on the way,' replied Ailie.

'Good idea,' said Sybil, although now she was wondering if the two other women had already met up before today, if they'd developed a deeper friendship between themselves. After all, they had more in common with each other than with her, not least that they were younger and had daughters around the same age. There was far more for them to talk about together. She shook her head and told herself not to be stupid – whatever friendship there might be between them wasn't a competition – even while wondering if Ailie and Rua would grow closer and squeeze her out. She hoped not.

When they got into the lift, she told them over the intercom the code they needed to tap on the panel beside the buttons so that the lift could access the top floor.

'It's very James Bond,' Ailie said. 'I wasn't expecting so much security.'

A few minutes later, the doors of the lift opened and they stepped out into the private hallway. Sybil was already waiting for them, the door to the apartment open.

'Come in, come in,' she said. 'I'm delighted you made it.'

'Of course we made it . . . Wow!' Rua broke off as she looked around her. 'Sybil, your home is beautiful.'

'Thanks,' said Sybil.

'It's breathtaking.' Ailie's eyes were open wide. 'I thought the whole code thing to get up here was dramatic, but this is like something out of *Lifestyles of the Rich and Famous*. *Are* you rich and famous?' she asked, turning to Sybil. 'Are we two massive eejits because we don't know who you are?'

'I'm not at all famous,' replied Sybil. 'As for rich, I'm . . . I guess I'm what you'd call comfortable.'

'I'm liking comfortable.' Rua took off her knitted cap and stuffed it into her bag. 'I love that herringbone-patterned floor. And the views are to die for. You can see all of Dublin from here.'

'I bought it because of the views,' said Sybil. 'They're stunning on a bright day like today. At night too.'

'It's like a glass box on top of the building,' said Rua. 'Can we go outside?'

'The terrace runs the whole way around,' said Sybil as she opened the sliding doors and led them out. 'I like sitting here during the summer, but despite the fact that there are heaters in the roof, it's too cold in winter. Anyhow, I don't like using the heaters – they're environmentally unfriendly – and quite honestly, I prefer sitting inside in the warmth and looking out.'

'I love it,' said Ailie, as she gazed across the bay. 'It's proper apartment living. I remember when Giorgio and I first moved in together, we lived in an absolute shoebox. There wasn't an inch of unused space. Nowhere to store anything either.'

'I was very lucky to get this place,' said Sybil. 'I was downsizing, but you're right, Ailie, a lot of apartments are so compact that they're not great for living in. This came on the market at exactly the right time. The original buyer changed his mind and I swooped in.'

'Will you give us a tour?' asked Rua.

'There's not much to tour,' said Sybil as they went inside again. 'The lounge is most of it. But I'm happy to show you around.'

'There aren't many apartments where the lounge is completely separate to the dining area,' remarked Ailie, as Sybil led them across the room and through the open double doors, where the dining table was set with the sandwiches and cakes she'd bought earlier. 'Oh, and what a spread!' she added as she saw them. 'We told you not to go to any trouble.'

'It truly wasn't trouble.' Sybil was about to say she'd bought everything from the deli, but she worried that Ailie and Rua might want to contribute to the cost. So she kept silent and instead carried on into the kitchen.

'I'm so envious,' said Rua as she looked at the white granite worktops and mink-grey wall-to-ceiling cupboard doors that kept everything out of sight. 'It's practically a professional kitchen.'

'Wasted on me,' said Sybil. 'I have a repertoire of three meals, two of which are salads. After that I'm hopeless.'

'Giorgio and I wouldn't have moved if we'd had an apartment like this,' remarked Ailie. 'It's bigger than our house.'

Sybil smiled, and then showed them the two guest bedrooms and the main bathroom, a blend of white and pink marble that added a certain luxury to the overall modernity of her home.

'You said you bought this place because you were downsizing,' said Ailie when they were back in the lounge again. 'Where did you live before?'

Sybil explained about Burrow Bay and pointed towards a red-tiled rooftop that was visible from the apartment.

'I can still see a tiny part of it,' she said.

'Doesn't that make you feel nostalgic?' asked Rua.

'Not really.' Sybil shook her head. 'We bought Burrow Bay because it was a good investment, not because we were madly in love with the house itself, although we were both very happy there. All the same, with only two of us, there was a lot of space to rattle around in. It was the garden that sold it to me, to be honest, and Theo was able to have his workshop out there. No matter how successful he became, he always liked working in a shed. But a big garden is way too much for me now.'

Ailie nodded in understanding. 'What did your husband do?' she asked. 'And you? Did you work too?'

'In a bank,' replied Sybil. 'Let's sit at the table and chat. It'll only take me a couple of minutes to heat up the soup, then I'll join you.'

Ailie and Rua took their places while she went into the kitchen and gently warmed the soup. She poured it into delicate porcelain soup bowls – a housewarming gift from Claire – then carried them into the dining room on a black lacquer tray.

'Looks delicious,' said Ailie as Sybil placed a bowl in front of her. 'Nothing beats soup in the winter.'

'Without a doubt,' agreed Sybil. 'Can I ask you, Ailie, how was Christmas for you and Flavia? Were you OK?'

Ailie exhaled slowly. Christmas had been something to be endured rather than enjoyed. She and Flavia had spent it with her sister and her husband, as well as their three adult children. She'd appreciated the bustle of the family Christmas at Deirdre's home, while thinking that her own would never be the same again. She'd cried herself to sleep that night.

'The first is always hard,' said Sybil. 'Grief changes shape but never entirely goes away. It gets easier, but never easy.'

'Exactly,' said Rua. 'Lilou, Brontë and I used to invite

my cousin and her partner to be with us for Christmas. I miss that.'

'It's such a terrible time for looking back.' Sybil shook her head. 'I try to look further back, to when I was a kid, to capture that magic of believing in Santa. But I usually end up remembering how Tansy and I fought like cat and dog over whose present was best. No matter what she got, she always wanted mine instead. She can still be a bit like that sometimes.'

The women laughed as they helped themselves to sandwiches.

'Tell us a little bit more about yourself, Sybil,' said Rua. 'How did you and your husband meet? What sort of life have you lived?'

Sybil took a bite of her sandwich to give herself time to gather her thoughts. She never usually talked about her life to anyone. She didn't consider it very interesting, and everyone who mattered knew it already. But Rua and Ailie were looking at her expectantly, and so she began at the point where she'd first seen Theo at the bank and had instantly fallen in love.

'How romantic,' sighed Ailie.

'Our eyes met across a massive computer processor.' Sybil chuckled. 'Back in the day, you had to have special authorisation to enter the so-called computer room. In fact, we were only short of having to wear protective clothing any time we went in. To protect the computer, not us. And I reckon that the entire computing power of that mainframe was probably less than a smart TV.'

She went on to tell them about their marriage, and the undercurrent of disapproval from her parents because Theo was working for himself and because he was younger than her. Only by three years, she added. It wasn't as if she was dating a teenager. And then she told them of the astonishment that the eventual sale of Echo had caused within the family and their disbelief that Theo had actually done something that had made them a lot of money.

They'd planned to use the money to invest in a new start-up. But before Theo's latest project was properly up and running, the company that had bought Echo offered him a job in the States, with a hefty salary and stock options. Theo had been uncertain, weighing up what they both agreed was a fantastic opportunity against putting the start-up on hold and having to work for someone else.

'I'm not really a team player, and the Americans are all about teamwork,' he told Sybil one evening as they sat in the garden talking about it.

'Whatever you want is fine with me,' she said. 'I'm happy here. I'd be happy in the States too. Being together is the main thing.'

And then he asked about her career and what she'd do if they moved to the States. His asking the question was what made Sybil know she'd chosen the right man to share her life. The job he was being offered was far more lucrative than her role in the bank, but he took her work seriously, especially as she'd been promoted to head of the audit section, a significant move for a female employee at the time.

'I'm prepared to see how things go in the States,' she told him. 'If we decide to stay there, I'll see what I can do about getting employment authorisation and a job. Truth is, computers and software are a big thing now. We bet on it before and it came up trumps. I think it's worth betting on again.'

So they sold their Sutton house and moved to California. It took time to settle in, but they grew to love it. Theo immersed himself in work, while Sybil took on some pro bono accounting for a local charity as well as helping to organise fundraisers that were attended by local celebrities.

'This sounds like the books my mum used to read,' remarked Rua when Sybil paused. 'All big business and glamour and sex and shopping.'

'I won't go into the sex and shopping.' Sybil laughed. 'Neither Theo nor I were into shopping. But we had a good life. Tech was booming, especially with the mergers and acquisitions that were going on all the time.'

In fact Sybil and Theo had been in California for a little over a year when the company that had bought Echo was itself the target of a takeover. Theo cashed in his stock options and went into partnership on a new start-up.

'Seems like our lives are in the States now,' said Sybil that night. 'And I love that for us.'

A year later, they bought a pretty little house in Menlo Park.

The day after they moved in, the phone call from Tansy came.

'Dad's had a stroke,' she said. 'It's not looking good. You have to come home.'

'Oh no.' Ailie looked at her now in sympathy. 'I'm sure that was awful for you.'

'It was certainly chaotic,' said Sybil. 'Theo offered to come with me, but I told him to wait until I knew how things were.'

The answer, she discovered, was not good. During her

flight home, her father suffered a second stroke and was in intensive care. Her mother was utterly distraught.

'You'll have to move in with her,' said Tansy.

'What?' Sybil looked at her sister in disbelief.

'She needs someone to care for her,' said Tansy. 'I have the children. I'm run ragged as it is. You've had your fling in the States. It's time for you to come home.'

'It's not a fling,' objected Sybil. 'I have to get back. Theo—'

'You know Mum.' Tansy shook her head. 'She and Dad were – are – inseparable. She can't cope without him. And she's not getting any younger.'

'She's in her early sixties,' said Sybil. 'That's hardly decrepit. But,' she added, as Tansy was about to speak again, 'I understand she needs support. I'll stay with her for a while longer.'

'Fine,' said Tansy. 'But Dad's prognosis isn't good. They're talking weeks rather than months. And Mum can't be on her own.'

Sybil understood that her sister was exhausted from the past couple of days. But she needed to nip in the bud any ideas of her moving in with Dolly on a long-term basis. She would help her mother through this hard time and then go back to her life in America.

Her dad died three weeks later. Theo had returned a couple of days beforehand and was quietly supportive, although he stayed in their own house so that he could work in peace, while Sybil remained with Dolly, who was inconsolable.

'You can't go back to California,' Tansy told her the day after the funeral. 'There's no way I can deal with everything on my own.'

'We bought a house there,' Sybil reminded her. 'It's our home now.'

'You said before that Theo can work anywhere,' said Tansy. 'Isn't he working at home right now?'

'Yes, but—'

'But nothing,' said Tansy. 'You've always skipped your responsibilities, Sybil. You married a weirdo, then fecked off to live your childless, hedonistic life—'

'I did not feck off to live a childless, hedonistic life. Though having children or not is entirely my own business.' Sybil knew that Tansy was stressed, but her sister's unvarnished views were hurtful. 'Why are you so dismissive of my choices? Just because you don't like them doesn't mean they're wrong. And just because you wanted to have kids doesn't mean I should do the same. Theo is a genius.'

'Theo is lucky,' retorted Tansy. 'Lucky he had you to support him when he wasn't earning a bean and lucky he was in the right place at the right time. Colin is a hard-working man and deserves more respect from you.'

'You know I respect Colin. Which, quite frankly, is more than you do with Theo. He's not a weirdo. He thinks differently, that's all. And he makes good choices.' Sybil's voice was firm. 'Look, I'm perfectly prepared to do what I can to help with Mum, but she's a relatively young woman. She doesn't need a nursemaid.'

But as it turned out, she did.

Chapter 12

'Oh, Sybil.' It was Ailie who spoke, her voice laden with sympathy. 'My own mum had Alzheimer's. It's so hard to have to look after a parent.'

'I might have been better at it if it was something clinical,' admitted Sybil. 'I'm not a patient person. I did my best, but it was very frustrating. And despite what Tansy thought, I needed to return to the West Coast. I hoped it might spur Mum on, but it didn't. She "took to her bed" as they say, and it was an effort to get her up again.'

When Sybil eventually persuaded Dolly to come downstairs and have breakfast, her mother insisted that her daughter couldn't leave her.

'I can't stay here forever,' Sybil said, as gently as she could. 'Theo needs me too.'

'Not as much as I do,' said Dolly. 'I'm a widow. I have nobody.'

'Theo will have nobody if I don't go back,' Sybil pointed out.

'He can come home to Ireland,' said Dolly. 'Hasn't he already made enough money? He doesn't need to be in America.'

'Reports of our wealth have been somewhat exaggerated.' Sybil made a face at her. 'There's no doubt he's done a lot better than he would have if he hadn't set up on his own, but he's running a new company now and it takes time for that to become profitable.'

'It'd be a lot more profitable if you were living here,' said Dolly. 'You could move in with me and save a load of money.'

'We couldn't possibly do that.' Sybil tried to keep the horror out of her voice. 'Perhaps we'll be able to come back in the future, but not now.'

'You have a duty to me,' said Dolly.

'I also have a duty to my husband,' said Sybil. 'I'll help you navigate all the stuff you need to do. But I can't stay.'

'I don't know how I raised such a cold, heartless daughter,' said Dolly.

'I'll be here a few more weeks, don't worry.' Sybil chose to ignore the fact that Dolly thought her cold and heartless. She wondered if she was. If other women more easily changed their lives for grieving parents. If she was missing some kind of empathy chip. She was happy to help, but not long-term. It frightened her that she could be dispassionate about it.

And yet she stayed, and the few weeks became a few months. Dolly retreated to her bed again and Sybil had intense discussions with Tansy about what to do. Her sister told her that their mother would get over it and that Sybil had to be patient with her.

'Patience isn't one of my virtues,' Sybil reminded her.

'We all know that,' said Tansy. 'But you have to try.'

She did her best, although she felt suffocated in her childhood home. She made valiant efforts to cook Dolly's favourite dishes and suggested daily walks by the beach or coffee at various cafés. She recorded her mother's favourite TV shows and told her that they were waiting for her when she eventually got out of bed. She did everything she could to entice Dolly back to life, but deep down she knew she was doing it with an undercurrent of resentment, and she hated herself for feeling that way. She resented that Dolly seemed to be more animated on the days that Tansy called around, that her mother and sister seemed to have an easy-going relationship that didn't exist as far as Sybil and Dolly were concerned. It irked her that she was putting in so much effort for what seemed to be so little return. And it bothered her that this irked her too.

'There's no way I would have been separated from Giorgio for months,' said Ailie, when Sybil paused in her storytelling. 'His family and I have a very complicated relationship, but if nothing else, he always stuck by my side.'

'It's different now,' said Sybil. 'Not simply because it's easier to keep in touch with people, which would make being apart easier too, but because there are more resources to call on. Not necessarily human resources,' she added. 'Not people. But groups and online help, stuff like that. I felt like I was the only person in the world in that situation, even though I knew I wasn't.'

'It must have been very hard with Theo so far away and no mobile phones or FaceTime,' remarked Rua. 'If he'd been in Cork or London, or even anywhere in Europe, he might have been able to come home at weekends. But not from the States.'

'I know.' Sybil nodded. 'I was miserable. It was getting to the point when I thought I'd never see him again.'

* * *

In those days, internet access was limited to dial-up modems that buzzed and crackled as they connected to the web, and this, as well as the eight-hour time difference between Dublin and the US West Coast, made Sybil feel utterly isolated from her husband. She knew he didn't particularly enjoy socialising, but she worried that he might meet someone else who'd take pity on him and start looking after him. At the same time, she also worried that he could be spending his days and nights hunched over a computer screen, not eating properly and generally going feral.

She told herself that she wasn't responsible for Theo in the same way she wasn't responsible for her mother, but she couldn't help feeling that both of them depended on her. She sent him long emails every night to which he never failed to reply, although not always quickly. He did, however, tell her that he missed her and hoped she'd be back soon. Sybil wondered whether, in part at least, he was perfectly happy without her, despite the fact that he always signed off his emails with the words 'love you' and some pixellated heart images.

It was a surprise and a relief when, out of the blue, Dolly eventually got out of bed. Little by little she went for the walks and the coffees that Sybil suggested. They also went on shopping trips to the city, where she bought herself new clothes, saying that all her other stuff was too big for her now with the weight she'd lost after Tony's death. Sybil began to hope that things were improving. But every time she talked about returning to the States, Dolly burst into tears and said that she couldn't cope without her.

Sybil worked very hard to make Dolly less reliant on her to look after the bill paying, meal planning and shopping. It was as if her mother had reverted to being a child, unable to make the tiniest decision of her own. Sybil knew that her parents had had a very traditional marriage, forged of its time, in which Dolly looked after the house and Tony took care of the finances. She sympathised as she tried to explain the idea of current accounts and credit cards to her mother, and showed her how to set up direct debits so that she didn't have to worry about bills going unpaid.

'I don't like it,' Dolly told her. 'I prefer paying by cash. I don't like cheques, I don't like direct debits – the idea that someone can lift money out of my account whenever they like is outrageous – and I can't be doing with credit cards. That's the same as buying on the never-never. Your dad and I did it with the television, and it cost nearly twice as much as if we'd saved up.'

Sybil recalled the purchase of the family's first television when she was a child. It had been a black-and-white model, in a walnut cabinet with sliding doors that closed over it so that, as Dolly put it, it was also a proper piece of furniture. Nobody except her father had been allowed to touch it. Sybil also remembered the gaunt man in a grey raincoat who'd called to the house every Friday to collect the weekly payment.

'Things have changed,' she told Dolly as patiently as she could. 'This will make it easier for you.'

'What's easy for me is you looking after it all,' said Dolly. 'I'm comfortable with going to the bank and taking out whatever cash I need for the week.'

Sybil had no luck in converting her mother to direct debits, although she did persuade her that it was useful to have a bank card that allowed her access to her cash from ATM machines. Dolly was enchanted by the idea that she could take out her money any time of the day or night and guarded her ATM card as carefully as if it were a piece of fine jewellery.

Sorting out the finances was something practical that Sybil was comfortable with. She was less assured in the evenings when Dolly sat in front of the TV (the old B&W having long since been upgraded to a very modern Sony) and watched all the recordings Sybil had made so she could catch up with her soaps and game shows as well as her favourite medical dramas.

After three months, Theo came back to Dublin for a visit. Dolly made a huge fuss of him and told him all his electronic gadgets would work from her house. Theo thanked her, then rented space in a local business centre.

'See how easy it is,' Dolly said, after he'd gone to work one morning. 'It's no bother for you both to live with me. It works for everyone. And there's plenty of space.'

'There really isn't.' Sybil hardened her heart. But she didn't know how to get out of the situation they were currently in.

'Any thoughts?' she asked Theo later that night when they were in bed.

'We can't stay here forever,' he agreed.

'I want to go back to Menlo Park and reclaim our lives,' said Sybil. 'But I feel awful for not wanting to stay here with her when she's struggling.'

'I understand that it takes time to recover from losing someone,' said Theo.

'I try to make her happy, but she's driving me up the wall,' said Sybil. 'Thing is, we were never that close in the first place. She always preferred Tansy. Or at least, they got on better. And now Tansy is too busy with her own family to help very much, and I totally understand that, but bloody hell, Theo, whenever she's around, Mum treats her like the prodigal son. Or daughter, I suppose.'

'What does Tansy do for her?' asked Theo.

'She brings her to mass on Sunday mornings.' Sybil propped herself on her elbow and looked at him.

'Anything else?'

'She's invited us over to dinner a few times. Mum loves going, but quite honestly, I find the kids a bit much. I'm a horrible person, aren't I?'

'No, you're not. You're my perfect wife and I love you.'

And after that, they stopped talking about Dolly and concentrated on themselves.

The following week, Theo told Sybil that he and his partner had been made an offer for the company.

'Already?' She looked at him in surprise.

'Hey, it's one of the few Silicon Valley start-ups genuinely making money.' He beamed at her. 'Why wouldn't someone want to buy it?'

'It's like a feckin' carousel,' said Sybil. 'How much are they offering?'

When he told her the amount, she gasped.

'That's even more than you got for Echo. Does Calvin want to sell?'

'It's the right thing to do.' Theo nodded. 'I can use the money to start again on my own. I can do it here if you like, Sybs. I don't have to be in the States. It would be more convenient, for sure, but it's not essential. I can go over and back. Easier for you, easier for your mum. And even if not entirely easier for me, I miss you. I want to be with you. In any case, I work better when you're around.' He leaned over and kissed her.

'I do love you, Theo Hansen,' said Sybil. 'You know I do.'

'Love you too,' he said, and kissed her again. 'I honestly don't care where I work,' he continued as she nestled in his embrace. 'But we'll buy a new place. I'm not living in your mother's house indefinitely.'

'I don't want to live here indefinitely either,' said Sybil. 'I can't be at her beck and call all the time. I'm sorry for her, I truly am, but she needs to fend for herself. I know that sounds mean. It's only been a few months since Dad died. She's grieving. It takes time, I get that. But she can't sit around the house and mope forever. At the same time . . .' she sighed, 'I can't walk away and leave her. She's my mum and I love her, even if she's driving me crazy.'

'You'll have to set boundaries.' Theo released his hold on her.

'What I'll have to do is get a job,' said Sybil. 'That way there'll be a proper reason for me not to be there all the time.'

'What about your bank?' suggested Theo. 'They were disappointed when you left. Perhaps they'd like you back.'

'I wouldn't have a clue about their systems now,' said Sybil. 'They'll have moved on. But I'll ask.'

In fact the bank was delighted to offer Sybil another job in the audit department. She rejoined shortly before Theo returned to Dublin for good. Dolly was both happy to know that they wouldn't be going back to the States and disappointed that they'd put an offer in on a house a few kilometres away and wouldn't be living with her. However, she was pleased that Sybil called to see her every evening on her way home and always stayed for a cup of tea and a chat. She tried to persuade her to stay for her evening meal too, but Sybil told her that she had to go home to cook for Theo. Dolly wondered aloud why Theo, working from his shed, couldn't cook for both of them, especially as Sybil was so bad at it herself.

'Dad never cooked a meal in his life,' Sybil told her one evening. 'Why do you think Theo should?'

'Because you're one of these modern couples who don't follow the rules,' said Dolly. 'It's the way the world is now. I'm not sure it's for the better, but if that's how it is, he needs to be pulling his weight.'

Sybil laughed at that and repeated the conversation to Theo, who looked panicked and said that he was a hopeless cook who'd existed entirely on takeout from their local Korean restaurant while he was alone in the States.

'It doesn't matter.' Sybil grinned. 'It's not like I'm putting gourmet meals on the table every evening. We'd starve without M&S.'

'All the same, you're doing a job and looking after me,' said Theo. 'I'll learn some cooking.'

He approached it like writing a computer program, buying recipe books and following the instructions precisely. The results were edible if not flamboyant. But when Sybil came home from Dolly's, there was always a meal waiting for her. She was very happy not to have to bother with lifting a pot or a pan again.

'Gosh, he was a keeper,' said Ailie. 'He was so good about your mum. Learning to cook too!'

'Women do that sort of stuff all the time,' remarked Sybil. 'We move countries for our husbands and we take up the lion's share of family commitments and nobody ever tells us how great we are. But,' she acknowledged, 'Theo was a one-off. A feminist for sure. Because a year or so after we came back, it was me who was offered an exceptional opportunity, and he insisted I take it.'

'What was it?' asked Rua.

'A two-year contract in Bermuda,' replied Sybil. 'The bank had an office in Hamilton and they wanted to move a stream of work there. They asked me to coordinate it all. It was a massive promotion.'

'All this stuff you were telling us about Theo, and meanwhile here's you being a power woman of your own,' said Ailie.

'I'm not sure about power woman.' Sybil laughed. 'I enjoyed my job and I was good at it. Also, I needed something for myself to counteract all the stuff with my mum. I suppose because Theo was so successful, I needed to think I was too. He was totally supportive about Bermuda and insisted it was too good an opportunity to pass by. He was quite happy to up sticks and move there with me. As long as he had a room of his own – or preferably a shed – he was grand.'

'How did your mum take it?' asked Rua.

'She was devastated,' replied Sybil. 'And Tansy was fuming. She told me I was being incredibly selfish to take a job I didn't need when my husband was supposedly a hotshot computer guy and leave her to look after Mum alone. She was so furious and I felt so bad that I nearly backed out. Theo wouldn't let me. He said I'd regret it forever. So I went, but it created a bit of a rift between myself and Tansy that's never quite healed. She thinks of me as hard-hearted and money-grabbing. I think my mother did too.'

'Surely not!' Ailie shook her head. 'You were entitled to

do something for yourself. You'd looked after your mother. You'd been away from your husband. Tansy must have understood that.'

'On one level possibly,' agreed Sybil. 'On another . . . well, I'm neither the daughter nor the sister either of them wanted.'

'You're doing yourself a disservice,' said Rua.

'I'm not so sure about that.' Sybil made a face. 'But as I say to Tansy, we're grown-ups now. All that stuff is in the past. I've no interest in reliving it even if it sometimes seems that she can't let it go.'

'Did you like Bermuda?' asked Ailie. 'I've never been.'

'My time there was amazing,' replied Sybil. 'I'd always felt uneasy that Theo was the one making the biggest financial contribution to our household. He'd say that he couldn't do it without me, but being truthful, he really was a genius. He could do anything. In Bermuda, I had loads of responsibility and my salary was very generous. Also, the bank provided a cute little house in a gorgeous location. It even had a tiny gazebo in the garden where Theo could do his thing. I loved working on the project. Everything about Bermuda was brilliant. Including the fact that the only people Theo and I had to worry about were ourselves.'

'How did your mother get on while you were there?' asked Ailie.

'She came to stay a couple of times,' said Sybil. 'I had to visit Dublin once or twice and she came back with me. The first time with Tansy and the second with an old friend because she wouldn't fly on her own.'

'Would you have liked to stay there?'

'It wasn't an option,' said Sybil. 'The contract was for a

very specific job, and so when the time was up and the project was finished, we had to go home. While we were away, we had Burrow Bay renovated and upgraded so it was ready for us to move back into. And that's pretty much it. Theo and I lived there and looked after the business, and everything was good until he became ill and . . . um . . . passed away.'

'He sounds like a great man,' said Rua. 'It seems that you had an exceptional marriage.'

'It had its ups and downs,' Sybil told her. 'But more ups than downs. He was an easy man to live with.'

'You must miss him terribly,' said Ailie.

'It's been hard,' agreed Sybil. 'But I've coped.'

'Unlike your mother.' Rua gave her a shrewd look. 'Is that why you're so independent? You didn't want to become her?'

'I . . . well, I'm the kind of person who gets on with things,' said Sybil. 'Theo wouldn't have wanted me to mope.'

'From what you've told us, you lost your husband at around the same age as your mum was widowed,' Rua said. 'She depended on you. You didn't want to depend on anyone. I think you still don't.'

Sybil said nothing. She was processing Rua's words. She'd never thought of it before, but the other woman had hit the nail on the head. When Theo died, she'd told herself, very firmly, that she wasn't going to turn into a version of Dolly. Instead she worked hard to be independent. To do things for herself. To continue to live her life, even if it was very different. But she also understood Dolly's grief a lot better. It made her feel guilty for not understanding enough back then.

Chapter 13

While Sybil was speaking, grey clouds had rolled in from the sea, obliterating the earlier clear blue sky and bringing a downpour of rain. The dining room darkened and she turned on the lights before making tea and coffee for her guests.

'I'm sorry for boring you,' she said as she sat down again. 'I'm sure you have better things to do than listen to me ramble on.'

'Not at all,' said Rua. 'It was interesting to compare things in the more distant past to life recently. If you don't mind me calling your youth the distant past,' she added with an apologetic smile. 'It sounds to me that you big up Theo, but you were part of his success and successful in your own right too. Did you stay in banking until you retired?'

'No.' Sybil shook her head. 'When I was fifty, the bank offered severance packages to some of its senior employees. I decided to take mine and then worked for one of Theo's smaller companies as their financial officer until he became ill. I know I've been talking about him setting up and selling companies like he was a real hotshot, but most of them were quite niche and were bought out because bigger companies wanted the technology he developed rather than the companies themselves. We were lucky to make good money from the deals and lucky that we both enjoyed working in the business. After Theo's diagnosis, I became a non-executive director in the main company. I'm still a non-exec; it gives me an interest and it keeps me in touch with the people. Makes me feel I'm honouring his memory.'

'Oh, Sybil.' Ailie reached out and squeezed her hand. 'You're an inspiration.'

'I wish.' Sybil smiled. 'Anyway, enough about me. How about you ladies?'

'My life is dreadfully dull by comparison,' Ailie told her, while Rua stayed silent. 'I trained as a dental nurse. Not everyone's idea of a fun job, but Dad was a dentist and I guess I kind of fell into it. Married young, divorced young. Fortunately it was all amicable. We both realised we'd made a terrible mistake and we wanted out as quickly as possible. Equally fortunately, no kids to worry about. Then, when I least expected it, I met Giorgio and fell madly in love with him. I understand the complications families cause because his caused a lot. And lately I'm super aware that everyone deals with grief differently. I'm afraid that I cry too much, or not enough. That I think of him too often, or not often enough. Sometimes I cook a meal he liked and I didn't and I make myself eat it and tell myself I really do like it after all. Or I watch TV shows that he enjoyed but that left me cold. The other day when I got home I listened to a bunch of podcasts that he used to scoff at – he said it was women nattering about nothing much. I enjoyed listening to them without him making his smart remarks, but then I felt bad about enjoying them. To be honest, I feel like my life isn't my own. That I haven't figured out how to live it without him.'

'That's perfectly normal,' said Sybil. 'It's all very raw for you and it takes more time than you expect to get over it. When Theo died, I revisited how I felt when Dad died, and when Mum died too. Each loss was different, but it was like opening old wounds.'

'Yes.' Ailie nodded in agreement. 'I did the same. Thought about my mum and dad.'

'You've lost both your parents too?' Rua asked. 'That's tough when you're young.'

'They both passed away in their early seventies,' said Ailie. 'I think I mentioned that Mum had Alzheimer's, which was difficult. More for my sister-in-law and brother than me, because they were the ones living closest to her. I used to go up to Donegal every second weekend to give them a break. Eventually Mum had to go into a nursing home because she was too hard to manage at home. I feel like we failed her, and yet I know it was the best thing for everyone.'

'I'm absolutely sure you didn't fail her,' said Sybil.

Ailie gave her a small smile. 'Thanks. Deep down, I know I did my best, but it's hard when you're not there all the time. I always think Dad died of a broken heart after Mum passed away. He couldn't live without her. By the way, I'm not that young,' she added. 'I'm in my fifties.'

'I would've said forties tops,' Sybil told her.

'I feel like I've aged a decade in the last few months.'

'Losing someone is an emotional thing, and it's physically draining too,' said Sybil. 'If you need help with anything, practical or otherwise, call me any time.'

'You're very kind,' said Ailie. 'I had an email from

Giorgio's solicitor in Italy the other day. It was in perfect English, so I think I'm going to be OK. He's putting everything together for me. My only concern is Flavia and that she's treated all right.'

'Are the Italian family in your life much?' asked Rua. 'I know you said they complicated your life with him, and I can relate to that. Lilou's relationship with her parents wasn't close. I only met them once before we got married, and very rarely afterwards. They were going through a divorce, and it was all a bit tense. I think they're both on their third or fourth marriages by now and have a selection box of children by different husbands and wives. Lilou was their only child together. I'm not sure they even remember her, let alone me.'

'How awful.' Sybil sounded horrified. 'I might not have always got on with my mother or Tansy, but we never stopped talking to each other.'

'Giorgio's family don't even want to acknowledge I exist,' said Ailie.

'Lilou's family don't care either way.' Rua's gaze dropped to the floor and she allowed her curly hair to fall over her eyes.

'Are your own family supportive?' Sybil turned her attention back to Ailie, as she got the impression that Rua was regretting blurting out what little information she had.

'Oh, all the Taylors get on well,' replied Ailie. 'Unfortunately we're scattered to the four corners of Ireland, which means we don't meet up that often. And everyone has their own stuff to get on with, so I don't want to burden them with mine. But the Marchettis – well, we don't do face-to-face at all. The day of Giorgio's funeral was the first time I'd ever met them.'

'That must have been difficult,' said Rua.

'Tell us about it,' said Sybil. 'If you want to, that is. Just because I dumped my life story on you doesn't mean you have to reveal anything you want to keep to yourselves.' She gave Ailie an encouraging smile, then glanced at Rua, who pushed her hair behind her ears but studiously avoided returning her look.

'My account might not be entirely unbiased,' said Ailie.

'I'm dying to know it all.' Sybil nodded. 'If you don't mind staying a little longer.'

'Rua?' asked Ailie. 'We were going to share a cab home. Are you OK for time?'

'Oh yes,' said Rua, who'd recovered her equilibrium. 'I'm enjoying myself.'

'Let's move into the living room,' suggested Sybil. 'We can relax in there.'

The three of them got up from the table. Sybil took some glasses from a cupboard and offered them their choice of red or white wine, or indeed anything else they fancied. In the end, they all opted for a rich Ribera del Duero red.

Once they were settled with their drinks, Ailie began by telling them that despite Giorgio's divorce from Sophia and his subsequent marriage, Signora Marchetti, and quite possibly his siblings too, continued to treat Sophia as his actual wife.

'Wow.' Rua shook her head in disbelief.

'How long were they together?' asked Sybil.

'Nearly fifteen years.'

'And how long were you and Giorgio married?'

'Twenty. I remember Giorgio wanting to celebrate the day we were together longer than him and Sophia. I asked him if he was keeping score. He told me that it was a milestone for him and that he loved me more then than he had when we got married.'

'How romantic.' Rua smiled.

'He was a very romantic man,' agreed Ailie. 'He loved the big gestures, like buying me flowers or booking an unexpected weekend away. At the same time, both of us were strong-willed and we argued a lot.' Her voice faltered. 'We argued before he died.'

Neither Sybil nor Rua spoke while Ailie tried to compose herself.

'I know it's silly,' she said. 'But one of our things was that we always, always sorted it out before we went to bed. And that day we didn't get the chance.'

'Oh, Ailie.' Sybil gave her arm a sympathetic squeeze. 'We all have things we regret. Things we said or didn't say. I'm sure you and Giorgio would have resolved whatever it was, like you always did.'

'Probably.' Ailie sniffed. 'I can't help feeling bad that we didn't.'

'Don't blame yourself,' said Rua. 'It's destructive.'

Ailie nodded, then took a tissue from her bag and blew her nose.

'I know you're right,' she said. 'We would have fixed it. Not like him and Sophia. According to Giorgio, they could go weeks without speaking.'

'Sounds to me that he made the right decision when he left her.'

'Yes, he did,' said Ailie. 'Mind you, his sister Sara used to refer to me as a marriage-wrecker, even though he'd divorced Sophia by the time I met him.'

'Why would she say that?' Rua looked puzzled.

'Everyone believed Sophia and Giorgio would get back together. They were kind of childhood sweethearts after all, and the family thought their separation was a temporary thing, because they'd been under a lot of strain. As well as which, she was, and still is, an integral part of the family business, whereas I haven't set foot in the Villa Farfalla in my life.'

'What exactly is the family business?' asked Sybil.

'It started out as an olive farm,' replied Ailie. 'Then they set up a *pensione*. Now they're trying to take it upmarket and turn it into a luxury hotel and wellness centre. They've started using the oil they produce as a base for beauty products. Somewhat ironically, the reason Giorgio left was because they didn't want to invest in it when he first suggested it, but in the last few years they've seen the light somewhat and had been coming to him for business advice. His son, Marco, seems to think that he can run with Giorgio's ideas.'

'Did Giorgio continue to have a financial interest in it?'

'That's one of the things I need to discuss with the Italian solicitor. I hated talking about it with Giorgio. I always felt I was intruding, daft though that sounds. But what bothered me more recently was that him becoming involved meant he had to occasionally deal with Sophia. It was what that last argument was about. She still lives in the hotel with the family.'

'You're joking!' Rua couldn't keep the astonishment from her voice.

'I told you it was complicated,' Ailie said. 'In many ways, the story isn't all that different from an Irish farm inheritance. You know how people feel about land here. Well,

Signora Marchetti feels the same about her house. She was brought up there. Her mother, Amelia, was the housekeeper, and the owners, the Barone and Baronessa Bianchi, left it to her when they died.'

'Goodness,' said Sybil. 'That was some inheritance. They must have thought a lot of her.'

'Their only son was murdered after the war. I get the impression the townspeople thought of him as a collaborator. They didn't have any other children, so it seems they looked on Amelia as part of the family and the daughter they never had.'

'Her own daughter, Giorgio's mum, was part of the family too,' Rua observed.

'Absolutely. Amelia's husband, Roberto, also acted as an occasional chauffeur and general handyman. The Bianchis couldn't do without them. Unsurprisingly, there was a lot of gossip when people heard she'd been left the house. It's big, and the olive groves that went with it are fairly substantial. So yes, Sybil, it was a very decent inheritance for Amelia. Fortunately Roberto worked in the local government and there was no official investigation.'

'Fortunately?' Rua looked at her with wide eyes. 'Because Amelia had done away with the Bianchis?'

'I sincerely hope not,' said Ailie. 'That'd make Signora Marchetti the daughter of a murderess, and quite honestly, she's a tough enough old boot without having those sorts of genes as well.'

Sybil laughed.

'What about Sophia?' asked Rua. 'When did she and Giorgio get together?'

'They'd known each other for years,' said Ailie. 'Childhood

friends, then childhood sweethearts. I'm not surprised he fell for her. She was stunning. They were in their early twenties when they married. Too young.'

'Not young for marriage forty-odd years ago,' observed Sybil. 'But definitely young now.'

'Signora Marchetti was delighted at the match,' Ailie said. 'The Rossis, Sophia's family, owned a lot of land adjoining hers, and as Sophia was an only child, she had a pretty decent inheritance too. I'm thinking that Signora Marchetti imagined joining the lands together.'

'Did that happen?' asked Sybil.

'No,' replied Ailie. 'A year or so after their marriage, Sophia's parents drowned in a boating accident, but she insisted on the land remaining separate. Obviously if anything happened to her they would be Giorgio's, but at that point they were living in the Villa Farfalla and she wanted to rent out the Villa Pomona, which was her old family home. She was quite the businesswoman herself.'

'I'd say good for her, except you obviously don't think so,' said Sybil.

'I'm quite happy for her to be a successful businesswoman,' said Ailie. 'The problem was more on the domestic side of things. Sophia struggled to get pregnant, and when she did, she miscarried. It happened three times.'

'Oh no.' Rua's voice was full of sympathy.

'I felt for her too,' said Ailie. 'Clearly it was very stressful and upsetting for her and for Giorgio. She turned to herbal remedies and religion. Giorgio's mother got the local priest to say a mass in the house every week. Giorgio wasn't a religious man himself, and he didn't want to go to the masses. So that was an issue. When she finally got pregnant again, she attributed it to the power of prayer and took to her bed for most of the pregnancy. Happily Marco was born safe and well, but Sophia believed it was due to God rather than modern medicine.

'Giorgio hoped things would go back to normal after that, but although the masses in the house stopped, Sophia and his mother went to church in the town every day. By then, Sophia had lost all interest in the business and was investing all her time and attention in her son. Again, understandable. But she and Giorgio began to drift. The Villa Farfalla wasn't making that much money, and he put together a plan to renovate and make it more profitable. It included using Sophia's family land. She wasn't having any of it. Signora Marchetti agreed that Sophia needed to look after her child and not worry about business. She said there was enough income for everyone to live happily in the Villa Farfalla. There was no need to renovate anything, just keep it maintained. In the end, Giorgio got frustrated and took a job in Rome. Sophia wouldn't go with him. She said it would be dangerous to move Marco from Trieste. Giorgio lived and worked in Rome during the week and came home at the weekends. But it all began to fall apart.'

'I'm not surprised,' remarked Sybil. 'I was worried that would happen when Theo was in the States and I was in Dublin.'

'There are definite parallels,' agreed Ailie. 'Except that you and Theo worked it out. Giorgio and Sophia didn't. What was equally painful for him was that his mother took Sophia's side in it all. There was nothing more important than Sophia giving him a son. She told Giorgio that as the eldest of her children he had a responsibility to the rest of the family and to the house, and that going to Rome was nonsense, despite the job there being quite prestigious and very well paid. Signora Marchetti also said that the Villa Farfalla was her mother's legacy and his proper job was to preserve it.'

'But surely upgrading it would do that?' said Rua.

'You'd think. I'm not sure how her mind works. But the bottom line is that she thinks he was wrong to go to Rome and that Sophia has more of a connection to the house than he did. From what I can gather, it was quite a rupture. It's why he didn't go back over the years.'

'That's so sad,' said Sybil. 'I know I have my run-ins with Tansy, but we've never got to the point of not speaking to each other for a prolonged period of time.'

'Well, it seems the Marchettis are good at holding a grudge,' said Ailie. 'Giorgio also felt that Sophia tried to weaponise Marco against him. That's why he was so indulgent with him when he was younger, and so supportive of him when he left college.'

'You get on well with Marco, don't you?' Rua asked.

'Oh yes.' Ailie nodded. 'I love him as much as I love Flavia. But,' she added, 'I don't want Giorgio's feelings of remorse about Marco to push Flavia to one side. According to her, Sophia has already got legal advice about Giorgio's will.'

'Right.' Sybil frowned. 'D'you know what's in it?'

Ailie repeated what Marco had said about being informed of the details when a full schedule of Giorgio's assets was available.

'Not that there should be much,' she added. 'But I want to make sure Flavia isn't overlooked. That she gets some kind of memento at least. She loved her dad so much.' She swallowed hard. 'And now she wants to do a gap year working for the Marchettis. She says Marco will sort it for her, but I'm worried it'll be a disaster.'

'Or maybe it's a way to repair things,' suggested Sybil.

'I'm not sure how much repairing there can be with Sophia around,' said Ailie. 'Over the years, she regained her interest in the business, so goodness knows how that's structured now.'

'Well, if there's anything we can help you with, say the word,' Sybil said.

'No question,' agreed Rua.

'You're both so kind,' said Ailie. 'Truly. I've been feeling overwhelmed lately and it's been a help to talk about it to you.'

'It was a good day when that eejit on the scooter ran into me,' Sybil said. 'It's brought us together.'

'Yes,' said Ailie. 'This has been a wonderful afternoon.'

'I've enjoyed myself immensely,' said Sybil. 'Thank you both for coming.'

'Do you want to tell your life story before we go?' Ailie asked Rua. 'Sybil and I have both unloaded. What was your time in France like? And do you want to talk about Lilou?'

'Perhaps some other time, if that's OK,' said Rua.

'Of course,' said Sybil. 'I asked you both for a casual lunch and a drink. I didn't intend for us to share all our secrets.'

'It was cathartic for me,' said Ailie. 'I've never really talked about the Italian side of the family before. Giorgio didn't like to, and it's only lately that Flavia has begun to take an interest. Well, only recently that I know about. She and Marco always get on well when he's here. It was silly of me not to think they'd be messaging each other and making plans while he was in Italy. But she never said anything.'

'Remind me how old she is?' said Sybil.

'Eighteen.'

'At that age you're lucky she talks to you at all,' said Rua, which made Ailie laugh.

'It's strange that Sophia never married again,' mused Sybil. 'If she's as gorgeous as you say, she must have had plenty of opportunity.'

'I'm pretty sure it's because she has no intention of letting anyone else get their mitts on either the Villa Farfalla or the Villa Pomona,' said Ailie. 'She has the face of an angel, but she's as strong-willed as Giorgio himself ever was.'

'Not that I'm taking sides, but maybe she simply comes across that way,' suggested Sybil. 'I'm sure the miscarriages affected her a lot.'

'They affected Giorgio too,' said Ailie. 'People assume that miscarriage doesn't have such an impact on men. Giorgio was broken-hearted about them. When he told me about it, he got very upset. But I do understand it must have been awful for her. I didn't think I'd get pregnant with Flavia, you know. I thought the chance had passed me by. I wasn't exactly delighted at first. I was anxious. And I was terrified that something would go wrong. Then she came along and everything changed.'

'It does, when you have a baby,' said Rua. 'Whether you planned it or not.'

'You didn't plan Brontë?' asked Sybil.

'Far from it.'

Sybil's phone buzzed, interrupting the moment when

both she and Ailie thought that Rua might change her mind and tell them her story after all.

'A message from Burt,' she said. 'He wants me to go to a performance of *Juno and the Paycock* at the Abbey next week. That man's got a brass neck on him. When I left him after our lunch, I assumed he'd never ask me out again.'

'Maybe he thinks you're playing hard to get,' said Ailie.

'Oh, please.' Sybil made a face. 'I'm too old to play hard to get. As for *Juno and the* feckin' *Paycock*, I haven't seen that since I was at school. I can't remember a thing about it, but then maybe it was because I was a teenager and not interested in some dreary play about Dublin in the 1920s. I prefer bright, uplifting things to grim stories about drunken men and long-suffering women.'

Both Ailie and Rua laughed, and after a moment Sybil did too.

'Maybe you should go and enjoy yourself,' said Ailie. 'If you hate the play, you hate the play, but why not give Burt a second chance? He might have been anxious and that came over as pushy. I know I'm not one to talk. I've been a virtual recluse over the last couple of months and I've no intention of ever getting together with another man. But I loved the concert and I've loved being here with you two today.'

'The concert and having a ladies' lunch with two fabulous women are very different to a play I probably won't like and a man who wants more than I can give,' said Sybil.

'Was there any spark at all between you?' asked Rua.

'I wasn't looking for a spark,' Sybil said. 'Though his megawatt teeth certainly light up a room.'

Ailie laughed and told her that in the dentist's surgery,

ultra-bright teeth were called Turkey Teeth because so many patients went to Turkey to get them.

'I don't know where Burt got them done,' said Sybil, 'but they're the youngest thing in his body, that's for sure.'

'If you feel the same way about him afterwards, then chalk it up to experience,' advised Ailie. 'But you might not have been in the right frame of mind before.'

'I'll see.' Sybil wasn't going to commit to anything.

'We should probably head off now,' said Ailie, putting down her empty wine glass and looking at Rua, who nodded in agreement. 'This has been the longest lunch I've been at in years.'

'Thank you both for coming,' said Sybil.

'It was great,' said Rua. 'I do hope we can meet up again.'

'Me too,' said Ailie.

'You sure?' Sybil glanced from one to the other. 'I was afraid you'd think I'd strong-armed you into it today.'

'Not at all.' Rua looked at her in astonishment. 'To tell you the truth, I was delighted to be asked. It's been such an interesting afternoon. I know I haven't given you the low-down on my own experiences, but one day I will. I'd like to.'

'We'll keep in touch so,' said Sybil.

'Definitely.' Rua leaned forward and hugged her.

'I've ordered us a cab,' said Ailie, looking up from her phone. 'It'll be outside in five minutes.'

She and Rua put on their coats.

Sybil saw them to the lift and watched on the monitor as the cab arrived and the two younger women got into it. Then she went into the kitchen and cleared everything she could into the dishwasher before rinsing the containers from the deli and putting them into the recycling bin. She washed the wine glasses by hand and left them on the drainer.

Afterwards she went back to the living room and sat on the sofa, where she gazed out over the city.

A few minutes later, she picked up her phone and started to type.

Hi Burt. Thanks for the invitation. I'd love to.

She took a deep breath, then pressed send.

Chapter 14

'I thought you'd gone to lunch,' said Brontë when Rua walked into the kitchen, where her daughter was sitting on the table eating a Pot Noodle. 'That's what you said.'

'And that's what I did.' Rua shrugged off her coat and hung it over the back of a chair. 'Time flew by.'

'So it seems,' remarked Brontë. 'It's nearly seven.'

'Sybil's apartment is in Sutton,' said Rua. 'It took more than an hour to get home, what with the rain and the traffic and everything.' She laughed. 'Why am I explaining myself to you? I'm your mother. I'm perfectly entitled to go to lunch.'

'You don't go out much, so when you do it's a big deal,' said Brontë. 'And when you stay out late, it's even bigger.'

'It shouldn't be,' said Rua. 'I should do it more often.'

'With the women you met today? Do you like them? Do you have much in common with them?'

'We've all lost a husband or wife,' said Rua. 'There's that.'

'Oh, Mum.' Brontë teared up. 'I know it's been hard for you. I should be glad you're going out and meeting new people. Are you interested in either of them?'

'Brontë!' Rua used her thumb to wipe away the tear that

trickled down her daughter's cheek, then looked at her in amusement. 'Ailie is in her fifties. Sybil is sixty-something. Both of them were married to men!'

'Well, you know how it is with some older people. They married someone of the opposite sex because they thought they should.'

'I don't think either Ailie or Sybil is a closet lesbian.' Rua was still amused. 'But thanks for looking out for my love life.'

'Would you?' Brontë's voice was suddenly serious. 'Would you find someone else?'

'It hasn't happened,' said Rua.

'But if it did?'

'Nobody will ever replace Lilou,' said Rua. 'Nobody ever could.'

'She was exceptional,' agreed Brontë.

'She was. And after listening to what Sybil and Ailie went through in their lives, I'm more grateful than ever that I had someone like her in mine. I'm grateful that I have you too.'

'That's good.' Brontë slid from the table and put her arm around her mother. Rua gave her a gentle hug in return. Although she was still gripped with sadness at the loss of her wife, she suddenly realised that the years when they were together had strengthened her and enriched her, so that for the first time she was beginning to think not of what she'd lost with Lilou's death but what she'd gained by knowing her.

'Tell me about your new friends,' demanded Brontë as they released each other and walked into the living room. 'Was it a bit like that scene in *Macbeth* where the witches peer into their cauldron?'

'Brontë Lehane!' Rua gave her a stern look, but her voice

bubbled with laughter. 'It's very anti-women of you to compare the three of us to witches.'

'Witches are cool.' Brontë grinned.

'Sybil is a lovely woman,' said Rua. 'She's one of those get-on-with-it types. Not much introspection from her, though an interesting past. I get the feeling that her family – or at least her sister – tend to put her down a bit; why, I don't know. Her husband seems to have made a lot of money in tech, but she had a good job in finance and I'm pretty certain she did somewhat better than she's letting on. Had a domineering mother, apparently. You don't know how lucky you are with me,' she added.

'Oh, I do,' Brontë assured her. 'Most of the time you're perfectly normal.'

'Lol.' Rua made a face, then gave her daughter a synopsis of Ailie's story. 'It seems very complicated no matter which way you look,' she finished up.

'I think she should connect with that part of her family if she can,' said Brontë. 'What wouldn't I give to have a relative with a beautiful boutique hotel overlooking the sea.'

'I'm not sure if it's a beautiful boutique hotel or a shabby pension,' said Rua. 'The boutique element was her late husband's plan, but he might have been outmanoeuvred by his mother and ex.'

'What did they think when you told them about Lilou?' asked Brontë.

'I didn't.' Rua got up from the sofa, went to the kitchen and poured herself some water. 'It was getting late and we'd done so much talking.'

'It'd be good for you to talk about her with someone other than me,' said Brontë.

'I suppose I got used to *not* talking about her,' said Rua. 'It was hard, and . . . well . . .'

Brontë gave her a quick hug, then asked when she planned to meet Ailie and Sybil again.

'Soon, I hope. I had a great time.'

And Brontë, looking at her mother's smiling face, really thought that she had.

The following Monday, Rua went into the office, which was located on the Sandyford business park, a twenty-minute drive from her home. She'd arrived early so that she could get a window desk, with a coveted view of the Dublin mountains from the fourth floor of the building, and was already engrossed in writing up her report when the CEO walked past.

'Morning,' he said. 'How are things?'

'Not bad.' She turned to look at him. 'The stats are good. I'm working on the analysis now.'

'That was quick,' he said. 'I wasn't expecting anything till next month.'

'It was an interesting project,' she told him. 'I realise it's very sad to say that I find numbers therapeutic, but I do.'

'We all need therapy from time to time.' He smiled. 'I'm not sure that twenty-four-seven working is the best therapy, though.'

'You're not supposed to say that to me,' she told him. 'You're supposed to be pleased that I put the company first.'

'You always do,' he assured her. 'And I'm very glad. But everyone needs some downtime. I was looking at your records a couple of weeks ago. You rolled over holidays from last year. You shouldn't do that.'

'Sorry,' she said. 'I'll take them this year, I promise. If it works, perhaps I could take a month, go to France.'

'A month is a lot.' He frowned. 'But let's talk about it when we're putting the schedules together. You have family in France, don't you?'

'We've rather lost touch,' Rua said. 'But I do have a house there. I haven't been back in a while.'

'Oh, to have a little Provençal cottage,' he said.

'It's not quite that,' said Rua. 'It's near Paris.'

'Even better.'

She smiled and turned back to the computer, while the CEO continued his walk to his corner office and wished that more of his employees were as dedicated as Rua Lehane.

Rua spent the morning on her report, and when she looked up from the computer again, she saw that all the desks in the office were now occupied. She got up and strolled over to one of her colleagues, a bearded man in his mid twenties who also worked in analytics.

'Hi, Henry,' she said. 'Haven't seen you in ages.'

He gave her a startled look. Rua wasn't known for engaging with the other staff.

'More like *we* haven't seen you,' he responded. 'I've been here every day for the past fortnight.'

Although it was a standard requirement that staff were physically present for at least two days a week, that could be lifted when someone was working intensely on a particular project as Rua had been. This was her first visit to her workplace since the beginning of the year.

'I find it easier to concentrate at home,' she said.

'So do I some of the time,' agreed Henry. 'Have you finished the Amber project?'

'Done and dusted,' she confirmed. 'I've scheduled in Topaz next.'

'I wanted to have a crack at Topaz,' said Henry.

'You did? What are you currently working on? We can swap if you like.'

'Seriously?' He looked at her in surprise.

'I don't mind,' she said.

'What happened to you over Christmas?' he demanded. 'You're not usually this accommodating.'

'I am,' she protested.

'Oh, come on.' He snorted. 'You pick your projects, you stick with them. You never ask anyone else.'

'I didn't realise it mattered to you,' she said. 'I go for whatever's available that looks interesting.'

'The rest of us collaborate,' said Henry. 'We talk about the stuff we'd like to do. But you're not here to join in.'

'I join the Zoom chats,' she reminded him.

'It's not the same.'

'I'll try to be here a bit more,' she promised. 'I'll make sure I don't rob projects that other people want to do.'

'It's not about robbing stuff,' Henry said. 'It's about . . . teamwork.'

'I guess that's not my strong point,' admitted Rua.

'Not really,' he agreed.

'I'll try harder,' she promised. 'I'm going to grab a coffee. Want me to bring one back for you?'

'Ah, here,' said Henry. 'Too much niceness in one day, Rua. The Christmas spirit still lingers, does it?'

'No.' She laughed. 'I'm simply embracing my inner coffee nerd.'

'Americano,' he told her. 'The tallest you can get.'

'Done.' She nodded and left him to it.

Henry's words echoed through her brain as she went about the rest of the day. She hadn't realised that people thought of her as a poor team member. She actually thought she was a good person to work with. Someone who kept out of the way unless there was something that needed doing. Someone who didn't interfere in anyone else's work. She'd never imagined that her colleagues might want more interaction from her. She was well aware that she'd kept herself isolated in the office, telling herself that she was a different generation to the twenty-somethings that made up the bulk of the company's workforce and that their interests were very different to hers. Yet her detachment had nothing to do with age. It was all about self-care. It was a long time since she'd felt comfortable being open with anyone, even Sybil and Ailie, in whose company she'd felt more relaxed than anyone's over the last few years.

I've allowed myself to stagnate, she thought. I've wrapped myself in cotton wool and I've concentrated all my attention on Brontë. I've regressed to who I was before and that's a mistake. I've wanted to be on my own since coming back from France and perhaps that's not a good thing.

She'd thought it was. Both for her and for Brontë. But now she recalled her daughter's words about wanting to work abroad for a time and her worry that Rua would be alone. She'd dismissed that concern, but it occurred to her that perhaps it was weighing more heavily on Brontë than she'd allowed.

She leaned back in her chair and gazed unseeingly out of the window.

Not for the first time, she needed to reassess her life. She needed to focus on more than her work so that Brontë felt good about getting on with things of her own. She gazed at the computer monitor in front of her and idly checked the internal social notifications. She saw a laser tag event scheduled for the end of the month. Rua knew that laser tag was very popular in the company, but she'd never bothered with it before. As she clicked on the link and saw videos of glamorous girls in vest tops and shorts stalking through corridors and pointing laser guns at people, she faltered. This really wasn't her thing. But then she told herself that she was reappraising her life. So maybe it *was* her thing after all. Who knew?

She signed up.

Bethany, the company's social director, arrived at Rua's desk as she was packing up her stuff to go home. She was a tall, athletic woman in her late thirties, and Rua could easily envisage her brandishing a laser gun in a vest top and shorts.

'Did you mean to sign up for laser tag?' Bethany asked.

'Yes.' Rua nodded.

'Well, delighted you're coming along. I wanted to make sure, as you've never joined us before.'

'First time for everything,' said Rua.

'New year's resolution?' asked Bethany.

'Spur of the moment.' Rua smiled. 'I thought it was time to be more involved, that's all.'

'That's good to hear.'

'I'm pretty sure my involvement will be limited to being immediately shot by one of the more experienced gamers,' said Rua. 'But you've got to start somewhere.'

'I'll look out for you,' promised Bethany. 'I'll make sure you're not assassinated in the first minute.'

'Glad to know you have my back.'

'I'm the social director. My job is to protect you.'

'I look forward to being protected by you,' said Rua, who then blushed as she realised that her words could be open to misinterpretation. 'But hopefully I'll be fine,' she added quickly. 'I've done some clay pigeon shooting in the past, so I'm not unfamiliar with shooting at a moving target.'

'In real life?' Bethany looked surprised. 'I do a little target shooting myself.'

'I only did it occasionally, in France, where I lived,' explained Rua. 'I don't know how well my skills have held up, so think carefully about what team you put me on.'

'I will.' Bethany smiled. 'I hope you have a good time with us.'

'I'm looking forward to it,' said Rua.

And she nearly meant it.

Chapter 15

Sybil went to the hairdresser on the morning of her theatre date with Burt Kennelly. He'd bought tickets for the matinee, which she thought was a good idea because that way she'd be home at a reasonable hour. Almost at once she chided herself for caring about what time she arrived home. She was retired. It wasn't as if she had to get up at the crack of dawn the following day. She could stay in bed as long as she liked. It didn't impact on anyone else. She shook her head, and Caitriona, wielding the hairdryer as though it was a weapon, told her to keep still.

When she'd finished, Sybil looked appraisingly at her reflection. She liked the shorter look she'd adopted during Theo's illness, but she'd asked Caitriona to leave a little extra length on this occasion, and as a result her appearance was slightly softer and less severe. Perhaps it was time to embrace a more gentle version of herself, she thought. Maybe she didn't need to look invincible all the time.

She changed into a jersey dress in light fawn, along with a pair of low-heeled suede boots, then added gold earrings and a heavy gold chain, as well as a selection of the narrow bracelets she'd bought when she worked in Bermuda. After that, she pulled on her winter coat and walked to the train station, where she caught the Dart into town.

It was decades since she'd been inside the Abbey, she realised as she walked through the door. The somewhat stark grey building had been modern and controversial when she was younger, but was now part of the landscape. It occurred to her that perhaps the last time she'd seen a play here had been in her final year at school, when her English teacher had brought the class to a production of *Grania*, by Lady Gregory, one of the theatre's founders. Sybil had remarked that building a theatre was a sure-fire way to have your play produced, a comment that had made everyone except their teacher laugh. She remembered Miss O'Hara lecturing her about the brilliance of Lady Gregory and the importance of a national theatre, although she couldn't remember a single thing about the play itself. Her only subsequent trips to live theatre had been for Claire, James and Darragh's school plays at the Helix. She'd enjoyed them more than Lady Gregory.

It took a couple of minutes before she spotted Burt, who was chatting to one of the ushers. He looked well in his charcoal grey suit and blue tie, and she was relieved she'd chosen the fawn dress, which was understated but stylish. When she went up to him, he kissed her on the cheek and they went into the auditorium together. There was an undeniable atmosphere of expectation, and she found herself looking forward to the play and hoping that she'd enjoy the experience.

'It's had excellent reviews,' Burt whispered as the lights dimmed. 'The critic said it was very relevant.'

The plot, centred around an Irish family during the Civil

War, slowly came back to Sybil as the drama unfolded. She supposed it was relevant in the way that unreliable men were always relevant, although she doubted that was what Burt meant. It was no wonder that the Irish were stereotyped as drunken louts when so many classic novels and plays portrayed them exactly that way. Another memory came back to her, of a TV programme with a scene set in a rural bar, where all the men had full pints of Guinness in front of them and the women were confined to 'the lounge', which was basically a few kitchen-style chairs set at unsteady tables. She'd been watching it with her parents and had asked why Ireland couldn't have sophisticated bars like you saw in the movies, where everyone was dressed in fabulous clothes and the women drank cocktails.

'You'd better move to America if you want that sort of thing,' Dolly had said. And indeed, when Sybil and Theo moved to California, one of the first things she'd done was to order a Manhattan in the stunning cocktail bar down the street.

'Did you enjoy it?' Burt asked afterwards, as he steered her out of the auditorium.

'Yes and no,' she confessed, telling him of the thoughts that had been going through her mind as she watched.

'That's the idea of theatre,' said Burt. 'It makes you think. If I'm strictly honest, I prefer musicals myself. But I thought you'd like this.'

'Why?' She gave him a puzzled glance.

'Well, didn't you bring me to the National Gallery? I thought the National Theatre was the next appropriate step.'

'Oh, Burt.' She laughed. 'I do like the gallery, but quite honestly, I prefer the cinema to the theatre. I have a weakness for action movies with wafer-thin plots and lots of explosions. If Keanu Reeves has a role, so much the better.'

He guffawed and told her it was good to know.

'Now,' he said, 'let's see if we can get a cab.'

'I came by Dart,' she said. 'It's only a few minutes to Connolly. Don't worry about me.'

'You're not thinking I'll let you run off without something to eat or drink, are you?' he said. 'I've booked us afternoon tea.'

'Oh.' She looked at him in surprise. 'I didn't realise.'

'I heard you talking about it with Tansy and Claire and I thought it would be a nice treat. Maeve always enjoyed an afternoon tea, though she usually went with one of her girlfriends. But I'm told that men are into it themselves these days, so I'm ready to give it a try.'

'Um, thank you.' Sybil was still taken aback. 'Where are we going?'

'The Merrion,' said Burt as they got into the cab.

It was a day for visiting places she hadn't been to in a long time. Her last trip to the Merrion, a stylish hotel on the other side of the city, had been before Theo was diagnosed. It had been a corporate event, Theo's company hosting a promotional lunch for some of its clients. He'd brought a tech innovator from the States to speak at it. Sybil had come along to meet and greet the clients as they arrived. She'd enjoyed it, even if most of the talk had sailed right over her head. But she'd felt part of it, part of something, as she always had with Theo. Their lives intertwined so much they always thought of themselves as a single unit, living and working in harmony, shifting and sharing responsibilities. Admittedly he'd been the innovator, but there was a time when she'd controlled the business administration and finance, as well as their years in Bermuda when her career had come first. They'd been a proper partnership.

She doubted that even if she wanted to, she'd ever find that again.

The taxi pulled up outside the Merrion and Burt led her up the steps. He'd reserved a table for them beside the fire, which was warm and welcoming after the cold air outside.

'This is lovely,' Sybil said as she sat back in the high-backed armchair. 'Thank you.'

'I don't think I gave it my best the last time we went out,' Burt told her. 'I pressurised you.'

'A bit,' she agreed.

'I want to make you happy,' he said.

'It's not your job to make me happy,' she told him. 'But a warm fire in elegant surroundings certainly helps.'

A waitress, whose name badge said *Dania*, arrived and asked if they'd like a glass of Prosecco with their afternoon tea.

'Oh, yes,' said Burt. 'I think we will.'

'Is it a special occasion?' She gave them a complicit smile. 'An anniversary, perhaps?'

'No,' said Sybil. 'We're friends.'

'Good friends.' Burt's words held a wealth of meaning as he beamed at Dania.

Sybil took out her phone and looked at her messages. There weren't any new ones. However, she simply couldn't think of anything she wanted to say to Burt, so she gave him an apologetic look and then faffed around with the phone as though she had something urgent to deal with. She didn't put it back into her bag until Dania returned with the Prosecco and a couple of menus detailing the sandwiches and cakes that were part of the tea.

'I'll be back shortly,' she told them when they'd made their selection of tea: Earl Grey for Sybil and a black Darjeeling for Burt.

'Everything OK?' asked Burt. 'You were a long time on your phone there.'

'Oh, a silly little thing that needed looking after,' she lied. 'It's fine now.' Then she stretched her feet out towards the fire. 'Imagine, this was once a home,' she mused. 'What must it have been like to live back then?'

'Great if you had the money,' Burt said. 'Pretty shit if you didn't.'

'Sadly I think my family would have been the downstairs rather than the upstairs inhabitants.'

'Mine too,' said Burt. 'But haven't we made enormous strides? Because aren't both of us sitting here toasting ourselves in front of the fire instead of you making it up and me cutting the logs for it.'

'You're right.' She smiled at him, and then at Dania, who'd returned with the tiered plates of cakes and sandwiches.

'Mother of God,' said Sybil. 'I'll never eat all that.'

'It looks more than it is.' Burt helped himself to a couple of salmon sandwiches. 'And sure, what you don't eat they'll bag up for you to bring home.'

'Save me cooking tomorrow, I suppose,' she said.

'Are you really not a good cook?'

'I get by,' she said. 'It's not my thing, that's all.'

'What is?'

'Hard to say.' She hesitated. 'I guess I spent such a long time working in both the bank and my husband's company,

I still see myself as that woman rather than someone who cares about cooking and homemaking. Being honest, my role within the company is fairly limited these days, so maybe I should make more of an effort at being domesticated. After all, I spend a lot of time at home.'

'The day after Tansy's party you were going to a meeting,' Burt recalled.

'Yes, but that's only a few times a year.'

'We've all got to slow down sometime,' he said.

'True. I guess I want it to be voluntary, though, and not enforced.'

'I was quite happy to retire,' he told her. 'And given what happened to Maeve, I'm delighted we had a few good years of travelling before she passed away. But you're right, Sybil, you need to keep yourself busy. You can't let yourself go. That's why I want to get out and about again. Hopefully do a few more trips, that sort of thing.'

'You're right to want that,' she agreed.

'It's why it's important to meet new people and make new friends.'

'I've made some new friends,' she said.

'Me, I hope,' said Burt.

'Actually some new girlfriends too,' Sybil said. She told him about Rua and Ailie. 'And I've you to thank for that, because if you hadn't got the tickets to the carol concert, I wouldn't have met them.'

'You never said before!' He looked at her accusingly. 'I asked if you had a good time and you never said anything about being run over by a young lad on a scooter.'

'I didn't want you to feel bad about it,' she told him. 'Anyhow, I was fine.'

'I suppose it's a good thing if it helped you meet some lady friends to chat to,' he said.

'Yes.' She nodded. 'Truthfully, Burt, I'm quite happy with my own company, but I know Tansy worries about me, so it's good to be able to tell her I have new people in my life.'

'I do hope you and I will be more than just friends,' said Burt as he selected more sandwiches. 'I like you a lot, Sybil.'

'I like you too.'

Even as she said them, the words sounded trite. As though she was about fifteen again. Not in the nervous way she'd been with boys at that age, but in the way of not knowing what to say and how to behave. She'd thought she'd long passed that stage in her life. But more than half a century later, she felt as though she'd been plunged right back into it.

'I was wondering if perhaps you'd like to come on a trip with me?' said Burt.

'Where?' she asked.

'We could do a weekend in Ireland,' he suggested. 'Maybe Parknasilla in Kerry? Or perhaps a city break in Europe. Do you like the sun? Well, you must. You lived in Bermuda!'

'I don't do much lying around in it,' said Sybil. 'City breaks can be fun. But . . .'

'But?' He looked at her.

'I'm not sure I'm ready to do that with you. I'm sorry if it's what you're looking for from me, and if all this . . .' she waved her hand to encompass the room, now almost full with fellow takers of afternoon tea, 'well, if all this is simply a prelude to getting me to go away. I know you said that time is short and you want certain things. I'm not sure I'm in the same place.'

'What's your problem with me?' He frowned. 'We've been getting along well today, haven't we?'

'We have indeed. I've no problem with you at all. It's me.'

Oh my God, she thought. I can't believe I've all but said 'it's not you, it's me' to someone for the first time in my life. The most clichéd line in the history of dating. And at sixty-eight years old, she'd finally managed to use it.

'You know what I think?' He poured himself more tea. 'I think you're afraid to put yourself out there. Afraid to take the chance.'

'I'm not afraid of anything,' she said.

'Then come away with me.'

Sybil said nothing. She sipped her tea and gazed into the distance, vaguely noticing the other people in the room and wondering what reason they had for splurging on the extravagant afternoon tea.

'Sybil?' Burt spoke again. 'What's the matter?'

'Nothing,' she said. 'Nothing at all. It's just that . . . well, I don't want to go away with you, Burt. I'm sorry. I don't know any other way of saying it. I've enjoyed our . . . our dates' – she mentally crossed her fingers, because she wasn't entirely sure that 'enjoyed' was the right word – 'but I don't think I'm ready to spend an entire weekend with you.'

'Will you ever be?' he asked.

'I don't know that either.'

'I see.'

'Maybe I'm too set in my ways,' she said, although she didn't think that at all, and was only saying it so that she didn't appear completely heartless.

'I can understand you being anxious about grasping a

second chance.' Burt nodded. 'It's hard to put yourself out there. It took me a while to realise that was what I wanted to do. But seriously, Sybil, you're not going to get many better offers. Most men my age are looking for women in their forties.'

Sybil spluttered into her cup of tea.

'And you think women in their forties want men in their seventies?' she asked.

'I'm seventy-two,' he said. 'Hardly ready for the knacker's yard yet.'

'No,' agreed Sybil. 'You're in great shape. You're an attractive man. But if I was in my forties, I'd want a man closer to my own age.'

'And yet here you are in your sixties – your *late* sixties – and you're rejecting a man close to your own age.'

'Not because of your age,' she said. 'Because . . . because I'm me, I suppose.'

'Tansy told me you were lonely,' Burt said.

'I *do* spend more time alone than I used to.' Sybil tried not to let her irritation at the thought of Tansy and Burt discussing her show. 'But I'm not lonely and I don't want to hook up with someone out of fear of future loneliness.'

'I don't want to be alone,' said Burt. 'I want someone to share my life with and I'm prepared to be accommodating to the right woman. I'm not expecting a huge romance. But I do expect her to appreciate me.'

'And that's why I'm wrong for you,' said Sybil. 'I appreciate everything you've done for me – the lunch at the Ivy, going to the Abbey, this excellent tea – but I probably don't appreciate you as a person enough.'

'Jesus Christ,' he said. 'You're hard as nails.'

'I'm not. Really I'm not,' protested Sybil.

'I took Tansy at her word,' said Burt. 'But she clearly doesn't know you as well as she thinks she does.'

'Maybe not,' conceded Sybil. 'Though she highlights my flaws to me often enough.'

'You should listen to her,' said Burt. 'Men don't want ball-breaking women.'

'I'm not a . . . Oh, for heaven's sake, I can't believe I'm sitting here listening to you saying what sort of woman I should be. Or indeed what sort of woman a man wants me to be.' She stood up and gathered her things. 'Thanks for today, Burt. But it's not working, it's never going to work and I guess it's better we don't see each other again.'

She carried her coat and bag to the reception desk and asked for the bill for the afternoon tea.

'Was everything all right?' asked the receptionist.

'Yes, but I have to go unexpectedly,' said Sybil.

She tapped her card on the payment terminal, paying for the tea and including a large tip, then walked out of the hotel. The doorman asked if she'd like a taxi, and when she said she would, he whistled at one driving up the street. It pulled up and she got in.

It was only when she sat back in the seat that she felt herself relax.

Chapter 16

At the dental surgery, Ailie was assisting with Sharon Keenan, another nervous patient, who found it difficult to remain still in the chair. From the moment the dentist asked Sharon to open her mouth, Ailie held her hand, assuring her that Mr Roberts wasn't going to hurt her and that she was doing brilliantly. She had sympathy for nervous patients – despite her familiarity with it, the sound of the drill set her own teeth on edge – and she liked that the surgery had a reputation for looking after them well.

When Sharon's small filling was complete, Ailie accompanied her to the desk, where she processed her payment.

'I know it's stupid to be afraid,' Sharon said. 'I tell myself how idiotic it is. But I can't help it.'

'We all have our fears,' said Ailie as she held the card machine towards her. 'And you're a lot better than you were a few years ago.'

'Thanks to you.' Sharon tapped her card. 'You're so calming. And I wanted to tell you that I'm sorry for your loss. I heard when I booked the appointment.'

'Thank you,' said Ailie. 'It's been difficult, but being back at work helps.'

Secrets Between Friends

Mr Roberts had told her not to rush back, but she found it hard to stay at home alone and was happy to return to the surgery. Flavia seemed to be coping by going out with friends, but Ailie struggled to leave the house. She noticed that fewer and fewer invitations to meet up with people were coming her way, and while in some ways it was a relief, because she didn't have to be sociable, it also scared her. Fortunately she had the support of Sybil and Rua; the almost daily messages they shared were a brief moment of joy in her world. However, going back to work was re-entering her comfort zone, predictable and controlled, even when the patients were as jumpy as Sharon.

At the end of a busy day, she got into her car and switched on the radio. As always, she had to stop herself from sending a voice message to Giorgio to tell him she was on her way home. Messaging him had been a reflex action. Two words. *Home soon.* So that he knew she'd be there, even though it would be at least an hour before he left the office. He'd liked her to do it. He said it was their thing. She cleared her throat and sent the message to Flavia instead. It was their thing now.

'Whenever, Wherever' by Shakira began playing. Ailie felt that she was being assaulted by memories, because it had been one of Giorgio's favourite songs. She sat in the car park with the engine running until it had finished, then wiped away her tears and drove home.

When she opened the front door, it was Taylor Swift's latest album playing at full volume that provided the music. Flavia's comfort zone was in her room listening to music as loud as she dared. They hadn't found a joint comfort zone yet. Ailie knew that the two of them were clashing more than usual, although after every argument they ended up hugging and saying how much they loved each other.

As she walked into the kitchen, the music was abruptly silenced, and she heard footsteps running down the stairs.

'You're home,' said Flavia.

'I am.'

'Busy day?'

'It's always a busy day,' said Ailie. 'How about you?'

'I've had a *fabulous* day.' Flavia beamed at her. 'Everything's sorted for the Villa Farfalla. I have a summer job. Marco organised it all.'

'He did? Already?' Ailie looked at her in astonishment.

Since their previous discussion, there'd been no further talk of going to Italy or working at the Villa Farfalla, and she'd assumed it was something Marco had said to Flavia without really meaning it. But now her daughter was confronting her with a fait accompli.

'A job doing what?' she asked.

'Chambermaid,' Flavia said. 'Cleaning. That sort of thing.'

'You're letting the Marchettis employ you as a chambermaid? Isn't there anything else you could do?'

'What's wrong with being a chambermaid?' demanded Flavia. 'I could do that anywhere. Why not somewhere I want to be?'

'Because . . . well, how do you know they're not going to exploit you?'

'Why would they do that? I'll be doing the best I can. I'm sure they'll appreciate it. Even if they do make me work extra hard, it's a well-known fact that chambermaids are exploited all the time, so it might as well be at the Villa Farfalla as anywhere else.'

'How much are they paying you?'

'We have to sort that out,' Flavia said. 'But I'll be getting my board and lodging, so it's not like I need a huge amount to live on. I'll be fine, Mum. Stop worrying.'

'I'm not worrying. I only want to make sure you know what you're getting into. And it's not that I don't want you to work—'

'It's that you don't like the Marchettis. I get that, Mum. I understand. But whatever went on between you guys doesn't matter to me and Marco. Beatrice either. She's finished her training to be a chef. She'll be doing work experience there for the summer too. It'll be awesome to be with my brother and my cousin for the whole summer.'

'Did Marco organise that for her too?'

'No, only me.' Flavia beamed at her mother. 'Beatrice has worked there during the holidays before. She was a chambermaid herself the first time.'

'And what are your plans for afterwards?'

'I haven't decided yet.' Flavia gave her an impatient look. 'Let's deal with the summer first.'

'Where exactly are you staying?' asked Ailie.

'I'll be in one of the spare rooms. The top two floors of the villa are taken up by Sophia, Sara and Mia along with their husbands. There's also an annexe with a couple of extra rooms; I'll have one of those.'

'It sounds a bit claustrophobic,' said Ailie. 'And it doesn't seem to leave a lot of room for guests.'

'Stop trying to find flaws. There are nine rooms for guests, which I guess is enough if you're trying to keep things exclusive. Though I agree with you, Mum. I can't imagine what it would be like to live with you for my whole life.'

She gave her mother a wide grin, and Ailie couldn't help laughing.

'Oh, all right,' she said. 'You'll be there with the entire brood. What about Signora Marchetti? Where does she live?'

'Chiara and Beatrice live with Nonna Flavia in the downstairs extension they built for her when she turned eighty. Antonio and his wife live in Venice, on the other side of the bay. That's where she's from.'

'You know far more about them all than I do,' remarked Ailie.

'Because I ask Marco,' said Flavia. 'And since the funeral, I've been in touch a lot with Beatrice too. She's very *simpatica*.'

'I didn't realise,' said Ailie.

'She's been super nice to me about Dad,' Flavia said. 'And she's very understanding about the whole Marchetti situation. After all, they weren't hugely sympathetic when Chiara got pregnant with her, and she doesn't see her own dad that often. She found it stifling living in the house with all of them and said it was a relief to head off to college. She wishes she'd come here to study, like Marco. She completely gets why Dad left too. She thinks they're all far too caught up in the house and each other. But she's happy to do her work experience there.'

'You've got it all worked out, haven't you?'

'I want to do this, Mum,' said Flavia. 'You're not going to be all silly about it, are you?'

'No,' said Ailie slowly. 'No, I'm not. But you do know that I haven't had a meeting with your dad's Italian solicitor yet, and there may be stuff that I have to deal with over there. The Marchettis might not like that and I don't want them to take it out on you.'

'What sort of stuff?' asked Flavia.

'Probably nothing important,' Ailie replied. 'But he could have left you a little something in Italy that they don't approve of.'

'I doubt it,' said Flavia. 'I didn't talk about Italy with him as much as I do with Marco. I think it's mad that you guys don't speak to each other over shit that happened more than twenty years ago. Marco, Beatrice and I don't care who was married to who or who owned what property when, or anything like that. All we want is to get on with it.'

'And you're sure everyone is OK with you being there?' asked Ailie. 'Nonna Flavia? Chiara? Sophia? Especially Sophia. Have you spoken to her?'

'No,' replied Flavia. 'But Marco says they're looking forward to having me.'

She looked so bright and excited and so very alive again after the last few months that Ailie couldn't and wouldn't say any more to burst her bubble. But she was crossing her fingers in hope that her daughter's time at the Villa Farfalla wouldn't be an unmitigated disaster.

Later that night, in bed, as she scrolled through her iPad looking at photos of herself and Giorgio, Ailie wished there'd been some kind of rapprochement between them all before now. At various times over the years she'd encouraged him to try to build bridges with his mother and his siblings, an almost impossible task while Sophia was living in the family home, as though she were more important to the family than he was. Ailie was aware that the Marchetti family were good at keeping the flames of division alive. She didn't want those flames to envelop and burn her precious daughter now. She wondered if she should contact Sara – the only Marchetti whose number she had, and that only because Sara had been in Giorgio's phone contacts – to ask if the whole thing was OK. Yet if she did, and Flavia found out, she'd be understandably angry at her interfering. It was hard to know what was the right thing to do.

What advice would Rua give? she wondered. After all, she must have gone through issues with Brontë about college and jobs. And Rua had family in France just as Ailie had family in Italy. She might have some insights. Perhaps Sybil would have some words of advice too. She mightn't have children of her own, but that could be an advantage and allow her to look at the situation without any prejudices. Although they were in touch by text, it had been a while since the lunch at the apartment. Getting together again could be both helpful and fun.

> Hi. I'm looking for advice and I thought you ladies might be the ones to give it to me. Perhaps meet up one evening? We could go to a new tapas place nearby that I've never been to but is getting good reviews. Next Thursday evening works for me 🙂 How about you? Ax

> Thursday at the tapas place sounds excellent. Send me details! Rxx

> I'd love to catch up with you both. Thursday is good for me too. Looking forward to it. Sx

Ailie looked at the messages and smiled. Sybil and Rua were turning into what Flavia would call her squad. And she was a hundred per cent there for it.

Rua dropped her phone into her bag after replying to Ailie. The only reason she'd known there was a message was the notification pulse on her wrist from her watch. The pub was far too noisy to hear anything except the person directly beside you. The person directly beside Rua was Bethany, who'd changed from the T-shirt and shorts she'd worn at the laser tag event into a pair of casual trousers and a white polo shirt. Her dark hair, contained in a tight bun at work, was now dishevelled, and resisting her attempts to tidy it with her fingers. Rua herself was wearing her usual outfit of black T-shirt and black jeans, and had only now begun to cool down after blasting her way around the course. Somewhat to her surprise, and, she supposed, the surprise of a lot of her colleagues, she'd been one of the highest scorers and one of the first to complete each mission.

'Remind me never to get on the wrong side of you,' Henry said when they looked at the leaderboard and saw she was in third place overall. 'When you came after me in Level 2, I was terrified.'

Rua had laughed, but now Bethany was saying almost the same thing.

'Clearly the clay pigeon shooting in France was a good basis for laser tag,' she said.

'I probably would've done better at clays,' Rua told her. 'The electronic environment made me dizzy. But I had a good time.'

'I hope you're going to come to more of the social events,' said Bethany.

'We'll see.' Rua shrugged. 'I guess it depends on what they are.'

'What are your interests?'

'If I'm being lazy, I like reading and finding quirky TV shows to binge on. I used to do a lot of hiking and bike rides. Not so much of those lately. I need to get into it again.'

'I do a bit of cycling as well as the target shooting,' said Bethany. 'I didn't have you pegged as an outdoorsy sort of person, but you so are.'

'Easy hiking. Nothing too strenuous on the bike rides either,' said Rua. 'I like being outside. I was brought up in the country. At one stage I used to go orienteering a lot.'

'I've done that too.' Bethany nodded. 'Though my speeds to the checkpoints weren't that great.'

'I don't think I'd be able to run at the pace I used to now,' said Rua. 'I'm not as fit as I used to be.'

'You were fit enough in the tag zone!'

Rua felt a sudden shift in her connection with Bethany. A feeling of more being said than the words the other woman had used. And she wasn't sure what to say in return.

She glanced at her watch and then picked up her bag.

'Time for me to be off.'

'Hey, sorry if I—'

'No, you're fine. No problem. I need to get home. My daughter will be waiting for me.'

'I think I saw her once in reception,' said Bethany. 'Flaming red hair like yours.'

'Sounds like Brontë.' Rua smiled. 'I've got to go. I'll see you in the office.'

'Hopefully soon,' said Bethany.

'I'll be in next week,' said Rua, and left.

Sybil was delighted to put an evening with Ailie and Rua in her diary. She hoped she'd be able to give Ailie advice on whatever was troubling her, though she felt she could do with advice herself following her abandoning of Burt Kennelly in the Merrion. She wanted to put it behind her, but she couldn't help replaying it over and over in her head.

Tansy had phoned her to ask how the date had gone.

'How did you know I was meeting him?' asked Sybil.

'He rang me and asked if I'd mind him hijacking the afternoon tea idea,' said Tansy. 'I told him to go right ahead. He said he was bringing you to the Abbey first. Clearly your dragging him around the National Gallery made him feel he had to top you in the cultural stakes.'

'He implied as much although that's daft,' said Sybil. 'The play wasn't bad. Unfortunately things didn't go exactly to plan at the Merrion.'

'Why not?' asked Tansy.

Sybil explained what had happened.

'You walked out on him?' Tansy was horrified. 'For heaven's sake, Sybil. That was a terrible thing to do.'

'It would've been more terrible if I'd snuck out when he was in the gents or something. As it was, I had to get up and go, which in itself was a bit terrifying. I've never done anything like that before.'

'I'm not sure many women have. My God, he was treating

you in one of Dublin's finest hotels and you couldn't stay long enough to even finish your tea.'

'I paid for it in the end. It was the least I could do. But I wasn't going to stay there and have him badger me about going away with him,' said Sybil.

'Would it have been so awful to go?'

'I didn't want to.'

'Why not?'

'Because . . . because I'm just not that into him,' finished Sybil triumphantly. She remembered the phrase being a thing when Claire was a teenager, and her niece telling her that a boy wasn't into her and wondering what she should do about it. Sybil couldn't remember exactly the advice she'd given Claire, but she was sure that being true to yourself was part of it. She told Tansy now that she needed to be true to herself and not pretend to like Burt simply because they were both widowed.

'I thought you *did* like him,' said Tansy.

'He's not the worst, but he's overbearing and not someone I want to spend more time with.'

'That's such a shame. I thought you'd be perfect for each other.'

'Absolutely not,' said Sybil. 'Besides, there are plenty more fish in the sea if I was that way inclined.'

'But there aren't,' protested Tansy. 'God is already fishing in your pond, Sybil. He's taking fish out all the time.'

'That's a cheerful way of putting things,' said Sybil.

'True, though.'

'What's true is that Burt suggested he was doing me a favour by being out with me because most men his age were looking for younger models,' Sybil told her. 'Why should I be grateful that an older man deigns to go out with me instead of a lithe and lissom forty-year-old? In all honesty, he probably would've preferred a malleable girl in her twenties.'

'Don't be ridiculous,' said Tansy. 'He has grown-up children of his own. Grandchildren too.'

'Being a grandfather – or indeed being a grown-up – doesn't save an awful lot of men from being complete eejits,' said Sybil. 'I'm not compromising on my life to make some man happy.'

'You did before,' said Tansy. 'You compromised on a family for Theo.'

'I've told you this a million times already: the decision not to have children was a joint one. I didn't make it alone. And I've never regretted it. So please, please stop making assumptions about me. Now, I'm going to have a bath, change into my jammies, then sit in front of the TV and watch *The Matrix*, which was one of mine and Theo's favourite movies. I won't be answering my phone to anyone.'

She ended the call and went into the bathroom, where she filled the bath and dumped in scented oil, even though she rarely had baths these days and the steam would probably mess up her hair.

She put her phone on silent and left it in the living room.

Afterwards, wearing her fleecy pyjamas, she curled up on the sofa and selected *The Matrix* from the list of available movies. She and Theo had watched it at least once a year ever since its release, preferring it to all the sequels. She'd continued the tradition by herself.

But she couldn't lose herself in the movie as she normally did. She was still mulling over the afternoon with Burt, and Tansy's reaction to her leaving him alone at the Merrion.

She knew she'd done the right thing, and yet in the corner of her mind was a nagging worry that part of the reason she was so against a relationship with him was the fact that she'd only slept with three men in her entire life, and one of them had been Theo. She was pretty sure that sex mattered to Burt Kennelly, but she couldn't help asking herself if her own lack of desire was simply fear of her inexperience showing. Fear of someone new seeing a body that was no longer smooth and supple. Was she doing the right thing for the wrong reasons?

Why is it, she raged to herself, that women feel they have to be perfect for men, even men they're not interested in? Why do I feel that way myself when I really don't care?

Maybe it was something Ailie and Rua could give her advice on when they met.

Chapter 17

Sybil arrived first for their get-together, ten minutes early as usual. She walked inside the stone cottage with its pillar-box-red shutters and doors and sat at the round table that had been reserved for them. The table was tucked into one of the many little alcoves in the restaurant, where the decor was dark and moody and the lighting subdued. It occurred to her that Burt might like it, and she shuddered at the thought that he'd made enough of an impression that she was gauging places based on his preferences.

She quickly switched her attention to the menu, with its offerings of *patatas bravas*, *jamón serrano*, *tortilla* and other less familiar dishes. Theo had always liked Spanish cuisine and had been a big fan of tapas. The night before he died, in a sudden bout of lucidity, he'd recalled a restaurant they'd been to in Madrid, where they'd gone for a long weekend. She remembered rich red wine, huge green olives and exquisite cheeses, followed by a stroll through cobbled streets that led back to their hotel.

Then he'd told her that he'd be happy if she found someone else, and she'd said that if that happened it would be a miracle and she didn't believe in miracles. Although she didn't say it out loud to him, she'd already decided that she didn't have the stamina for a relationship that would require the kind of commitment she wasn't prepared to give again. As soon as she could, she changed the subject, because the last thing she'd wanted to do, knowing that he was slipping away from her, was talk about her future.

'Sybil. You're here already!' Ailie arrived at the table and Sybil stood up to greet her. She thought the other woman looked better than before, with more colour in her cheeks, her hair glossier and her eyes brighter. However, she also had a slightly worried air, and Sybil hoped that they'd be able to help her with whatever issue she wanted advice on.

Before they had time to sit down, Rua arrived. There were hugs all round and a brief exchange of pleasantries, then Sybil said that it would be best to get the ordering out of the way so that they could concentrate on their talk.

'I know there's a bit of a tradition in Ireland to chat about a hundred other things before getting to the issue at hand,' she said, when the ordering had been done and a bottle of Rioja and a large carafe of water were on the table in front of them. 'But I lived in the States, where people cut to the chase. What's the matter?'

She poured the wine while Ailie reminded them that Flavia had been hoping to work in Italy, and that now that it had come to pass, she was concerned that her daughter was walking into a hornets' nest. She was afraid that if the Marchettis treated her badly, her stay with them would ruin whatever relationship she might have with them in the future.

'Brontë worked as a chambermaid in a small hotel during her first year at college,' Rua told her. 'She insists she never worked as hard in her life. According to her, the housekeeper was a slavedriver, and that's not unusual.'

'I don't mind Flavia having to work hard,' said Ailie. 'It's good for her to have to work. But I don't want them taking advantage of her because of who she is.'

'Did everyone in the family work in the hotel when they were younger?' asked Sybil.

'I think so,' replied Ailie. 'Sophia is the hotel manager, but I don't have a clue what the sisters do there now. Flavia says Chiara's daughter, Beatrice, worked as a chambermaid before and she'll be there as a chef this summer. Marco has worked there since college. I guess that ultimately it's his inheritance.'

'They were probably all taken advantage of in some way or another when they were younger, even if they're the ones taking advantage now,' Sybil said.

'It doesn't matter if Flavia's doing long, hard hours if it's something she really wants to do,' said Rua. 'She'll learn from it.'

'I don't want Sophia to pick on her or make her feel unwelcome,' said Ailie. 'I don't want her to think she can get at me through my girl.'

'You've clearly raised Flavia to stand up for herself, and I'm sure Marco and Beatrice will support her too,' Rua said. 'It sounds like she gets on well with them. Anyway, it would be counterproductive for Sophia to give her a hard time. I don't think you have to worry.'

'You haven't heard back from the Italian solicitor yet, I take it?' Sybil looked at Ailie questioningly.

'I sent him a couple of emails last week and got a holding reply but nothing of substance.'

'Might be no harm to have Flavia on the spot,' said Rua. 'She might learn something.'

'I did think that,' confessed Ailie. 'But I don't want to turn her into some sort of spy. And yet . . .' she paused. 'They don't realise how good her Italian is. She might overhear something useful.'

'Now I'm imagining her sending you coded texts every evening.' Rua grinned.

'Oh, God, I'm a complete madwoman, amn't I?' Ailie couldn't help laughing. 'What am I thinking? Of course she should go, and make the most of it. It'll be good for her to have a bit of diversion with Marco and Beatrice.'

'I have a suggestion,' said Sybil. 'Let her loose and keep your fingers crossed that everything's OK. Make an appointment with the solicitor for about a month after she gets there, whether he's done anything or not. It's a good reason for visiting yourself, one she'll understand, so she won't think you're checking up on her, but obviously you can see if everything's working out or not.'

'That's rather a good plan,' said Ailie. 'Legal stuff in Italy seems to move at a glacial pace, but Flavia's job doesn't start until sometime in April, so I have plenty of time. And I did say to her that I might have to go to Italy at some point, so it wouldn't be a big surprise.'

'Sounds perfect,' agreed Rua.

'Did you worry incessantly about Brontë after Lilou died?' Ailie asked her. 'Did it become . . . Well, what I'm afraid of is that I'm projecting my fears and insecurities and grief on Flavia. I'm constantly second-guessing how she's feeling.'

'I worried more immediately afterwards.' Rua released a slow breath. 'We had to deal with the police and the whole system . . . They were kind, but I was in total shock. And then there were Lilou's parents. As a family, they were never close, even before the divorce. When Lilou left home, she had very little contact with them, or with Max, Valery's son, who'd lived with them for a while. Her relationship with him was nothing like Flavia and Marco. Although I have to say, nobody in that family bore grudges. It was more . . . an absence of feeling, I guess. I didn't want Brontë to notice that. I wanted her to believe that everyone loved Lilou.'

'How long did she know her?' asked Sybil. 'From little, or did she only come into your lives later?'

'Oh, almost forever,' said Rua. 'As far as Brontë was concerned, she had two *mamans*, and that was fine by her. She's pretty much always been around women. It's a wonder she can cope with men at all. But she seems to get on fine with them.'

'Does she have a boyfriend?' Ailie asked.

'These days it all seems to be group friends,' said Rua. 'I'm never a hundred per cent sure what the situation is. But Brontë seems relaxed about it. We've always been close, and although I'm sure she has her secrets, she's generally open with me.'

'So how was it you ended up in France in the first place?' asked Ailie. 'Did you go there to work?'

Rua said nothing.

'You don't have to tell us.' Sybil spoke gently, sensing Rua's reticence. 'Only if you want to.'

'It's a safe space with you two, isn't it?' Rua gave them an anxious smile.

'Always,' said Ailie. 'What happens in the group stays in the group.'

'The lips of the Merry Widows are sealed,' said Sybil.

'Merry Widows?' Rua looked confused, while Ailie smiled.

'Sorry,' said Sybil. '*The Merry Widow* is an operetta that we performed at school one year. It's basically a romcom about a rich widow and the men who want to marry her for her money. It's quite entertaining. I heard one of the arias on Lyric FM recently and thought of the three of us . . . Sorry, it's probably not very appropriate.'

'I'm not sure I'm quite merry yet,' said Ailie. 'But I'm doing my best to move forward. Meeting you two has helped me so much already. And it's a good name for our WhatsApp group.'

'Agreed,' said Rua. She paused. 'I'd like to tell you about Lilou and me. And what happened before we ever met, if that's all right.'

'Of course it's all right,' said Sybil. 'We want to know. And there's no judgement among the Merry Widows. Ever.'

Rua kept her voice flat and unemotional as she told them about the rape. Neither Ailie nor Sybil said a word, allowing her to reveal her story at her own pace. She paused when she reached the point where she'd returned home and practically collapsed in the hallway.

'You poor, poor thing.' Sybil reached across the table and covered Rua's hand with hers. 'I hope he was locked away for a very long time.'

Ailie stayed silent. Rua had voiced the subliminal fear she felt every time Flavia went out on her own. She knew her daughter was a strong, capable young woman and well able to look after herself, yet no matter how strong or how capable, she'd never be a match for a man with violent assault on his mind. She too reached across the table and took Rua's other hand. They stayed like that, in an unbroken circle, nobody saying a word, while Rua breathed in and out, slowly and steadily, as she'd learned to do when she was stressed.

It still hurt almost physically to speak about what had happened to her. For years she'd relived the rape on a daily basis, each time focusing on a different moment in time, wondering if there was anything she could have done to prevent it. Would he have stopped if she'd screamed? If she'd tried to scratch his eyes out? If she'd tried to run. She reminded herself that the shed was isolated and nobody would have heard her. She'd struggled as hard as she could. But had she given in too quickly? Been too passive? Had she somehow encouraged him despite her protestations? She remembered Davey saying at one point that no matter what she said, she really wanted it. She wanted to know what it was like to be with a man, he said. Part of her questioned if he'd been right. She couldn't stop questioning it. Questioning herself. Feeling as though something about her had invited it.

Even more agonising was that she couldn't help asking herself if her mother believed it was her own fault. Because when she managed to sob the story out, Mary Lehane said there was no point at all in going to the garda station, sitting down in front of Sergeant Dessie Mullery, Pearse's brother and Davey's uncle, and telling him that Davey was a rapist.

'Do you think he's going to believe a word of this tale?' she demanded. 'And even if he did, do you think he's going to do anything about it?'

'It's not a tale, it's the truth.' Rua's teeth were chattering. 'And it's his job to do something about it.'

'It may well be,' responded Mary. 'But it'll be your word against Davey's, and I know who they're going to believe.'

'Bring me to a hospital. They can find evidence.'

'What sort of evidence can they find?' asked Mary.

'DNA,' said Rua. 'Plus, he hit me. He assaulted me. There's plenty of evidence.'

'Don't be ridiculous. This isn't *CSI: Miami* or whatever,' said Mary. 'This is Loughmore.'

'It's not Loughmore in the 1970s when you were a teenager,' protested Rua. 'Ireland is a more modern country now. Bring me to Cork University Hospital. They'll look after me.'

'They won't look after you like I'll look after you,' said Mary. 'Sit down there now and I'll make you a cup of tea and we'll work it all out.'

'Mam! It's not tea I want. It's Davey Mullery in prison. He assaulted me, and that's a crime!'

'Jesus, will you keep your voice down,' hissed her mother. 'I don't want the entire neighbourhood hearing all this.'

'Are you trying to pretend it never happened?' asked Rua. 'Because it did.'

'I'm trying to do what's best,' said Mary. 'And what's best isn't always going to the police.'

'Yes, it is. It has to be.'

'I'm telling you, it's not. Listen to me for once, Rua Lehane, and put your fancy notions of justice to one side. Ireland isn't half as modern as you think. The world isn't on the side of women in these situations. Pearse Mullery has his finger in a lot of pies in the town and the county. In the country too, for God's sake, given he's a TD. As well as owning a chunk of the company your dad works for.

You think he won't do whatever it takes to save his son? You can bet your bottom dollar he will, even if it means throwing our entire family to the wolves and blackening your name.'

'But Davey assaulted me.' The tears were falling down Rua's face. 'He raped me, and you're saying to let him get away with it. For what? To save Dad's job?'

'He's only getting away with it if you think of it like that,' said Mary. 'You know he's going to say that you went with him. That it was consensual but afterwards you were ashamed. That you got cold feet. That you regretted it. That's what every single one of them says and people believe them because they want to believe them. You're not going to be able to prove otherwise even if you have a scratch on your cheek or a bruise somewhere you shouldn't have a bruise. You'll end up in court and you'll be trashed like so many young girls in this country have been trashed. They'll want to know why you were out walking on a dark night. Why you went to Charlene's in a tight top, pretty skirt and high heels when the weather forecast was bad. They'll want to know why you were wearing a lacy bra. Why you chose that bright red lipstick you like to wear. They'll ask why you got into the car. Why you didn't run away from him. I'm not having my only daughter's reputation dragged through the mud like that. I'm not.'

'But—'

'You're right about one thing. I want to protect you. I want to protect your father, and Stan too. Conal is putting you both through college so you can have a better life than us. We have the money, but he's stretched to the pin of his collar all the same. He can't afford to lose his job, and he will if you start flinging accusations about Davey Mullery around. What price your education then?'

'They can't fire Dad,' said Rua. 'There are laws.'

'You might be nearly twenty, but you've a lot to learn about the world yet,' said Mary. 'The Mullerys have power. We don't.'

'You're talking as though we live in a feudal society.' Rua put her head in her hands. 'Davey Mullery committed a crime and you want him to get away with it.'

'God Almighty, I do not,' cried Mary. 'But if you think the law is going to help you, you have another think coming. I don't want you to be blamed for ruining his life. And that's what they'll say.'

'What about *my* life?' demanded Rua.

'There are better ways than the law. That's the God's honest truth.'

'What better ways?' asked Rua.

'I have to come up with them yet,' replied her mother. 'But I will.'

Rua didn't go back to college the following week. She told Charlene that she had the flu and felt terrible and that she was staying home till she improved. She was sure that her friend would see through her lie, that somehow she would sense that something terrible had happened. Charlene had been her first girlfriend, back when they were both in their early teens. Their tentative romantic relationship hadn't lasted, but their close friendship had. Yet Charlene simply told her to get well soon and said she'd see her when she got back.

The flu story meant she could stay in bed without anyone

bothering her. Mary brought her breakfast each morning and soup later in the day. At the end of a week during which Rua didn't leave her room, Mary told her that she'd come up with a plan.

'What?' Rua looked at her from eyes that glittered feverishly.

'I'm going to ask Pearse Mullery for money to keep it quiet,' said Mary. 'That seems fair.'

'You're going to blackmail him?' Rua could hardly believe what she was hearing. 'That's a crime too. Are you mad?'

'It'll be more successful than bringing a case against his son,' said Mary. 'Because all that would happen in a trial is that people in this town would line up to give character references for Davey and say what a great young lad he is and how he's a fantastic hurler and his dad is a pillar of the community. If you were very lucky, they'd find him guilty on a minor charge and give him probation.'

'Not if I give evidence,' said Rua.

'*Especially* if you give evidence,' countered Mary. 'Leaving aside the fact that the whole thing wouldn't get to court for years and would leave you in a legal limbo with everyone whispering about you—'

'They'd be whispering about him too,' interrupted Rua.

'But they'll give him the benefit of the doubt,' said Mary. 'With you they'll say that you wanted to go out with him and he turned you down and you're getting your revenge.'

'That's so unfair!' cried Rua. 'Why don't people believe women? And what if you're wrong? What if Ireland really is better than that now?'

'It's not just Ireland,' said Mary. 'It's every damn country in the world. A young fella's future is far more important in the eyes of the law than a woman's life. That's the way the judges see it. And they're mostly men too.'

'What if he doesn't pay you?'

'He will,' said Mary. 'If he knows what's good for him, he will.'

Rua didn't want to believe that her mother might be right, but she knew she had a point. Unable to face college yet, she researched news stories of rape victims – such as there were, since very few women either reported the crime or saw it actually prosecuted – and she could see why Mary thought the way she did. One of the stories had been of a woman raped in a town similar to Loughmore. At the trial, a number of local men, including the parish priest, had lined up to shake her attacker's hand and wish him well. Despite the fact that the rapist was convicted, the woman was shunned and her family struggled with the unwanted attention that had been brought on them. Rua could see the same thing happening in Loughmore. She could almost hear people asking her if she was happy that she'd ruined Davey Mullery's life and shamed his father, who did so much for the community (even if he'd never fixed the potholes in the road, she thought grimly). She could hear the muttered comments about her asking for it. She could imagine it all and it made her sick to her stomach.

She thought about her own father, who would undoubtedly find it difficult to be part of local gossip. He was aware that something had happened to upset her, but Mary had dismissed it as 'women's problems', and as far as Conal was concerned, that made it none of his business. Rua didn't know how he'd react if he discovered the truth, and there was a part of her that wanted to protect him from it. At least, she wanted to protect his idea of her. Stan, away in London for a year, didn't know anything. She'd never confided in him and she wasn't going to start now, but she wondered what he'd think of her mother's scheme. She was pretty sure her brother would want Davey Mullery punished. And yet she had a feeling that he too wouldn't want the family in the limelight.

But with Mary's plan, Davey Mullery would never face accountability for what he'd done. She hated to think it. And yet the idea of going through what had happened again and again, of allowing people to judge her over and over, was daunting. Perhaps her mother was right after all.

Nevertheless, the decision not to report the rape gnawed away at her, and she found it difficult to return to her normal life. Her weight loss was rapid, as she was unable to eat, and her sleeping patterns were erratic. She was afraid to go to sleep in case she dreamed of Davey. It was one thing him invading her thoughts when she was awake – at least she had some control over them then – but the idea of him being part of her unconscious state was unbearable.

Charlene texted and asked when she was returning to college. Rua replied that she was recuperating, that the dose had been worse than she thought. She wanted to tell Charlene everything, but now that her initial anger had dissipated, all she felt was shame. She didn't want to be tainted in her former girlfriend's eyes.

'Go for a walk,' said Mary one afternoon. 'You need to get out of the house.'

Rua didn't want to go for a walk, but the day was crisp and clear and so she dressed in jeans and a roll-neck jumper, pulled on her boots and wrapped a scarf around her neck, twisting it high so that it covered half her face. She took the path by the river, noting that the landscape was unchanged, that the ducks still glided by and the birds still sang in the trees, unaware that her life had been pushed off course forever.

Then she saw the three men walking towards her. Her heart began to pound in her chest, and when she recognised them as Davey and his best mates, Trevor and Cian, she felt her stomach tighten and a throbbing pain behind her right eye.

'How'ya,' said Davey when he reached her.

She couldn't speak.

'You're looking well. Better than ever, in fact.'

Her sight was fuzzy and his words sounded as if they were coming from miles away.

'See you around.' He brushed against her as he walked by.

He said something to his friends, and they laughed. Rua felt her legs crumple beneath her. She sank to her knees and rolled herself into a ball at the side of the river.

It was Bridie Horan, a neighbour walking a dog, who found her there thirty minutes later and brought her home.

'She hasn't been well,' said Mary when she opened the door. 'A bad dose. I thought she was feeling better so sent her for a walk. Thanks for helping her, Bridie.'

'You're welcome.' Bridie frowned. 'Is everything OK?'

'Hunky-dory,' said Mary as she put her arm around Rua's shoulders and ushered her inside. 'Everything's hunky-dory.'

'I'm sending you away,' she told Rua that evening.

'What d'you mean, sending me away?' Rua looked at her. 'I'm an adult. You can't send me anywhere.'

'You're not doing well here,' said Mary. 'You're not putting it behind you. Plus, you're running the risk of another incident like today by being in Loughmore. Better to leave for a while.'

'I want to go back to college,' protested Rua, although without conviction. 'But not yet. It's Davey Mullery who should be sent away, not me.'

'I met with Pearse earlier.'

'What did he say?' Rua looked at her mother from wide-open eyes.

'He told me that whatever horseplay Davey might have got up to, he was a good lad, and that you were exaggerating.'

'Horseplay!' cried Rua. 'It wasn't horseplay. It was an assault.'

'It's exactly like I said.' Mary shook her head. 'They won't believe you. Nobody will.'

'I wish *you* bloody believed me,' muttered Rua.

'There's three sides,' said Mary. 'His. Yours. And what actually happened. What I'm doing is trying to find the best way out of a bad situation for everyone. And I've found it, because Pearse is going to appoint your dad to a management role in the company and he's given me a few bob to pay for a bit of a break for you. He says you're overwrought.'

'I'm not overwrought, and I told you exactly what happened.' Rua bit the inside of her lip so hard it started to bleed.

Mary handed her a tissue. 'You'll be better off out of here for a while,' she said. 'I rang Francine. She'll take you for a few months.'

'Francine? Your cousin Francine? But she's in Paris.'

'Exactly.' Mary gave her a look of satisfaction. 'I told her there was a bit of a situation with you and a young fella and you needed to get away. She says you can stay with her until you feel better, and in the meantime spend time in a place you've always wanted to revisit.'

Rua blinked. She'd been to Paris for a school trip a number of years previously and had loved the vibrant city. She hadn't seen Francine then, and in truth she didn't know her mother's cousin well; indeed, the only time she'd met her was at her grandmother's funeral years earlier. But she liked the older woman's style and independence.

'Her housemate is abroad for a few months,' said Mary. 'Francine says she'd be glad of the company.'

Maybe her mother was right, thought Rua. Maybe leaving Ireland was for the best. She could return to college when she got back. She'd be better then. No matter what, she wasn't going to let Davey Mullery ruin her life.

She was stronger than that.

Chapter 18

'Oh, Rua,' breathed Sybil. 'You poor woman. Bad enough what happened, but your mother's reaction! So very much of the time. Or at least, as you said yourself, a previous time. Thinking as she would have thought at your age. Making decisions on your behalf. Sending you away like that. I understand her reasoning, but it must have been terrible for you.'

'It was very difficult,' said Rua. 'It took plenty of counselling to get myself into a place where I wasn't going demented with guilt and rage every single day.'

'Your mother didn't suggest going to London for an abortion when you realised you were pregnant?' asked Ailie.

'Ah, well.' Rua shrugged. 'She didn't suggest it because she didn't know. I didn't know either. Not when I left Cork, in any case.'

'Surely you went to the doctor?' asked Sybil. 'Even if you kept quiet about the rape, you must have got some medical attention.'

Rua shook her head. 'I didn't even leave the house for the first few days. My mother wanted me at home, and she certainly didn't want Dr Lynch examining me. She gave me . . .' She hesitated.

'The morning-after pill?' Ailie's tone was sympathetic. 'It didn't work?'

'Um, no. It wasn't the morning-after pill. I'm not sure that would have even been available in Loughmore at the time. It was some kind of concoction she blended herself. It made me really ill,' said Rua.

'You have *got* to be joking.' Sybil stared at her. 'Your mother gave you a home remedy? Was she crazy?'

'She's a countrywoman steeped in country traditions.' Rua sighed. 'She thought she was doing the right thing.'

'She could've killed you,' cried Sybil.

'Back then, I probably wouldn't have cared.'

'D'you mind me asking – did she know you were gay?' Ailie spoke gently. 'Was it something you'd talked about?'

'We never talked about sexuality in our family,' said Rua. 'My mother would make occasional comments about me needing to find a man, and I'd say I wasn't interested in men, and she'd say that one day I would be. She didn't understand, she didn't want to understand, and she wasn't going to let it be part of us.'

'I knew women like her.' Sybil nodded. 'How about your dad?'

'Like my mother, he's very much a don't-ask-don't-tell kind of person. He likes a quiet life. As soon as he heard the words "women's problems", there was no way he was going to ask questions. As far as leaving college for France was concerned, he reckoned it was me being stroppy and Mam doing her best for me.'

'So how did it work out in France?' asked Ailie. 'Did your mum's cousin look after you? Or was she a chip off the old block?'

'She was my lifesaver,' replied Rua, her voice infused with warmth. 'Which means that, much as I hate to admit it, my mother may have been right in sending me away.'

Francine met her at Beauvais airport.

Rua spotted her at once, a tall woman whose flame-red hair, so similar to her own, marked her out as less likely to be a Parisienne, but who carried herself with the innate elegance of so many of the women who lived in the city. She kissed Rua on both cheeks, then led the way to the bus that went to Porte Maillot, from where her apartment was a ten-minute walk.

The apartment block had been built in the sixties, Francine told her, and had recently been refurbished so that the facade was bright and modern. The narrow street where it was located overlooked a small park that contained cedar trees, wild flowers and a children's play area. Rua was pleased to see the green space, but she was too tired from the early-morning flight and queasy from the bus journey to take anything in properly, so as soon as they were inside, she asked if she could lie down for a bit. Francine showed her the bedroom that would be hers, and she stretched out on the bed, falling asleep almost immediately.

'The queasiness was probably from being pregnant,' she told Ailie and Sybil. 'I'd been unwell for a few days after taking my mother's concoction, and I'd had a little light bleeding, which put the whole pregnancy issue to rest as far as I was concerned. Because I'd lost so much weight, putting some on again didn't strike me as odd. Besides,' she added with a smile, 'Francine insisted on us eating out a lot. She said it was important for me to enjoy good food, and there were dozens of excellent bistros within walking distance of the apartment.

'My mother hadn't said anything to her about rape, and at first she thought I was recovering from a bad break-up. When I told her what had actually happened, she was wonderful. The most amazing woman I ever met in my life. She saved me, and that's the truth. She always accepted things as they were, good or bad. No matter what happened, she chalked it up to experience. She wasn't one of those insanely positive manifesting-happiness kind of people, but she was determined to see good in everything. A bit like you, Sybil.'

'I'm not as positive as all that,' said Sybil. 'You're talking about her in the past tense. Did she . . .'

'She passed away last year,' Rua said. 'She was nearly ten years older than Mum. Losing her, especially after losing Lilou, was very hard.'

'Of course it was,' said Ailie. 'I don't know how you've coped.'

'The last couple of years have been tough,' agreed Rua. 'I thought I'd rebuilt my life after the assault. I thought Lilou, Brontë and I had a future. That's the hardest thing.' She swallowed the lump in her throat. 'Seeing the life you expected being ripped away from you.'

'I don't think I'd have coped as well as you,' said Sybil.

'I'm not sure how well I'm coping,' admitted Rua. 'I feel like I keep on having to start over. It's exhausting.'

Ailie refilled their wine glasses and then asked her how she'd reacted when she realised she was pregnant. 'I'm guessing you hadn't met Lilou at that point?' she added.

'For those first few weeks, it was just Francine and me.

She was the one who wondered if I could be pregnant. I was going to the loo a lot, and at first she thought I might have an infection. But after a while she suggested that pregnancy was another potential cause. I told her it was very unlikely. She insisted on getting me a test and, well . . .'

Rua didn't tell them how horrified Francine had been when she explained about her mother's home-made concoction. 'I love Mary, but she's a complete fool,' she'd said. 'I'm not entirely convinced she shouldn't have let you go to the guards either, even if I understand her reasoning. But how dare she play fast and loose with your health like that.' And she'd immediately arranged an appointment with the local doctor.

'Dr Allard laid out the options for me and explained the rights and benefits I had in France,' said Rua. She also gave me the name of a counsellor I should see. I didn't tell her about the rape,' she added, 'but I did say that the pregnancy was very much unplanned. She was kind and professional and that was exactly what I needed.'

On her journey back to the apartment from the doctor's surgery, Rua contemplated the options that had been given her, although it wasn't so much options she had to think about as the consequences of the option she chose. After all, the choice was binary. Have the baby or have an abortion.

The thought of giving birth to Davey Mullery's child made her feel ill. She didn't want to think that any part of him was now a part of her, or that his actions had put her on a course that would change her life forever, although she conceded that had already happened. After all, if it hadn't been for him, she'd be in Cork right now, studying for her degree. But the idea of any baby, let alone his baby, was too much to even process.

The doctor, in telling her that an abortion was available to her, also assured her that there was no reason she couldn't conceive again when she was ready to be a mother. Rua had never given much thought to being a mother before. In the rare moments it had crossed her mind, she assumed that in a relationship where she and her partner wanted a child, they'd go down the route of sperm donation and IVF. She wasn't sure how viable an option it even was. In that scenario, she'd somehow always imagined her potential partner would be the one having the baby, not her. She'd never seriously considered being pregnant herself. Yet here she was, very much pregnant at twenty years of age.

And she had to accept that this might be the only chance she'd ever have to be a mother.

'It must have been a very difficult and confusing time for you,' said Sybil. 'Those decisions are extremely tough.'

'Oh, it was. I didn't know what to think or what I should do. But Francine was brilliant. I made an appointment with the counsellor, who was fantastic. So was Ségolène.'

'Ségolène?'

'Francine's girlfriend.' Rua laughed. 'My mother hadn't realised she was sending me into Sappho's lair when she hustled me off to France. Like I said, she didn't want to know about my sexuality. I honestly think she believed it was a phase I was going through. That I was a bolshie feminist woman. She's mellowed over the years and accepted it – she even voted yes in the marriage equality referendum – but it was a big adjustment for her. Back then, it clearly never occurred to her that Francine's housemate was in fact her lover.'

'Are you absolutely sure your mother didn't know about you?' asked Ailie. 'Mothers usually do. I'm surprised she didn't know about Francine either.'

'Deep down she may have had a good idea, but there was no way she was going to let that thought come to the front of her brain,' replied Rua. 'I don't think she considered Francine at all. They weren't especially close, and as far as Mam is concerned, gayness is a modern thing. She used to believe that older women living together were simply close friends. Possibly a convenient arrangement for two women who hadn't managed to find men who'd marry them.'

Both Sybil and Ailie laughed.

'It must have been a shock when she learned the truth,' observed Sybil.

'I'm sure it was. She found out everything at the same time: me having a baby, me being gay, Francine and Seg . . . Poor Mum, it was the one time in my life I truly felt sorry for her.'

'You mentioned that Ségolène wasn't there when you first arrived,' recalled Ailie. 'Was she OK about you turning up?'

'She and Francine talked a lot while she was away, so she was up to speed with everything and very supportive,' replied Rua. 'When she returned to Paris, she was as kind and generous as Francine. They were a perfect couple. Perfect people. Thankfully she's still in good health and living at the apartment. We FaceTime regularly and she's been to Dublin to visit me once or twice. Anyhow,' Rua returned to the topic, 'Francine phoned my mother when I had the baby. I couldn't do it myself.'

'You mean you didn't speak to her all the time you were in Paris?' Ailie was aghast. 'All the time you were pregnant?'

'I was very angry with her,' Rua said. 'Even though I'd learned to live with what happened, I resented her for making me believe it was best not to report Davey. I understand she had good reasons, and when you see how women are treated now, even in high-profile cases, I know it would have been a nightmare to go to court, but sometimes I still feel it was a mistake.'

'It's very hard, especially as you were so brave in wanting to press charges in the first place,' said Sybil. 'I remember reading a while back that ninety per cent of cases don't end in a conviction. Maybe that's what your mum was thinking too.'

'Oh, look, I know all the statistics, same as I know he probably wouldn't have been convicted. I hate admitting that she might have been right, that's all.'

'Have you thought at all about reporting it as historical abuse?' asked Ailie. 'The gardaí are far more sympathetic now.'

'That's true.' Rua nodded. 'But there are loads of restrictions on historical cases. It's not just me I have to think about either, it's Brontë too. I never told her, you see. She thinks her dad is someone I had a one-night stand with in Cork and that I headed off to France because I was pregnant. I told her I wanted to go. It's very believable as far as she's concerned. If I try to bring a case against Davey, she'll have to hear all the gory details of what happened. It's a lot to say to a child that they were the product of an assault. A lot for her to live with, especially as she's also gone through the mill with the loss of Lilou and Francine. And you know yourselves, with the Mullerys' high profile in politics, it would inevitably end up in the media and I'd totally lose control of the narrative. I love my daughter. I don't want to do anything to upset her.'

'It's tricky,' agreed Ailie.

'Has she ever tried tracing her father?' Sybil asked.

'Not yet,' replied Rua. 'But I live in fear of it. Thing is, she's only ever known me and Lilou, and for the most part she's been perfectly satisfied with that.'

'If she asks, will you tell her?' Ailie looked at her enquiringly.

'I'll have to, won't I?' said Rua. 'I've been thinking about it for quite a while. By not telling her, I'm sort of behaving exactly like my mother. Doing what I think is best, even though I know it might not be in the end.'

'What did your mum say when she found out about Brontë?' asked Sybil.

'She freaked out,' said Rua. 'And then she turned up on our doorstep.'

Mary arrived without any notice and threw Rua, Francine and Ségolène into complete disarray. Ségolène immediately absented herself from the family reunion, saying that Rua and her mother needed time together.

'You should've told me before now,' said Mary as soon as Ségolène had left. 'I had a right to know. It's disgraceful that none of you had the decency to inform me.'

'Why?' asked Rua. 'So that you could come up with another plan given that nearly poisoning me didn't work? One that involved me giving up the baby, for example? So that there'd be no trace of her in Loughmore? No trace of anything to upset the Mullerys.'

'We don't need another plan,' said Mary. 'You're here. People will think you got pregnant here. There's no need to disabuse them.'

'So it's all worked out exactly how you wanted,' said Rua. 'You managed to get me and my inconvenient baby out of the country, and you can keep pretending nothing bad ever happens in Loughmore.'

'I wish you understood my point of view,' said Mary. 'I wish you could see that everything I've done was for the best.'

'How's Dad?' asked Rua. 'How's the new job going for him?'

'Your father is fine,' said her mother. 'He's doing well.'

'And Stan? Happy at college in London?'

'Yes.'

'I'm glad I did something to help the family.'

'It's not like that at all,' said Mary. 'You're twisting it around to suit yourself. All I ever wanted was to keep you safe and make the best of a bad situation.'

Rua said nothing.

'Where's the child?' asked Mary.

Rua indicated the bedroom, where a small cot took up the only free space. She watched her mother walk inside. At first there was silence, and then she heard Mary speak.

'Ah, you little dote,' she whispered. 'A blazing redzer like your mother. The Lehane genes are strong in you. That's a good thing, isn't it, pet?'

Rua felt a lump in her throat at the softness of Mary's words. She hadn't imagined her mother would be loving. She'd assumed she'd be cold and hard-hearted about her baby, ready to tell her to give her up. Her sudden tenderness was completely unexpected.

'She's beautiful.' Mary walked back into the living room where Francine and Rua were sitting, the baby in her arms. Rua watched as she gently rocked the tiny infant. There was something natural about the way she held her, Rua thought, far more confident than she herself was when she picked up her daughter.

'So how are you planning to cope?' asked Mary.

'We haven't come up with a plan yet.' It was Francine who spoke when Rua remained silent. 'But we'll work it out. We have excellent childcare here.'

'You're not farming her out to childminders, are you?' Mary sounded outraged.

'Not right now,' said Rua. 'But at some point, when I start working, we'll have somcone care for her.'

'I sent you here to Francine for a break,' said Mary. 'I wasn't expecting it to be forever, and I surely wasn't expecting her to have to put up with you *and* a baby. You can't assume she wants to expand her household to include you both.'

'We're not putting up with Rua,' said Francine. 'She's very welcome here.'

'But you don't have any space,' said Mary. 'Not for you and your friend and Rua and a baby.'

'We have two bedrooms.' Francine's tone was mild. 'That's enough. And although Seg and I have to work, we can help look after the baby. We want to. She's a welcome addition to the family.'

'I'm not sure . . .' Mary's face turned pink. 'You and your . . . your . . .'

'Seg and I are grand,' said Francine. 'We've been together for years. Don't worry about us.'

'But a baby. And Rua.'

'I'm grand too,' said Rua. 'And I'm especially grand here with two people who understand me.'

'Understand you?'

'Oh, for God's sake, Mum. Davey Mullery is a pig, and he may well have done what he did to me regardless of who I was, but half the pleasure he got from it was knowing that I'd never had sex with a man before and had no interest in having sex with a man ever. He said it to me. The absolute shit.'

'Rua. Language.'

'I've given birth to my rapist's baby and you think my language is the issue here? For fuck's sake, Ma.'

'Jesus and His Holy Mother,' said Mary. 'I don't know what to say. To think. To do.'

'That's a bloody first,' muttered Rua.

'So tell us about Lilou.' Ailie filled their water glasses and Rua took a large slug. 'If you don't mind continuing on.'

'I spent the first few months mostly in the apartment with Brontë,' said Rua. 'You know yourself, a small baby is a tsunami of demands and needs. I was in charge of the domestic arrangements while Francine and Seg were at work. They both had good jobs, Seg with UNESCO and Francine with the EU Commission, which meant they travelled a lot. They were glad to have someone at home and I quite enjoyed cosplaying trad wife in a non-trad way. But I wanted to get a job and contribute to the household. I also wanted to find myself a flat. Even though Francine told Mum there was plenty of space, there really wasn't.'

'You didn't think of going back to Ireland?' asked Ailie.

'Not at all. I lost touch with everyone at home. As far as I was concerned, I was never going back.'

When Brontë was six months old, Rua enrolled her in a *crèche collective* and began job searching in earnest. With her significantly improved French and agility with numbers, she was soon offered work in a data analytics centre. She liked having a job that meant not having to interact with too many people. She was nervous around anyone she didn't know, and DataForm allowed her to keep herself to herself. She built up a reputation of being someone who was organised and efficient and who could be depended on to complete her projects on time, although she guarded her privacy fiercely and rarely socialised with her colleagues.

'You do know that there's more to life than going to work,' Ségolène told her one Saturday afternoon as they sat in the park with Brontë, who had started to crawl and loved being outside. 'You must make friends, Rua.'

'I don't need friends,' Rua replied as she scooped up her daughter, who'd made a bid for freedom and was squirming towards the pathway. 'I have you and Francine and I have Brontë.'

'Brontë is your daughter, not your friend,' said Ségolène.

'True, but we'll become friends.'

'Will you? Perhaps this is just me, but I would say that parents and children should never be friends. That they have a good relationship, that they can depend on each other – or certainly that a child can depend on its mother or father – but friends? *Non.*'

'I've never heard you sound more French,' Rua told her.

'I *am* French. We believe in setting boundaries.' Ségolène gave a shrug so Parisian that Rua couldn't help laughing.

'But I am serious too,' she went on. 'And in your case it is also different. You love Brontë, that much is obvious. Nevertheless she is a reminder of what happened.'

'I know.' Rua's eyes clouded over. 'Oh, Seg, you see it so clearly, don't you? I'm besotted with Brontë, I adore her. But sometimes I look at her and I see Davey. And it doesn't make me love her any less, honestly it doesn't, but she shares his DNA and that's sometimes hard to accept.'

'I understand perfectly.'

'I thought you'd tell me not to be silly.'

'There is a tendency in this world to want things that are not perfect to be perfect,' said Ségolène. 'To want every child to be loved even when some are not. To force ideas of perfect parenthood, perfect families on those that will never be perfect. As though any family is perfect – such a nonsense that is. And there's a desire to project a way of living and being that suits us on everyone else. But the world is a very diverse place, *chérie*, and every single person is different.'

'I wish you'd tell my mother that.'

'She also is doing her best,' said Ségolène. 'You need to be kind to her.'

'I'll be happy if Brontë loves me.' Rua scooped her daughter into her arms. 'Maybe that's enough.'

After her conversation with Ségolène, however, Rua began to socialise a little more. Although she kept in the background, almost invisible in her anonymous black T-shirt and jeans, she joined a group of Irish people living in Paris and, despite never having been to a match at Croke Park in her life, went to events where the All-Ireland GAA Championships were shown live from the iconic venue. She also went to the St Patrick's Day parade (something she'd never done in Ireland either) and to a céilí, where long-forgotten steps to the Irish jigs and reels she'd learned in dancing classes as a child came back to her. With her red hair and grey-green eyes, she knew she looked like a cliché of an Irish character, but she didn't mind. She was happy. She was enjoying herself.

And then she met Lilou.

She was in the park again, this time reading to Brontë from one of the interactive picture books Francine had given her, when a woman walking past gave a short yelp and then swore loudly. Rua looked up to see that she had dropped a takeaway coffee and was hopping from foot to foot in her ridiculously high-heeled shoes.

'Are you OK?' she asked.

The woman looked at her. She was as tall as Rua was petite, with corn-coloured hair pulled back into a single plait. The blue of her eyes matched the gilet she was wearing over a long-sleeved white T-shirt and white trousers now stained by the coffee.

Rua realised that she shouldn't really have said anything at all. Although she didn't find the residents of Paris half as rude as they were portrayed to be, they weren't generally welcoming of casual conversation from strangers. Especially if the stranger was commenting on a faux pas they'd committed.

'I'm fine,' replied the woman. 'Thank you.' And then she gasped and pointed at the baby, because Brontë had picked up a handful of grass and was about to eat it.

Rua removed the grass from her daughter's hand and remarked that nobody could say that Brontë was a fussy eater. The woman laughed, then, instead of commenting politely and walking on, she introduced herself as Lilou, complimented Rua on her accent and said that her baby was very pretty.

Rua heard the other woman's words but was more conscious of the sensation that had suddenly enveloped her. Her heart was racing, her mouth was dry and it seemed as though an entire meadow of butterflies were fluttering in her stomach. She was unable to take her eyes off Lilou even while a part of her was conscious of Brontë on the rug beside her.

She'd never felt like this before. Sure, she'd been attracted to other women, and her relationship with Charlene had been sweet and intense, but this . . . this was on a completely different level. She wanted to say something clever and witty, something that would make Lilou feel the same way about her. But she could think of nothing to keep this woman here, to stop her walking away into the Parisian evening.

It was Lilou who spoke again, asking about Brontë, and Rua, who never discussed her daughter with anyone at the office or indeed anyone in the Irish-in-Paris group, was suddenly talking about how adorable she was but how she came with sleepless nights and unpredictable days and yet was now the most important person in her life.

'And her father?' Lilou glanced around. 'He is here? Or working perhaps?'

'Not here. Never will be here. He was a mistake.'

'Oh.' Lilou's eyes met hers, and once again Rua was overcome by unfamiliar sensations. But this time they were ones of connection. Of knowing that this woman would be important to her. Of knowing that she was in the company of someone who would make a difference to her life.

'I need to go home and change.' Lilou glanced at her stained trousers. 'But if you are free, would you like to meet me later? Do you have someone to look after Brontë? Such a pretty name for such a pretty child,' she added. 'And if there is no one to care for her, there is an excellent bistro not far from here where they are particularly welcoming of small children.'

'I do have someone to care for her, and I'd love to meet you later,' said Rua.

Lilou gave her the name of a bistro, then air-kissed her before striding out of the park. Rua stood motionless, her fingers resting on the place that Lilou's cheek had almost touched. Then, with Brontë in her arms, she hurried back to the apartment and asked Francine if she'd be able to look after the little girl for the evening. Francine, noting her flushed cheeks and sparkling eyes, asked if this was an important outing, and Rua said that she didn't know exactly but that she was meeting someone very *sympathique*, if that was OK.

'You don't have to ask my permission to meet someone,' said Francine.

'But I'm asking you to babysit out of the blue, which is a bit cheeky.'

Francine said that she and Ségolène loved looking after Brontë, so Rua went into her bedroom and changed out of her dark jeans and top, taking a soft wool dress in moss green from her wardrobe and putting it on for the first time since she'd come to France. She was relieved that it fitted her, even if the low-cut V of the neckline emphasised her now generous boobs more than it ever had before. She twisted her hair into an updo, then changed her mind and brushed it loose again. Then she applied her red lipstick – also unused since her arrival in France – and walked into the living room to an appreciative look from Francine.

'It is nice to see you in a different colour for a change,' she said. 'I have something for you.' She went into her bedroom and returned with a silver pendant from which hung a green stone. 'It goes with the dress,' she said. 'And your eyes.'

'It's beautiful,' said Rua. 'Are you sure you want to lend it to me?'

'Given to me by my first girlfriend.' Francine grinned. 'I kept it because it's a nice stone, but Seg doesn't like me wearing it. She's not an especially jealous woman, but this always bugs her. I'm sure she won't mind me lending it to you.'

'Thank you,' said Rua. 'It's perfect.'

She kissed Brontë goodbye and then went to meet the woman who would become the love of her life.

'A meet-cute in Paris.' Ailie gave her a dreamy look. 'How romantic.'

'It was love at first sight,' agreed Rua. 'And I never expected it. I thought it was going to be me and Brontë against the world forever. But with Lilou . . . it was as if she'd always been there. It took some time for us to get together properly as a couple. Shortly after we met, she was sent to Switzerland as part of her job. She was a chemist, and the company she worked for was Swiss. But she came back for weekends and I went to Switzerland from time to time. When she got a job back in Paris, we moved in together. Which I'm sure was a relief to Francine and Seg.'

'Lilou was OK with Brontë?' said Sybil.

'She adored Brontë. She was a very adorable baby,' Rua told them, her maternal pride shining through. 'And my wife was a very adorable woman. I was never as happy as when I was with her. And even though I've lost her, I also feel grateful for having had her.'

'It's wonderful that you feel that way,' said Sybil. 'Did you visit Ireland with her?'

'A couple of times.' Rua's lips tightened. 'My mother wasn't entirely happy about me parading around Loughmore, as she put it, with my baby and my fancy Frenchwoman in tow. There were plenty of different stories, but nobody ever figured out the timeline, and the general gossip was that I'd got pregnant in Paris.'

'Useful gossip,' observed Ailie.

'Partly,' said Rua. 'There was a bit of me that wanted Davey Mullery to know Brontë was his daughter, being raised by me and another woman. And yet I didn't want us to have anything to do with him or his family. I know that sounds a bit crazy. It was important to me that she grew up with some Irish heritage, which is why I let her stay with my parents when she was a bit older, but I never felt comfortable returning to Loughmore. I still don't. Mam loves Brontë, which is a massive bonus, but I can't relax around her. Too much has happened for us to be comfortable with each other.'

'I see your point of view, but it's sad,' Ailie said. 'I get that you feel your mum should've supported you in reporting the rape, but like I said before, you could probably report it now.'

'I don't know what good it would serve. Not for me, because I don't need it. And especially not for Brontë. She thinks I was experimenting with my sexuality when I got pregnant. Honestly, kids today are so good with the kind of stuff that would've had my mother lighting candles in front of a statue of the Virgin Mary and praying for my eternal soul. The funny thing is that my mam is a much better grandmother than mother, which is why Brontë enjoyed staying with her and Dad. But I was always terrified she'd run into Davey and he'd guess.'

'Wouldn't it be better to tell her the truth before she finds out?' Sybil's tone was sympathetic. 'Because I can't help thinking she will some day, somehow. And you don't want her resenting you for keeping it from her.'

'You're right,' said Rua. 'I know what I need to do. I'm just too damn scared to do it.'

Chapter 19

In the brief interlude that followed Rua's story, Sybil excused herself and went to the ladies. She was full of admiration for the younger woman and how she'd overcome the assault and its consequences. She recalled the darker periods of Irish life when it came to how women were treated. She knew that many young women today would find it hard to believe: the tragedy of fifteen-year-old Ann Lovett, who died, along with her baby, giving birth in a grotto outside the country town where she lived; Joanne Hayes, who was falsely accused of murdering a baby and treated abominably by the state; and the countless stories of women who were sent to Magdalene laundries, shamed for becoming pregnant while the fathers of those babies continued with their lives as though nothing had happened.

Both in the US and in Ireland, Sybil had gone on marches for women's rights, and she knew things had improved over the years. Yet there were still double standards, complaints that women's rights had 'gone too far', and it remained the case that women were invariably held accountable for the actions of men, rather than men being shamed for their own behaviour.

She was washing her hands, deep in thought, when the door to the ladies swung open. She glanced up, and her eyes widened in surprise as she recognised her sister.

'Tansy?' She looked at her in astonishment. 'I didn't expect to see you here.'

'Same.' Tansy's expression was shocked, and Sybil could hear tension in her voice. 'What are you doing here?'

'I'm meeting my new friends. The two widows I told you about.'

'But why here? It's miles out of your way.'

'They both live this side of town. It was convenient for them.'

'Not for you.'

'They came to me last time,' said Sybil. 'It was my turn to travel. And you? This isn't hugely convenient for you and Colin, though I believe it's the current in-place on the Southside. Are you having a romantic night out together?'

'What's with the twenty bloody questions?'

Sybil was startled at her sister's tone.

'Sorry.' Tansy shrugged. 'I'm out with a friend, that's all.'

'We have half a bottle of wine left between us,' said Sybil. 'We'll probably leave after that. D'you guys want to come and say hello?'

'No, it's fine. You do your thing and I'll do mine,' said Tansy. 'I'll give you a shout later. Maybe we can come here ourselves sometime.'

'Sure,' said Sybil. 'Have fun. Talk soon.'

Rua was telling Ailie more about Lilou's family when Sybil returned.

'Her dad, Valery, was a farmer,' she said. 'He had quite

a substantial amount of land, although over the years he sold a lot of it. Alize was originally from Paris, but when she divorced her first husband, she bought a florist's shop in the town near Valery's farm. His then wife used to buy flowers from her. Valery came in one day and asked her to stop selling flowers to Emmeline because it was a wasteful extravagance. Alize told him to eff off, and from what I can gather they then had a shag in the back room.'

'Rua! You're kidding.'

'Nope. Lust at first sight. Valery divorced Emmeline and married Alize, though eventually they both had affairs and split up. They were perfectly pleasant when I met them, but very much caught up in themselves and their various love affairs. I haven't heard from them since Lilou died.'

'I feel like I inhabit a different world to both of you,' said Sybil. 'I have the phone number of every single person in my family and I know where they all live. There are no divorces or remarriages – a bit odd, I'll admit, in this day and age, but so far everyone's stuck together. Nobody's ever dropped off the radar completely. James would be the nearest to that, I guess, because he lives in Brussels and I don't see him much, but every so often he sends me a photo of a famous politician or president he's met, and I send him an occasional jokey meme. But I could contact any of them any time. In fact,' she added, 'Tansy came into the bathroom when I was in there.'

'Your sister?' Ailie looked at her in surprise. 'Where is she now? Why didn't you bring her over to say hello?'

'I asked her to join us for a few minutes, but she said she was with a friend,' replied Sybil. 'She was a bit flustered at seeing me. This is slightly off the beaten track for her, and even more so for me. So she was surprised to find me here.' She glanced around her. 'I guess she's in one of the booths.'

'Sybil! I know you said no divorces or remarriages in your family, but maybe she's having an illicit encounter herself and that's why she was flustered,' suggested Rua.

'That's so not Tansy.' Sybil shook her head, but frowned.

'Are you sure?'

'Now that you say it . . .' She hesitated, and thought of her sister's uncharacteristic dismissal of her earlier. 'I find it hard to believe it's anything romantic, but she's hiding something, that's for sure.'

'Why wouldn't it be an affair?' asked Rua.

'Because . . . because . . . Tansy! It's impossible.'

But the more Sybil protested, the more she wondered if her new friends were right. She simply couldn't believe Tansy would cheat on Colin. Not a paragon of traditional family values like her sister. Yet there was certainly something out of character in her behaviour.

She poured the last of the wine into their glasses and tried to put Tansy out of her mind while she listened to Ailie and Rua chatting about their daughters. She wasn't upset by being unable to take part in the conversation; instead, she mentally explored, as she often did in these situations, her own feelings about being childless. After Theo died, Tansy remarked that Sybil was lacking the support network she would have had if she'd had a family of her own, and that her stupid decision to live a child-free life was coming back to haunt her. A few days later, her sister had called around with two enormous boxes of home-cooked frozen meals and loaded her freezer with them. 'Because you've nobody else to look after you and you have to eat properly,' she'd told her. 'I don't want you wasting away.'

Sitting alone that night, Sybil had wondered if her grief would have been easier to bear with a child of her own, yet listening to Rua and Ailie talk of how much they'd tried to protect Brontë and Flavia, she doubted it. Anyway, you made decisions based on the best information you had at the time, she thought. The most important thing was being able to live with them. And she could live with hers, even if Tansy thought she was mistaken.

Could her sister be having an affair? It truly did seem very unlikely. It was much more plausible that Tansy was secretly meeting an architect or interior designer because she wanted to get work done to the house and knew Colin wouldn't approve. Or she might have some other scheme to surprise her husband. Less dramatic than the scenarios Rua and Ailie had come up with, but infinitely more plausible.

Ten minutes later, with their conversation having reverted to Ailie's plans for Italy, Sybil spotted Tansy again. This time her sister walked straight towards her.

'I'm off home,' she said as she stopped at the table. 'But I thought it would be nice to meet your friends after all.'

'Right.' Sybil introduced her to them. 'Would you like to join us for coffee?'

'No, thanks,' said Tansy. 'I have to get back. I'm late as it is. I'll be in touch, OK?'

'Sure,' said Sybil.

'Nice to meet you all.'

Sybil watched as she left the restaurant.

'Well?' She looked at Ailie and Rua.

'She's a good-looking woman,' said Ailie.

'Seems friendly,' added Rua.

'Having an affair?' asked Sybil.

'If she isn't, why didn't her friend come to the table with her?' Ailie mused.

Less than a minute later, a man carrying a briefcase walked by. He didn't look in their direction.

'If she's having an affair with him, I know who he is,' said Ailie, her eyes following the man out of the door. 'His name's Watson Drury and he's a patient at the dental clinic where I work.'

Chapter 20

Sybil was tempted to follow Watson Drury outside and see if he was meeting Tansy, but she stayed where she was and instead asked Ailie what she knew of the man.

'Divorced,' she replied. 'In his fifties. His wife left him a couple of years ago.'

'How would Tansy know him?' wondered Sybil.

'If your sister is a patient at our clinic, she might have met him there,' replied Ailie. 'I don't know her, but then I don't know every patient. Him I do know because he got a number of crowns done with us and didn't complain about the price. Nearly everyone complains about the price,' she added. 'That's why they go abroad.'

An image of Burt's gleaming smile flashed across Sybil's mind, and she shuddered.

'Watson Drury is a plastic surgeon, so maybe that's why he doesn't complain,' said Ailie. 'He knows how much things should cost.'

They dropped the topic as the waitress came with their bill, then left the tapas bar promising to keep each other updated on how they were getting on, and agreeing to meet again the following month.

Once home and curled up in front of the TV, Sybil put on her reading glasses and opened her iPad. She searched for Watson Drury, and his name appeared immediately as a consultant at a private clinic. Was Tansy thinking of having some work done? wondered Sybil, as she scrolled through the various procedures covered by the clinic. Yet her sister had never been someone who was overly concerned about appearing younger. She looked after herself, Sybil knew, with regular facials and massages and other more pampering treatments. But it was a big step from a bit of exfoliation to a face-lift. Surely if that was what she was thinking, she wouldn't be meeting Waston Drury in a tapas bar. No, there was something else going on and Sybil wanted to know what it was.

But, she reminded herself, she wasn't going to give unasked-for advice.

She wasn't Tansy, after all.

Ailie was also sitting in front of the TV with an iPad on her lap. She was feeling very relaxed after the tapas with Rua and Sybil, who'd eased her anxieties about Flavia's work experience at the Villa Farfalla. In particular, Sybil's suggestion of turning up after a month on the pretext (or possibly the genuine reason) of having a meeting with the solicitor was an excellent one.

She opened a browser and searched for the villa. She'd never done this before, and realised that might seem bizarre to people who routinely googled people and places, but it had never been important to her. All she'd ever cared about was making sure that Giorgio was happy with his decision to live in Ireland. And as far as she knew, he always had been.

Nonetheless, he'd kept things from her. She hadn't been

aware of his chats with Flavia about the Marchettis, nor even considered he'd been in advanced discussions with Marco about development plans for the villa and the estate. She'd tried the oils Marco had given her for Christmas and had been impressed by their silky smoothness and delicate perfume. It seemed to her that they were undoubtedly a luxury product that could be a commercial success if marketed well. However, she didn't know how advanced any plans for the beauty business were, or if they were viable; or indeed if the wellness centre was a big project or a small add-on to the hotel. She was completely in the dark about all of it.

The website was modern and well designed. It opened with a rolling banner of the Adriatic coastline and the hills rising behind it before transitioning to a video of the villa itself. Definitely shabby chic, Ailie decided, as she studied the exterior carefully. The main building was tall and oblong, the open shutters dark green against the rusty ochre walls. A gravel pathway led to the front door, which had large pots containing laurel bushes on either side. It looked peaceful and easily marketable as a get-away-from-it-all destination. A good location for a spa, she acknowledged. Marco was right about that.

She clicked on the rooms. Each was unique in size, shape and decor, but all had wooden floors, coloured woven rugs and dark furniture. The bathrooms were very modern, with elegant porcelain tiles and rainfall showers.

The villa's breakfast room had a long refectory table in the centre as well as a couple of smaller tables near the windows. As with the bedrooms, the furniture was dark and a little gloomy for Ailie's taste, but it fitted in with the overall ambience of the building. The hotel didn't provide evening meals, but lunch and snacks were served on an upstairs terrace overlooking the bay. There was a sample menu of antipasti, salads and fish, which Ailie presumed Beatrice had devised. The pictured dishes looked both appetising and healthy.

She clicked on another video, this time of the olive grove, with a link to buy the Villa Farfalla's totally organic and natural products: prettily packaged soaps as well as the body oils that Marco had given her, and both plain and flavoured oils for cooking. Another tab brought her to a brief list of treatments available at the wellness centre, although there were no videos of the spa itself.

Before leaving Italy, Giorgio had been very keen on developing the wellness aspect of the villa, but Ailie knew his mother and Sophia thought it required far too much investment. Given the limited treatments they currently offered, and despite the new products and Marco's enthusiasm, it seemed they still hadn't developed that aspect of their holiday offering very much.

Nevertheless, she thought as she clicked on *Book Now* to check the prices, the Villa Farfalla was in a fabulous location, even if visitors would need a car to get into the city to explore the restaurants and nightlife. She selected some random dates in May and saw to her surprise that the villa was already booked out. It was probably just as well, she decided; staying with the Marchettis wouldn't necessarily be a good idea. They might not want her in the house given Flavia's status as a summer employee. She was certain her daughter wouldn't want her there cramping her style either.

Then the door opened and Flavia herself came in and flopped on the sofa beside her, so Ailie closed the iPad and spent the rest of the evening watching what to her seemed inane YouTube videos with her daughter.

* * *

Rua was having breakfast the following morning when Brontë walked into the kitchen dressed in a reasonable facsimile of an office suit: dark blue skirt, white blouse and a navy jacket that Rua recognised as hers. She raised an eyebrow.

'I'm going for an interview for a Saturday job,' said Brontë. 'A jewellery shop. They like their sales associates to look smart.'

'You usually go shopping on Saturdays. Why are you now deciding you want to be behind the counter instead?'

'They had a notice up in their window and I thought I'd try for it,' replied Brontë. 'No harm in earning a bit of money if I can. They might keep me on for the summer.'

'You're planning to stay in Dublin rather than travel again?'

'I honestly haven't decided. But I thought doing the interview would be good practice.'

'Fair enough,' said Rua. 'I applaud the initiative and I think it's a good idea to dress the part.'

'And what about you?' Brontë gave her mother an appraising look. 'You're dressed for the office yourself. Trousers rather than loungers.'

'I need to go in for a few days,' said Rua. 'New project. New people on the team. I want to meet them and get to know them.'

'Get to know them?' Brontë raised an eyebrow.

'Introduce myself.'

'You've never done that before.'

'Of course I have,' said Rua.

'Hmm. So are you taking the car or the Luas? My interview is in Dundrum. You could drop me there on your way.'

'Won't you be early?'

'Yes, but I'll get a coffee and read my book while I wait.'

'OK.' Rua got up from the table and put her cup in the dishwasher. 'I need to bring some tech with me, so I have to drive. Makes me feel better about it if there's two of us in the car.'

'I have my uses.' Brontë laughed.

Rua put on her jacket, then picked up her keys, bag and a large box filled with a variety of cables and other accessories, and the two of them left the house together.

'I miss Les Hauts Champs, but I like living here,' Brontë said as they drove off. 'There's a lot more going on and it's convenient to everything, even if the house is small.' She sighed. 'Not that I'll ever be able to afford even the tiniest of shoeboxes myself, ever.'

'You will,' said Rua. 'Eventually. You have plenty of time to do the things you want.'

'At my age you were living in France with a newborn baby. Me, I mean,' Brontë added, as though Rua might be confused about the number of children she had.

'So I was.' Rua joined the traffic on the main road, thankful that it wasn't as heavy as she had expected. She detested driving in rush hour, but nor did she like being in a crowded space on the tram for her commute. Other people's bodies pressed close to her made her anxious. It was another reason she preferred working from home.

'Do you ever wish it hadn't happened?' asked Brontë.

'What?'

'Sleeping with your guy instead of sticking to women. Having me.'

'We've talked about it before.' Rua glanced at her. 'I made a mistake. But you're an incredible person and I can't imagine not having you in my life.'

'That's not the same as not regretting me,' remarked Brontë.

'I don't regret you,' said Rua.

'The thing is,' Brontë continued, 'I can't imagine having a baby at my age. Not at any age, to be honest. It's mind-blowing. Being pregnant, giving birth, all of it. It's so far off my radar that I literally can't process it.'

'When the unexpected happens, you *have* to process it,' said Rua.

'I get that. But you're such a sensible person, Mum. So particular and organised. I'd have thought you'd have dealt with birth control ahead of trying it out with a man.'

'Like I said, I made a mistake.'

'Exactly!' Brontë's voice was triumphant. 'I was a mistake. What I don't understand is why you didn't . . .'

'What?'

'Get rid of me?'

'I'm not sure this is the time and the place for this conversation.' Rua tutted with annoyance as the car in front of her indicated at the last minute, forcing her to brake suddenly.

'We've never had it,' said Brontë. 'We should.'

'We've had lots of conversations about how much I love you and how much you matter to me,' said Rua.

'But not about whether you thought of getting rid of me. You must have.'

'It was an option, certainly.'

'So given that my father was nowhere to be found and that you had your whole life in front of you – why didn't you?'

'Could we not have this discussion right now?' asked Rua. 'Another time. Tonight if you like.'

'I'm out tonight,' said Brontë.

'We *will* talk about it,' promised Rua. 'Truly. But in the appropriate setting.'

'OK.' Brontë got out of the car and closed the door.

Rua watched her walk to the tram stop.

'I don't know if I'm ready,' she whispered to herself. 'I don't know if I can say the right thing.'

The SUV behind her beeped loudly as she missed the green light.

The rest of the team were already at the office when she arrived. Rua put her equipment on the last available desk by the window, and then Henry, along with the new team members, Sasha and Zhi, joined her in one of the creative spaces (she used the firm's terminology, even though the creative space was nothing more than an enclosed office). She spoke to them about the project and allocated responsibilities, checking that they were all confident about what was expected from them. She was impressed by the self-assurance of both Sasha and Zhi, whose questions were brief and to the point. Henry, as always, presented a laid-back approach to the work, although she knew that he was both competent and efficient.

'OK,' she said when they were finished. 'Weekly catch-up every Friday.'

'Here?' asked Henry. 'Or online?'

'Here,' said Rua. 'At least for now.'

'Cool.' He leaned back in his chair. 'It'll be good to see more of you.'

'I'm glad you think so.'

'Seriously,' he said. 'Also, now that we all know you're a deadly hotshot with a laser gun, we'll be on top of our game.'

Rua laughed and left the office. She brought her laptop with her and took the elevator to the ground-floor café. As she sat at one of the tables with a large mug of black coffee, she saw Bethany get up from another table and walk over to her.

'Hey,' said Bethany. 'You're in the office again.'

'Everyone seems to comment on my office appearances,' said Rua. 'I didn't realise I was a rare species.'

'You're the only one who can work from home as she pleases. It leads to speculation from time to time.'

'It was one of the conditions of me working here,' Rua said. She hesitated before adding, 'I'd just returned from France and I was going through a difficult time. Fortunately the company was very understanding, and since then they've realised that I get a lot done at home, so it's worked out pretty well. Nobody's tried to make me come in more often.'

'Our esteemed CEO said you were the most focused woman he'd ever met.'

'He hasn't met enough women in that case.' Rua grinned. 'D'you want to sit down? You're towering over me there.'

Bethany nodded and sat opposite her.

'So what else do people say about me?' asked Rua.

'They mostly comment about how dedicated to the work you are.'

'Makes me sound dreadfully boring.'

'I know about your hard time.' Bethany's tone was cautious. 'You lost your partner. I'm very sorry.'

'Thank you,' said Rua. 'It was difficult, but I'm fine now.'

'I'm glad to hear it. Sorry, this isn't the time or the place to bring up personal stuff. I didn't mean to embarrass you.'

'You haven't embarrassed me and there's no need to apologise.'

'I don't want you to feel uncomfortable around me,' said Bethany.

'Why should I feel uncomfortable? People lose their partners. It's a fact of life. I wish it wasn't for me, but it is. You don't have to tiptoe around me.'

'I suppose it's because you're not here that much. Nobody really knows you.'

'My fault, not yours,' said Rua. 'That's why I'm trying to be a little more involved.'

'Well, it's good to see you,' Bethany told her. 'Did you enjoy the laser tag?'

'More than I expected.'

'You did exceptionally well for a first go.'

'My super focus obviously helped.' Rua smiled.

'Would you like to come to another event?'

'What sort of event?' she asked.

'Nothing to do with work this time,' replied Bethany. 'Remember I mentioned that I did some target shooting? I'm in a gun club. We're trying to recruit more women members. I thought of you, given how deadly you were with the laser, and you did say you'd shot clays before.'

'So is this clays?' Rua experienced a momentary flashback to one of the days she, Lilou and Brontë had gone clay pigeon shooting on their neighbour's farmland. It had been a glorious spring day and the clays were vibrant orange circles against the blue sky. They'd enjoyed themselves immensely and afterwards had hot chocolate and brioche back at the house.

'Targets mainly.' Bethany's reply brought her back to the present. 'You don't need your own gun; one is provided for you. Rifles obviously.'

'I can manage a rifle.'

'It's a good day out,' Bethany assured her. 'As I said, we're trying to get more women, so it would be fantastic if you came.'

'Could I bring some female friends along too?'

Bethany looked surprised, but she gave Rua a cheery smile. 'Sure,' she said. 'The more the merrier.'

'It's a couple of women I hang out with,' Rua told her. 'Other widows. We've been supporting each other a bit. I don't know if they'd be interested, but it would be nice to ask.'

'No problem.' Bethany sounded more confident in her reply. 'I'll send you a link to the website. The outing is next Saturday.'

'Thanks for inviting me,' said Rua.

'Thanks for saying yes. I hope you'll enjoy it.'

'Is it wrong to say I get a kick out of shooting things?'

'Not to me.' Bethany smiled. 'We could chat about it a bit more if you like. D'you have any lunch plans for today?'

'No.'

'Would you like to go for a sandwich?'

'Sure. But it'll be closer to two before I'm free.'

'Sounds good. See you in reception then.' Bethany got up, taking her coffee with her.

'See you then,' said Rua.

She glanced at her open laptop, but her legendary focus had deserted her.

She was thinking of Bethany, and how she'd smiled at her as she'd turned to walk away.

Chapter 21

Sybil and Ailie were taken aback by Rua's invitation to go to the shooting club. Both replied that they'd never shot anything before, and Sybil remarked that innocent bystanders were more likely to get plugged by her than the target. But Rua sent them the link to the website and suggested that it would be a change from simply meeting up for lunch. She added that Brontë was coming with her because both of them had a little experience from their time in France and she thought her daughter might enjoy it. In fact Brontë had been very keen when Rua mentioned it to her, and Rua, surprised at her unbridled enthusiasm, was delighted. Ailie asked if Flavia could join them too, although she wasn't sure if she'd want to. But Flavia had liked the idea, and so the following Saturday morning the five of them met up at the small wooden clubhouse, a few kilometres from Kilmacanogue and the iconic Sugar Loaf mountain.

It was a bright day with a cool easterly wind that whistled through the early spring leaves and made Sybil glad that she'd worn a woollen beanie along with her quilted jacket. As she got out of her car, she saw that Ailie and Rua were already there, and identified which daughter was which by their hair:

Brontë's fiery mane was pulled into a messy plait, while Flavia's darker locks were being whipped across her face by the wind.

'Hello, all,' she said as she crossed the gravel car park to meet them. 'This is different.'

'When Flavia sprung the Italy trip on me, I decided I wouldn't turn down any invitations I got myself,' Ailie said as she rubbed her hands together to keep them warm. 'I'm not entirely sure this was what I had in mind, though, when I told myself I had to get out and live my life to the full.'

'It's good to step outside our comfort zones,' Rua said. 'That's Brontë, by the way.' She waved at her daughter, who was deep in conversation with Flavia.

'And Flavia is with her,' added Ailie as both girls walked over to them.

'Nice to meet you both,' said Sybil. 'Are you any good at this?'

'I did a little clay pigeon shooting in France,' Brontë told her. 'I was OK but not brilliant. I'm not sure how I'll be at stationary targets.'

'Here's Bethany!' Rua spotted her colleague with a group of other shooters and waved. Bethany saw her and hurried over, greeting them all and saying that it was fantastic to have so many women show up.

'There are some female members,' she told them, 'but we'd like more.'

'I can't guarantee that we'll all become members,' said Rua. 'Or even that you'd want us to.'

'I can probably guarantee that I won't,' Sybil said. 'It's a bit of a trek for me and I'm not at all convinced I'll be any good. But hey ho, I'll try anything once.'

Bethany led them to the range, where she went through

a detailed explanation of gun safety before showing them how to load a rifle and take up a prone position at the range.

'The hardest part for me will be getting up again,' observed Sybil as she aligned her body as Bethany told her. 'Neither my knees nor my hips are as forgiving as they once were.'

'Take aim at the target,' Bethany told her. 'The wind will affect the flight of the bullet, but let's not worry about that yet. Let's see how you get on with firing the rifle first. Keep in mind that it'll recoil and it's quite a jolt on your shoulder. Good that you're wearing a nicely padded jacket.'

Sybil didn't tell her that it had been her Christmas present to herself: Hugo Boss, very expensive and not intended for lying on a grubby mat at the foot of the Wicklow Mountains. However, she followed Bethany's advice and squeezed the trigger gently, gasping at the shock of the recoil.

'You hit the target!' Bethany was looking through a range finder. 'High and wide, but at least you got it.'

She left Sybil to perfect her aim and turned her attention to Ailie, who told her that she'd never make a soldier because lying like this was very uncomfortable. But when Ailie hit the outer ring on the target, she forgot her discomfort and, like Sybil, began working on her aim.

Rua had already taken a couple of shots by the time Bethany came to her. Like Ailie, her first hit the outer ring, but her second was closer to the centre.

'Not bad at all,' said Bethany as she wriggled her body down beside Rua's and looked along the range. 'Have another go.'

She stayed with Rua while her aim got progressively better, saying that Flavia and Brontë were being looked after by Anya, the club chairperson.

'They'll like Anya,' she said. 'She's only twenty-five and a brilliant shot. She's won quite a few competitions.'

'I think I was more useful at the clays than this,' Rua remarked. 'Seems like I'm better at moving and firing than being slow and steady.'

'We do clay pigeon shooting on Sundays,' Bethany told her. 'You could always come again tomorrow.'

'Let's see how much of an eejit I make of myself today first.'

'You're not making an eejit of yourself at all. You're really good. You have an aptitude for it.'

'I'm not sure how good a thing it is to have an aptitude for shooting targets,' said Rua.

'It's just a sport.' Bethany sounded amused. 'And we only ever use circular targets. We never put up human-shaped ones. It's not what we're about. In fact, I find it a bit gross when people do that.'

'I would too.' Rua released a slow breath and pulled the trigger. 'Bullseye,' she said with delight.

'You're a natural.'

'Maybe.' Rua drew back the bolt and reloaded the gun.

'Nice and easy,' said Bethany.

'Nice and easy it is.'

She hit the bullseye again and released a sigh of satisfaction. She'd been good at shooting clays on the farmland behind her home in Les Hauts Champs, but she hadn't been sure that the skills would translate. She was pleased they had. And pleased that Bethany had invited her to be here today.

Eventually Flavia, who'd steadily improved her aim, declared that her shoulder was sore and she needed a break. Brontë, in the prone position beside her, suggested they go to the clubhouse for coffee, so the two young women made their way to the green-painted building, where they got hot drinks and snacks from a machine.

'It's bizarre how our mums met,' said Flavia as she sat at one of the wooden tables outside and unwrapped a Kit Kat. 'But nice that they've become friends.'

'Yes,' agreed Brontë. 'Quite honestly, I despaired of ever getting Mum out of the house. She was a positive recluse when we came to Ireland after Lilou died. At first I didn't mind. I was around the same age as you when it happened, and I guess I was happy to have her undivided love and attention. But after a while it became tedious.'

'It's suffocating all right,' agreed Flavia. 'My mum keeps asking me if I'm OK and wanting to keep tabs on where I am and who I'm with . . . Exhausting.'

'She's concerned about you, that's all,' said Brontë. 'Mums are like that.'

'And you had two of them! What was that like?' asked Flavia.

'It's all I ever knew,' replied Brontë. 'Mum was Mum and Lilou was Maman, and that's how it was.'

'I used to call my dad Papà,' said Flavia. 'Not when I was with my friends, they would've given me a terrible time for it, but at home. He liked it.'

'How are you getting on without him?' asked Brontë. 'Not you and your mum. You.'

'Oh, you know.' Flavia wrapped her hands around her coffee and released a slow breath. 'Sometimes I forget he's dead and I think of things I want to tell him when I get home. And then I remember and it's like a kick in the stomach.

Other times I miss him so much it hurts. Then there are days I don't think about him and I feel bad about that.'

'I totally get it,' said Brontë. 'Lilou was such a vibrant person it seemed impossible that she should have died. It was so random and unfair that it took me a long time to accept it. It probably wasn't until we came to live here that I did.'

'How did you feel about leaving France?' asked Flavia.

'It's all a blur, to be honest,' replied Brontë. 'When we first came, we stayed with my grandparents and that was both good and bad. Mum has a tricky relationship with Granny. I think Granny was angry at her for getting pregnant with me. Let's face it, even twenty years ago it was something she should have taken precautions about. I get on really well with Granny and Gramps, but I was sort of relieved when we moved to Dublin.'

'And do you prefer it to France?'

'It's like you said. If we'd stayed there, I would've kept waiting for Lilou to come home. Because she never lived with us in Dublin, it's different.'

'I get that.' Flavia nodded.

'Interesting that we both have parents from different countries,' said Brontë. 'How do you get on with your Italian relatives?'

'How much time do we have?'

Brontë raised an eyebrow, and Flavia gave a brief résumé of the enmity between her mother and the Marchettis.

'All the same, you're going to spend the summer with them,' said Brontë when Flavia finished by telling her about the offer of a job at the Villa Farfalla.

'Yes. I'm looking forward to it but I'm a bit nervous too. What if they're as horrible as Mum thinks?'

'You can always come home,' said Brontë.

'As an abject failure,' said Flavia. 'I want them to like me. I want to like them. It's for my dad as much as for me.'

'You get on with your half-brother, though.'

'Marco's a pet,' said Flavia, 'but I've only ever known him in Ireland. What if he's all . . . oh, I dunno . . . all Italian over there?'

Brontë laughed, and after a moment Flavia did too. Rua, recognising the sound, looked around from her position on the range and smiled as she saw the two young women together. Perhaps they'd become friends just as Rua had with Ailie and Sybil. She waved at Brontë, who didn't notice and was continuing her conversation with Flavia.

'So how's your mum doing now?' she asked. 'Obviously she's got into a little group with mine and that older woman, Sybil, which is nice for them all. Is she OK?'

'Some days she's good, other days not so much,' replied Flavia. 'Being friends with your mum and Sybil has helped. I think it was good for her to meet people who didn't know Dad. I know the Marchettis are Dad's family, but they didn't know us as a family. It's why I'm sort of looking forward to going to Italy. Does that sound weird?'

'Not a bit,' said Brontë. 'I went to counselling when we came back to Ireland. I felt so uprooted and confused that I was finding it hard to cope. The counselling put my mind at ease, I guess. Mostly I felt guilty about us leaving France and about feeling better in Ireland. But it seemed disrespectful to Lilou to leave her behind. Although we didn't,' she added. 'Mum has her ashes. She keeps them on the top shelf of her wardrobe, which is a bit freaky.'

'You're kidding! That's where my mum keeps Dad's ashes too.'

The two young women chuckled.

'Anyhow, are you doing all right now?' asked Flavia.

'Is anyone ever all right?' Brontë sighed. 'Isn't there always something to make you worry?'

'Oh, God, yes.' Flavia's reply was fervent.

'Well, look, if you're ever feeling worried – either here or in Italy – and there's no one else you can talk to, message me,' said Brontë. 'Whether it's worry about yourself or your mum, I'm sure we can work it out between us.'

'Seriously? That's so kind of you.'

'Not at all,' said Brontë. 'The older women are sticking together. Us younger people should do the same.'

Sybil was next to abandon the range in search of coffee. Her shoulder was throbbing, her hip was sore and the biting wind meant that she needed to warm up. Flavia and Brontë were finishing their own snacks when she arrived, but both of them stayed with her and asked if she was enjoying herself.

'It's not bad,' she replied. 'I get a great sense of satisfaction when I hit the target, even if it's nowhere near the centre. I'm not sure it's something I'd do on a regular basis, though.'

Flavia remarked that Brontë had shot clays in France so she had an advantage.

'Oh, yes, your mum mentioned that.' Sybil nodded.

'I'd forgotten how exhilarating it can be,' said Brontë. 'It was mainly with our neighbour, although I did go shooting once with my *grand-père*. He was brilliant at it, but then he's a real country person.'

'Did you get on well with him?' asked Sybil.

'I only met him a couple of times.' Brontë shrugged. 'Neither Mum nor I were very important to him. Sometimes I think Lilou wasn't either.'

'Rua told me that he and your grandmother both married again and moved away.'

'Yes.' Brontë nodded. 'Alize and Valery were like everyone's idea of a French farce. They had affairs, they got married, got divorced, got married again!' She laughed. 'I hardly knew them. But I miss Lilou so much.'

'She sounds like a wonderful person.'

'She really was.' Brontë's smile was wistful. 'But we have to accept what happened, don't we?'

'It's not always easy.'

'We were talking about Lilou and my dad earlier,' said Flavia. 'How hard it is to accept.'

'Life can be unfair,' said Sybil. 'It'll always hurt, remembering them, but after a while you remember more of the good things and it's a comfort. It's lovely to have met you young ladies.'

Flavia tried to hide a grin at being called a young lady. Sybil noticed, but said nothing.

'Ah, your mums have decided to take a break too,' she said. 'I'm going to head off myself.'

'Oh, stay for another session,' urged Rua, when Sybil told her she was leaving.

'I enjoyed it more than I expected, but I'm done,' said Sybil. 'My shoulder is aching.'

'Wait until I get your targets,' said Bethany. 'We can total up your score.'

'I don't mind you getting the targets, but don't say the score out loud,' implored Sybil. 'I don't want to embarrass myself.'

Bethany went into the back of the clubhouse and Sybil smiled at Rua.

'I like her,' she said.

'So do I.'

'Someone you might get close to?'

'Maybe,' said Rua. 'We went to lunch together last week and had a good old natter. We like a lot of the same things. Regardless, though, I'm not losing the Merry Widows.'

'I'm glad to hear it,' said Sybil. 'I love our little group. But if you and Bethany have a connection, you should nurture it. At the very least, let it develop.'

'We'll see,' said Rua. 'It's different to the connection I have with you guys.'

'I love our group too,' said Ailie. 'And it looks like Flavia and Brontë are getting to know each other as well. So that's another benefit.'

'Definitely,' said Sybil. 'Today was different but very enjoyable. Perhaps we can meet up again in a few weeks?'

'Sounds good,' agreed Ailie.

'It's my turn to organise us again,' Sybil said. 'You did the tapas, Rua did this. So I'll message you all, unless something else exciting comes up first.'

'Perfect,' said Rua. 'Oh, here's Bethany with your targets.'

Although Sybil's shooting had been rather erratic, she'd scored more than she expected, and she took her leave of the women feeling quite pleased with herself. It wasn't ever going to be a new hobby for her, but it was nice to have.

And as always, meeting Ailie and Rua had lifted her spirits.

Rather than take the motorway route that her satnav suggested, Sybil elected to go home via the coast, where the views were prettier. She made better time than she'd expected, so she decided to stop off at Dun Laoghaire, a pretty coastal town that had once been small and quaint but was now perpetually busy and bustling. She parked near the harbour and strolled along the seafront until she arrived at a small café, where she ordered tea and a slice of carrot cake. She was hungry from her exertions at the shooting range, and the coffee at the clubhouse, while welcome, had been nothing more than tepid brown liquid.

As she gazed across the bay towards her own home in Sutton, she tried to remember the last time she'd been in Dun Laoghaire. She and Theo had visited quite a lot at one stage, as they'd had friends living in the town, but they'd drifted apart over the years. She recalled that Clarissa had signed the online book of condolences when Theo died, which was kind of her. She took out her phone to see if she had their contact information, but Theo must have been the one to keep it, as there was nothing in her address book. In any event, even if she knew where they lived, she could hardly ring the bell after all these years and ask how they were getting on. They could have divorced. Remarried. Died. Sybil knew that this was something she'd thought about when she'd first seen all the condolences from people she'd lost touch with. Anything could have happened in their lives, just as the unthinkable had happened in hers. It was true that you never knew what was going on in someone else's world. And it was why she was now significantly less judgemental than she'd been in the past.

Her attention was caught by a woman in a bright yellow rain jacket walking past the café. She hesitated for a moment, then, leaving her carrot cake unfinished, hurried to the cash desk and tapped her card to pay the bill. She was in time to see the woman turning at Marine Road, and she hurried up the street to catch up with her.

'Tansy!' she called. 'Wait!'

She hadn't seen her sister since the day at the tapas bar, although they'd texted a number of times since. Most of the messages were inconsequential, Tansy asking Sybil if everything was OK with her and Sybil replying yes but never adding what she really wanted to say, which was 'By the way, are you having an affair with a plastic surgeon?'

Tansy had stopped outside an old building with a renovated facade and was looking around to see who'd called her.

'It's me,' said Sybil breathlessly as she caught up with her.

'Sybil. Why do I keep bumping into you on the Southside? Are you stalking me or something?' Tansy seemed agitated.

'I stopped for tea on my way home from Kilmacanogue,' replied Sybil. She glanced at the building they were standing in front of. The lettering on the plate-glass window said *WellWishers* and proclaimed it to be a wellness and beauty centre.

'What were you doing in Kilmacanogue?' asked Tansy. 'That's a long way from home.'

Sybil explained about the shooting expedition.

'You're joking.' Tansy looked at her in astonishment.

'Why should I be joking? You're always at me to do new things. I'm doing new things.'

'But target shooting! You can hardly see ten yards without your glasses, for heaven's sake.'

'You're wrong there.' Sybil kept her voice mild. 'My distance vision is excellent. It's reading that's the bugger.'

'Either way.' Tansy shook her head. 'Target shooting with

your widow friends is unusual to say the least. You haven't seen or heard from Burt recently, I take it?'

'You've asked me that at least half a dozen times over the last few weeks. No, I haven't,' replied Sybil. And then, before she could help herself, she added, 'What about you? Have you been out and about with anyone yourself?'

'What's that supposed to mean?'

'Nothing. Or maybe everything. Oh, look, I don't want to pry, but, well . . . your name has been, um, linked, shall we say, with a man by the rather improbable name of Watson Drury. I can't not tell you.'

'Who have you been talking to?' demanded Tansy.

Sybil didn't reply.

'And what makes you think that I have anything to do with Watson Drury?' her sister went on.

'Perhaps you're thinking of getting a bit of work done?' Sybil glanced from Tansy to WellWishers. 'Though I thought he worked out of an actual clinic, and this is more of a tweakments place.'

'For feck's sake, Sybil, there's nothing wrong with trying to improve my looks a bit.'

'So you *are* seeing him as a plastic surgeon,' said Sybil. 'Isn't it a bit odd outside his surgery?'

'It's none of your business.'

'Hey, it's none of *your* business when you try to interfere in my life either,' retorted Sybil. 'I'm returning the favour, that's all.'

'How are you planning to interfere?'

'Oh, for heaven's sake! I'm not going to interfere at all. Of course I'm not. I suppose I was surprised to hear you'd been out with him. I guess I thought you and Colin were solid.'

'We are,' said Tansy.

'Good. So what's the story with Mr Drury?'

'Did you see him at the tapas bar with me?'

'Not *with* you. He left shortly afterwards. Perhaps too shortly afterwards. And you were so shifty when I was talking to you, I put two and two together. If I've got five, I'm sorry.'

'How did you recognise him?'

'Ailie did. He's a patient at her dental surgery.'

'For feck's sake.' Tansy snorted. 'You can't do a thing in Dublin without someone finding out.'

'Which is why it's hard to have an affair.'

'I'm not having an affair.'

'What then?'

Tansy looked at her watch. 'I've got an appointment for fillers in five minutes,' she said. 'Go have another cup of tea and I'll meet you there.'

'I was in the café around the corner,' said Sybil.

'See you there shortly,' said Tansy, and she went into the wellness centre.

Sybil returned to the café and ordered another pot of Earl Grey, although she decided to lay off any more carrot cake. She scrolled through her phone as she waited for Tansy and smiled at the photos Rua had forwarded of them all stretched out on the ground, rifles at their shoulders, intent on their targets. There were a couple of Brontë and Flavia too, both in the prone position and later standing beside their targets looking pleased with themselves. Sybil smiled. She liked the two girls and always felt rejuvenated after chatting with younger people, buoyed up by their energy and enthusiasm, remembering how, when her own life had stretched in front of her, she'd been fired with energy and enthusiasm too. Not that she'd lost those feelings entirely. But in her youth, alongside Theo, she'd been filled with excitement for all the adventures ahead of her and the new things she expected to do. Now her life had become well ordered and predictable.

Though since she'd met Ailie and Rua, slightly less predictable than before. And it didn't have to be predictable at all, she thought suddenly, as another notification from the travel company she'd forgotten to unsubscribe from popped up on her screen. She could do whatever she wanted, whenever she wanted. Even take the cruise they were promoting if she felt like it. Instead of swiping past the notification as she usually did, she clicked on it and was astonished to see how good the offer for a Mediterranean trip was. According to the website, the cruise ship was luxurious and intimate, catering for eight hundred passengers. Sybil wouldn't have called eight hundred people an intimate gathering, but perhaps in the context of cruising it was, and maybe it was also the sort of gathering she could lose herself in. Take herself out of her comfort zone among people who didn't know her and who she'd never see again. Be unpredictable, she told herself. Do something unexpected.

Before she had time to change her mind, she took out her credit card and booked herself the best available cabin.

She was still asking herself what had possessed her when Tansy walked into the café half an hour later. Her sister went to the counter and ordered herself a frappé and a biscotti, then sat at the table opposite Sybil.

'Good job on the fillers,' said Sybil. 'You'd hardly notice.'

'You're supposed to notice an improvement at least,' Tansy told her.

'I do. Your face is fuller but not inflated.'

'Thanks.'

Sybil broke the silence between them. 'It's ages since we've had coffee outside of your house or mine.'

Tansy tipped half a sachet of sugar into her cup and busied herself stirring it.

Sybil didn't say anything more.

'You'll be annoyed with me,' said Tansy eventually.

'About what?'

'Watson.'

'Go on.' Sybil's words were cautious.

'I did meet him at the dentist's,' said Tansy. 'We got chatting in the waiting room. He was – is – very charming.'

'OK,' said Sybil slowly.

'And I was attracted to him. He's smart and intelligent and interesting to talk to.'

'So what happened?'

'He's divorced,' Tansy said. 'He kind of came on to me a bit. I . . . well, for the laugh I said I was getting a divorce myself.'

'Tansy!'

'I know. I know. It was a mad thing to do. But the dentist's makes me nervous and being a bit flirty kind of took my mind off it.'

'Jesus wept,' said Sybil.

'We chatted about his work. He mostly does reconstructive surgery in a private hospital but also takes on some cosmetic procedures.'

'At that wellness place?'

'No, you're right, it's mainly injectables there, and that's not his thing. He does the cosmetic stuff in a clinic.'

'Have you had Botox too?' Sybil gave her an appraising look.

'I do get a little around the eyes,' admitted Tansy.

'I've always thought you were ageing better than me. It's too late for me to care at this point, but you're right to do it if it makes you feel good. So you were thinking of a facelift?'

'I was not,' retorted Tansy. 'I don't mind the tweaks, but the idea of actual surgery when I don't need it for a medical reason – not a chance! But I did go to his consulting rooms to talk it through, and when I said I wasn't ever going to have surgery, he said he was happy about that because it meant he could ask me out. He wouldn't have if I'd become a patient.'

'Right.'

'And so I went out with him.'

'To the tapas bar.'

'Yes. But I didn't plan to have an affair with him. I'm not having an affair with him.'

'Why did you meet him in that case?'

'Initially . . . for the adventure. Don't be judgy. I feel like I'm in a bit of a rut. The kids are all grown up with their own lives – even Darragh, if he ever leaves the feckin' house. Colin and I are at a point where we know each other so well that nothing is very exciting any more. I love him and I'd never do anything to hurt him. I don't want to leave him, far from it. But a little excitement . . . meeting a different man, talking to him like a woman instead of, well, a mother and a housewife . . . it was good to do.'

'I see.' Sybil understood perfectly what her sister was saying. It was important to have your own status that had nothing to do with your relationship to someone else, whether that was your partner or your children. Theo had understood that, which was why he'd been so supportive of her accepting the Bermuda job all those years ago. But Tansy, who'd built her life around her husband and family, had allowed herself to become subsumed by them. All the same, telling a man she was getting a divorce and then meeting him at a tapas bar could have unwanted consequences. And no matter what she said, Colin would be very hurt if he knew.

'It was unfortunate I bumped into you in that case.'

'I nearly threw up,' confessed Tansy. 'I felt so guilty, even though there was nothing to feel guilty about.'

'You were kind of deceiving Watson,' Sybil pointed out. 'You said you were getting a divorce.'

'I know,' said Tansy. 'I didn't care.'

'So where does this leave you?'

'Oh, look, I told him I couldn't see him again. That Colin and I were making another go at it. I think he was freaked out that I'd been copped by my sister in a place I assured him nobody would ever recognise me.'

'Not that it should have mattered if you were getting a divorce,' remarked Sybil.

'I know, but I told him I wanted to be discreet.'

'So everything's OK with you and Colin now?'

'It always was,' said Tansy.

'Not really,' Sybil said. 'Not if you were looking for adventure.' She studied her sister thoughtfully. 'It's not my thing, but maybe you'd like the shooting range.'

'I'm actually thinking about dance classes,' Tansy said.

'You were a good dancer when we were kids. I was terrible, especially at the Irish dancing. I could never get a jig right.'

'I'm going to go and check a session out. I might be able to persuade Colin to come along. He's pretty nimble on his feet too.'

'And so Watson Drury is consigned to the scrapheap?'

'Well . . .' Tansy looked at her thoughtfully.

'What?'

'I did think when I was talking to him that he'd be a great fit for you.'

'Mother of God, Tansy, you've got to be kidding me.'

'Not at all.' Her sister's tone was cheerful. 'He's very well off, so no worries he might be a freeloader.'

Sybil made a face at her.

'He's also charming and interesting to talk to,' continued Tansy. 'And only fifty-nine, which means he fits into your mould of going for younger men.'

'For crying out loud!'

'He's an interesting man. I can see how you'd prefer him to Burt. He's a completely different personality.'

'I'm not sure how many times I have to tell you. I'm not looking for a man.'

'Not looking, but if one dropped into your lap?'

'No,' said Sybil.

'I'm not giving up on you,' Tansy said. 'You're a good-looking, vibrant woman. You deserve a second chance at happiness.'

'Tansy, darling, I *am* happy.'

'There's always room for a little more happiness,' said Tansy.

And Sybil had nothing to say in return.

Chapter 22

As she parked at the airport, Ailie couldn't believe how quickly the last few weeks had gone by. At first, the days since Giorgio's death had moved at a glacial pace, November, December, January and February all melding into one long, dark month of heavy skies, cold weather and misery, the only bright spots being the times she met up with Sybil and Rua and the messages they regularly exchanged. But the days were longer now, the sky seemed higher, and Ailie's heart, while still burdened by her loss, was lighter. Although not perhaps today, because today was the day Flavia was leaving for the Villa Farfalla.

There had been scenes earlier in the morning as Flavia, her case packed since the previous weekend, suddenly began adding more clothes, declaring that she needed additional T-shirts and shorts and wailing that she didn't know why she hadn't put them in in the first place. Ailie reminded her that she was already at the limit of the weight allowance for her baggage and that she'd have to take something out; Flavia then burst into tears because she didn't want to leave anything behind. Ailie sat on the end of the bed, put her arm around her and gently reminded her that Italy was the home of fashion and she'd surely be able to find some very stylish clothes there to add to the already ample selection of tops and skirts and trainers and shoes that she'd originally selected. After another minute of sobbing, Flavia sniffed and said that Ailie was probably right and that maybe she'd be able to afford something by Prada or Gucci by the end of the summer. Then she took out her phone to google designer shops in Trieste. At which point Ailie had quietly finished the packing for her and locked the case.

Now Flavia was cheerfully wheeling it into the terminal while Ailie tried not to feel emotional.

'You'll text me as soon as Marco picks you up?' she said for at least the tenth time, after she'd watched her daughter drop off the bag.

'I already told you I would.'

'And you'll let me know how it's all going?'

'Yes.'

'And you won't let them take advantage of you?'

'Mum!'

'OK, OK. I'm sorry. You'll make sure you have time to enjoy yourself?'

'I'm going to have a great time.'

'I know you are.' Ailie hugged her tightly and Flavia squeaked in protest.

Ailie released her and waited while Flavia went through the fast-track security that Ailie had gifted her. When her daughter was out of sight, she walked slowly back to her car. She got in, rested her head against the steering wheel and allowed a few tears to fall. Then she sat up straight again and sent a text.

Flavia safely on her way to Trieste and the lion's den. I'm proud of her and terrified at the same time. All messages saying that I'm an idiot to be worried very welcome.

Sybil was on the train from Galway to Dublin when she saw Ailie's text, and she immediately replied with words of encouragement. She was glad the group had already made a date to meet up again soon, conscious that for Ailie this would be the first time she'd been entirely on her own since her husband's death. She was hopeful that she and Rua would be able to give her any extra support she might need.

She herself had spent the last couple of days with her friend Juliette, whose own daughter and family had gone on a trip to Dublin. It was Saoirse who'd suggested Sybil stay with Juliette while she was away, and Sybil was delighted to fall in with the plan. Although she loved meeting up with her new friends, Juliette was someone who'd known her and Theo as a couple, and it was nice to be able to reminisce with her about times they'd all shared together. Juliette had also been very interested in the Merry Widows group and had extracted as much information as she could from Sybil about Ailie and Rua.

'But how could that woman not know a thing about her husband's family?' she asked when Sybil recounted Ailie's history. 'I know everything there is to know about Kevin's. And in fairness to his sister, she's tried to keep the lines of communication between us open. Not that I particularly want to communicate with her; she's the sort of wan that'd tell Kevin everything. But there isn't an ounce of badness in her.'

'I get the impression that there *is* some badness in the Marchettis,' said Sybil. 'Though maybe it's simply a cultural thing. People from different countries look at life in different ways.'

'You're probably right,' said Juliette. 'As for that poor pet Rua, losing her wife like that! It's very, very unfair.'

'She's such a positive person,' Sybil said. 'I hope she finds someone else.'

'And you?' Juliette gave her a shrewd look. 'What about you?'

Sybil filled her in on the Burt episode, followed by Tansy's 'date' with Watson Drury and her subsequent suggestion of him as a potential partner for Sybil, which left Juliette chortling with laughter.

'That Burt guy sounds utterly wrong for you at any rate,' she said. 'And I can't believe Watson Drury would suit you either. What on earth is Tansy thinking?'

'That getting me fixed up with anyone is better than me being single,' said Sybil.

'Are you sure she's telling the truth about the plastic surgeon?' asked Juliette. 'I mean, her meeting him for the sake of adventure. Telling him she was getting divorced when she's not. Sounds more like something a bloke would do. Is there more to it than she's letting on?'

'I think I believe her,' said Sybil, although her voice held a trace of doubt. 'After all, she was perfectly prepared to push me at him. She'd hardly do that if she wanted him for herself.'

'Diversionary tactics,' suggested Juliette.

'Maybe.' Sybil sighed. 'I can only wait and see how things turn out.'

'And the cruise?' Juliette turned to the other topic of conversation. 'That's so unlike you.'

'I suppose it was thinking I don't do enough different things these days,' said Sybil. 'It's only a week, so if it's shit, I'm sure I can put up with it.'

'You'll be grand,' declared Juliette. 'Sure, if the worst comes to the worst you can lounge on your balcony and get room service for the whole seven days.'

'Exactly. Also, some of the ports look interesting. There's a trip to Pompeii. Theo and I went when we were first married, and I'd love to revisit.'

'You'll have to send me loads of photos.'

'I will,' promised Sybil.

'Meantime I'll keep my ear to the ground for gossip. A friend of a friend had surgery with yer man Drury. She knows his PA.'

'You're not serious.'

'Tansy was right when she said you can't do anything in Dublin. All of Ireland is a village. I'll let you know if I hear anything.'

'Thanks,' said Sybil.

Now, on the train, she mentally rehashed her own conversation with Tansy. She hoped her sister had been telling the truth about her relationship with Watson Drury. But in all honesty, she couldn't be sure.

Rua also sent Ailie a message of encouragement, telling her of her anxieties when Brontë had gone away the previous year but assuring her that everything had worked out fine in the end. She added that she knew Ailie had different concerns, but pointed out that Flavia was in a place with at least one person who was looking out for her, whereas Brontë had travelled all over Europe with a motley collection of friends.

You're right, I know. But I'm going to be a nervous wreck till I hear she's arrived and an equal wreck until she texts after her first day. I'm mad. I realise that.

You're a mother. It never ends.

Indeed xxxx

Rua allowed herself a wry smile. She was going to have to be a different sort of mother tonight, the one who would tell her daughter everything she wanted to know about her conception. And she wasn't looking forward to it one little bit.

Brontë hadn't broached the subject since the day of her interview. But Rua was now ready to tell her everything, and believed her daughter had the right to know. She was aware that Brontë was planning an evening in, so tonight was the ideal opportunity.

She was in the kitchen cooking when Brontë walked into the room, sniffing appreciatively at the aroma of *poulet basquaise*, one of Rua's signature chicken meals and one that both Brontë and Lilou had loved. Lilou had been a talented cook but was always delighted when Rua made an effort for her. Rua, while deferring to her wife's greater culinary expertise, had tried to do her fair share when they'd lived in France, but now she didn't bother as much with the dishes that had once been so common for them.

'That smells delicious,' Brontë told her as she flopped onto a kitchen chair. 'Takes me right back.'

'Me too,' said Rua.

'Is that why you haven't cooked it in so long?'

'Maybe.'

Brontë went into her bedroom and returned a few minutes later in a pale blue and cream striped top and blue leggings. She'd tied up her curls with a cream ribbon. Looking at her, Rua couldn't help thinking that her daughter had absorbed by some kind of osmosis the chic way that Lilou or Francine or Ségolène had of pulling an outfit together, no matter how informal it was.

'What?' asked Brontë as she opened the bottle of Pinot Noir that was on the table, and realised that Rua was staring at her.

'I was thinking how French you still are.'

'Not any more.' Brontë shook her head. 'I think I've lost it. When Lilou was alive, I used to think in French all the time, but now I don't.'

'What language do you dream in?' asked Rua.

'Gosh, I haven't a clue.'

'If I dream about Lilou, I dream in French,' said Rua. 'If I dream about anything else, it's usually in English.'

'That's a bit mad, isn't it? Will I pour this out? Is the *poulet* ready?'

'Yes. Go ahead. I want to talk to you about something and I don't know if it's better before or after eating.'

'That sounds serious.'

'It kind of is.'

'Oh.' Brontë looked at her anxiously. 'Is something wrong? Are you OK?'

'I'm totally fine,' Rua assured her. 'Couldn't be better.'

'Granny? Gramps?'

'Everyone's peachy,' said Rua. 'It's something else. What we were talking about before. About me being pregnant in France with you.'

'Oh,' said Brontë again.

'You have a right to know,' said Rua.

'I know I do.' Brontë took a sip of wine. 'I always felt there was more to it than you were letting on. I'm not a child, Mum. You can tell me anything.'

Could any mother tell her daughter anything at all? wondered Rua. And even if she could, should she? Were some things better off left unsaid? But she'd started down this road now and she couldn't draw back. Brontë was looking at her expectantly. Rua turned the heat down on the food and began to talk.

Neither of them spoke after she'd finished. Brontë twirled her wine glass between her fingers, an inscrutable expression on her face. Rua wanted to ask her what she was thinking and how she was feeling, but she knew that she had to allow Brontë time to process what she'd told her. She wondered if her daughter was blaming her for not saying anything before now. She reached across the table for the bottle of wine and refilled the glass in front of her. She hadn't realised she'd finished it.

'Did Lilou know?' asked Brontë eventually.

'Yes.'

Brontë was silent again. And then Rua realised that her daughter was crying, the tears rolling slowly down her cheeks. She took a handful of tissues from the box on the counter and gave them to her.

'I can't believe it.' Brontë blew her nose. 'I can't believe that happened to you and you kept it quiet and that Granny kept it quiet too. It's . . . it's . . . well, it's incredible.'

'It was the times,' said Rua. 'Lots of things were kept quiet.'

'It was only twenty years ago.' Brontë sniffed.

'It was very different, though.'

'Maybe not all that different. I mean, a girl gets raped now and the same sort of shit goes on. Maybe it's not as shameful a thing in the court of public opinion, but she's going to feel exactly the same way you did. As though she did something wrong. As though it was her fault. It *wasn't* your fault.'

'I know that.'

'But Granny acted as though it was. What about Gramps? What did he think?'

'We kept it from your grandfather,' said Rua. 'It wasn't something I felt I could tell him and your granny was determined that it was for the best to stay silent. Her view was that the fewer people who knew, the better. As far as she was concerned, it was Davey Mullery's word against mine, and people were going to give him the benefit of the doubt because people always give men the benefit of the doubt. So that was why she didn't want me to say anything.'

'Do you wish you had? To the authorities and to Gramps?'

'I desperately wanted to report it,' said Rua. 'Of course that way your grandfather would have had to know too. But your granny was adamant that it was a bad idea, and over the years I can see why. It's like you're assaulted twice. Once by the man and then again by the system.'

'I hate it!' Brontë's voice, which had been shaky, was now forceful. 'I hate that I'm the result of a man assaulting you. That my father,' she almost spat the word, 'felt he had the right to do this to you. I hate it.'

'I hated it too,' said Rua. 'But please never forget how much I love you.'

'Do I look like him? Do I sound like him?' demanded Brontë. 'Do I behave like him? He thought he was entitled. Am I like that? I don't want to be, but maybe I am. I have his genes.'

'You're not at all like him,' replied Rua. 'Though your eyes . . . sometimes I think you have his eyes. He was good-looking. So are you.'

'Oh, stop.' Brontë blew her nose again. 'Stop trying to find a nice thing to say about him. Who is he exactly? The name sounds vaguely familiar.'

'He's a politician. The local TD in Loughmore and the junior minister for fisheries.'

'It's no wonder you never want to go back.' Brontë looked at her in understanding. 'A damn politician.'

'He wasn't when he raped me,' said Rua. 'His dad was. Davey took over the seat a number of years ago. He stood for election, but it was a foregone conclusion. The Mullerys are the local mafia in Loughmore and the surrounding area. That probably influenced your gran's thinking.'

'Why didn't you out him when he was running for election?' asked Brontë. 'That could have been the right time to do it. You might have been believed then.'

'I think they'd have believed me less, to be honest.'

'He's in a position of power.' Brontë frowned. 'He really shouldn't be. He's a criminal.'

'And yet think of all those women who speak out years after the event. They're accused of looking for fame or money and the men get nothing but support.'

'Not all the time.'

'Pretty much all the time.' Rua sighed. 'I disagreed profoundly with your grandmother's approach. I wish I'd reported him to the guards back then and hang the consequences. But I've moved on.'

'He shouldn't get away with ruining your life!' cried Brontë.

'He certainly changed it,' agreed Rua. 'I won't sugar-coat things; there were times when, yes, I thought it was ruined. But I rebuilt it, and I have you. I love you, Brontë, and I always will. I made a conscious decision to keep you and I've never regretted it.'

'Not even sometimes?'

'Not even when you were going through the terrible twos and your moody teenage years.' Rua smiled faintly.

'You saying that, well, it makes me feel that all women should put up and shut up,' said Brontë. 'That they should force themselves to keep their child even if they don't want to. That they might feel there's something wrong with them if they don't love it. And I don't think they should feel that way at all.'

'Neither do I,' agreed Rua. 'It worked out for me in the end. It might not have. I know that. I was lucky because I was surrounded by love. Francine and Ségolène were unbelievably good to me, and to you. Lilou was utterly wonderful. It makes a difference.'

'I'm ashamed that I was conceived by force.' Brontë worried at the quick of her fingernail and winced as it came away, drawing blood. She stuck her finger in her mouth and sucked it.

'*You* shouldn't feel the slightest bit of shame,' said Rua. 'If there's shame to go around, it's all Davey Mullery's. And if you want to have some counselling about it, we'll organise that.' She looked straight into Brontë's eyes. 'I'm being totally honest with you here. Given my lifestyle, I thought it would be very unlikely I'd ever have a baby, and that horrible though how it came about was, this was my chance. In the end, I felt I had to take it. That it was the one positive outcome from the assault. But I couldn't be sure. Right up until you were born, I wasn't a hundred per cent certain. All I can say now is that you've been the most amazing person in my life for the past twenty years. You've made me who I am. I can't imagine ever not having you here.'

'I'm glad you think that, but at the same time . . . what about all the women who make a different choice?'

'They need to make the right choice for them,' said Rua.

'You don't think that every woman who gets pregnant unexpectedly should do what you did and then fall in love with her baby?'

'I don't think every woman could or would,' said Rua. 'Everyone has their own story. Their own reasons. I made my decision based on a number of different things. I made the right one.'

She got up from her chair and put her arms around her daughter.

'Is it OK to hate him?' Brontë's voice was muffled, her face squashed against Rua's shoulder.

'I try not to hate,' said Rua. 'That's giving him control of my feelings. But I do continue to think and to hope that somehow, in some way, justice will be served.'

'Me too,' said Brontë. 'Me too.'

Chapter 23

Flavia had expected the arrivals hall at Trieste airport to be as busy and crowded as that in Dublin, and had worried that she wouldn't be able to find Marco. But the airport was a lot smaller than she'd imagined, and it was easy to see the people waiting for the latest arrivals. Unfortunately, Marco wasn't among them. She stood beside her suitcase, anxiously scanning the crowd and wondering if she should phone him. She didn't want to appear like a naïve young traveller unable to cope for five minutes on her own, and kept checking her phone to see if she'd missed a message from him. So far there was nothing. She'd texted him before the flight and hadn't heard back, but she hadn't particularly expected to. Marco wasn't the kind of person who jumped to attention when he was called. All the same . . . She shuffled from one foot to the other. He'd promised he'd be here waiting for her. And he wasn't.

She knew Ailie would've tracked the flight and enabled notifications for when it landed, and would be expecting to hear from her soon. But she would also have added time for retrieving luggage and getting through security, all of which had taken less than twenty minutes. So Flavia had time before her mother started panicking. She would be less worried herself if she wasn't feeling the pressure of having to tell Ailie that everything was fine when it seemed as though she'd been abandoned at the airport.

She opened WhatsApp and sent a message.

> Hey. Have arrived in Trieste. No sign of my brother. Hope he hasn't forgotten me. Fx

She pressed send.
The reply came almost immediately.

> Don't worry. He's probably been delayed by traffic or something. Bet he left it till the last minute to leave the house. Men are desperate like that. Call me
> if you need anything. Bx

She smiled, already feeling reassured. She was very glad she'd met Brontë at the shooting range and bonded as they chatted about their respective mothers. Brontë had been easy-going and supportive, and she hadn't talked down to Flavia, as so often girls even just a year older did.

Marco was now fifteen minutes late.

Flavia wondered if she should get a taxi to the Villa Farfalla. But what if he turned up and she'd gone? She took a deep breath. She could message him from the cab. Not a problem.

The last group of people from her flight had left the arrivals hall and it was now quiet. She moved to one side so that she didn't look quite so conspicuously abandoned and took out her phone.

> I'm here but you're not. So I'm going to get a cab

'*Ciao! Sorella mia!!*'

Her heart leaped and she felt a flood of relief wash over her as she looked up.

'Where were you?' she demanded as Marco held out his arms and then folded her in a bear hug. 'I've been waiting ages.'

'Your flight was early and I was a little delayed,' he replied. 'You weren't worried, were you?'

'A tiny bit,' she confessed. 'I was about to text you.'

'That's the problem with the youth of today,' he told her with mock severity. 'No patience. You'll learn it at the Villa Farfalla.' He reached for the handle of her case and began wheeling it, ignoring her protests that she could do it herself.

'I'm sure I'll be too busy to learn patience,' she said as she followed him.

'You'll learn to be patient with the guests.' He grinned. 'Some are easy to deal with, but others are very demanding. You'd think we were running a five-star boutique hotel.'

'Is that not what the Villa Farfalla is trying to be?' she asked a little breathlessly. Marco was a quick walker and she had to hurry to keep up with him.

'We're not there yet,' he said. 'But hopefully one day. Anyway, you'll get to know it all this evening, and tomorrow you start.'

'Tomorrow?' She looked at him in surprise. 'But that's Sunday.'

'And you don't think the hotel is open on a Sunday?' His tone was amused.

'Of course I do,' she responded. 'I thought—'

'That you would have a little holiday first?' They'd reached his car, a black Mercedes with a sleek leather interior. 'No time for lounging about, I'm afraid. It's going to be all work and no play for you for the rest of the summer.'

She said nothing, but gazed straight ahead as he drove out of the car park and negotiated the tollbooth before merging onto the motorway. Then she took out her phone and sent the same message to Ailie and Brontë.

> In the car with Marco now on the way to Villa Farfalla. So exciting 😈

'You OK?' he asked.
'Yes. A little overwhelmed, maybe.'
'No need to be.' He casually overtook a small Fiat. 'This is your homeland too.'
'Yes. I want to get to know it.'

They were both silent then. She watched the countryside whizz by: green trees and occasional glimpses of the azure-blue sea beneath an equally blue sky. It would be all right, she told herself. The Marchettis would welcome her, and yes, it would be hard work but she would make the most of the opportunity to get to know Italy and her Italian family.

> Have a good time and stay safe xxx

She snorted at her mother's text but didn't reply.

> Send me pix 😊

She smiled at Brontë's and sent a smiley emoji in return. 'Ailie?' asked Marco, his tone suddenly gentle.

'Yes. She's anxious about me. Well, you know her. She would be. Though she was grand about me heading off to Australia. Mind you, I was with a few friends then and all the mums had a WhatsApp group so they could keep in touch with us and each other.'

Marco laughed.

'It's mental,' said Flavia. 'They don't need to know what we're doing every second of the day, but they feel they should.'

'My *mamma* was paranoid whenever I went to see you guys in Ireland,' said Marco. 'Especially when I went to study there.'

'Yeah. I know. I heard Mum and Dad talking about it.'

'What did they say?'

'Only that Dad had to give Sophia daily reports.'

'Daily? Are you serious?'

'That's what they said. I don't know if he did or not.'

'I hope not,' said Marco.

She laughed, and suddenly the atmosphere in the car was lighter.

'I'm a little anxious too,' he told her.

'About what?'

'I want you to have a good time, but my mother and the others have mixed views about you working with us. And so I'm trying to be strict with you to give you an idea of how they are.'

'Marco, please don't be someone else for them,' begged Flavia. 'You're my brother.'

'I'm sorry.' He leaned across and squeezed her hand. 'I guess I was being a bit of a dick. Now . . .' His tone changed as they turned a corner and the Gulf of Trieste opened up in front of them. 'What do you think of that for a view?'

'It's magnificent,' she breathed.

'You don't get to see it from your room,' he said. 'You're Cinderella, after all. You can only see some straggly trees from your window. But there are plenty of spectacular views elsewhere at the villa.'

'How on earth could Dad have left?' She shook her head.

'How indeed,' murmured Marco as he turned another corner and stopped the car outside a pair of dark green iron gates. He pointed a remote at them and they opened slowly inwards. He nudged the car up the gravel driveway and stopped in front of a tall ochre building with a terracotta roof and green shutters at every window.

'*Benvenuta alla Villa Farfalla*,' he said, and cut the engine.

Ailie was relieved when she saw that Flavia had been picked up by Marco. She'd been quietly afraid something would go wrong and Marco wouldn't show up. She chided herself for her lack of faith in her stepson and reminded herself not to expect a call from Flavia this evening because she would be finding her way around her new surroundings and getting to know the Marchetti family. She gritted her teeth at the thought.

She sat at the kitchen table with her iPad, and scrolled through the emails she'd exchanged with Avvocato Silvestri about Giorgio's Italian affairs. He'd provided a lot of information about wills and inheritance, but it was difficult to follow and said nothing concrete about Giorgio's own will. Ailie hoped that meeting the *avvocato* in person would provide greater clarity. She looked at her diary and highlighted the week she thought would be best to make an appointment with him while giving Flavia plenty of time to settle in at the Villa Farfalla.

Then she browsed hotels near Trieste. There was plenty of availability for the dates she wanted at a whole variety of price points, but she couldn't stop herself checking the Villa Farfalla again. Fortunately it remained fully booked, which meant she didn't have to make a choice.

Flavia will be busy, she thought. And I suppose Sophia is happy that the hotel is full.

At the thought of Sophia, she felt her body tighten. She hoped that Giorgio's ex-wife would be kind to Flavia, but worried that she wouldn't. She was tempted to FaceTime her daughter there and then and remind her to take no guff from Sophia, but she thought better of it and closed the cover of her iPad. Then she made herself a cup of tea to calm her nerves.

Until now, with her mind on Flavia and her journey, she'd ignored the disconcerting silence that had taken over the house. She told herself that it was often silent. That there had been plenty of days in the past when she was alone there, with Giorgio working late and Flavia out with her friends. Today's silence wasn't any different, and yet it felt as though it was. She'd never before been in the situation where she'd be spending a night at home by herself. Either Flavia or Giorgio had always been there. But tonight neither of them would. And Ailie had never felt so abandoned in her life.

She sipped the tea and suddenly realised that tears were sliding down her cheeks into the pink-patterned cup on the table in front of her. Salty tears, salty tea, she told herself in an effort to cheer herself up, but all that happened was that she cried even harder.

She cried for herself and for Flavia, and for Giorgio, who had been a good man, a good father and a good husband. She cried in a way that she hadn't after he'd died. Then it had been about gentle tears, emotion bubbling up and being clamped down again as she held it together for herself and for her daughter. But now there was nobody to hold things together for. Nobody to see her cry and nobody to care.

She was still sobbing when the text message came through, and she hastily wiped her eyes in case it was Flavia wanting to call her (her daughter never called without messaging first. She insisted it was unbelievably rude to interrupt someone with a phone call).

> Hey. Hope Flavia got away OK and you're feeling all right. Rx

Ailie smiled through her tears at Rua's message. It was kind of her to think of how she might be feeling.

> Having a little cry. I'm sure I'll be fine later.

> Do you want to meet for a quick coffee?

> I'm not fit to go out, but if you'd like to drop by, you're very welcome.

> Be with you in fifteen.

Ailie responded with a thumbs-up emoji (another no-no as far as Flavia was concerned; apparently it was passive-aggressive, although Ailie didn't understand why), and then went into the bathroom to splash cold water on her face. By the time she'd made herself presentable by adding some tinted moisturiser and a soft pink lip balm, Rua's car was pulling up outside the house. Ailie watched her get out and take a small bouquet of flowers from the back seat.

'For you,' Rua said when Ailie opened the front door.

'Oh, that's very kind. Unnecessary, but sweet of you.'

'I find flowers very uplifting,' said Rua. 'Also, I made these yesterday, so I brought some with me.' She held out a small box of pastries. '*Chouquettes*,' she said. 'Little sugar puffs. Brontë loves them.'

'By the look of them, I will too.' Ailie gave her a faint smile. 'Not sure about my waistline, though.'

'They're tiny,' Rua said. 'Hardly any calories at all.'

Ailie's laugh was shaky but genuine. She put on the kettle, then snipped the ends off the flowers and deftly arranged them in a vase.

'Tea or coffee?' she asked Rua.

'Tea's fine.'

Ailie made a pot and put it on the table along with two pretty pink plates that matched the cup she'd been drinking from earlier.

'I'm not normally someone who mainlines tea,' she said, 'but sometimes it's the exact right thing to have. Oh my God,' she added, having popped a *chouquette* in her mouth. 'This is delicious. And far too moreish.'

'It's been a while since I baked them, yet they're so easy to do,' Rua said, taking one for herself. 'Brontë thinks it's for her benefit.'

'Oh? Why would she think that?'

Rua explained that she'd told her daughter about the assault, and the name of her father.

'She thinks I'm trying to love-bomb her because of the trauma.'

'*Is* she traumatised?' asked Ailie. 'I'm sure it was very difficult to talk about for both of you.'

'Naturally she was upset, and angry too,' said Rua. 'Both about what happened and about me keeping it from her. It's hard for her to accept her father is a rapist – not that I blame her for that. Nobody would want to know that they were the product of an assault. My worry is that she internalises things, so I'm trying to keep a dialogue going with her. It's hard, though. I've suggested counselling, but she doesn't want to talk about it right now.'

'I can understand that.'

Rua nodded and took another *chouquette*. 'I'm taking it as easy as I can with her,' she said. 'Hopefully things will work out. Meantime, how about you?'

To her annoyance, Ailie felt herself tear up again.

'I'm grand really.' She sniffed. 'I guess somewhere deep down I didn't think Flavia would actually go, and now that she has, I'm even more anxious than before.'

'She'll be fine,' said Rua. 'She's a sensible girl, and from what you've told me, she gets on well with Marco. There might well be difficulties with the rest of the family, but I'm sure she'll overcome them. Also, if it helps, I know she's texting with Brontë.'

'They were very pally at the shooting range,' recalled Ailie. 'I didn't realise they were in regular contact.'

'As far as I can gather, they message each other almost daily. I mentioned to Brontë earlier that Flavia was off to Italy, and she gave me a kind of pitying look and told me she knew that already because they'd texted about it loads of times since the shooting day.'

'Really?' Ailie was surprised. 'That's . . . well, that's good.'

'I guess they have a lot in common,' said Rua. 'And it's nice for them to be friends.'

'Yes,' agreed Ailie. 'She'll tell Brontë stuff she won't tell me.'

'Definitely,' said Rua. 'Not that Brontë will pass any info to me. But at least you can be sure she has another person to talk to. Same as I have you. And we share stuff we wouldn't with our children too.'

'True. Speaking of which . . .' Ailie went on to tell Rua how disconcerting it felt to be in the house on her own. 'I know it shouldn't matter, but it does. It's kind of brought home the finality of Giorgio. That he's never coming back. I mean, I knew it before, and yet with Flavia around, I could sort of ignore the feeling. I can't any more.'

'There were times after Lilou's death when I locked myself in the bathroom and didn't come out for hours,' said Rua. 'I couldn't bear to be in the house alone, but I was used to being in the bathroom alone, so it was the only place I felt half normal. That's why I ended up coming back to Ireland. I thought I'd be OK in a place that didn't have any associations with Lilou. But Brontë and I ended up spending time with my parents, which was even harder. I was relieved when I got the job in Dublin.'

'It's been very difficult for you,' said Ailie.

'Oh, look, you and me both have had to deal with being alone. Sybil too, for all that she presents a composed face to the world. She was with her husband since her twenties. She must have been devastated.'

'She said one time that she was lucky because he became ill and they had time to say goodbye,' recalled Ailie. 'I'm sure it was awful after he died, but she did have time to adjust. I didn't. Neither did you.'

'No,' agreed Rua. 'It's so horrible that one day everything in your life is perfectly fine and the next it's turned completely upside down.'

'It happened with Giorgio,' said Ailie. 'And I feel it's happening with Flavia going away too. It's like I've been disconnected from the two of them.'

'I felt exactly the same when Brontë went travelling last year,' said Rua. 'I wanted her to call me every day. She laughed at that and told me not to be so controlling. But after a while she settled into a kind of routine of calling or at least texting every second day or so. It was hard not having her presence at home, but in the end I think it was good for both of us.'

'You think it'll be good for me and Flavia too?'

'I honestly do,' said Rua. 'Because we have to let them go, don't we? And being a good mother means being able to do that, knowing that we've equipped them to cope with the world.'

'Hmm. I'm not sure I've managed that with Flavia yet,' said Ailie. 'She's only eighteen.'

'She's a very level-headed young woman.' Rua spoke firmly. 'And even if she's doing something you're not a hundred per cent happy about, she's kept you informed the whole time.'

'More or less,' agreed Ailie.

'So relax,' advised Rua. 'Don't let her know how anxious you are. Every time she calls, tell her you're excited she's having a good time. Say you miss her but you're getting lots of things done yourself.'

'You're so wise,' said Ailie.

'Not a bit of it,' said Rua as she took another *chouquette*. 'But I do my best.'

Chapter 24

It was her nephew James, back in Dublin for a few weeks, who drove Sybil to the airport. The cruise was departing from Rome, and Sybil was overnighting there before heading to the port of Civitavecchia to embark on the ship. Tansy had been astonished when she'd heard about her sister's holiday, via Claire, to whom Sybil had imparted the news.

'You're going on your own?' she asked, when she phoned Sybil to talk about it.

'It was a kind of a snap decision,' replied Sybil. 'I saw the ad and booked it without talking to anyone. I thought you'd think it a good idea. I'll have to socialise with people. You're always on at me to do that.'

'All the same, you'll be travelling by yourself,' said Tansy.

'As I've done many times before,' Sybil reminded her.

'This is different,' protested Tansy. 'Unless . . .'

'What?'

'Are you finally looking for love? Have you decided this is a good way to do it? Is it one of those silver surfer type cruises? Will it be mainly older people?'

'I hope not,' said Sybil, answering the last question first. 'It's a child-free cruise, I do know that, but I'm hoping that

I'll be dragging the average age up rather than down. It's supposedly a small ship and I guess there'll be some other solo travellers, but I'm not going in order to meet someone.'

'Maybe a little bit of a sexual adventure,' suggested Tansy. 'Apparently if you hang a picture of an upside-down pineapple on your cabin door, it indicates you're a bit of a swinger.'

'Are you insane!' cried Sybil. 'I've no interest in . . . Just because you thought you wanted an adventure with Dr Plastic doesn't mean I want the same.'

'I didn't want . . . Honestly, Sybil, you're such a cow sometimes. I was trying to help you, that's all.'

'And I appreciate your help,' said Sybil even as she made a face at the phone. 'However, this is a holiday to catch a bit of sun, see some interesting places and eat good food.'

'Hmm.'

'Seriously. If I'd wanted to find love, I'd've done it before now.'

'Maybe you're coming around to it, though,' said Tansy.

'Truly not,' Sybil said. 'But if some handsome European prince sweeps me off my feet, you'll be the first to know.'

Tansy had insisted on her sending photos from every port, and Sybil, beaming widely, got James to take one of her outside the terminal building.

'Have a great time,' he told her as he handed her phone back. 'And don't fall for any moochers.'

'Moochers?' She frowned.

'You know. Deadbeat men trying to mooch in. So that they can spend time with you whenever they want. Stay in your house. Live off you without any commitment.'

'Don't worry, there'll be no moochers.' Sybil laughed.

As she walked into the airport, she thought of all the times she'd done this in the past, sometimes with Theo, sometimes not. More recently for her overnight city breaks to London, Brussels and Paris. However, there was a different feeling to going on a week-long holiday by herself, without anybody to share the excitement. But at least she *was* feeling excited. It was good to be doing something different.

The flight to Rome was on time, and when she exited Fiumicino airport, she hailed a cab to take her to the hotel she'd booked for the night, a small, stylishly converted palazzo, almost adjacent to the Colosseum. The interior was cool white marble and warm travertine, while the rooms were decorated in the sumptuous reds, golds and purples of Imperial Rome. A rooftop cocktail bar overlooked the Colosseum itself and was where Sybil took a photo, framing the bellini she'd ordered in front of the ancient monument. She sent the resulting picture to Ailie and Rua as well as Tansy, with the caption that she was already enjoying the high life.

That looks stunning (both the drink and the background). Ax

Wish I was there! Rx

Have you found any other shipmates? Tx

Sybil reacted with smiling emojis to the first two messages and a laughing one to Tansy's. She doubted that many of the other cruise passengers were staying at the hotel, but even if they were, she wouldn't know them. She finished her bellini, then went to the small trattoria next door and ordered pasta and a glass of red wine. After that, she went to her room and fell asleep.

Her pre-booked car arrived on time to transfer her to the port the following morning. Although it was dwarfed by another cruiser moored nearby, the *Azure Queen* still looked like a pretty big ship to Sybil, and she worried that she'd made a terrible mistake.

Her cabin on the port side was perfect. It had a king-sized bed, a separate bathroom and a small sitting room, as well as a large outside balcony with comfortable loungers. On the sitting room table was a vase filled with fresh flowers and an ice bucket containing a bottle of champagne, along with a box of pink truffles. She wasn't quite ready to drink an entire bottle of champagne, but she did pop one of the truffles into her mouth and pour herself a glass of water. Then she sat on her balcony watching other passengers embark until she heard a tap at the door and a steward brought in her case.

'I can unpack it for you,' he said, but she shook her head and told him she'd do it herself.

When she'd finished, she replaced her shoes with a pair of flip-flops and went to explore the ship. There were plenty of people around, but it wasn't overwhelmingly crowded, and most of the other passengers were familiarising themselves with their new surroundings too. Sybil found a couple of swimming pools with plenty of lounging options, as well as a library and a small shopping mall. There were also a number of different dining rooms. She suddenly thought of Burt. Undoubtedly if he'd been with her they would've reserved their table for the evening meal and finished the champagne already.

She continued to wander around the various decks before returning to her cabin, taking her book from the shelf and settling down to read the murder mystery set in Venice. She was so engrossed in the story that she didn't even realise they'd set sail until they'd cleared the harbour.

Their first port of call was Naples, and as Sybil had already booked the Pompeii excursion, she went to the scheduled talk about the ancient city, where the guide handed out some printed information. She took the maps and leaflets, thinking that the cruise organisers had pitched their offering firmly at her age group rather than at a generation that wouldn't know what to do with paper. As she skimmed through the information, one of the crew asked her if she was settling in well, and reminded her that there was a get-together for solo travellers in the morning.

'I'm booked on the tour in the morning,' she told him, 'so I've plenty to keep me occupied, but thank you.'

'There are get-togethers every morning in the Club Café,' he told her. 'We'd love to see you there.'

'Perhaps,' she said non-committally, appreciating that this was his job, but wondering why people in general were uncomfortable at seeing others on their own. She understood the need for company. She understood the attraction of having someone to share with. But she wished that the rest of the world understood that being alone didn't always mean you were aching for someone to join you. And then she recalled Tansy's comments about the pineapples, and wondered if she herself was the one who was out of step.

She was conscious of her solitary state once again in the dining room that evening, where she'd asked for a table for one. The crew clearly felt that a woman alone needed special attention, because she barely managed to read a single page of the book she'd brought with her without a waiter coming to fill her glass, or ask if there was anything more she needed, or check that everything was good with her meal. Notwithstanding the interruptions, she enjoyed her dinner as well as the glass of champagne she had in one of the bars afterwards, though this time she kept her nose firmly in her book and sent off signals that very clearly told everyone that she was far too engrossed in it to talk.

The sun came out for her trip to Pompeii and the sky was an unbroken blue. Sybil wandered through the ruined city, listening to the guide and recalling the story of the eruption from her previous visit with Theo. As she walked along the cobbled streets, she pictured the shocked residents seeing lava and smoke shooting into the air, and the chaos that would have ensued. She imagined families trying to make a decision about staying or going, worrying about each other and their houses, trying to find transport to leave the city and hoping that everything would be all right if they couldn't. Although they must have known it wouldn't be all right, she thought. They must have known that a catastrophic event had taken place.

As the official tour ended, she found a shaded spot near the forum and sipped from her bottle of water, gazing across the site at the huge crater in the volcano that had brought an end to the city. She thought of how such an event would be reported today – documented on social media, an influx of twenty-four-hour news reporters coming to the area, the warnings to leave and, she supposed, the people who didn't listen. As well as those who would probably consider the catastrophe an opportunity to loot or steal or make money from desperate people, along with the inevitable conspiracy theorists who would suggest that 'they' had known it would happen and had kept the information to themselves.

Do we learn anything at all from the past, she wondered, as she got up and brushed grass from her shorts. Or do we repeat the same mistakes over and over, hoping that at least for ourselves, things will turn out differently?

It was over thirty years since she and Theo had visited the site, yet she could recall it clearly. She remembered laughing at the sign for the brothel with him, and both of them wondering about the bakery, and their awe at the magnificence of the public bathhouses. Now, as she walked back to the coach along one of the perfectly straight streets, its stones grooved from the wheels of the ancient chariots, the sense of him being beside her was so intense that she stopped and looked around. She wouldn't have been surprised to see him, beanpole-tall, in frayed jeans and scruffy trainers, running his hands through his hair as he talked. But the only people nearby were the other tourists visiting the site that day.

Although she didn't believe in an afterlife or psychic presences or half the things that Tansy, with her fixations on wellness and spiritual worlds, did, Sybil acknowledged that sometimes she felt connected to Theo in ways she couldn't quite explain. He was gone but not gone. He was unreachable yet somehow close by. Perhaps that was why she didn't want to find someone else. Or perhaps it was simply that she'd worked on being happy by herself and she didn't want to mess that up. It *had* been work, she acknowledged. It was still work. Because although people said that things became easier after the first year, what they didn't realise was that at this time of your life, a year was the twinkling of an eye. So that even though five years had passed since Theo's death, those years were nothing to Sybil. She could turn around at any time and any place and imagine her husband by her side. And she didn't think that was ever going to change.

She took more photos as she continued along the path, although she knew that she had taken more or less the exact same ones thirty years earlier. She sent a few to Rua and Ailie with captions on her favourites, which included the sign for the brothel and the bathhouses.

> Hope you're taking the opportunity for some R&R as well as exploration and have booked yourself a spa treatment on the ship. Rx

> Please stay away from brothels but enjoy the cruise lol. Ax

She was almost the last to get back on the bus.
Lost in both the distant and the more recent past, she hadn't realised how late it had become.

Although she had her evening meal on her balcony that evening, she went to the ship's theatre later, where they were putting on a performance of songs from musicals. She spent a very pleasant couple of hours humming along to well-known pieces like 'I Dreamed a Dream' and 'Wait For

It', even though she'd been bored when she went to *Les Misérables* in Dublin and hadn't seen *Hamilton* at all, not really embracing the concept of musicals in principle. (Another reason, she thought, why she and Burt would never have got on, given that he liked them so much.)

The next day was at sea. She didn't bother with the solo traveller meet-up, but headed to the pool with her book. Much of the poolside conversation that she overheard was about that evening's formal dress code. As Sybil had known there'd be formal days on board, she'd brought an appropriate dress, but she didn't decide until later in the afternoon to make the effort and wear it.

At seven o'clock, having spent quite some time applying more make-up than she ever wore these days, and battling with the zip on the full-length lilac evening dress that she hadn't taken out of the wardrobe since she bought it, she was ready to mingle. She was thankful for the chiffon sleeves that hid arms that were less firm than even a couple of years ago, and for the fact that the dress was loose and floaty, which meant that it still fitted. She slid her feet into the matching shoes and walked tentatively around the cabin, terrified that she'd topple off the unaccustomed high heels. Like riding a bike, she told herself after she'd made a couple of circuits. Wearing heels came back to you.

She left the cabin and made her way to the small cocktail bar on the top deck. Only one unoccupied table remained, so she sat at it and ordered a bellini, which had become her go-to cocktail for the trip. She sipped it as she surveyed her fellow passengers, thinking how well men looked in tuxedos, remembering the times Theo had dressed up and she'd had to help him adjust his dickie bow while he complained that it was all nonsense really; though afterwards he'd enjoyed the evenings, especially the part where he untied the bow and let it hang around his neck. He'd always insisted on one that tied rather than one that clipped around his collar, and as he was utterly incapable of doing it himself, she had to master tying it for him. She'd once remarked that if only he'd cut his hair, he'd look like a young Sean Connery in his James Bond role, and Theo had lifted an eyebrow and said, 'Licensed to kill,' in a faux-Scottish accent that had made her laugh.

She smiled at the memory, then glanced up as another tuxedoed man walked into the bar and looked around for a seat. She recognised him from the trip to Pompeii. He'd boarded the coach back to the ship in front of her, and been seated a couple of rows ahead. She remembered him because of the silver-tipped cane he'd used to steady himself. He was, she reckoned, a few years older than her, with a surprising amount of wavy silver-grey hair. He wore heavy-rimmed glasses and was sporting a deep maroon dickie bow to go with his tux. The cane was an almost stylish accessory.

'This seat is free,' she told him, conscious that he might need to sit.

'Thank you.' He smiled at her and eased into the comfortable chair. 'I haven't seen the bar this busy before, but I suppose we all want to show off tonight.'

She smiled and glanced away as the bartender came over and welcomed the passenger as Mr McGuinness, asking if he'd like his usual.

'I'll try the special gin cocktail tonight,' he replied. 'Might as well push the boat out, so to speak.'

Sybil had taken out her phone and was scrolling through it lest the new arrival think she wanted to talk to him. He in turn took his own phone from his pocket, glanced at it briefly, then replaced it as the bartender returned with his cocktail.

'Cheers,' he said to Sybil.

'Cheers.' She raised her glass.

'I haven't seen you here before,' he said.

'I haven't been here before.'

'I like it for a pre-dinner drink,' he told her. 'Small and quiet. Good for a night like tonight.'

'I'm a fan of small and quiet,' she said.

'Fergus McGuinness.' He extended a hand. 'Nice to meet you.'

'Sybil Hansen.' She shook it. 'Nice to meet you too.'

'Are you waiting on someone?' he asked. 'I don't want to take up a seat you were holding.'

'I wouldn't have told you it was free if I was keeping it for someone,' she said with a smile.

'Fair point.'

'Your accent.' She frowned slightly. 'Northern Ireland? Via somewhere?'

'Holywood,' he said. 'County Down, not California. Via Perth, Australia, and Southampton in the UK. And you?'

'Sutton. County Dublin, not Coldfield, UK. With a little time in Bermuda.'

'Your accent is definitely Southern Ireland, with nothing else added.'

'It's been a long time since Bermuda,' she said.

'It's a long time since Perth and Southampton too.' He smiled. 'I have a son in Perth and a daughter who was born in Southampton and now lives in Oxford. How about you?'

'No children,' she said. 'Not even a cat. But I'm good with that.'

'And why wouldn't you be?' He grinned. 'No responsibilities.'

Another assumption people made when you said you were childless. But before she had the chance to say anything, he gave her a contrite look.

'I'm sorry, I'm sure you have plenty of responsibilities,' he corrected himself. 'You get to our age, you've lived life, there's always something.'

'But not today,' she acknowledged. 'Right now, it's not-a-care-in-the-world time for me.'

'Are you here alone?' he asked. 'I didn't see you at the solo travellers' coffee meet-up.'

She hesitated before admitting that she was indeed travelling alone, but that she'd avoided the coffee mornings.

'Possibly a good move,' said Fergus. 'To tell you the truth, I like travelling by myself. Candy, my daughter, thinks I should go on group holidays, but I don't like organised tours. I prefer to do my own thing.'

'Me too,' agreed Sybil. 'Having said that, I'm sure I saw you on the Pompeii trip.'

'It's the best way to get there,' he said. 'I'm sorry. I didn't see you.'

'I was at the back of the coach,' said Sybil.

'It's a very moving place,' said Fergus, and went on to talk a little about the trip. Sybil nodded in agreement. She realised, as he carried on speaking, that she was enjoying chatting with him. He was knowledgeable without being overbearing, and he listened to what she had to say too. Eventually they ran out of Pompeii-related conversation and Fergus asked her if she usually travelled alone.

She told him about Theo, and he nodded sympathetically.

'I have to confess to two divorces,' he said. 'I married young in Perth; it was a mistake from the start, but Myra got pregnant shortly after we married and we tried to make a go of it. Sadly, it didn't work. Then I remarried when I went back to the UK. Another mistake, ultimately, but at least that marriage lasted a bit longer.'

'How long have you been single?'

'Over ten years,' he replied. 'When you've mucked something up twice, you're not quite so keen to try again.'

She nodded. 'Do you see your children often? Obviously with your son in Australia, that's a bit of a trip.'

'I go there every couple of years or so,' he replied. 'In fact I've a month-long visit planned directly after this trip. Jake's in his forties now, with two kids of his own. I'm better with the grandchildren than I ever was with my son and daughter. Candy comes and visits me in Holywood, sometimes with her family, sometimes by herself. Even if there wasn't the distance between Jake and me, I reckon girls take more responsibility for their parents than boys. Candy's always checking up on me, asking what I'm eating, making sure I'm taking care of myself, urging me not to hibernate at home.'

'What did you work at?' Sybil asked, while thinking that his daughter sounded a lot like Tansy. 'I take it you're retired?'

'I was in construction,' said Fergus. 'It was a good option for Irish emigrants to Australia back in the seventies.'

'Did you go on your own?'

He nodded.

'Must have been lonely.'

'Ah, not really. I made some pals quickly enough. Fellas like me from the North and the Republic. We got jobs working on big projects back then. Office buildings and the like. Jake recently sent me a photo of one I worked on. It was being renovated. I couldn't quite believe that something I helped build from the ground up was now in such a state that it needed to be restored! A bit like myself, I suppose.'

Sybil laughed.

'After a few years in Perth, one of the lads and I set up our own construction company,' he continued. 'We did smaller jobs, but we were good at it. The company grew and we employed a lot of people. Over time, we merged with an international firm. I went to the UK, as I was divorced by then, stayed there until my second divorce and then decided to return to Holywood.'

'Did you do well out of it all?' Sybil had already noted that his suit was expertly tailored and that he had the certain style that enough money brought.

'I did OK,' he acknowledged. 'When I went back to Holywood, I bought a site and built a home for myself. It was different doing something like that, but very enjoyable. Since then I've advised on one or two small developments, but I'm mostly retired. And you? Are you also retired?'

She told him about Theo's companies and her work at the bank, and he raised his eyebrows at the mention of Ambitec, saying he was a small shareholder.

'Oh goodness, I hope you're doing OK with them,' she said.

'Every year I sell some shares to fund my summer holiday.' He smiled. 'So yes, it's all good.'

He was an easy-going man, thought Sybil. She was enjoying his company and was happy to continue their conversation over dinner when he invited her to join him at his table.

The waiter asked if they'd like wine, and she said she'd

have a glass of white. Fergus suggested they share a bottle, and when she agreed, he gave her the list to make the choice. She recognised a Gravina Bianco that Theo used to like, so she ordered that, and when it came, she was the one who tasted it.

'Fruity,' said Fergus when he took a sip. 'Apples, maybe a bit of peach . . .'

'Are you a wine buff?' she asked. 'Have I chosen something awful?'

'Not at all,' he said. 'I don't think I've ever had this before, but I like it. As for my apples and peach blarney, I'm never all that sure about what I taste in a wine, but I make some ill-educated guesses.'

'I don't know much either,' Sybil confessed. 'I was at a tasting once where a person said that one of the wines had notes of coal in it. And I couldn't help wondering how they even knew what coal tasted like.'

'When Kimberley, my first wife, was pregnant, she loved the smell of coal, but she was addicted to the taste of lilly pilly,' Fergus told her. 'It's a red berry. She cooked it, made jam with it, used it in cakes . . . everything! Then after Jake was born, she couldn't touch the blasted things, though he loves them. Grows them at home as shrubs as well as eating the fruit.'

'How about your second wife?'

'No cravings that I remember,' said Fergus. 'Not even me in the end.'

'Oh dear.'

'I wasn't the best of husbands. I was too selfish and I took Genie for granted. It was my wives who filed for divorce, not me . . .' He broke off and made a face. 'I'm not painting myself in a very good light, am I?'

'It's OK,' said Sybil. 'I'm not interviewing you for the position.'

Fergus laughed. 'Let's move away from this sort of stuff. What are you interested in, besides cruising?'

Sybil told him that this was her first cruise, but filled him in on some of the yacht trips she and Theo had taken from Bermuda, which he said sounded marvellous.

'You never thought about staying there?' he asked, when she'd finished telling him a little more about her time on the island.

'I think I enjoyed it so much because I knew I wouldn't be there forever,' she replied. 'It was a marvellous experience, but I would've gone mad if there hadn't been an end date. I liked – and will always like – the buzz of life in the city. I realise that Dublin is small in comparison to other major capitals, but I feel at home there.'

'Despite the name, Holywood isn't exactly the bright lights,' said Fergus. 'But it suits me now. Candy thinks I've become reclusive and is always at me to get out and about more. She doesn't quite get that I'm very happy in my house.'

'Do you have any pictures of it?' asked Sybil as the waiter took away their empty starter plates.

'Sure.' He took out his phone and scrolled through it before handing it to her.

'Oh my goodness, that's spectacular!' she exclaimed. 'I can see why you're happy to stay home. It's very *Grand Designs*.'

His home was a glass and steel structure enclosed by varnished wooden slats, with an angular roof at two different levels, the whole thing surrounded by a landscaped garden.

'Can I scroll more?' asked Sybil.

'There's about a dozen photos. Feel free.'

She looked through them all, intrigued by both the interior and exterior designs that seemed to make the house a part of the landscape.

'How long did it take to build?' she asked. 'Did you have terrible moments when it all seemed to go wrong and you had to work through the night?'

'My job was to not let that happen,' he said. 'So I wouldn't have made a good candidate for a makeover programme, because although I did go marginally over budget, the house was finished on time.'

'It truly is beautiful.' She handed the phone back to him.

'I like it myself,' he said. 'It's good for living alone, and is future-proofed because although there are a few small steps inside, they can be fitted with ramps. And there's no upstairs.'

'D'you think you're going to need ramps at some point?' She glanced at the silver-tipped stick.

'Hopefully not, but who knows? That' – he nodded towards the stick – 'isn't a long-term thing. I sprained my ankle a couple of days before coming away, saw the stick in a shop and thought it would be a kind of cool accessory. The ankle is still a bit sore, but I could get by without a cane. In fact,' he added, 'if you like, later on, we could go to the Sunset Bar, where they have dancing. I could manage one or two gentle sorties around the floor.'

'I'm perfectly happy to go to the bar with you,' Sybil said, 'but I'm the world's worst dancer. I can't do ballroom dancing. I was a teenager in the disco era, after all.'

'My mother sent all of us to ballroom dancing classes when we were youngsters,' said Fergus. 'It was an embarrassment at the time, but it's handy now.'

The waiter arrived with their mains, and their conversation

moved to how good the food on board was. When they finished the meal, they took the lift to the Sunset Bar, where there were plenty of people sashaying their way around the floor.

'Come on.' Fergus left his stick beside a table and took her by the hand. 'Stay with me and I'll show you what to do.'

'I'm not very good at following instructions,' said Sybil as she bumped into him.

'It doesn't matter as long as you're having fun.'

And she was. She enjoyed dancing with him because he made her feel as though she knew what she was doing, and he didn't complain even when she stepped on his toes. She also enjoyed sipping another bellini with him after he'd told her his ankle was beginning to ache, as well as swapping thoughts about their fellow passengers and sharing anecdotes about their lives back home.

By 11.30, she was beginning to feel sleepy, and told Fergus she was going to her cabin.

'Too many bellinis,' she said, and he smiled at her.

They left the bar together.

'What deck are you on?' he asked as they approached the lifts.

'Five. I'm midships, in 525.'

'Top deck. Nice.' He nodded appreciatively. 'I'm 425, immediately below you, so I beg of you, no practising those new dance moves in the middle of the night.'

She laughed.

They got into the lift. When the doors opened on his floor, he stepped outside.

'It was a real pleasure to spend this evening with you,' he said. 'Perhaps I'll see you again tomorrow?'

'That'd be great,' she said.

He nodded and turned towards his cabin.

The doors slid closed.

Sybil waited for the lift to go up. If this were a movie, she thought, he'd press the bell again and the doors would open and . . . well, who knew what might happen, if it was a movie.

But it wasn't.

When she got to her cabin, the red light was blinking on the cabin phone, indicating a message.

'I really enjoyed myself tonight and I do hope to see you again tomorrow. I'm booked for one of the shore excursions. It would be ideal if you were too, but if not, perhaps a coffee or something stronger before we sail away again? Sleep well.'

She smiled as she turned out the light and got into bed.

But she didn't go to sleep straight away. She lay in the dark and recalled her conversation with Fergus, and how different it had been to her conversations with Burt. How Fergus seemed genuinely interested in her. How he waited for her to finish a sentence before chiming in with his own opinion. How, like her, he seemed to be happy in his own company, even if his daughter worried that he was too reclusive, just as Tansy worried about her.

And she thought of how nice it had been to dance with a man for the first time in years, even if she had stepped on his toes too many times.

Chapter 25

Ailie checked and rechecked the information on the airline website before booking her ticket to Trieste. She'd finally received an email from Avvocato Silvestri telling her that he could meet her in his office the following week, or if she preferred, he could arrange a Zoom discussion sooner. Aside from her desire to visit Flavia, Ailie definitely wanted to speak to the solicitor in person. She disliked virtual meetings and she reckoned there was more chance new questions would occur to her if she was with him in his office. In any event, it was nearly a month since Flavia had gone to work at the Villa Farfalla, which she felt was a reasonable amount of time to wait before visiting her.

From what she could gather, things were going well at the villa. Flavia FaceTimed her every few days to update her on daily life at the hotel, and sent short, cheerful videos from around the estate. She also brought Ailie on a live virtual tour of the house, which was too dark for Ailie's taste, although the exterior tiled areas were bright and cheerful in the sunshine. The tour included a panoramic view of the olive groves, which Ailie noted were very extensive and surely a big income-generator for the Marchettis.

Her daughter also sent photos of the exterior of the Villa Pomona, although at the time she hadn't been inside, either to see the treatment rooms or to watch the production of the oils.

Flavia couldn't really answer many of Ailie's questions about her aunts and grandmother, as she didn't see that much of them during the day, and in the evenings they tended to meet on the small patio off old Signora Marchetti's room, a gathering to which she was never invited. Sometimes, though, they lingered on the larger garden patio after dinner, and on those occasions she had the opportunity to join them, although she usually kept herself to herself and didn't engage in conversations that mainly revolved around the business of the hotel. She socialised with Marco and Beatrice, who, she assured Ailie, were looking after her brilliantly. Her main point of contact for work was Sophia, who, as the hotel manager, was in charge of Flavia's schedule; a schedule Ailie thought was very demanding, given that she started at 6.30 in the morning and didn't finish until the early evening.

'It's fine, Mum,' Flavia told her when she said this. 'Cleaning the rooms and making the beds takes a lot of time, especially as Sophia is such a perfectionist. But in the high season, everyone's busy. My Italian has come on in leaps and bounds.'

Ailie thought it was ironic that Sophia had turned her daughter into someone who cleaned and made beds without complaining, something that never happened in Dublin, where her room was a constant disaster area and her acquaintance with the washing machine was fleeting at best.

'What's Sophia like?' she asked.

'All right.' Flavia's tone was cautious as she recalled her

first meeting with Marco's mother. Sophia had called her into her office, with its heavy mahogany furnishings and velvet drapes, and told her that she needn't think she'd be getting any special treatment because she was Giorgio's daughter.

'I wouldn't expect it.' Flavia had responded in English, as Sophia had spoken to her in English, and she didn't say that her Italian was probably more fluent than the heavily accented words coming from her late father's ex-wife.

'I am your manager. You report to me.'

'Of course,' said Flavia.

'Our standards are high.'

'Well, you do call it a luxury hotel.' Flavia glanced around. Sophia's office, despite its somewhat gloomy decor, was extremely luxurious.

'If there are complaints, I will let you know.'

'I hope there won't be any complaints.'

'So do I,' said Sophia, who then dismissed her with an impatient gesture.

Flavia had left the office with a sigh of relief.

'She's been polite though distant towards me,' she told Ailie now. 'She's very precise about things. Very disciplined. A lot of the family chat seems to be about the next steps for the hotel and how they should develop the business. They all seem to have different ideas, but nobody except Marco has any sort of a plan. And his plan is pretty much Dad's plan, from what he tells me.'

'What about old Signora Marchetti?'

'I think Nonna would like things to stay exactly as they always were,' replied Flavia. 'She's a bit deaf and she forgets stuff. Sometimes she calls me Sara or Mia.'

'How about Marco's luxury oils? How are they coming along?'

'They're a hot topic,' said Flavia. 'Sara and Chiara talk about them a lot. They don't want Marco to sink too much money into developing a whole line. I tell him what they're saying because they never notice me and chat away in front of me. I'm on his side in this. Not to stereotype anyone, but Italian men are very good about personal grooming, and the oils are gorgeous.'

'He's treating you all right?'

'Wonderfully well,' Flavia assured her. 'Him and Beatrice both. Honestly, I'm busy and I'm exhausted by the end of the day, but I'm having a good time. I went to an open-air concert with them at the Castello di San Giusto last night. It was brilliant. And we're doing a boat trip along the coast the day after tomorrow.'

'You know I'll be over at some point to see the *avvocato*?'

'Yes. But the villa is booked up for the next six weeks. There aren't any spare rooms.'

'My schedule depends on Signor Silvestri, but it would probably be better if I stayed somewhere else, maybe closer to town.'

'I'll check out places and send you links,' said Flavia.

'Thanks, sweetheart. I'll let you know when I'm coming.'

That conversation had been a couple of weeks earlier. Ailie thought that perhaps Flavia believed she'd chicken out of any visit to Italy. But now she had a date for her meeting with the *avvocato*, and she was going to fly to Trieste and learn what business ties Giorgio had with the Villa Farfalla, and how, if at all, the wishes set out in his will might impact on her or her daughter.

She realised that she was nervous about what the lawyer might have to say, but she was looking forward to finally moving things along. Giorgio's Irish affairs had been reasonably simple to deal with, as she'd anticipated. But she had no idea what, if anything, she might be facing in Italy. And no idea of what kind of opposition she might face from the Marchettis if there were clauses in the will they objected to.

She sent Rua and Sybil a WhatsApp message telling them of her proposed visit and asking them to wish her luck.

Do you want to meet for a quick good-luck drink before you go? Rx

Absolutely 🙂

That tapas place?

Perfect. Tuesday at 7?

See you there.

It was a few hours later before she heard back from Sybil.

When are you arriving?

Early on Thursday.

The ship docks in Trieste on Thursday morning!!!! I could meet you if you like.

Seriously? I didn't know you'd be there.

I didn't realise it myself until I boarded and looked at the itinerary. I thought the ship went to Venice, but we're actually docking in Trieste and there's a day tour to Venice.

Oh, but I'm sure you want to go to Venice.

I've been there a few times already. But not Trieste. Happy to meet you instead.

It would be fantastic, if you don't mind interrupting your holiday.

Text me when you arrive. I think it's cool to meet in Trieste.

Will do.

Ailie looked at her phone and smiled. It was good to know that her friends had her back. Both women brought different views and experiences to the table and each buoyed her up in different ways. Knowing that she was going to see them before and during her trip to Trieste was excellent news.

She was feeling both nervous and excited as the plane touched down in Trieste, where the early-morning sky was a bright cornflower blue dotted with an occasional fluffy white cloud. By the time she stepped outside the terminal building, there was a hint of warmth in the air.

'Mum!'

She turned around in surprise. Although she'd sent Flavia her flight information, she hadn't expected to see her at the airport.

'It's such a treat to see you, but what are you doing here, especially so early?' Ailie asked in delight. 'I thought you'd be too busy to come.'

'I asked Sophia if it would be OK if I slipped out. She was reluctant at first, but then said it would be fine as long as I have all the rooms cleaned before lunchtime. The guests will only start to come down to breakfast around now. I wanted to welcome you to Italy.' And Flavia flung her arms around her mother, hugging her tightly in a way that she hadn't in ages.

Ailie hugged her back, inhaling her familiar scent while noting that she was also wearing a new floral perfume that hinted at long, lazy summers.

'You look gorgeous,' she said when she finally let her go. 'Being here suits you.'

'It's the good weather and fantastic food,' Flavia told her. 'Beatrice is the best cook, Mum, you wouldn't believe the recipes she comes up with. Oh, here's Marco now with the car.'

'Marco came too?'

'Of course. Otherwise I would've had to spring for a taxi, and they're not paying me enough for that.' She laughed. 'Come on.'

'Ailie.' Marco took her bag and put it in the boot of the Alfa. '*Benvenuta in Italia.*'

'Thank you.'

'Flavia says you're staying at the Stella Maris.'

'Yes. It's convenient to the city and the solicitor's office.'

'I'm sorry you're not staying at the villa.'

'It was already booked up.' Ailie didn't say that she preferred to be somewhere else.

'Your room at the Stella will hardly be ready yet.' Marco glanced at the dashboard clock. 'It's only nine thirty. Would you like to come to the villa first?'

'I arranged an early check-in,' said Ailie. 'And I'd really like to freshen up, so perhaps I could come over later? Meet you and Beatrice. And whoever else is there.'

'People should be around sometime later this afternoon or early in the evening,' said Marco. 'They all know you're visiting.'

'Right.'

'They're delighted you've come to Italy at last,' Flavia assured her. 'Truly, Mum, everyone's been very kind to me and nobody's said a bad word about you, even when they don't know I can overhear them.'

Ailie didn't say anything in reply. She didn't want to put Flavia in an awkward position by being more probing with her questions, especially in front of Marco. So she sat back and watched the countryside flash past, glad that her stepson was a competent and safe driver.

Half an hour later, he pulled up outside the hotel, with its views over the bay. As she got out of the car, Ailie could see the sleek white lines of a cruise ship docked in the port. She wondered if it was the ship Sybil had sailed on.

'This is a good location,' Marco told her as he took her case from the boot. 'The Piazza Unità is a short walk from here, and there are nice bars and cafés in the streets nearby. It's only a fifteen-minute drive to the Villa Farfalla. If you call me when you're ready, I'll come and collect you. Perhaps lunch?' he suggested. 'We have a pretty upstairs terrace where we serve light lunches. It'll probably be too early for you to meet the family, but it would be an excellent way for you to sample the Villa Farfalla in your own time.'

'That sounds ideal,' she said, pleased at the idea of being able to scope out the villa without the family there.

'Fantastic.' Flavia beamed. 'I'm so happy to see you, Mum.'

'Likewise.'

'I'd better get back to work.' She glanced at her watch. 'Come on, driver.' She gave Marco a friendly dig in the ribs. 'Let's go.'

Ailie's hotel room was small but pretty, and well stocked with fragrant soaps and creams, which, she learned on reading the information leaflet, were supplied by a local business. She wondered if the Villa Farfalla sold products to any of the city's hotels, or if their nascent beauty venture was strictly for themselves.

She made herself a cup of coffee, then decided to text Sybil before having a shower.

Her friend replied almost immediately.

Sitting on the deck of the ship looking towards the city. According to my map it's a five-minute walk to the main square. If you like I can meet you there?

About to pop under the shower. Let's say thirty minutes?

Apparently there's a nice café bar called Harry's. How about there?

Does every Italian city have a bar called Harry's? Sounds good. See you soon.

Ailie couldn't quite believe that this morning she was in Dublin, and now, a few hours later, she'd arranged to meet a friend in an Italian bar. It was so not the life she'd led. And not that she didn't wish she was here with Giorgio, but it was sort of exciting to travel on her own and make her own plans.

She dressed in a pale pink cotton skirt and matching top and typed the directions for Harry's bar into her phone. As Marco had said, the square was a short stroll away, and she listened to the babble of foreign languages around her as she walked. Groups of tourists were already rambling through the town, and she guessed that many were from the cruise ship she could see moored close by. If that *was* the ship Sybil had sailed on, she now understood how her friend was able to make an arrangement to meet her so quickly.

She entered the square and looked around, appreciating the beauty of the classical buildings and trying to imagine what it must have been like centuries earlier, when merchants, traders and princes would have paraded through the streets. Making her way to the bar, she broke into a smile as she saw the tall, silver-haired woman already sitting at one of the outside tables. Sybil was positively glowing with good health, her arms bare in a classic blue linen dress, a pair of oversized sunglasses perched on her head. Ailie waved at her and Sybil stood up, waving in return.

'I can't believe we're both here at the same time!' she exclaimed as Ailie joined her at the table. 'And in such a beautiful place too.'

'It's gorgeous, isn't it.' Ailie smiled. 'I was so anxious about coming, and anxious about meeting the solicitor, but right now . . . right now I feel like I'm on holidays.'

'And that's how you should think of it,' said Sybil. 'What'll you have? I ordered an Aperol spritz.'

'Aperol spritz?' Ailie looked shocked. 'It's only just gone eleven.'

'Yup. But people have been having late-morning spritzes in every port I've visited so far. I've embraced the concept. You should too. You're not meeting the solicitor till tomorrow, right?'

'Right.' Ailie nodded, and when the waitress arrived with Sybil's Aperol spritz, she asked for the same. 'Though it should be a cappuccino, shouldn't it, at this hour?'

'Nope.' Sybil's tone was firm. 'We're tourists being touristy. We're allowed the alcohol.'

Ailie laughed and shifted her chair so that the sun was warming her shoulders. It was good to be here, she thought. She wished that she'd come years ago with Giorgio and had him show her around his birthplace. It was such a shame that his relationship with his family had fractured, and an even greater shame that they'd never managed to repair it.

'I can't get too pissed,' she told her friend when the drinks arrived along with a small dish of olives. 'I'm going to the Villa Farfalla for lunch.'

'Goodness,' said Sybil. 'Straight into the lion's den.'

'I don't think any lions will be there,' Ailie said. 'According to Marco, the family won't be around until later in the afternoon, so I'll be lunching alone.' She explained how he and Flavia had met her at the airport. 'It was so thoughtful of them. Flavia seems to be happy here.'

'Good,' said Sybil. 'I was going to suggest we have lunch somewhere ourselves, but if you've got arrangements, perhaps we could meet again before the ship sails this evening. No stress if you feel you have to be around for a family gathering – whatever suits you.'

'I feel bad about messing up your Venice trip,' said Ailie. 'Especially as I'm twice as confident when you're around. Now I'm messing up your lunch too.' She hesitated. 'How would you feel about coming with me to the villa?'

'I don't want to intrude,' said Sybil. 'Besides, I haven't been invited.'

'*I'm* inviting you,' Ailie said. 'It would be good to have the company if nobody else is there, and if any lions do show up, it would be equally good to have someone on my side.'

'If you'd like me to, and if you don't think Marco will mind, I'd be happy to come along,' said Sybil.

'I really would.' Ailie leaned back in her cushioned chair with a smile of relief.

Am spending the day with my friend. Having lunch at her in-laws'. Should be interesting. Hope you're enjoying Venice.

It's hot and there are far too many tourists, not that I can say anything, looking like a boiled lobster myself. But I'm loving the history.

Theo and I used to visit in October. It's a better time.

Perhaps we could come together some day?

Memories of walking the narrow streets and taking the *vaporetto* flashed across Sybil's mind. Sipping cocktails at the small palazzo outside their elegant hotel. Crêpes and cappuccino for breakfast at the nearby trattoria overlooking a narrow canal. Dressed up for a performance of *Tosca* at the Teatro La Fenice. She gazed at Fergus's text and thought of what it would be like to do those things with someone else. She suddenly recalled Burt Kennelly and shuddered. But Fergus McGuinness wasn't Burt Kennelly.

She typed quickly.

Sounds like it could be a plan.

Then she added an emoji of a gondola followed by a little heart.

Having decided against another spritz, Ailie and Sybil were finishing glasses of iced water when Marco pulled up at the square. They paid the bill and strolled to the car, where Ailie introduced Sybil to Marco and explained about her arriving on the cruise.

'What an amazing coincidence,' said Marco.

'Isn't it?' Ailie nodded. 'I thought she was going to Venice.'

'Venice is overrated,' Marco told them. 'Lunch at the villa will be much better than anything you'd get there.'

Ailie remarked that his picking them up made her feel as though Marco was a chauffeur.

'That's exactly what I am,' he acknowledged with a smile. 'Guests can ask for a transfer from the airport, and that's one of my jobs.'

'Nice car to pick them up in,' remarked Sybil.

'Company car,' Marco said.

'It must be hard when the family and the company are the same thing,' she said.

'Not in Italy.' He looked over his shoulder and beamed at her. 'We're all one big happy family.'

Ailie and Sybil exchanged glances. Sybil winked at her. And Ailie, much to her own surprise, laughed.

Although she'd already seen the Villa Farfalla through the virtual tour on the website as well as Flavia's FaceTime version, Ailie thought it was both more and less impressive in real life. Half hidden by a row of cypress trees, the electric gates and gravel driveway made her think of stately country homes. But the building, while possessing a certain grandeur, desperately needed attention, with the paint peeling both on the stonework itself and on the slightly warped wooden shutters. Nevertheless, the overflowing floral window boxes were bursting with scent and the view towards the bay was spectacular.

'Shabby chic,' murmured Sybil when they got out of the car. 'Very on trend.'

'More shabby than chic,' whispered Ailie. 'But it's an impressive building.'

Marco led them into a hallway with a polished hardwood floor, a green and gold runner along the centre. A gold chandelier hung from the ceiling, while the walls were papered in a multicoloured floral print. A small glass-topped desk was placed in an alcove near the end of the hallway. There was nobody at the desk, on which was a computer, some files, and leaflets about the area, as well as an old-fashioned push bell.

'It's very quaint,' said Ailie as Marco brought them through a large square room containing sofas, armchairs and occasional tables.

'And magnificent,' said Sybil after following him up a short staircase and stepping out onto a terrace that appeared to run right around the house. She inhaled the scent of pine trees and hibiscus plants and commented that it was uplifting.

'We grow lavender too,' said Marco. 'As well as adding it to the oils, we dry it and make it into sleep sachets for the rooms. Lots of the guests buy them to take home. One of my innovations that's very popular. Come on,' he said. 'The tables are on the other side, overlooking the bay.'

They walked along the terrace to the dining area. Six tables were set with white linen tablecloths and silver cutlery, and each had a small vase of flowers in the centre. Currently there was nobody sitting there, and Marco told them that two couples were due to eat later.

'We ask at breakfast,' he said. 'So Beatrice knows what to prepare.'

'And what about the rest of your family?' Sybil decided she'd put the question. 'Ailie said they were out. But is there anyone else here to join us?'

'Sadly not for lunch,' replied Marco. 'Nonna had a hospital appointment, so Chiara brought her. Sophia and Sara are at a meeting with suppliers, and Mia is overseeing some work at the Villa Pomona. That's Sophia's original family home, where we now have the wellness space,' he added. 'My uncle Antonio lives in Venice and only drops by occasionally.'

'I'll see them later, in that case.' Ailie was relieved that stress about the Marchettis potentially showing up wouldn't spoil lunch with Sybil.

'Perhaps you should leave meeting them until tomorrow,' said Sybil. 'After your discussion with the solicitor.' She noticed Marco frown at her words. 'After all,' she added, 'that's why you're here. To see how things stand.'

'And to see Flavia,' added Ailie.

'She's helping out in the kitchen right now,' said Marco. 'I'll send her up to you when she's free. But meanwhile, what would you like for lunch?' He indicated the chalkboard menu hanging on the wall.

'It doesn't matter that we didn't order this morning?' Sybil asked.

'Not at all. We ask for advance booking so there's no food waste, but it's not critical.'

'In that case, I'll have the Mediterranean salad,' said Sybil.

'Same for me,' said Ailie.

Marco nodded and left them sitting at one of the tables.

'It's quite rude of your relatives not to be here,' said Sybil.

'Sounds like they're busy. That's a good thing.'

'They knew you were coming. Someone besides Marco should've welcomed you.'

'Maybe I'm not welcome,' said Ailie softly.

'Don't let them walk all over you,' said Sybil. 'You've got to be firm.'

'You're right.' Ailie got up from the table and walked to the iron railing that surrounded the terrace. 'I don't know how Giorgio left all this for Dublin,' she said as she took in the view, where small boats skimmed across the azure blue of the bay. 'It's so beautiful.'

'Yes, but possibly claustrophobic if you're surrounded by family all the time,' observed Sybil. 'I'd kill Tansy if we both lived in our old family home, even though it was in a great location. It doesn't surprise me that Giorgio needed to do his own thing.'

'He absolutely did,' agreed Ailie. 'And yet he was restless, particularly recently. With Marco becoming more involved in the hotel management, Giorgio wanted to encourage and help him, and I think he regretted being at a distance.'

'I can see why talking to Marco about developing the business might have triggered his interest in the hotel again,' said Sybil. 'But I doubt he regretted his divorce and leaving in the first place.'

'He didn't regret divorcing Sophia,' agreed Ailie. 'He regretted the rupture with the family. It was so crazy that they took Sophia's side,' she added. 'And that they never let up, not after all those years.'

'Let's see how things are after you meet the solicitor.'

'I'm certain Giorgio will have done something to support Marco's position in the company,' said Ailie. 'He had a lot of faith in him.'

'He seems a competent young man,' said Sybil. 'Who knows, perhaps Giorgio and Marco might have come up with things together that everyone would have agreed on.'

'Perhaps.' Ailie blinked away a tear. 'My concern now is that if he thought he had a lot more time and could have changed things later, he might have treated Flavia very differently to Marco in his will. It would be understandable. In fact, I *expect* there to be some kind of different treatment.

Yet I don't want her to be hurt by anything her dad did. She adored him.'

'Do you want me to come with you to the solicitor tomorrow?' asked Sybil.

'But won't you have sailed somewhere tonight?' Ailie looked at her in surprise. 'I thought you only stayed a day in each port.'

'My package only has one more port of call,' Sybil told her. 'It doesn't matter to me if I leave the ship now or tomorrow.'

'But you've paid . . .'

'One day makes very little difference. It doesn't bother me in the slightest to change. Only if you'd like me to. I don't want to pressurise you.'

'What about your flight?'

'I'll change it to one from Trieste. It's entirely up to you, Ailie. If you want moral support, I'm here. If you want to do things alone, that's perfectly fine with me.'

'If you're certain . . .' Ailie smiled at her. 'I'd love you to come with me. You make me feel so much stronger. But won't you have to get back and pack and disembark and everything?'

'I can do that after lunch. The ship doesn't sail until six. Plenty of time. Anyway, this city is beautiful and I'm happy to spend an extra day here. What's the name of your hotel? I'll see if I can get a room there for the night.'

Ailie gave her the details of the hotel, and Sybil was making an online reservation when Flavia appeared on the terrace with a large jug of lemon water. She beamed at Sybil.

'I can't believe you're here too. It's a lovely surprise to see you.'

'I'm thrilled to visit. The villa is heavenly,' said Sybil. 'I hope you're enjoying yourself.'

'I'm run off my feet,' replied Flavia. 'There's so much to do. But I love it.'

'And you're being treated well?'

'Me, Beatrice and Marco are having a grand old time. The aunts are very polite, though poor old Nonna isn't always with it. But I'm glad I came.'

'Can you sit and join us?' asked Sybil. 'Or are you too busy?'

'I have to bring you your salads first,' said Flavia.

She hurried away, and Sybil smiled at Ailie.

'She looks well,' she said. 'And she really is pleased to see you.'

'She might be the only one,' said Ailie as she gazed down towards the sea.

Chapter 26

As soon as they'd finished lunch, Sybil asked Marco, who'd joined them for coffee, if it would be possible to drive her back to the ship. She didn't say anything to him or to Flavia about staying in Trieste, but she told Ailie she'd see her soon.

Back on board, everywhere was quiet, most of the passengers being away on the various shore trips and excursions. Sybil hurried to her cabin and packed her case, then made her way to the purser's desk to tell him she was disembarking, explaining that she was staying with a friend in Trieste instead of continuing to the final port. When all the paperwork had been completed, she sent a message to Fergus to tell him what she was doing and asking him when he expected to be back from his Venetian trip.

She was standing on the balcony of her cabin when her phone rang.

'You're leaving!' Fergus sounded shocked. 'I thought you were just meeting your friend for a drink.'

'She needs a bit of support.' Sybil had given him a brief rundown on the situation between Ailie and her late husband's family at dinner the previous night.

'Isn't there anyone else to give it to her?'

'Not really,' said Sybil. 'I'm truly sorry, Fergus. I was looking forward to our dinner this evening – I look forward to it every evening – but I've grown close to Ailie over the last few months and I'd like to be there for her tonight.'

'The tour is due back to Trieste at around four thirty,' said Fergus after a moment. 'Can we meet up then?'

Sybil suggested Harry's bar at five, as she would have disembarked before he returned.

'I'll see you there,' he said.

She was sitting at the same table where she'd waited for Ailie when he turned up at exactly five o'clock.

'I can't believe you're abandoning ship,' he said, after he'd greeted her and ordered Prosecco for both of them.

'I would've been leaving tomorrow anyway.'

'I know. But I was prepared for tomorrow. Not today.'

'Same here,' said Sybil. 'But I think Ailie needs me more than you do. Though I'm being conceited in suggesting you need me at all. You're well capable of being perfectly happy on your own.'

'I can cope on my own, but I'm not always perfectly happy,' said Fergus. 'I was perfectly happy thinking we'd be sharing a table tonight. But,' he added as she was about to speak, 'I do understand about your friend. I know it's been a hard time for her and I think you're doing the right thing, even if, selfishly, I'd've preferred if you weren't doing it.'

Sybil smiled at him.

'Would you like me to stay here too?' he asked. 'I could, if you wanted.'

'Oh, Fergus, that's so kind of you,' she said. 'And there's part of me that would love you to stay. But I'd feel terrible about ruining your cruise. You've got another week, and after that you're heading off to Perth. You should stick to your plan. After all, I'm here for Ailie so I wouldn't be able to give you any time.'

'You wouldn't be ruining anything, but you're right. I'd be in the way.' He toyed with the stem of his glass. 'What about when we both get back to Ireland?'

'You'll be in Holywood. I'll be in Dublin.'

'So that's it? After today, I'll never see you again?'

Sybil took a long, slow sip of her Prosecco.

'Meeting you has made the cruise so much more than I expected,' she said. 'I look forward to seeing you every day. I haven't felt like that about anybody since . . . well, since Theo died.'

'Are you still in love with Theo?' asked Fergus.

'Ah, no.' She shook her head. 'I love my memories of him. I love who he was. I love who I was when I was with him. I'll always love that. But life goes on. I've gone on.'

'You're not ready to be with someone else, are you?'

She ran her finger around the rim of the glass while she considered what to say next.

'I told you about Tansy, and how she feels that I need to snap someone up. When I sent her one of the photos of us, she was ecstatic that I'd met you. She was practically writing the wedding invitations.'

Fergus grinned.

'I told you about Burt too.'

This time Fergus guffawed. 'I hope you're not comparing me with him.'

'Well, I am. But favourably.' She smiled, and then carried on in a more serious tone. 'The thing is, Fergus, I didn't think I'd ever care about anyone after Theo. I didn't want to. I've worked hard to make my life a good one for me, by myself. And it is. I was ready to get the most out of the cruise by myself. I wasn't looking to meet anyone. And yet you've made it all so much better. Every day has been a joy. I know I'd like to see more of you. At the same time, I'm not sure exactly what that means for me, or for you. I'm sorry if that makes me sound selfish and hard.'

'It makes you sound like someone who thinks things through,' said Fergus. 'Which is more than I've always done when it comes to women. Two divorces isn't an enviable track record.'

'You're a bit obsessed with your two divorces.'

'Because I think of them as failures on my part,' he told her. 'I don't like to fail.'

'Life is all about failing,' said Sybil. 'Then picking yourself up and getting on with it.'

'I don't think you've failed very often. But you're certainly good at getting on with it.'

'So are you. You went to Australia. You made a life. Some things didn't work out. You moved to England. You made another life. Some things didn't work out. You came back to Northern Ireland. You made a life.'

'Are you suggesting that if you became part of it, something wouldn't work out?'

'No,' said Sybil. 'But how much a part of it would you want me to be? After all,' she added, 'we haven't even slept together.'

'I didn't want to pressure you into it!' cried Fergus. 'But for heaven's sake, Sybil, I'd have been very happy to take you to bed.'

'I appreciate both that you wanted to and that you didn't try to,' said Sybil. 'I appreciate everything about you.'

'But you don't love me.'

'I think it's a bit soon for that. Do you think you love me? Or do you love the idea of me?'

'Ah, feck it, you're so cool and logical,' he said. 'I love the opportunity that you might be.'

'You've nailed it!' Sybil beamed at him. 'We have an opportunity and as yet we don't know where it will lead.'

'But there's a chance of it leading somewhere?'

'There's always a chance,' she said. 'You're a good man and I'm lucky to have met you.'

'The luck is entirely mine,' said Fergus.

He raised his glass and touched it off hers. Then he looked at his watch and said he'd better get back on board.

'I'll walk as far as the ship with you,' said Sybil.

He called the waitress over and paid the bill. Then he asked her if she could take a photo of him and Sybil.

'Of course,' she replied.

He rested his hand lightly on Sybil's shoulder as they stood side by side, the water of the bay behind them while the waitress took the photos.

Then he scrolled through them and forwarded one to Sybil.

'Tansy will definitely approve of that.' She nodded. 'We don't look half bad in it.'

'We look sensational,' he said as he took her arm and they began to walk towards the boat.

'Make the most of your remaining days on board,' she told him when they reached the security barrier. 'Enjoy the ports and the fantastic dinners. Have a great time in Perth with your son and your grandchildren too. I've never been, so photos would be appreciated.'

'I'll do my best to have a good time, but it won't be as good without you. I hope everything goes well for Ailie.'

'Fingers crossed.'

He leaned forward and kissed her on the cheek.

'I'll miss you,' he said.

'Likewise.' She looked up at him.

He leaned forward again. This time he kissed her on the lips. She'd forgotten what that felt like. Soft and firm. Gentle and hard. Her heart beat faster and instinctively she put her arms around him and drew him closer.

'We'll meet when you're back from all your travels,' she said.

'Is that a promise?'

'Yes,' she said as she broke away. 'It is.'

She watched as he presented his ID at security. Her heartbeat had returned to normal, but she could still sense the touch of his lips on hers. She wondered what it would have been like to have been with him tonight. What sort of lover he would have been. What sort of lover she would have been.

Maybe just as well it wouldn't be happening, she thought. All the underwear she'd packed was practical and supportive. If she was going to show off her lingerie, she'd like it to be prettier stuff.

As for sleeping with a man who wasn't Theo . . . She'd never thought she would. But she'd never told herself she wouldn't. And she'd find out what it was like eventually, if that was what they both wanted.

Fergus turned at the bottom of the gangplank and waved at her. She waved in return.

As soon as he'd disappeared from view, she took a deep breath and walked purposefully in the opposite direction.

Later that evening, Ailie and Sybil had a FaceTime chat with Rua, who'd texted to find out how things were going.

'You two look glowy and happy,' she said when they'd brought her up to date. 'I'm envious. It's lashing rain here today.'

'We should all get away together somewhere warm and sunny,' said Sybil. 'Later in the summer maybe?'

'I'd love that,' agreed Rua.

They chatted about possible locations, and then Brontë's face appeared on the screen.

'Hi, ladies,' she said. 'Are you enjoying Italy? Have you met up with Flavia?'

'Indeed we have,' said Ailie. 'I'm surprised she hasn't texted you already. She said she's in touch with you all the time.'

'We get on well,' said Brontë. 'We share information on our mothers.'

'Oh, God.' But Ailie laughed.

'See you soon,' said Rua when they'd chatted some more. 'Good luck tomorrow. Keep in touch.'

Ailie closed the cover on her iPad, then told Sybil that she was going to bed because she'd been up since the crack of dawn and could hardly keep awake. Sybil nodded and said she'd meet her for breakfast in the morning.

When Ailie had gone to her room, Sybil left the hotel and walked into the square again. The berth where the *Azure Queen* had been moored was now deserted. She felt a sense of loss as she pictured Fergus alone at their table in the dining room, and imagined the waiters bustling around him, maybe even asking where she was and why he was eating alone. Or perhaps he wasn't alone. Maybe he'd gone to the bar and been invited to join another table for dinner. Or he'd taken advantage of an upside-down pineapple sign on a random cabin door.

She hesitated before sending a text.

Beautiful evening here. Miss you.

It was a couple of minutes before her phone buzzed in reply.

Missing you too. Nhat was asking where you were.

Nhat was their waiter.

She sent some smiley emojis in reply.

Fergus returned the message with a trio of hearts.

Feeling a little like a teenager, she took a selfie in front of the fountain and sent it to him, then dropped her phone into her bag and turned back to the square, where people were taking advantage of the balmy summer evening, sitting at the bars and restaurants and strolling arm in arm. She wondered how much of a wrench it had been for Ailie's husband to leave Italy, and if his frustration with his family had made it an easy choice. After he met Ailie, the choice was different; true love trumped everything, even the most beautiful of locations.

She bought herself a vanilla gelato and thought of how love changed everything. It had for her and Theo. As for Fergus – not yet love, she thought, although she'd felt a definite thrill when he'd kissed her. But perhaps an acknowledgement that she didn't always have to do it alone. As she'd said to him, life was about moving on, even when it moved in unexpected directions. She'd always embraced the unexpected before. She could do it again.

Her thoughts turned to Ailie and the unexpected direction *her* life was taking. She wondered about the reception her friend would get from the family, especially Sophia. She hoped very much that the trip to the solicitor would clarify everything for her. And that Ailie would be happy with it and feel strong enough to face whatever Giorgio's family might throw at her.

She deserved some happiness.

And she deserved to be treated with respect.

The following morning, they arrived on time at Avvocato Silvestri's offices on the first floor of a restored neoclassical-style building, a short walk from their hotel. A well-dressed young man brought them to a high-ceilinged room with a deep-pile carpet and white Louis XIV style furniture, where they waited for the solicitor to arrive.

Ailie had already visualised him as someone grey-haired and older, to fit with the vibe of the room, but Alessandro Silvestri, tall, slim and wearing an impeccably tailored suit, looked to be in his late forties at most, although his short dark hair was lightly flecked with silver and he had fine lines at the corners of his eyes. The lines deepened as he smiled at her and put a pile of folders on the desk in front of him, speaking in fluent English as he said that it was a pleasure to finally meet her.

'This is my friend Sybil,' said Ailie. 'She's here for moral support.'

'I'm sorry that it has taken this long to bring everything together,' said Alessandro, after he'd shaken Sybil's hand. 'But these things always take time. Now you have come, we can prepare papers for signing and move things along.'

'Are there a lot of papers to sign?' asked Ailie.

'The law would not be the law without lots of paperwork, and there will be more later too, but I will explain it all, and there are also English translations for you.'

She nodded, feeling slightly more at ease.

'We're here to talk about Giorgio's will,' she said. 'I wanted to check with you that it's OK for us to have this conversation without the rest of the Marchetti family here too.'

'But of course.' He nodded. 'Many people have the idea that there must be a formal reading, like in the movies. That is not necessary at all. I can tell you everything now.'

'Before the Marchettis?'

'I sent them an email with a copy of the will shortly before you came. Some of them, including Sophia Marchetti through her own *avvocato*, wanted to know the details sooner, as she felt entitled to make various claims. But it is better everyone knows at the same time.'

'What sort of claims?' Ailie looked at him anxiously. 'Is there anything special I need to know about?'

'Nothing you need to worry about,' replied Alessandro. 'Most are for trinkets and are a matter of family discussion, not law. Others are without merit, as I have already told Avvocato Fognini. Let me explain everything. The laws of succession and inheritance are different in Italy than in the UK and Ireland. There are taxes that will have to be paid as soon as probate is granted. So we don't rush that.'

'Will I have a tax liability?' Ailie frowned. 'How will I pay it?'

'Do not worry. I will take care of everything for you,' the solicitor assured her.

'Did Giorgio have many assets here?' Ailie asked.

'Signor Marchetti was the sole shareholder of the company that runs the villa as a hotel and wellness centre, and he had other personal assets that we will discuss.'

'The sole shareholder?' Ailie looked puzzled. 'I thought the family ran everything. What about Sophia?'

'The company – Farfalle – was set up after the divorce,' Avvocato Silvestri reminded her. 'Sophia, Mia, Chiara, Antonio and Sara Marchetti are directors and receive a generous monthly fee for that, but they are not shareholders.'

'Surely they all would have wanted a share?' Sybil, who'd stayed silent until now, posed the question.

'Signor Marchetti had been left a share of the house and contents when his father died,' the solicitor explained. 'He transferred this share to the family in order to be the sole shareholder in the company. The Marchettis were happy with that. I think there was a feeling that the company was a means to run the business, but that the house was more important.'

'The house was always important to them,' Ailie agreed. 'All the same, I'm a little shocked they were OK with it.'

'For many years he left everything to do with the running of the hotel to the family. He signed the accounts at the end of the year, but that was all. In the last few years he has been more actively involved, although clearly from a distance.'

'That makes sense.' Ailie nodded slowly, then turned to Sybil. 'I told you he seemed more distracted before he died. He was in contact with Marco a lot more too.'

'Does his ex-wife have a share in the Villa Farfalla?' asked Sybil. 'The house itself, I mean, not the company.'

'No.' Alessandro shook his head. 'Sophia's family home was the Villa Pomona, and she retained ownership of it after the divorce. Signor Giorgio also made a generous cash settlement to her. The result was that she doesn't have a share in the house or the company or any other of Signor Marchetti's Italian assets. But she does receive a very generous salary as the manager of the hotel, and she also leases the Villa Pomona to Farfalle for the wellness business.'

'Well, isn't she the smart cookie,' said Sybil. 'Do you mind me asking if the business is profitable?'

'You would need to talk to the accountants for their assessment. But it is profitable enough for the directors to take their money every month.' He took a card from the files and passed it to her. Giorgio's accountants had offices in the same street as the solicitor.

Ailie was relieved at what she was hearing. She didn't care whether the company was profitable or not, although for the sake of the Marchettis, and Marco in particular, she hoped it was; certainly if it was managing to support them all it had to be doing pretty well. Nor did she want to have a row with Sophia over anything Giorgio had done. In any event, it was an equal relief that it appeared there was nothing to worry about there either.

'So what happens to the company now?' she asked. 'Does the family take it over?'

Avvocato Silvestri shook his head.

'No. Farfalle has been left in equal shares to you, Marco Marchetti and Flavia Taylor-Marchetti.'

'What!' Ailie stared at him. 'Me, Marco and Flavia, my daughter? Not the original Flavia, Giorgio's mother? We own it now?'

He nodded.

'And they know this? You told them by email? Marco too?'

She was gripped with a sudden panic that she would be ambushed by the family, furious that she'd been left something that she was sure they believed should be theirs, no matter how little value might be attached to it.

'Yes, although I spoke to Marco shortly before you arrived. It is a surprise, but not a complete surprise. Signor Marchetti had already indicated to them that Marco would be his successor as owner of the business. He told Marco there would be some family input. The surprise for Marco was that the input was to be from you and Flavia and not the Italian Marchettis.'

'Oh my God,' said Ailie. 'They'll go ballistic.'

'I have dealt many times with Marco Marchetti and he is a sensible man. He is prepared to work with you and Signorina Flavia. As for the others, I reminded them in my email that the house has always been the most important thing to them and that this has nothing to do with Signor Marchetti. One little point. Sophia Marchetti owns the Villa Pomona and its lands outright. The Villa Farfalla does not form part of the company assets. But the land does. That might be something the family will wish to negotiate with you.'

Ailie exhaled sharply. There was a lot of land. And a lot of olive trees on the land from which Marco was developing his luxury oils. Even if the hotel was only barely breaking even, the land would surely be valuable.

'Additionally there is the apartment,' the *avvocato* went on. 'Although that is a separate asset.'

'What apartment?' asked Ailie.

'Signor Marchetti bought a small apartment a couple of years ago in a town further along the coast and had it renovated.'

'Oh!' Ailie turned to look at Sybil, a sudden realisation in her eyes. '*That's* what he was talking about the day before he died.'

'The apartment?'

'I thought it was something to do with adding apartments to the hotel, but it sounded so peculiar I wanted to know more about it. He told me he'd tell me when the time was right and I yelled at him to stop keeping secrets and he called me stupid and walked out, and when he came back he collapsed in front of me and died.' Ailie covered her face with her hands and began to cry.

Avvocato Silvestri took a box of tissues from a drawer and pushed them across the desk. Sybil plucked out a handful and gave them to Ailie.

'He was trying to do something good for me,' Ailie sobbed. 'And I yelled at him.'

Sybil let her cry for a little longer, then took her hand.

'Listen to me,' she said. 'You told Rua and me that you and Giorgio argued but that you always made up. He was probably going to explain it to you and make up when he came into that room. He wasn't upset with you. He didn't die angry. He died knowing that he'd looked after you and Flavia and Marco to the very best of his ability.'

Ailie scrubbed at her eyes with the tissues.

'He sounds like a decent, caring man,' said Sybil. 'You were lucky to find him, Ailie. And he was lucky to find you.'

'I hope you're right.' Ailie's voice was shaky. 'I've felt so terrible about that last fight. I blame myself—'

'Do *not* blame yourself.' Sybil's voice was firm. 'He didn't blame you. He didn't rush upstairs and change his will. He loved you. And Flavia. And Marco. And he trusted you all.'

'Oh, Sybil, you're such a rock of sense.'

'Not always,' said Sybil. 'But about this, I'm one hundred per cent certain.'

'Signor Marchetti bought the apartment in the names of both of you,' said the *avvocato*. 'It is yours now, Signora Marchetti.'

Ailie was startled at his use of the name. She hadn't changed hers when she married, either the first or second time. Hearing herself referred to as Signora Marchetti made her feel as though she were a different person.

'What should I do with it?' she asked. 'Is it empty, or is there a tenant?'

'He started renting it out after the renovations were completed last year,' he told her. 'To my niece, Gina. Legally. A proper arrangement. The rental went into a separate account. My niece is not expecting it to be a long-term lease. Signor Marchetti was happy to have it occupied while he wasn't here. You can sell if you wish and I will be happy to handle the sale for you. You can continue to rent to Gina. Or you can use it yourself as he originally wanted, a place to stay in Italy.'

'Why on earth didn't he discuss any of this with me?' Ailie rubbed her forehead. 'Buying apartments, making me a shareholder in his family company – he never said a word!'

'All I know is that he wanted to make sure you and his children were well provided for,' said the solicitor.

'I didn't expect . . .' Ailie took another tissue from the box. 'I can't believe he did all this for me, and yet he didn't tell me anything about it.'

'He might have wanted to keep his Italian and Irish lives and assets separate,' said Sybil. 'He probably thought he had plenty of time to tell you all about it. He was still young, after all.'

'He should have confided in me.' Ailie rolled the tissues into a ball and looked at her friend. 'But he was always a little secretive. Always someone who wanted to do things his own way. He was looking after me. Looking after Flavia. I wish . . . I wish . . .'

'Ailie.' Sybil spoke gently. 'He was married to you for twenty years. Of course he was looking after you.'

'But even after twenty years, some men do stupid things.' Ailie reached for yet another tissue.

'That is true.' The solicitor nodded. 'But Signor Giorgio wasn't stupid. He always tried to make sure everything was properly done and accounted for. When we talked about his will, he expected to live for another twenty or thirty years. But he also wanted to be sure that if anything did happen to him, you and Flavia would be all right. As far as the apartment is concerned, you can keep or sell it, whatever you wish. The same for the company. If you want to sell your shares to the Marchettis, to Marco or to your daughter, it is entirely your choice. You will let me know and it will be my honour to deal with it.'

'I know you're shocked, but this is all very positive,' said Sybil when they were standing in the street outside the office.

'I wasn't expecting him to have anything worth leaving,' said Ailie. 'I already knew he'd given up his stake in the house when he and Sophia got divorced. As far as I was concerned, the business was simply a family-run hotel, although I understood that he'd wanted to grow it and make it more successful. I assumed his involvement was to help Marco. But I am very glad he treated Flavia and Marco the same. I hope Marco's OK with that. After all, he's been the one running things. As for Sophia and the family, if they suspected any of this at the funeral, it explains why they were so cold to me. Oh, Sybil, my head is absolutely spinning.'

'Come on, let's get ourselves a drink.' Sybil led her to the square, and once again they stopped at Harry's bar and sat at an outside table. Sybil ordered Prosecco for both of them. Ailie made no comment about the time of day they were consuming alcohol.

'What you've got to remember is that Sophia is part of his past,' said Sybil. 'He's taken care of her already. She's had the benefit of the Villa Farfalla and everything to do with it over the years. She also has her own house, that other villa you talked about She's been pretty shrewd in renting it back to the business. Quite cheeky of her, in fact. She and the family could have chosen to follow Giorgio's development plans, but they didn't. And maybe it was because he saw that Marco was developing plans of his own that he did what he did. He obviously saw something in Flavia too. And you, Ailie.'

'I wish he'd told me what he planned.' Ailie took a larger than usual sip from the Prosecco the waiter placed in front of her. 'I should've asked him questions instead of feeling like I was intruding any time the hotel or the Marchettis or particularly Sophia were mentioned. He might have been perfectly happy to tell me if I'd brought it up. Thing is, he never asked me about my first marriage. We spoke about it once, he accepted it was over, and that was that. So I thought I should be the same.'

'You didn't want to appear needy,' observed Sybil.

'Exactly.' Ailie nodded. 'And as far as looking after us was concerned, I knew he had a good life assurance policy that paid off the mortgage. I got a lump sum when he died too. I assumed that was that. The main reason I came here was to look after Flavia's interests. I do hope Marco doesn't resent her being sort of foisted on him as a partner.'

'It looked to me like Marco genuinely cares for both of you,' said Sybil. 'In any event, the solicitor seems very much on top of things.'

'Yes, he does. I have confidence in him.'

'Can I ask you one silly thing?'

'What?' Ailie gave Sybil an anxious look.

'Why is the company called Farfalle but the villa is Farfalla?'

'One is plural and the other singular,' replied Ailie. '*Farfalla* means butterfly. Apparently there are lots of butterflies around during the summer. Oh, Sybil, I'm dreading seeing the Marchettis. Maybe I should go home.'

'Look, they'll have had time to absorb everything,' Sybil

told her. 'The only thing to worry them is you coming in like an avenging angel for the company, and I don't think you'll want to do that.'

'No.' Ailie shook her head. 'But what d'you think will happen tonight?'

Marco had texted earlier that morning to say that both she and Sybil were invited to dinner at the villa. Ailie had been hopeful that it would be something of a reconciliation. Now she wondered if it would indeed be an ambush.

'I guess they'll quiz me about everything,' she mused. 'I'm not sure how I'm going to deal with it. Or with Sophia. I'm terrified of meeting her.'

'Don't worry,' said Sybil. 'I'm there to take the heat off you. You'll be fine.'

She squeezed her friend's arm, and Ailie smiled at her. Somehow Sybil's strength of purpose always made her feel better.

Chapter 27

Marco collected them and brought them to the villa that evening. He kissed them both on the cheek when they met, told Ailie that there would be time for them to talk later, then opened the door to the car and played music by Ennio Morricone on the short drive at a volume that made it impossible to hold a conversation.

It was still bright when they arrived at the house, but anti-mosquito candles were burning around the garden patio, where the entire Marchetti family was already gathered. The patio was a homely space with terracotta tiles and tubs full of flowers, a low balustrade surrounding it and a small wall fountain to one end, but to Ailie it seemed like a stage setting for a play.

A long marble table was prepared like a luxurious advertisement for Italian living, with decorative lemon-scented candles, yellow crockery and delicate blue glasses along with baskets of bread and small dishes of olives. There were carafes of red wine on the table and bottles of Prosecco in silver wine buckets.

'*Benvenute, signore.*' It was Sara who stepped forward. 'Good of you to come.'

'Thanks for inviting me,' said Ailie. 'This is my friend Sybil.'

'You must meet Mamma.' Sara nodded in acknowledgement to Sybil, then led Ailie to the chair where the old lady was sitting.

'*Salve*, Signora Marchetti,' said Ailie.

'So you're here,' said her mother-in-law in Italian. 'Only when my son dies do you think it's worth visiting.'

'That's not true,' Ailie replied in the same language. 'I would have liked to visit sooner. The time was never right.'

'It's not right now either,' said the old woman. 'And it's not right that my eldest son has died away from home.'

'Ireland had become his home,' said Ailie. 'But he spoke of Italy often.'

'Hah.' There was a sudden spark in the other woman's eyes, and she stared at Ailie without speaking.

'Sit down, everyone.' Beatrice interrupted the growing silence as she walked onto the patio followed by Flavia, both carrying trays of antipasti.

The group did as she asked. Ailie found herself seated between Sara and Sybil, while Chiara was opposite, alongside Mia, Antonio and his wife, Celestina. Signora Marchetti was at the head of the table, her sons-in-law, Fabio and Donatello, nearby. Sophia, who hadn't appeared until they were about to sit down, was at the other end, looking chic and elegant in a sheath dress of midnight-blue silk, a single strand of pearls around her neck and matching drop earrings hanging from her ears. Ailie couldn't help feeling even more like she was taking part in a play.

Beatrice and Flavia put the large plates of antipasti in the centre of the table, then filled everyone's glass with Prosecco before sitting down close to their grandmother.

'*Salute.*' Sara raised her glass, and everyone else followed suit. 'So,' she said in English, 'first of all to make sure we all know each other, I will say everyone's name.' When she got to Sophia, the other woman locked eyes with Ailie, then wrinkled her nose slightly and looked away. Ailie felt Sybil reach for her hand and squeeze it, and she turned briefly to her friend, who gave her a look of encouragement.

'You are here, Ailie, with a friend, and your daughter is also here claiming her birthright as a Marchetti,' continued Sara. 'A crowd of Irish people all interested in us.'

'Three,' said Ailie. 'Not really a crowd.'

'I thought that was the expression.' Sara frowned.

'Three's a crowd?' said Ailie. 'Only when it should be a couple and there's an extra person.'

'Ah. Rather like Giorgio and Sophia,' said Mia.

Ailie almost choked on her Prosecco.

'Although as they were divorced before he met Ailie, it's nothing at all like Giorgio and Sophia.' Sybil's voice was firm and authoritative.

'Yes, we divorced,' said Sophia, 'but that doesn't mean we weren't still a partnership.'

'Not a romantic partnership,' said Sybil. 'So's we're all clear.'

'You seem to be very knowledgeable about my brother's relationships,' said Sara.

'I'm a close friend of Ailie,' Sybil reminded her. 'But even if I wasn't, everyone knows that divorce is the end of a romantic relationship. You can sometimes stay friends and that's a good thing, but both people are entitled to find someone new. Did you?' She switched her gaze to Sophia.

'I remained true to my vows,' said Sophia.

'And to the family,' said Chiara.

'What do old vows matter when you're divorced?' Sybil spoke again. 'As for being close to the family, I assume it's because the family is also the family business?'

'I have always been close to the Marchettis. My family, the Rossis, lived next door, after all.' Sophia's voice was taut. 'Marco is the son of Giorgio and me and it's important for him to have a good relationship with his grandmother, his aunts and uncles. Family matters to us in Italy.'

'It matters in Ireland too,' said Sybil, not allowing herself to think of how many times she'd wanted to throttle Tansy. 'Ailie wants Flavia to be close to her Italian family as well as her Irish one. Which is why she was very happy for her to work at the villa with you. From what I hear, you've made her feel very welcome, which is so kind and caring of you. You're happy working here, Flavia?' She turned to her.

'For sure,' said Flavia, although she couldn't keep a slight anxiety from her voice. 'The Villa Farfalla is a fantastic place to work.'

'It really is,' Beatrice chimed in. 'You've been such a help over the last few weeks, Flavia. It's brilliant having you here.'

'No doubt at all, *sorella mia*,' said Marco.

Flavia smiled at both of them, a look of relief on her face.

'The kids are all right,' murmured Sybil, loud enough for Ailie and those nearby to hear. 'Things can only get better.'

'So we have spoken with Avvocato Silvestri.' Antonio switched the conversation to Italian. 'We all know my brother's wishes.'

'Yes.' Ailie didn't elaborate.

'We do not know why he has treated us like this.' Sophia spoke with a quiet fury. 'Treated me especially this way. I should be part of the company. I am the manager of the hotel, after all.'

Ailie glanced around the table. Everyone was looking at her. Marco's gaze was thoughtful. She wished she'd had time to speak to him before this gathering.

'*Porca puttana!*' Sara swore under her breath, then raised her voice. 'What was he thinking?'

'That we would be better at running a business than you?' suggested Ailie.

'*Come osi dire ciò?*' Sophia glared at her and then switched to English. 'How dare you say that? We have been running the business perfectly well for over twenty years. We have nurtured it. I have made it very profitable.'

'I understand you might feel upset,' said Ailie. 'But you've all lived well from the business and you'll continue to live well from it. You've been generous to yourselves with the fees you've taken. Plus you continue to live here rent-free.'

'You are right, Ailie, that everyone has been cared for by the Villa Farfalla,' said Marco, before turning to Sophia. 'Mamma, you know that the last few years I've been the one making financial decisions, in consultation with my father, and they've been good ones. Like him, I have a vision. This family is excellent at making things run smoothly but not at thinking of the future. You, Mamma, are like a forensic detective in how you monitor everything and ensure it's all good. And you . . .' he looked at his aunts and uncles, 'Fabio and Donatello, you have your own careers. And good incomes from them too. And I know, Zia Sara, Mia, Chiara, you like to be involved in things. Like fabrics for the rooms, or the layout of the interior, or talking to the guests – those things. Which are important. But for the company, Farfalle, I am the big-picture person.'

'What about her?' Mia jabbed her finger in Flavia's direction. 'She knows nothing. Except being a chambermaid.'

'Flavia will be studying business administration at college,' Ailie said, noticing the colour rise in her daughter's cheeks. 'That's why her father trusted her. She'll be an excellent shareholder.'

'He should have left it to me.' Sophia's voice crackled with anger. 'I am and always will be his true wife.'

There was another uncomfortable silence around the table. Flavia's eyes flickered towards Ailie.

'And yet you were divorced. And you've been divorced longer than you were married,' remarked Sybil.

'That makes no difference,' said Sophia. 'None at all.'

'Giorgio once said to me that divorce was the end of a mistake.' Ailie looked up, her voice trembling slightly. 'You're lucky, Sophia, that you didn't stay together and begin to hate each other. I guess you do sort of hate Giorgio because he left you, but you love the memory of him.'

'Don't you dare tell me how I feel,' snapped Sophia.

'He loved you too. When I first met him, he was struggling to come to terms with the end of your marriage.'

'It's his own fault. He left me.'

'He couldn't stay here with you. With all of you. Maybe there are people who can live together with their families around and make it work. But it didn't work for you and Giorgio. He had to leave and he was happier for leaving.'

'It was the biggest mistake of his life,' cried Sophia.

'Mamma.' Marco spoke gently. 'It was not. Papà was happy with Ailie. He loved her. He loved Flavia too. I was there. I know. And although I am sorry that it didn't work out between you, I'm also glad that he found happiness and I have a wonderful sister who means so much to me.'

'If I could have given him more children . . .' Sophia, dark eyes reflecting her anger, looked down at the plate in front of her. 'It was because of the children that he left.'

'I'm very sorry you lost your babies,' said Ailie softly. 'It was a terrible thing for you to go through. I can't imagine what that was like.'

'No, you can't. And neither could he.' Sophia was angry again. 'So he ran away, instead of staying and making it work.'

'He stayed with you for, what, five years after Marco was born?' said Sybil. 'That's hardly running away.'

'I wanted more children,' said Sophia. 'He didn't. Until her.' She pointed at Flavia, who shrank back in her chair. 'She should have been mine. A true Marchetti.'

'That's enough.' Once again, it was Sybil who spoke, her voice hard. 'Flavia is Ailie and Giorgio's daughter and she's as much a true Marchetti as anyone. You shouldn't talk about her the way you do.'

'If I—' Sophia was about to speak again but Sybil cut her off.

'I don't share your experiences and I can't share your feelings,' she said. 'Nevertheless, Sophia, it's very clear that you've allowed yourself to wallow for years in some mistaken belief that your husband is to blame for everything. And yet you've lived well since he left. Maybe it's not the life you expected, but it's a good life all the same, surrounded by people who love you in a place you clearly love very much yourself. How we live, how we deal with the things that go wrong, how we appreciate the things that go right

– it's a choice. Your choice, Sophia. You can spend the rest of your years feeling hard done by, or you can be thankful that you loved a man and had a son who you love and who loves you. You should be grateful, not aggrieved.'

'Who are you to talk to me like that?' demanded Sophia.

'I'm someone who lost a husband too,' replied Sybil. 'Theo was a good man and he died five years ago. It's been bloody hard. But I've learned to live again and to open my heart to new people and new experiences. That's partly because of Ailie, who's a kind and generous person and has been such a good friend to me. I hope you have good friends, Sophia. I'm sure Giorgio's sisters are good to you. But you need to stop resenting him and resenting Ailie, get off your arse and live a little.'

Sophia, finally silenced, stared at her in disbelief. Nobody had ever spoken to her like that before in her entire life.

A rasping sound echoed around the table. It was old Signora Marchetti laughing. 'I wish *you* were part of our family,' she said. 'You have fire and spirit.'

'You have chosen a strong friend, Ailie,' said Marco.

'My mum is strong too.' Flavia looked around the table. 'She allowed me to come here even though I know in her heart she didn't want me to. She's been nothing but supportive since Dad died. She's an awesome person and you guys will be lucky to have her helping Marco with the company.'

'And you,' said Ailie. 'You own part of it too.'

'We'll see how that works out,' said Flavia.

'I'm sure you'll both be brilliant,' said Marco. 'Papà always valued your opinion, Ailie, and he was delighted you were going to study business, Flavia. I am happy to have you as part of Farfalle. And I want to say, Mamma and everyone, that I know Dad wasn't a saint. He didn't always think of other people as much as he should. He made decisions without consulting us. He liked to . . . to play his cards close to his chest in everything he did. But he was a good father to me, and I know he mourned the loss of the babies. He told me so, many times. I also know he wanted you to be happy, Mamma. He often asked if you were.'

Sophia said nothing.

'He made his decisions based on what he thought was best,' continued Marco. 'I promise that I will look after the interests of every Marchetti in Italy and in Ireland. Always.'

'You and I and Flavia will sit down and talk about it together,' Ailie said to him. 'I'm sorry we didn't have time earlier. And don't worry,' she added. 'I've no intention of interfering.'

'I will be happy to hear your advice,' said Marco. 'But I might not always take it.'

'Exactly like your father,' she said.

Beatrice cleared away the plates and bowls and returned with large pots of coffee. There had been a truce while they ate, the conversation drifting around the younger people and their studies and plans and steering clear of contentious issues. Then Sara made a comment about the business, and the others stopped talking to listen.

But Signora Marchetti closed down the conversation.

'There is no need to talk of these things again.' She shook her head. 'We are not a business. We are family. That's the most important of all.'

'Of course it is, Nonna.' Beatrice leaned across the table

and took her grandmother's hand in her left and Flavia's in her right. 'And look at us. All here. All together.'

'But not my eldest son.' Tears formed in the old woman's eyes. 'Not my Giorgio. And not my Claudio either.'

Ailie felt a lump in her throat. 'I truly wish we had visited while he was alive,' she said.

'Why did you stop him?' asked Sophia.

'I never stopped him,' Ailie replied. 'He didn't want to come.'

'You think you wouldn't have been able to keep him if he saw me again?' Sophia gave her a triumphant look. 'He would have stayed with me?'

'Nonsense,' said Marco, before Ailie could speak. 'You and he were divorced for a reason. We are all part of one family. There should be no disagreements.'

'Ailie's not a Marchetti,' said Chiara.

'Certainly she is,' said Marco. 'Her and Flavia both.'

'Thank you,' said Flavia.

'It's not the same.' Mia looked obstinate.

'You're all equal but some are more equal than others?' Sybil paraphrased one of her favourite quotes, and to her surprise, it was Fabio who laughed.

'She's right, this woman,' he said. 'You are talking about how much of a Marchetti someone should be. But we are no more than a family with a small business and we all want it to go well. It isn't make or break for me and Mia financially. Or for Sara and Donatello. But the villa itself matters to our wives because it is their home. And this is it, I think. We are talking about the emotional part of running the hotel, not the business part. Because we know and trust that Marco can do that. And we should trust that Ailie doesn't want it to go wrong because of Marco and because of her own daughter, who is as much a Marchetti as him and as Beatrice and as any of our children.'

'I promise you, all I want is for the hotel to be a success,' said Ailie.

'Me too,' said Flavia. 'I love it here.'

'It will always be a success,' said Signora Marchetti. 'This house has stood for more than a century. Our past and our future is in its stones. It will not let us fail.'

'To the Villa Farfalla.' It was Marco who raised his glass. And even if some of the Marchettis might have been reluctant, they all stood for his toast.

'Come on,' he said to Flavia and Beatrice after they'd drunk the Prosecco. 'I told Luigi and Lorenzo we'd meet them in half an hour. We should go now.'

Flavia walked around the table and kissed her mother on the forehead.

'See you later,' she said.

'See you,' said Ailie. 'Stay safe.'

'I'll look after her.' Marco smiled. 'I always do.'

The three younger people left the terrace. The adults remained at the table in silence.

It was Signora Marchetti who broke it.

'More Prosecco,' she said, holding up her glass. 'I think we deserve it.'

Chapter 28

Rua and Bethany were sharing a wrap in the village café where they'd stopped after their bike ride around the foothills of the Dublin mountains.

'I'm so out of practice at this,' said Rua. 'I thought the online gym stuff was keeping me in shape, but I think my legs are going to fall off.'

'That'd be a shame.' Bethany told her. 'You have nice legs.'

'Likewise.' Rua smiled in return, then picked up her phone as it beeped with a message alert.

She smiled at the photo of Sybil and Ailie standing on the prow of a boat; they'd taken a ferry from Trieste to the small town where Ailie's newly discovered apartment was located, and Ailie had sent a selection of pictures of both the apartment and the boat ride there and back.

Looking fab. See you soon. Rx

Loads to talk about. Ax

The three of them had already chatted on Zoom the previous night after Ailie and Sybil had returned from the Villa Farfalla.

It appeared that relations, while not exactly cordial, had reached a stage where the elderly Signora Marchetti was willing to believe that Ailie only wanted the best for the house and the family, while Sophia was putting all her faith in Marco to keep her in check. Signora Marchetti's change of heart was partly due to Flavia. She'd got to know her namesake granddaughter over the last few weeks, she told Ailie. And she liked her. So she was ready to give her mother the benefit of the doubt.

Meanwhile Marco and Ailie had talked about Giorgio's wishes. Marco had been aware that his father had wanted to involve Ailie and Flavia in the business at some point in the future, but he hadn't known the provisions of the will. In any event, he assured Ailie, he was happy to work with them and get their input into the company. Flavia already had some good ideas that he would be interested in following up. Ailie, for her part, told him that she had faith in him to always do what was right.

Rua was thrilled for her friend. She hadn't quite got to grips with the intricacies of the family business, but she could see that Ailie was keen for everything to work out, even if she had no interest in being directly involved. And from their discussion, she gathered that Sybil had been firm and decisive at the family dinner, giving support to Ailie and encouraging her to express her opinions in a way that she might not have done before.

'We're good for each other,' said Rua aloud.

'You and me?' Bethany asked.

'Us too.' Rua smiled. 'But I was talking about my gal pals.'

'Your Merry Widows?'

'Yes. It does seem strange that we've only known each

other a short time and we've become so close, but Ailie and Sybil are great people.'

'And me?' asked Bethany. 'Am I great people too?'

'You're certainly needy people,' said Rua. 'What's the matter?'

'You seem to get on better with them than me.'

'Differently.' Rua put her mobile face-down on the table. 'I get on differently. We have a shared experience and that counts for a lot. But you matter to me, Bethany. You know you do. This last week or so . . .' Her eyes locked with Bethany's. 'I've loved spending so much time with you.'

They'd met regularly, going for walks after work, or for occasional dinners, and spending more time in each other's company than Rua had spent with any one person since Lilou's death.

And she'd revelled in it. Revelled in being with Bethany, at sharing time with her, laughing with her, living life with her. Although she'd been cautious too, unsure of where her feelings were taking her.

Brontë had noticed her mother's sudden interest in going for long walks, and when Rua told her about Bethany, Brontë had given her seal of approval. She'd liked her at the gun club, she told Rua, and then asked if it was leading anywhere.

'Would you mind if it did?'

'Not in the slightest,' said Brontë. 'If you're happy, I'm happy.'

And Rua *was* happy. More light-hearted and spontaneous. Less closed in on herself. Even once abandoning scheduled time at her laptop to have a drink with her new girlfriend.

'I've loved being with you too,' said Bethany now. 'But were you only there for me because your friends were away?'

'Don't be daft.'

'It's just . . . I don't know where I stand.'

'Where do you want to stand?' asked Rua.

'I love you.' Bethany said the words abruptly. 'I want to be with you. All the time.'

'Bethany!'

'Do you love me?'

'I can't . . . We hardly know each other.'

'That's fine.' Bethany shook her head. 'I understand. I'm sorry if I've made you feel uncomfortable.'

'You haven't.'

'I have. I'm putting myself out there, saying stuff that I haven't said to a woman in years, and you're not ready to hear it.'

'I'd like to be ready,' said Rua slowly. 'It's nearly three years since Lilou died and I feel I should be further along. Yet talking to Sybil makes me realise that it's an ongoing process, and, well, I'm not sure exactly where I am in that process. Sometimes I feel . . . healed. Other times I can't believe I won't wake up beside her. When I'm with you, I don't think about her, but afterwards I sometimes do. I care about you a lot, Bethany, and I feel great about it, but it's not fair to you when I still miss my wife.'

'I've never experienced a loss like yours,' said Bethany. 'I've nothing to compare it to.'

'It's not like splitting up with someone,' Rua told her. 'It's deeper. More profound. But,' she added, 'that depth of emotion isn't forever. I can feel myself changing and I know that's partly because of you.'

'And your Merry Widows.'

'They'll always be my friends,' said Ailie. 'But that's very different to being a lover.'

'I love you, but I'm not even your lover,' Bethany pointed out. 'You've kept me at arm's length.'

'There's something else you need to know about me first,' said Rua.

'What?' asked Bethany. 'What could I possibly not know at this stage.'

'Let's get another coffee.' Rua ordered for both of them, and when the lattes were on the table, she took a deep breath and told her about Davey Mullery and the rape.

'Oh my God.' Bethany's voice was full of compassion. 'You poor thing.'

'I'm over it,' said Rua. 'In as much as anyone can be. I didn't want it to be the defining thing about me, and after I met Lilou, it wasn't.'

'I see.'

'It wasn't only her,' Rua said. 'It was Francine and Ségolène too. But Lilou made me complete again.'

'And nobody else will ever be able to do that. Nobody can compete with her.'

'It's not a competition.'

'It feels like it.'

'It's not,' repeated Rua. 'You've got to know, Bethany, that when I'm with you . . .' Having started the sentence, she struggled to complete it, but then she continued in a rush, 'I'm a better person when you're around. A happier person. A more hopeful person.'

'But not a person in love with me.'

'I do love you,' said Rua. 'But I'm scared to be "in love" again.'

'And with what you've told me, I can't feel hard done by, because you've been through so much more than I ever will and you've got the moral high ground on being hurt and scared,' said Bethany.

'Now you're being silly. Look, it took me time and work to get over Davey. It's taken time to get over Lilou too. I know that one day I will.'

'But not today.'

'It's a process,' repeated Rua.

'Right.' Bethany stood up, leaving her untasted coffee on the table. 'I'm heading off. I need some time. It seems you do too.'

'Oh, Bethany, don't go.'

'I have to. I can't be here right now.'

Rua watched her walk away, striding quickly towards the exit.

'Shit,' she said.

She thought of Lilou.

What she'd do in the same situation.

Lilou would run after Bethany.

But Rua stayed sitting on her chair and watched her walk away.

When she got home later that evening, the aroma of *poulet basquaise* was once again filling the house. She walked into the kitchen, where Brontë was standing at the cooker.

'What's this?' asked Rua.

'I'm cooking dinner,' said Brontë.

'So I see. But what have I done to deserve it?'

'You're my mum. That's enough, surely. Are you OK?' She frowned. 'You look upset about something.'

'I'm fine,' said Rua. 'And this is so lovely of you. Is there an ulterior motive?'

'How little faith you have in me,' said Brontë. 'Go and change, and the food will be ready when you get down.'

Rua did as she was told, putting some drops in her eyes and applying a little blusher to brighten her face. Fifteen minutes later, they were sitting at the table, their plates full and two glasses of red wine in front of them.

'Dammit, you always make this better than me,' said Rua after she'd tasted it.

'Lilou was a good teacher.'

'She taught both of us. You inherited her flair for clothes and her flair for cooking. I do sometimes wonder what on earth you got from me.'

'Your organisational skills,' said Brontë, which made Rua laugh. 'Seriously,' her daughter continued, 'I've done some organising and I wanted to let you know.'

'What sort of organising?'

'I'm going away for a few days.'

'Where?'

'Italy.'

'What?' Rua looked at her in surprise.

'I'm going to see Flavia. They had a last-minute cancellation at the Villa Farfalla and we were talking and she said if only I could come, and I thought, why not, and so I checked out flights and I'm heading off the day after tomorrow. Flavia reserved the room for me, so we're sorted.'

'Goodness.' Rua was taken aback. 'Can you get time off from the jewellery shop?'

'No problem,' said Brontë.

'And you've booked everything.'

'That's what I said.'

'I didn't realise you and Flavia were so close,' said Rua. 'I mean, I know you've been in touch and everything, but . . .'

'We get on well together,' said Brontë. 'She's going through what I went through after Lilou died. Not exactly the same, of course, but not all that different either. Her father's death was so sudden that she didn't even have time to say goodbye. At least I had that with Lilou. I don't know if it helped her that we were there, but it helped me. I feel for Flavia that she didn't have that.'

'I'm sure it's been hard for her,' agreed Rua.

'And now she's in Italy and she's trying to get to know her dad's family, but it's tricky. I get that too, not that I can really help her there because I never got to know Alize and Valery. I might as well not exist as far as they're concerned. But Flavia gets on well with her half-brother and her cousin and she wants to build on that to have a decent relationship with her aunts and uncles too. She said they've been a bit nicer to her since her mother went there with Sybil, and she's getting on quite well with her grandmother now.'

'How does you going to stay help that along?'

'It doesn't,' admitted Brontë. 'But she wanted them to see that she's not totally dependent on the Marchettis, that she has another life and other people in it.'

'I'm delighted that you've become friendly enough for her to want to ask you.'

'We click,' said Brontë. 'Like I said, I get what she's going through. I like her.'

'Isn't she supposed to be working?'

'Yes, but she's got lots of free time in the evenings. We can go into town, sample the nightlife – she's put lots of pics on her socials and it looks sensational. We'll have a good time.'

'I'm sure you will,' said Rua. 'I'm glad you're going, though I feel a little left out. Sybil and Ailie have both been to the Villa Farfalla and you're going too now. I'm the only one who hasn't made it.'

'Perhaps later in the summer.' Brontë grinned. 'Can you imagine if it turns into a place where we'd like to holiday?'

'I'm happy you're going by yourself,' said Rua. 'You don't need me hanging out with you.'

'I don't,' agreed Brontë. 'But I'm glad that it wouldn't worry me if you were.'

Flavia had finished cleaning the rooms and making the beds when she heard the Mercedes pull up outside the house and the doors open and close. She put her cleaning equipment into the cupboard and ran to the front door.

'*Ciao, bella!*' she cried as she saw Brontë standing at the entrance. 'It's great to see you.'

'You too,' said Brontë. 'I can't believe I'm here.'

'I can't believe it either, but how fantastic is it?' Flavia beamed at her as she led her up the stairs to her room. 'Nonna is looking forward to meeting my Irish friend.'

'How are you getting on with her? With them?'

'Like I said to you, better since Mum was here. I was so worried at her coming and all the complications that seemed to be around Dad's will and everything. But somehow her being here changed everything. Suddenly she wasn't the big bad wolf, she was an ordinary person. And when she talked about Dad, well, they could see how much she loved him.'

'And Sophia?' Brontë opened her case and began unpacking.

'I guess from Mum's point of view she was her opposite big bad wolf. But after dinner they spoke briefly to each other without fighting. So perhaps things will improve in the future. At least they shouldn't get worse.'

'It's so hard having to worry about our parents,' said Brontë. 'And look at you, with shares of your own and an apartment nearby. You're a regular nepo baby.'

'I couldn't believe it when I heard about the apartment,' said Flavia. 'I haven't had time to go there myself, but Mum says it's very cute. The pics are fab. It's small, but nice for one person. She might keep it, and I could live there for a bit before I go back to college.'

'You wouldn't want to live here?' Brontë extended her arms to encompass the Villa Farfalla.

'I love it here, but I'd go bonkers with the aunts around all the time.' Flavia shook her head. 'I'm clearly more like my dad than I thought. But I love the idea of the apartment and I love the idea of working on the development of the luxury oils sometime in the future. Marco suggested it's an area I could help with after I graduate.'

'It's very exciting,' said Brontë. 'It's an opportunity at any rate. Listen, I also wanted to say thanks for being there for me when I called you about my own . . . well, the man who fathered me. It was difficult to process.'

'Oh my God, Bron, I couldn't believe it when you told me. Your poor mum too. What happened to her was awful.

And your dad being the son of a TD and now the TD himself – it's terrible. Makes him untouchable.'

'Maybe not,' said Brontë. 'I haven't decided how I'm going to deal with that yet.'

'Would you out him? Does your mum want to? Have you talked to her about it?'

'We sort of talk around it. She worries I might want to get to know him. But he's a criminal abuser, so why would I want that? The good thing for me is that it makes everything about Mum and her relationship with my grandparents so much clearer.'

'She should have told you sooner,' said Flavia.

'She thought she was protecting me.'

'Parents say that all the time, but sometimes I think it's themselves they're protecting.' Flavia smoothed the sheets on the bed as Brontë took her case from it and stowed it in the corner of the room.

'You don't have to tidy up after me,' said Brontë.

'I can't help it.' Flavia laughed. 'I've become an expert at making beds over the past few weeks. Any little wrinkle drives me crazy. My mother won't know me when I get home. Now come on.' She opened the door. 'Time to show you around the Villa Farfalla.'

After escorting her around the house and gardens, Flavia brought Brontë to see her grandmother, who was sitting on her patio, her head bent over a tablet on which she was rapidly scrolling.

'Nonna, this is my friend. She's staying with us.' Flavia pushed Brontë forward.

'You are bringing your friends to stay now,' said Signora Marchetti. 'How will we make any money?'

'She's a paying guest,' said Flavia. 'You have to be nice. And she's booked a facial treatment too. She'll let lots of people know about the Villa Farfalla.'

Signora Marchetti laughed while Flavia translated the conversation for Brontë.

'This is part of your plan to make the hotel famous?' the Signora asked.

'I've added Instagram to Nonna's tablet,' Flavia told Brontë. 'She's addicted now.'

'I'll post loads of pix,' Brontë promised.

'You are a *brava ragazza*,' said the old woman. 'Good. Good.' And she went back to her scrolling.

That evening Marco drove Flavia, Brontë and Beatrice into the city, where they walked around the narrow streets eating gelato and exclaiming at the beauty of the buildings and the perfection of the view over the bay.

'Tell me more about your history,' Brontë asked Marco, when they were sitting at a café drinking iced lemon.

'The history of Trieste or of my family?' he asked.

'Both,' said Brontë.

And so he told them about the Barone and Baronessa Bianchi, and about the status of Trieste during the war, and they looked around at the streets filled with tourists and marvelled at how things could change in an instant.

'I used to think about that in Les Hauts Champs too,' said Brontë. 'There's a war memorial in the town square. To the fallen. It's only a small town, a few hundred people, but there are at least thirty names on the memorial.'

'My God,' said Flavia. 'That must have been devastating.'

'Nonna talks about the war sometimes,' said Marco. 'Not

often. She was only a child back then, but obviously there are some things that affected her. I don't think she likes to remember.'

'I understand, but we . . . young people like us . . . we shouldn't forget these things.' Beatrice swirled the ice cubes in her drink. 'We should know our history, try not to let it repeat itself.'

'That's why we should encourage the older generation in our families to get on,' said Flavia. 'We've made a start with my mum and the Marchettis.'

'And we're all friends.' Beatrice smiled at her. 'You know we love having you here, Flavia. I'm so glad you came. You're a great help to me in the kitchen too.'

'Not at first,' Flavia conceded.

'But now. Now you make an almost perfect tomato sauce.'

They all laughed.

And Flavia felt the warmth of having a family surround her.

Chapter 29

Rua was delighted when Brontë returned from her stay in Italy sun-kissed and happy and full of stories about the Villa Farfalla, the Marchettis and Flavia's handsome half-brother who'd brought them out every night. It was a long time since she had been so enthusiastic about anything, and Rua was sorry that she had to leave her for a couple of days while she went to a conference in Cork.

'How about I come down on the last day?' suggested Brontë. 'We could go and see Granny and Gramps. I haven't seen them since Christmas.'

'I'd love you to come,' said Rua. 'I'll let your gran and grandad know we'll pop by.'

'Not pop by,' said Brontë. 'We'll have to stay the night.'

'If it's OK with them,' said Rua.

'It's never a problem to stay,' Brontë told her. And then she looked at her mother, realisation dawning. 'But it is for you? Of course it must be. Because of *him*. How could I be so stupid!'

'Ah, I'll be fine. No worries.' Rua smiled, but as always, the idea of spending a night in Loughmore made her stomach tighten.

Now, as the final session of the conference drew to a close, she was on a high from the presentations she'd attended and was thinking that she could adapt one or two of them herself for the office. She'd never wanted to give a presentation before, but listening to the various speakers over the course of a couple of days, she'd seen what they did well and what didn't work, and she was thinking that it was something she might be able to do herself.

It was the most confident she'd been in years.

She took out her phone, and then hesitated as she looked at the thread of messages with Bethany.

They hadn't spoken or texted since the coffee after their bike ride over a week ago. Rua hadn't gone into the office since then, and although she'd thought about texting her, she didn't know what to say. Clearly Bethany had nothing to say either.

It seemed like their relationship, such as it was, was over. And although there was an ache in her heart about it, Rua was also a little relieved. She'd dipped her toe back into the dating scene and it hadn't been as traumatic as she might have expected, but she'd felt tugged in different directions whenever she thought of Lilou. Nevertheless, her time with Bethany had been worthwhile. It had made her see life differently. Made her want to be out and about more. Made her realise that she could have feelings for someone else again.

And feck it, she thought, as she waved goodbye to a few of the other attendees, she'd go back into the office on Monday. She liked being back in the office.

Nothing and nobody was going to stop her.

* * *

She checked out of the hotel and drove to Kent station to meet Brontë's train. Almost immediately she spotted her daughter standing on the platform in a short white summer dress, her hair flowing loose around her face in a tumble of flame-red curls. They greeted each other with hugs, and Brontë put her small wheelie case in the boot beside Rua's.

'Granny does know we're coming?' she said as she settled into the passenger seat.

'I told her about the conference and said I might drop by. I texted last night to say you'd be with me. She replied that she had the guest bedrooms made up.'

'You didn't tell her that I know about Davey Mullery, did you?' Brontë glanced at her mother, and Rua shook her head. 'Maybe you should've,' she continued. 'In case the subject comes up.'

'Are you planning on saying something?' Rua tried to keep her tone neutral.

She'd been aware as soon as Brontë said she wanted to see her grandparents that it was something her daughter might raise, but she hadn't wanted to make a big deal of it.

'Perhaps we should,' said Brontë. 'Get it all out in the open.'

'I was hoping that I could mend some bridges with your grandmother,' said Rua. 'Be kinder, less abrasive with her. I'm not sure that rehashing the past will do that.'

'What about Gramps?' asked Brontë. 'You always seem to get on a bit better with him.'

'Possibly because he doesn't know anything about it. Like I said before, we kept it from him back in the day. I've never said anything since, and I doubt your gran has either.'

'I can't believe it of Granny. She's so chatty normally.'

'She can keep a secret when she wants to. She thinks I hold it over her.'

'Do you?'

'A little,' Rua said. 'She knows I think it was wrong not to report it, and I suppose I've never given her cause to think that I understand why she acted the way she did.'

'It's so odd to think of you sweeping it all under the carpet,' said Brontë. 'We've never done that. I've always been able to tell you everything.'

'Keeping your mouth shut was normalised when I was a girl,' said Rua. 'Perhaps it was a little different in the cities, but in Loughmore . . . well, let's say rural towns were very judgy. And young girls were judged the most.'

'No change there.' Brontë made a face. 'When and where are we not?'

'True,' said her mother. 'I'd like to think women are believed more, but even now that's not the case. Rape is probably the only crime where the victim is blamed for being the victim. And although there's more acceptance of different lifestyles, you all live your lives on social media and you can be judged by the entire world instead of a few dozen nosy neighbours.'

'I suppose we can delete social media,' mused Brontë. 'But you can't delete your neighbours. It must have been hard to think that every time you walked out of your house someone you knew in real life was judging you.'

'It never properly happened to me,' said Rua. 'I was packed off to Francine and Ségolène, and when I came back with you, well, yes, I was judged, but it was in a kind of "your wan headed off to France, see what happened to her and let that be a lesson to you" kind of way. Like a warning to all the other young girls of the perils of going abroad.'

'And that was better?' Brontë raised an eyebrow.

'Different at least,' said Rua.

They lapsed into silence and she turned on some music. By the time they turned into the driveway of the family home, Cyndi Lauper was telling them cheerfully that girls just wanted to have fun.

The door opened as they got out of the car, and Mary hurried out to greet them. Rua never understood why her mother didn't simply wait for them to ring the bell, why she had to come out of the house herself, and she suddenly wondered if it was her way of putting up some kind of barrier before they even stepped inside.

'Hi, Mam,' she said.

'Well, isn't it well for you and your all-expenses-paid conferences in that swanky new hotel,' said Mary. 'And now you're slumming it here with me.'

'Don't be silly, Gran.' It was Brontë who replied. 'Mum worked hard at that conference. She didn't have time to swan around. Not even a spare hour for a massage, although the hotel has an award-winning spa.'

'Maybe next time,' said Rua as she followed her mother and daughter into the house.

Her father was in the living room watching sport on the TV, but as soon as he saw her, he switched it off and got up to hug her.

'This was a surprise. It's lovely to see you both.'

'I'll put the kettle on,' said Mary. 'Or would you like a coffee from the fancy machine you got me?'

'Water is fine. Can we have it in the garden? It's such a nice afternoon.' Brontë smiled at her.

'Whatever you like, sweetheart,' said Mary.

Rua went up to the guest room and took her toiletries out of her bag. Then she crossed the hallway into her old room, where she sat on the edge of the bed and recalled all the times she'd sat there before, worrying about her life; whether it was something to do with school, or her friends, or lack of interest in boys, or her (even then) tricky relationship with her mother, or her brother, or anything and everything to do with living in Loughmore. But more intently, she remembered the hours of sitting there after Davey Mullery's assault, trying to block it out of her mind, trying to tell herself that it wasn't her fault, trying not to feel guilty for following Mary's advice and leaving the police out of it. She'd been angry both on her own behalf and because he could do the same to someone else. Not that she'd heard that he had. Or if it had happened, any other victims had stayed quiet, just like her.

Even if it hadn't resulted in pregnancy, she knew that what Davey had done to her would stay with her all her life. It had changed her as a person. Changed the way she viewed the world. Changed everything about her.

She wondered if men who raped women ever sat in their own bedrooms and regretted it. If they had any remorse. If they realised the impact of their actions. Or if, instead, they rationalised it to themselves, telling themselves that they'd been tricked or led on, or if they used some other form of words to make themselves feel all right. Rua was pretty sure Davey Mullery hadn't regretted it for a second. She shuddered as she remembered him pushing past her at the riverbank, knowing that he was untouchable, that he'd never be called to account for his actions.

Even if she wanted to do something now, she couldn't help thinking it was far too late. After such a long time, no one was going to go against the local TD, who had (according to his website) brought investment to Loughmore and secured a grant for the GAA pitch, and who promised on all his election material to work tirelessly for the people of the town so that their lives would be better.

Davey probably thought of himself as a good and decent man. He'd say what had happened between them was a youthful indiscretion and he'd be believed. He probably believed it himself, after all these years.

People would want to believe him.

He still lived in the town, after all.

She was the one who'd left.

When Rua came downstairs, the others were sitting around the large wooden table in the garden. Mary had brought out a jug of iced water along with a pot of tea and a plate of biscuits.

'So, Granny, Gramps, Mum has something to say to you.' Brontë spoke as Rua sat down.

Rua shot her an anxious look. 'I haven't . . .' She shook her head.

'Well, OK, it's me that has something to say.' Brontë's voice was steady. 'It's that I know about what happened with Davey Mullery, and while I concede that you might have done what you thought was best, Granny, it really wasn't. You should have gone to the gardaí and had him prosecuted for rape.'

There was total silence around the table.

Conal looked at Rua, and then at Mary, bewilderment in his eyes.

Rua dropped her gaze to the table.

Mary opened her mouth and closed it again.

Brontë took a sip from her tumbler of water.

It was Conal who spoke first.

'Rape?' he said. 'What rape?'

It was a moment before Rua spoke, and when she did, her voice wobbled.

'Davey Mullery raped me when I was nineteen, and Mum persuaded me not to go to the police,' she said.

'Davey Mullery is my father,' said Brontë.

'I thought . . . I thought you got pregnant in France.' Conal was shocked.

'Didn't you ever work it out from the dates, Gramps?' asked Brontë.

'I never thought . . .' He looked at Mary again. 'Why didn't you say anything?'

'I did what was best,' said Mary.

'Davey Mullery.' Conal stared at her. 'I worked for Pearse for years.'

'Yes,' said Mary.

'I worked for that man, and his son . . .' Conal balled his fist. 'His son . . . my daughter . . . I don't fucking believe it.'

Hearing her father swear shocked Rua. She'd never heard him utter more than a gentle 'dammit' before. She wondered what would have happened if Mary had told him that night. Looking at him now, she was afraid he might have gone after Davey Mullery and administered his own justice in the form of a beating. And where would that have left them?

'Why are you telling me this now?' he demanded. 'Why not then? When I could have done something? When I was fit enough to have throttled that . . .' He broke off again, unable to continue. 'You kept it from me,' he said to Mary, when he'd composed himself. 'Deliberately.'

'Yes,' said Mary. 'I did. I kept it from everyone for the sake of our daughter.' She looked at Conal and at Rua and at Brontë. 'And you may all think I did the wrong thing, but I stand by it.'

Conal got up, went over to Rua and put his arms around her, holding her tightly.

'And I stand by you,' he said. 'Now and always. I would've done more back then if I'd known. You should have told me.'

'Oh, Dad.' Rua felt her eyes brim with tears. 'I thought you'd blame me too.'

'I never blamed you,' her mother said. 'But I knew you *would* be blamed. There's a big bloody difference. Anyhow, it all worked out. I got the money for you to go to France, where you were happy. You met Lilou. Your dad did well in Pearse's company. I'd do it all again in a heartbeat.'

'What d'you mean, you got the money?' asked Conal.

For the first time, Mary's voice faltered, as she told him that she'd demanded compensation from Pearse.

'I don't know who I married.' Conal looked at her in disbelief. 'And I don't know what I'm going to do about this. But I can tell you something. I'll not let it rest.'

He strode into the house, leaving the three women at the table.

'Why did you have to say that?' Mary turned to Brontë, her face flushed. 'Just because your mother told you something that she didn't have to tell you, why did you have to bring it all up? Everything was fine. Your dad was fine. Your mother was fine. I—'

'Don't say you were fine too!' cried Brontë. 'Nobody is

fine, because nobody admitted what happened. Of course she had to tell me. She should have told me sooner. We need to know these things, Gran. We need to talk about them.'

'Why?' demanded Mary. 'Why not leave secrets well enough alone? It's not like anything will change now.'

'Because they fester,' said Rua. 'They fester and they grow and they affect us all in different ways.'

'Mum's right,' said Bronté. 'All the times we visited and I knew there was something wrong but I could never put my finger on it. Yet we only needed to open up and talk—'

Mary interrupted her. 'You young ones think that talking about everything, sharing everything, is the only way to do things. You can't keep a damn thing to yourselves. But there are other ways. Better ways.'

'You think your way was better?' asked Bronté.

'It kept everyone happy for twenty years,' replied Mary.

'No, it didn't!' Bronté shook her head. 'You can't seriously think that Mum was perfectly happy after being shipped off. And then for me to be her disgrace.'

'You weren't her disgrace,' said Mary. 'Everybody loved you. I protected her is what I did, and you're too naïve to see it.'

'Pretending something never happened isn't protecting anyone,' said Bronté. 'It's wrong, Granny. It really is.'

'So tell me, missy, what's your plan now? Confronting Davey in the main street? He's a TD, you know. He's powerful.'

'He sounds like a right shit,' said Bronté. 'I'm mortified to be his daughter.'

'We've lived with Mullerys in this town for generations,' said Mary. 'They'll always be the ones with the power. But

I got what I wanted from his father, and it was a damn sight better than dragging your mother's name through the mud.'

'You extorted money from him!' Brontë exclaimed.

'I got what was due.' Mary's tone was stubborn. 'You're young and foolish. You see things in black and white. But one day you'll see that nothing is ever clear-cut.'

She got up from the table and left her daughter and granddaughter sitting alone together.

'That didn't go as well as I'd hoped.' Brontë sounded chastened. 'I thought perhaps she'd be happy to finally talk about it. And that it would be good for Gramps to know. I knew he'd be angry, but I thought it would be with Davey Mullery, not Granny.'

'It went exactly as I expected,' Rua told her. 'Your grandmother is a different generation, and it can't have been easy for your grandad to realise he was kept completely in the dark by her.'

'I thought older people were cooler now,' said Brontë. 'I thought they understood. I mean, think of Francine and Ségolène. Francine was older than Granny, and she was fantastic.'

'Not everyone is Francine and Ségolène,' Rua pointed out. 'And Granny is who she is.'

'Gramps was pretty steamed up,' said Brontë. 'I hope he's not going to have a row with Granny, or go off and do something stupid.'

'He'll cool down, he always does. But I'm sure he and Granny have a bit of talking to do.'

'Is this why you didn't want to talk about it yourself?'

'Partly,' agreed Rua.

'I'm sorry.'

'Don't be.' She gave Brontë a consoling smile. 'You're right. It's better to have it in the open. At least as far as the Lehane family is concerned.'

Mary went to the attic bedroom that Conal used as a den. She found him there, smoking a cigarette through the open window, something he occasionally did still, although he'd given them up ten years earlier.

'I could smell it,' she said as she walked into the room. 'I always can, even through an open window.'

'Good for you,' he said. 'Keep on top of us all, knowing what we do. Planning our lives for us.'

'Conal. Don't be silly.'

'Don't be silly!' He turned to face her, grinding out the cigarette in the ceramic ashtray on the window ledge. 'You've kept information from me for twenty damn years and you're asking me not to be silly. I'm not silly. I'm fuming.'

'I understand why're you're angry. That's why I didn't say anything back then.'

'Back then I would've been angry with that bastard Mullery. Now I'm angry with you.'

'I thought I was doing the right thing. I still think I did the right thing. But I admit I should've told you.'

'You let me work for that poxy bollix knowing his son assaulted my daughter and knowing he'd paid you money to keep it quiet. He was probably laughing at me every single day.'

'I'm sure he wasn't. He treated you well, didn't he? You got promoted.'

'One of the biggest shocks in all this is knowing I married

a woman who would have negotiated up the thirty pieces of silver that were given to Judas.'

'The money was a side issue,' Mary said. 'I was protecting her, Conal. You've forgotten what it was like back then. You've forgotten that girls lost their jobs and their reputations, that they were shunned by the neighbours, all of it. They were blamed. Always. I helped her.'

'It's as well I'm retired,' said Conal. 'Because I wouldn't be able to set foot in that place again. And if I see that fucker on the road, I won't be responsible for what I say or do.'

'You'll say and do nothing,' said Mary. 'You're a good man, Conal Lehane, and Rua is a good girl. Her lifestyle isn't exactly what I'd've chosen for her, but she's happy. She's a remarkable mother and Brontë has grown into an exceptional young woman.'

'Are you trying to say that everything you did was justified?'

'No. But it wasn't unjustified either. I hope eventually you'll see that.'

Rua and Brontë, hearing raised voices from the open window though unable to make out what was being said, decided to give Conal and Mary some time and space alone and walked into the town together. Given the warmth of the early evening, there were plenty of people around, many of them sitting on the benches in the square, each with a small plaque reminding anyone who sat there that the seat had been erected thanks to local funding obtained by Davey Mullery. Brontë and Rua walked past the square and bought ice creams in Daisy's Dairy, an artisanal shop set up a few years earlier by one of Rua's former schoolmates. There was no sign of Daisy herself, although Rua would've liked to compliment her on the quality of the ice cream.

On the outskirts of the town, she pointed out the Mullery houses.

'That's Southwinds,' she said, indicating the largest.

Brontë stared at the house. 'So that belongs to my grandfather.'

It jolted Rua to hear Brontë call Pearse Mullery her grandfather.

'And which one is my father's?' she asked.

'The one to the left of it.'

'Big enough,' remarked Brontë.

'He always liked big, flashy things.'

'I googled him,' Brontë said. 'Married. Four children. Two boys, two girls. My half-siblings. All a lot younger than me.'

Rua nodded.

'Did he know?' asked Brontë.

'Know what?'

'That you weren't into men.'

'That was why he did it,' said Rua.

'He's a pig,' said Brontë.

Rua said nothing.

'You don't want to say horrible things about him because he's my father,' said Brontë.

'I don't know what I want to say.'

'I love you,' Brontë told her. 'I admire you. You're a role model for me.'

'Thank you.' Rua swallowed the lump in her throat. 'Do you want to see him, though? Speak to him? We can go up to the house right now if that's what you want.' She turned to Brontë. 'I've always felt sick at the thought of ever seeing him again. One of the reasons I didn't like coming back here was that I could have bumped into him unexpectedly. But with you here beside me, I could face anyone or anything. If that's what you want.'

'I feel he should be punished,' said Brontë. 'He's had a good life, while you—'

'I've had a good life too.' Rua interrupted her. 'Not the one I expected. But good all the same. I met Lilou and she made me happy. You make me happy. I know I've been affected by what he did, but I'll never let myself be defined by it.'

'I love that you say that.' Brontë linked her arm with her mother's. 'I'm glad for you, I really am.'

'Maybe the right thing to do would be to report it,' said Rua. 'But even if it is, I'm not ready to do it yet. I thought I might be. But I'm not.'

'I understand.'

'Thank you.' She looked at her daughter. 'How do you feel?'

'Furious on your behalf,' Brontë said. 'Sad that he's my dad. I thought I might be ready to see him, but now that we're here, definitely not on this trip. Maybe not ever. But who knows, perhaps when the next election comes around I'll get in touch with him. Or get in touch with the media. That'd give him a fright, wouldn't it? For now, though, let's go home and try to fix things with Granny and Gramps. I'd hate to be responsible for them never speaking to each other again.'

Chapter 30

A few weeks later, the Merry Widows group met for a long walk around Howth Head before returning to Sybil's apartment for lunch. The three women laughed and joked during the walk, happy to be outdoors under a glorious midsummer-blue sky and taking selfies with the backdrop of the sea sparkling beneath the high sun. Sybil had ordered in the same sandwiches as before, although this time they ate them on her enormous balcony overlooking Dublin Bay.

'I know the views from Trieste were impressive,' she said as they watched the sailing dinghies skim across the water. 'But this is magical.'

'No place like home,' agreed Ailie. 'Even if Flavia is thinking of the Villa Farfalla as her second home now.'

'How are you getting on without her?' asked Rua.

'It's lonely,' acknowledged Ailie. 'But I've been busy at work, so that's keeping me occupied. As has dealing with all the stuff from the Marchettis.'

'It's good that you're friends with them now,' said Sybil.

'The word "friends" is doing a lot of heavy lifting there.' Ailie grinned. 'But with Alessandro in the middle of our negotiations and Marco being very proactive, things are moving along quite nicely.'

'It was worth visiting so,' said Rua.

'Without a doubt,' agreed Ailie. 'I hate the word, but it was a kind of closure for me too. Not of everything, because my role in the business, at least for as long as I'm involved, is completely new to me, but it was a closure on Giorgio's relationship with them and how it always affected me. And on my feelings of guilt that our last words to each other were in anger. You were right, Sybil, when you said he'd probably come to fix things between us. That was how he was. How we were. So it isn't nagging at me any more. And I have to say, despite my reservations, working at the villa has been good for Flavia. It's helped her so much with her grief over her dad.'

'I'm glad,' said Sybil.

'The apartment is a wonderful bonus too,' added Ailie. 'Flavia wants me to keep it – Alessandro's niece showed her around and she's fallen in love with it.'

'Who wouldn't want to have an Italian bolthole?' asked Rua.

'I'm feeling a lot more positive about it,' said Ailie. 'Not rushing into anything yet, though.'

'You've plenty of time,' agreed Sybil.

'You were such a pet to end your cruise early and stay with me,' Ailie told her. 'It made all the difference.'

'What about the man you met on board, Sybil?' asked Rua. 'Fergus? Are you in touch with him at all?'

'I wasn't sure I would be, but yes, I am,' said Sybil.

'Go, Sybil!' Rua gave her a thumbs-up.

In all honesty, she'd been both pleased and a little surprised that Fergus continued to message her regularly. Despite their conversation on the quayside, she'd been quite prepared for him to forget about her, or decide that it wasn't worth keeping in touch with someone who lived nearly two hundred kilometres away. At first he sent her various photos from the remainder of his cruise, and later some from his son's home in Perth, where he said he was having a wonderful time but was looking forward to getting back to Ireland and seeing her again.

'He messages me every day,' she told Ailie and Rua. 'It's sweet.'

'I'm so pleased that after you leaving him on the ship for me, it's all working out for you,' said Ailie. 'And I know you said you weren't prepared to invest in a man again, but it seems to me that this man might be right for you.'

'I'm not entirely sure where it's going,' confessed Sybil. 'I haven't seen him since Trieste, because he's in Australia, but I'm willing to see how things turn out. It's been a bit of a revelation being with someone again, even if it is a long-distance relationship.'

'He sounds perfect,' said Rua. 'What are you unsure of?'

'It became so important to me to prove to myself that I could be happy alone that I've struggled to imagine being happy with someone else in my life,' replied Sybil. 'I'm having to rethink that and see where it leads me.'

'D'you think Fergus feels the same way?'

'He's been divorced twice and feels quite bad about it. Considers himself a bit of a failure in the marriage stakes. I told him I wasn't rushing to marry anyone so he didn't have to worry. He's been very . . . respectful of me, and I like that. Of course Tansy thinks I could do nothing better than race up the aisle with him.'

'Seriously?' Ailie laughed.

'She told me that if I didn't put a ring on it, I'd regret it forever.' Sybil chuckled. 'I'm looking forward to seeing him again, but I'm also prepared for the fact that a chunk of time has gone by and he might feel entirely differently when he's back home than on the ship. Whatever happens, I know I'm not the grumpy, selfish old woman festering away on my own that my sister seems to think. She was right about me not having enough friends before,' she conceded. 'But I *am* making more of an effort, and with you ladies, I'm well served in the friends department. And I like that you know me as me, and not Theo's wife.'

'Yes.' Ailie nodded. 'With you guys I'm Ailie, not Giorgio's widow.'

'I suppose I've always been a little weird about who and what I am,' said Rua slowly. 'Being in a same-sex marriage was different. Not for me and Lilou, but how people perceived us. Yet I was blissfully happy with her. I'd like to be blissfully happy again, but I've made rather a mess of that.'

'Have you met someone?' asked Ailie. 'Did it go wrong?'

'It looked like it might work out, but then it didn't,' said Rua.

'Bethany?' Sybil looked at her enquiringly.

'How did you know?'

'You seemed close at the firing range.'

Rua told them how things had seemed to be going well but how hard it was for her to commit in the way Bethany wanted.

'She seemed like a nice woman,' remarked Ailie. 'I'm sorry it hasn't worked out.'

'She was. Is,' said Rua. 'I'm sorry it hasn't worked out too. But when she told me she loved me, I panicked. I'm not ready for that.'

'But do *you* love *her*?' asked Ailie.

'I'm confused,' Rua replied. 'I loved being with her, but Lilou was always in the back of my mind. I couldn't let her go and that wasn't fair on Bethany. I know I hurt her, and I regret that.'

'Is it awkward at work?' asked Sybil.

'Not really. At first I stayed home, but then I realised I was being silly. After all, we work on different floors.'

'I remember when I fell for Theo at the bank,' Sybil said. 'We were on different floors too, but we kept making excuses to visit each other.'

'Bethany and I are doing our best to avoid each other,' said Rua. 'Oh, look, it was a start. At least I know that I can feel something for someone again. I never thought I would. And I think Lilou would be happy about it.'

'I'm sure she would,' said Sybil.

'At least you're open to love and romance,' Ailie said. 'I'm happy for you. And you too, Sybil, if you build something stronger with Fergus. But whatever happens, we'll always be friends, won't we?'

'For sure we will.' Rua nodded. 'And not trying to change the subject, but Brontë and I stayed with my folks after the conference. Things happened there too.'

She told them about Brontë speaking out, about her parents' reaction and Brontë's subsequent decision not to have any contact with Davey Mullery.

'Which makes me happy, to be honest,' she said. 'Part of me was expecting her to want a relationship with him, and

I was terrified of how that would make me feel. Another part of me was even more terrified that she'd want to confront him or his family about what had happened. She feels I should have my revenge on him.'

'And you don't want revenge yourself?'

'Sometimes I do,' acknowledged Rua. 'But I got myself into a good space when I was in France. It wasn't perfect, but I was able to live with what had happened and the choices that I made and that were forced on me. When Lilou was killed, things inevitably went a bit pear-shaped. Back in Loughmore, I wondered if outing Davey Mullery would somehow make me feel better about losing her. After a few weeks feeling like that, I went to counselling again. It helped hugely, although the truth is that I retreated into myself a lot. Quite honestly, until I met you ladies, I was totally closed up. These last months have made me feel normal. Talking to Brontë has made me realise that Davey Mullery doesn't matter to me any more. She can make her own decisions about him and I'll stand by her no matter what. As for me, all I care about is living my own life.'

'How is Brontë herself doing?' asked Ailie.

'Pretty OK, I think. I know she's been in touch with Flavia, so I assume she's talked to her about it.'

'Flavia hasn't said a word to me,' said Ailie. 'But I wouldn't expect her to. It's nice that the girls have each other to confide in.'

'How about your parents?' Sybil asked Rua. 'Obviously it was a big shock for your dad when Brontë spilled the beans.'

Rua recounted the scene at the house and told them that when she and Brontë returned, her parents were sitting together in the garden, although the atmosphere was tense. Brontë had urged her grandmother to come inside and make tea while Rua stayed with Conal.

'I'm so sorry that I didn't know,' he said. 'I would've killed Davey Mullery and that's a fact.'

'That's probably why she didn't tell you.'

'Your mother always thinks she knows best.'

'I found it very hard to forgive her,' Rua said. 'In fact I probably haven't, at least not fully. But I've accepted that she thought she was doing the right thing.'

'That doesn't mean she didn't make a wrong decision. And she didn't trust me enough to tell me. If she had . . .'

'Oh, look, Dad, I've struggled with keeping it all quiet myself. But Brontë has decided that she doesn't want to have anything to do with him right now, so going after him would affect her as much as me, and I don't want that. It's such a loss for him not to know her. In some ways, that's revenge enough for me.'

'Are you sure about that?'

'Yes,' she said.

He hugged her, and she hugged him, and they sat together chatting until Mary and Brontë came out with the tea.

'And then, same as always, we pretended nothing had happened.' Rua sighed now. 'My mother switched the conversation to something about one of the neighbours, and I was quite happy not to talk about Davey Mullery any more.'

'So you'll not do anything?' asked Sybil

'Maybe if Brontë takes a different view herself later on, I'll think about it. But for now it would be such a cataclysmic thing, and the truth is that I've got my life on track. Brontë's happy. I'm happy. Why would I jeopardise all that?'

'In that case, let's get back to your love life.' Sybil took the bottle of wine from the cooler and topped up their glasses. 'Do you want to repair things with Bethany if possible, or would you like to find someone new?'

'I cared about Bethany. She made me feel more alive than I had in ages. But I couldn't . . .'

'Couldn't what?' asked Sybil.

'I don't know.' Rua shrugged helplessly. 'It's like Lilou is still there. Like I haven't really said goodbye.'

'Oh.' Ailie and Sybil exchanged glances.

'I'm bound to her,' added Rua.

'How?'

'Emotionally. Physically too, I guess, when I think of our house in Les Hauts Champs.'

'You still have a house in France?' Sybil looked surprised.

'I haven't gone back since the funeral,' said Rua. 'I couldn't.'

'It's been empty all this time?'

'One of the neighbours has a key. She opens the windows once a week, runs the water, that sort of thing. But nobody has lived there or stayed there since Brontë and I left.'

'Perhaps you need to deal with that before you can move on with Bethany,' said Ailie.

'It sounds so stupid, doesn't it?'

'Not at all.' Ailie shook her head. 'Isn't it exactly what I've had to do with the Marchettis?'

'That's different,' objected Rua. 'You had a whole inheritance to sort out.'

'It's still about a physical place. A house. A home. Although in my case I had to go there to understand it. You need to go to leave.'

'Maybe.' Rua looked doubtful.

'Is it your house?' asked Sybil.

'Oh, yes.' Rua nodded. 'It was Lilou's. Left to her by her grandmother. She was the sole owner. And when she died, it came to me. But I couldn't live there with Brontë. It was too hard. So I came home.'

'And now you need to return to France and sort it out,' said Ailie. 'Why don't you ask Bethany to go with you?'

'I couldn't.' Rua looked at her in horror. 'I couldn't bring her to the place where Lilou and I lived. It would be wrong on a million different levels.'

'I understand.' Ailie nodded.

'Why don't *we* go with you?' suggested Sybil.

'You?'

'Ailie and me. After all, we were very successful in Italy. No reason we couldn't have equal success in France.'

'Crikey, you're setting us up as some kind of globe-trotting consortium,' exclaimed Rua.

'The Merry Widows on Tour.' Sybil laughed. 'Why not?'

'Why not indeed?' Ailie's eyes brightened. 'We could spend a week or so in France. It doesn't have to be in your house, Rua. We could stay nearby. We wouldn't impose.'

'It wouldn't be an imposition,' Rua said. 'Besides, there isn't a hotel in Les Hauts Champs. Not even a B&B. The nearest place is about fifteen kilometres away.'

'We can hire a car,' said Sybil. 'That's not a problem.'

'You're staying in the house,' said Rua firmly. 'There are three bedrooms. Two doubles and a single. None very big,' she added, 'but all lovely. Well, maybe not now. It's been such a long time since I was there.'

'We can make it lovely,' said Sybil.

'I guess . . .' Rua began to smile. 'I guess it could be a good trip.'

'Of course it could,' said Ailie.

'When I get home, I'll check my work diary,' Rua said. 'See what time I can take off. You do the same.'

'My diary is always free.' Sybil smiled. 'I'm the pensioner here. I'll fit in with whatever suits you both.'

'OK then.' Rua nodded. 'It's agreed. There'll be a Merry Widows trip to France soon.'

'I'll drink to that,' said Sybil.

They raised their glasses and laughed.

After the others had gone, Sybil continued to sit on the balcony, although she exchanged the wine for water. She was excited about the trip to France and cheered by the fact that both Ailie and Rua seemed to be excited too.

She watched a ferry approach Dun Laoghaire harbour in the distance and thought about the people disembarking, their reasons for travel, the journeys they still had to make. It used to be a regular occurrence, but it was a long time, she reflected, since she'd had a holiday twice in one year. My life has moved on, she said to herself. And that's a good thing.

She finished the glass of water, then went inside, fetched her laptop and opened the photo app. She'd taken lots of pics on the cruise and she wanted to delete the unnecessary ones. Unlike people who kept thousands of digital photos and never looked at them again, Sybil found editing them and putting them into albums a therapeutic thing to do. Sometimes at night, instead of watching TV, she looked at slideshows of her and Theo on their travels. They always cheered her, even if she grimaced at how she'd changed over the years.

Now she cropped and deleted, enhanced and filtered her cruise photos. Many of them were scenic, and a large quantity featured Pompeii, but the later ones also included shots of her and Fergus – some selfies and some taken by the cruise staff – as well as others of her, Ailie and Flavia at the Villa Farfalla. It was undoubtedly a beautiful house in a wonderful location, she thought as she zoomed in on the pretty fountain, but it did need some TLC.

She thought of Fergus's designer home in Holywood and wondered when she'd get to see it. And if she'd be comfortable staying there. If he'd be comfortable staying with her. It would mean some big changes. It was quite a while since she'd had to consider any big change in her life.

It suddenly occurred to her that wondering about lifestyle changes was quite a nice thing to have to do at sixty-eight. At least it proved that she had a future that mattered.

She scrolled through some photos of Theo. She hadn't taken any of him in the last months of his illness because she hadn't wanted to record how thin and gaunt he'd become. She would always remember him as a fit, strong man. A partner in life. In reality, the only partner she'd ever needed.

Her phone rang, and she saw Tansy's name.

'Hi,' she said. 'What's up?'

'Just calling to see how you are,' said Tansy.

'I'm fine. My friends were over for lunch earlier.'

'The widows?'

'Yes.'

'Hmm.'

Sybil knew that Tansy was both intrigued and somewhat unconvinced by her friendship with Ailie and Rua. That she had put them all into a kind of sad, bereaved box and worried they spent all their time reminiscing about their pasts and sobbing about their late spouses. It was as though she couldn't see them as individuals, only as women joined in sorrow, although Sybil had already pointed out that she and Ailie had spent a fantastic few days in Trieste together. Now she told her that they were thinking of a trip to France soon too.

'I'm glad you're getting the opportunity to travel with friends,' said Tansy. 'Better than doing it alone or locking yourself away in the apartment like Rapunzel. Meanwhile, there's one little thing I wanted to bring you up to speed on.'

'Oh?'

'Burt Kennelly is engaged.'

'Engaged!' Sybil choked back a laugh. 'Isn't getting engaged an unnecessary step at his point in life?'

'It takes a couple of months to organise a wedding,' said Tansy. 'Why shouldn't he get engaged first?'

'You're right,' conceded Sybil. 'I was being silly.'

'It could've been you,' said Tansy.

'It couldn't.'

'He's very happy.'

'I wouldn't have been.'

'You're too damn picky.'

'I'm truly not.'

'Oh, well.' Tansy stopped baiting her. 'He met his fiancée at the musical society.'

'I knew he liked musicals, but I didn't realise he was in a musical society. He never mentioned it.'

'You probably didn't give him a chance.'

'I'm delighted he's found love.' Sybil was sincere. 'He deserves it.'

'Monica Russell deserves it too,' said Tansy. 'In her late forties, never married. Youngest of five. Looked after her elderly mother for years. Mrs Russell died a few months ago.'

'Possibly a good match so,' said Sybil. 'At least she doesn't have anyone to compare Burt to, and he's also done well in getting himself a younger woman to look after him.'

'You're so cynical. What about your cruise man? Any joy there?'

'He's invited me to visit.'

'Sybil! Tell me you said yes.'

'I did indeed say yes.'

'Hallelujah!' exclaimed Tansy. 'When?'

'In a few weeks. When he's back from visiting his son in Australia.'

'Pity he's away. Get in there as soon as you can. Don't delay or you could be in another Burt Kennelly situation and some other woman might swoop in.'

'I'll bear that in mind,' Sybil assured her.

But she didn't tell her just how much she was looking forward to seeing Fergus McGuinness again.

Chapter 31

Rua drove them from Paris to Les Hauts Champs in the Renault Espace they'd hired at the airport. She drove cautiously, using the satnav until they were out of the city, but put her foot to the floor as soon as they reached the motorway. Sybil, who was sitting in the back, grabbed the armrest with trepidation. She was relieved when they eventually exited onto one of the long, straight D roads emblematic of rural France, cutting through carefully cultivated farmland occasionally punctuated by lines of upright plane trees. On a road like this, she felt they should get stuck behind a clapped-out Citroën, or a large, rumbling tractor, or even a young girl riding a bicycle, her hair flowing in the wind as she wobbled through a traditional village, but the truth was that the other traffic was mainly modern saloon cars like their own, and almost every town they passed through was bordered at each end by a bright modern petrol station.

'It's kind of commuter territory,' Rua said, when Sybil expressed her thoughts aloud. 'I know there's farmland, but most people don't work on the farms any more. Lilou's dad was an exception, and even he gave it up in the end. A lot of the smaller towns like Les Hauts Champs are being abandoned, or the houses are being bought by overseas tourists who want a slice of French life even if they often can't hack the reality.'

'I suppose that's like everywhere.' Sybil winced as Rua zipped past a motorcycle with what seemed like inches to spare.

'It's a shame,' said Rua. 'Though at least the working-from-home thing has helped a bit. And French people in general aren't as tied to their work as people in other countries.'

'Isn't that stereotyping them a bit?' asked Ailie, who was unfazed by Rua's driving.

'A stereotype I embraced wholeheartedly.' Rua chuckled, then pulled into the next petrol station which, she said, was a good spot to stock up on basic foodstuffs. When they'd bought all they needed they got back into the car and Rua followed a narrower road, which, to Sybil's relief, meant their speed slowed dramatically. In the distance, she saw a tall church spire and remarked how elegant it looked.

'The Église Saint-Rémy,' said Rua. 'It's the church of Les Hauts Champs. Not far now.'

Ten minutes later she turned into the main square of a much smaller town than any they'd passed through earlier. She exited at the southern corner before pulling up outside a two-storey stone cottage with blue shutters at the sash windows and a low wall surrounding a slightly overgrown garden.

'*Nous sommes arrivés*,' she declared as she switched off the engine. 'Here we are. Le Petit Nid.'

'The Little Nest?' hazarded Ailie, working on the assumption that the French and Italian words for nest were similar.

'Exactly.' Rua beamed at her and got out of the car. '*Bienvenue.*'

She pushed open the gate to the cottage and inserted the key into the lock on the front door, which was painted in the same blue as the shutters.

She hesitated for a moment, then took a deep breath and turned the key.

The memories came flooding back. The aroma of Lilou's cooking wafting from the kitchen. The scent of the fresh flowers that she liked to buy from the florist, the occasional pungent smell of manure from the nearby field.

The cottage had originally been part of the farm outbuildings, but Lilou's grandfather had bought it and renovated it as a home when the farm had downsized. It had two main rooms downstairs, a kitchen and a living room, along with a large space beneath the stairs where he'd installed a compact bathroom with a shower. Upstairs were the three bedrooms, and a full-sized bathroom with an enormous bath in its centre.

Rua took another deep breath before opening the door that led to the kitchen. It was exactly as she'd left it. The scrubbed-pine table with four wooden chairs took up most of the space, while the walls were lined with shelves and cupboards that still contained crockery and a variety of tins and other containers. Like the external woodwork, the cupboards were painted in duck-egg blue. A picture window overlooked the field at the back of the house, while a set of French doors led to a sun-drenched paved courtyard with a round bistro table and chairs.

'It's so pretty,' said Ailie, who'd followed Rua into the kitchen. 'I'm sure you loved living here.'

Rua, her eyes brimming with tears, was unable to reply. Neither Ailie nor Sybil spoke, allowing her time to compose herself.

'I thought it might have changed,' she said, her voice

shaky. 'There's no reason why it should, I know. And yet with the time that's passed . . .'

'I know,' said Sybil. 'A few months after Theo died, I had to go to a meeting in the company's office. I couldn't believe that everything was exactly the same as it had been when he was there. It was disconcerting to say the least.'

'I feel that way every time I walk into my house,' Ailie said. 'I keep thinking something will be different, but it never is. It took me weeks to move some newspapers Giorgio had left on the armchair in the front room. I couldn't make myself do it for ages.'

'I'm glad you both came with me.' Rua sniffed. 'It would be unbearable by myself.'

Neither Ailie or Sybil spoke, but they both put their arms around her and held her close.

Later that evening, they ate in the town's only restaurant, a small but inviting space that Rua told them opened three nights a week in the summer but remained closed during the winter months. It was at the opposite corner of the square, past the *boulangerie* and the florist. According to Rua, the florist only opened in the mornings, and the *boulangerie* opened until mid afternoon.

'But there's a supermarket about ten kilometres away, and of course we have our pizza dispenser,' she told them as they took their seats in Tante Amelie's.

'A pizza dispenser?'

'A machine that cooks hot takeaway pizza,' Rua said. 'You choose from a digital menu and it delivers it in a few minutes. It was an absolute staple for Lilou and me when we were both working in Paris.'

'You're joking.' Ailie looked aghast. 'In France?'

'We have a baguette dispenser too,' Rua informed them. 'Beside the *boulangerie*. For your Sunday and emergency baguette needs.'

'So far, except for your gorgeous cottage, you've destroyed every preconception I had about living in France,' said Sybil. 'I'm shocked at the lack of restaurants and at the notion of food dispensers.'

'It's progress of a sort,' said Rua. 'But,' she added, 'the food in Amelie's is out of this world and will utterly restore your faith in French cuisine.'

'You might be right,' said Sybil as she studied the handwritten menu. 'What's *salade périgourdine*?'

'A warm duck salad,' replied Rua. 'With potatoes, bacon and walnuts.'

'That suits me.' Sybil closed the menu. 'It's surprisingly warm this evening and I don't think I could manage anything hot.'

'The *confit de canard* is her signature dish,' said Rua. 'I have it almost every time.'

'I love the sound of that, but like Sybil, I'm wilting a bit in the heat,' said Ailie. 'I'll go for the truffle omelette'

'It's delicious,' Rua assured her, and then stood up from the table as a woman in her mid thirties approached them and held out her arms.

'Rua, *ma chérie*!' she exclaimed. 'It's so good to see you again. I hope you are well?'

Rua introduced her to her friends as the titular Amelie and owner of the restaurant.

'I will have to be on the top of my game for your guests.' Amelie switched to English and smiled at them before disappearing into the kitchen again.

'She was so kind to me after Lilou's accident,' said Rua. 'She sent cooked meals to the house every day for weeks.'

'You had a good life here?' Sybil looked at her enquiringly. 'You were part of the community?'

'Yes and no,' replied Rua. 'Lilou more than me because she used to visit when she was younger and lived here with her grandmother for a time. So everyone knew her. I was nothing more than a blow-in, and it was hard to socialise and be accepted. Not,' she added, 'that there was much socialising going on here anyway, as you can already tell from the available nightlife options.'

'Is there a pub?' asked Ailie.

Rua shook her head.

'Crikey, even the most remote town in Ireland has a pub. I can't imagine having nowhere to go.'

'That's why people move to the cities,' said Rua.

Their conversation was interrupted by Amelie's return with some floury bread rolls, followed by their meals, which did indeed restore their faith in French cooking.

Afterwards they returned to the cottage and went to their rooms, all of them tired from the day's travelling, the sultry heat of the evening, the good food and a bottle of excellent wine.

Alone in the bedroom she'd once shared with Lilou, Rua stood at the window and looked out over the fields. She'd missed this view and she'd missed this house. She'd missed her life in the country town too. Despite its drawbacks, she'd loved it here, but it had been impossible to stay after Lilou's death. She hadn't realised how hard it would be to keep going. To wake up every day and get dressed. To go to work, even if that was simply down the stairs. To keep up with all the administrative things that you had to do when you owned a house. She couldn't find the energy for any of it. And her priority was trying to hold it all together for Brontë's sake.

She hadn't wanted to leave, but she couldn't stay. And although Francine had offered her and Brontë a room in the Paris apartment, it wasn't practical now that Brontë was older. Besides, her daughter had desperately wanted to go back to Ireland to see her grandparents. She wanted to be near people who were her family. Rua didn't have the heart to refuse.

But being in Les Hauts Champs now made her realise how much of a home it had been to her.

She turned away from the window and opened the wardrobe door, then caught her breath. She'd forgotten there would be clothes on the hangers, the kind of clothes she didn't wear any more, the full skirts and wide belts and fitted tops that she'd liked so much when Lilou had first introduced her to them, telling her that her black jeans and T-shirt look was far too limiting, no matter how well it suited her. She'd embraced a palette of strong colours in France and enjoyed wearing them – her tops were always blocks of red or green or blue and her skirts delicately patterned to pick up those shades. She remembered not wanting to pack them for her return to Dublin. She remembered thinking there was no joy in her life any more. But somehow she'd forgotten that she'd left them here on the rails.

She took out one of the skirts and held it to her. She probably wouldn't fit into it now, she thought, remembering one of the occasions she'd worn it, a dinner in Paris to celebrate Lilou's promotion. She put it back in the wardrobe and closed the door. Then she began placing her Dublin clothes, the T-shirts and jeans she'd reverted to on her return to the city, in the tall chest of drawers at the end of the bed. She noted that there were still scented sachets in the drawers, and that despite the fact she hadn't been here in so long, the house itself didn't smell musty or uncared for.

In fairness, Madame Gasquet was very good about coming in and checking on it every week. Rua knew that it was partly because the other woman was interested in buying it. She'd told Rua as much on the day she'd left France, saying that she hoped to have first refusal in the event of a sale. Rua had given the thought of selling serious consideration, but she knew how hard it was to offload country houses – despite the popularity of English speakers moving to France or Spain or anywhere else, there were more remote houses than people willing to buy them. She'd told Laure Gasquet that she hoped to come back for the summers at least, although that hadn't happened. Now she wondered if her neighbour was still interested in the house. Although she wasn't at all sure that she was ready to sell.

Her phone pinged.

I heard you'd gone to France. I hope everything is OK. Bx

She stared at the message, unsure of what to say, or indeed if she should say anything at all. How had Bethany discovered she was away? Had she been looking for her? Asking about her? And if so, what did that mean? And if she replied? Would that mean something too? Bethany would have seen that she'd looked at the text. She couldn't ignore it. She didn't want to ignore it.

All is good, thanks. Rx

Bethany reacted to Rua's message with a pink heart.
Rua felt her own heart beat faster.

Ailie sent Flavia a photo of the view from her room, which overlooked the main square.

Ooh fab 😍

Flavia's reply was so swift that Ailie assumed her daughter must have already been scrolling through her phone. Then a photo appeared. It was a selfie of Flavia, Marco, Beatrice and some other young people Ailie didn't recognise.

Out sampling the best Trieste has to offer. Loving my life. Fx

Glad for you. About to go to bed. Am old woman without your youthful stamina.

Ailie added some laughing emojis.
Flavia sent a hug in return.
Ailie put her phone on the bedside table and sat on the edge of the bed. She was more tired than she'd expected, and not only from the travelling. She'd received an email from the *avvocato* while having coffee with Rua in Dublin airport, telling her that he was drawing up the final contracts regarding the business. She would soon be a director of Farfalle. On reading the email, she felt the weight of the last few months slide from her shoulders. Mostly she was

thankful that things had worked out, but she was also grateful that Giorgio had been thinking of her future and looking after her and Flavia. She wished he'd confided in her. Yet he had always liked to present her with solutions to problems that she hadn't known existed, problems he'd kept from her because he didn't want to worry her. And it was typical of him to want to leave her without worries for the future because he'd sorted it all.

'I miss you,' she murmured, opening the photo app on her phone and scrolling to one of her favourite pictures of him, standing on the beach at Brittas, looking strong and handsome and healthy. 'I miss everything about you, even the arguments. Because they were a part of us. The quiet moments, the loud moments, the disagreements, the making up. It made us who we were. And we were good together.'

She closed the app and got into bed.

She hadn't expected to, but for the first time since Giorgio's death, she fell asleep straight away.

Like Ailie, Sybil had also received messages on her phone.

> How's France? Is the house nice? Saw Burt today with his new lady friend. She's not in as good nick as you even if she is twenty years younger. Tx
>
> Hope you had a pleasant journey today. Send pix of the house. You know I like seeing different places. Fx
>
> Mum says you've gone to France. You're totally living your best life these days. A role model for me when I'm older for sure. Cx

Claire had also attached a photo of Tadgh and Sorcha in a paddling pool in the back garden.

I'm not sure I'm a great role model. But I'm very glad you think so. Sx

The house is gorgeous. France isn't exactly what I expected but we had the most fantastic meal tonight so that's ticked the cuisine box even if there are other food stories to tell. Will FaceTime you tomorrow and bring you on a tour of the town. Off to bed now. Why are you not asleep? It's the middle of the night in Perth. Sx

France is fantastique. House cute. Glad that Burt has his lady friend, honestly. Tho thanks for implying she's not as attractive as me! Sx

Late night chatting to Jake then couldn't sleep. Was looking at our cruise photos. We do look well in them. Fx

Fergus was the only one who'd sent a further message. Sybil wondered what it would have been like to come to France with him.

Enjoyable, she thought, as she reacted to his message with a smile.

Something she might suggest when she saw him again?

Chapter 32

Rua woke the next morning to a narrow shaft of sunlight sliding its way through the pretty cretonne curtains on her bedroom window. She knew by the light that it was early, and when she rolled over to look at the time on her phone, she saw that it was a little after six. She lay gazing up at the ceiling and let her mind drift. She realised, somewhat to her surprise, that despite waking early, she'd had a solid seven hours' sleep, something she couldn't remember happening for years. And now she was wide awake, so she pushed away the light duvet and got out of bed. Opening the curtains, she saw the rosy pinks and golds of the rising sun illuminate the stone buildings of Les Hauts Champs. She put on a cotton T-shirt and leggings and slid her feet into her trainers. Then she cleaned her teeth and brushed her hair before tiptoeing down the stairs, taking a hat from the coat stand and letting herself out the front door.

The air wasn't yet warm, but nor was it cold. She opened the iron gate that led to the street and walked briskly to the square, which she crossed in front of the Mairie, the town hall, where the French flag fluttered in the gentle breeze. She followed the road past Amelie's restaurant towards Benoit St Jacques's equestrian centre a couple of kilometres outside the town. Lilou had enjoyed horse riding, but it was something Rua had never quite got to grips with, even though Benoit had always put her on the most placid of his mounts and allowed her to trot gently around his field while her wife galloped into the distance.

Thirty minutes later, she'd arrived in front of the centre. She could hear the gentle whinnying of the horses, and Benoit's calming voice as he talked to each of them. She'd always liked Benoit, a gruff man in his fifties, who had over twenty years of competitive show-jumping behind him and who now trained young people in the sport. She walked into the yard and saw him moving bales of hay.

'*Bonjour*, Benoit,' she said.

His face broke into a smile as he saw her, and he enveloped her in a bear hug.

'Rua, *ma petite*. It's good to see you again.'

'Good to be here,' she said.

'You've returned?'

'Only for a visit.'

'You are well? And Brontë? She is well?'

Brontë had ridden horses with Benoit too. She'd been considerably better (and braver) than Rua.

'Very well,' she told him.

'You are here to ride?'

'It's been a long time,' she said. 'So I'm more here to sit on a horse that knows what it's doing.'

'*Bien*.' He nodded. 'You have brought your riding hat?'

'Always wear a hat,' she said, swinging it from her fingers.

'Come on,' he said. 'I will put you on Maisie. She is so gentle you'll hardly know you are moving at all.'

'Thanks.' She smiled as he went to one of the stalls and opened the door. The grey Percheron he led to her was bigger than she'd expected, but she could sense that it was placid and docile. Benoit gave her a leg-up into the saddle, and as Rua settled into position, she remembered the feel of the animal beneath her and the instructions both Benoit and Lilou had drummed into her.

'A gentle squeeze is all you need,' he reminded her. 'She will bring you around.'

'Thank you,' said Rua.

She urged Maisie forward and the horse reacted immediately, ambling towards the gate that led into the large field. As she gained confidence, Rua allowed her to walk a little faster, and eventually to break into a gentle trot. The sun was higher in the sky now and warm on her shoulders, and even at the pace she was moving, she felt exhilarated. She remembered all the times she'd trotted behind Lilou, who inevitably grew impatient with her and told her to keep with her baby walking while she cantered and then galloped away. She'd admired Lilou's easy ability to be one with the horse, something she'd never quite mastered herself.

She circled the field a number of times, allowing her thoughts to drift and allowing herself to feel happy. It occurred to her, as she passed the gate for the third time, that allowing herself to feel happy wasn't something she'd done a lot of over the past few years. Every time happiness had crept up on her, she'd damped it down, guilty at the emotion when she was without the one person who had made her life complete, angry at herself for forgetting, even for a second, that Lilou's life had been cut tragically short. Of course she hadn't tried to be unhappy. She'd even insisted to Brontë that they do things that were fun. But beneath it all was a feeling of disrespect that she should be enjoying herself without her late wife.

I wish you were here, she thought now. I wish I was watching you in the distance, envious of your ability to control your horse while I never quite managed to have a bond with mine. But then you were born to it. And even if I, like you, grew up in a small town, I was always trying to get away and I never wanted to get involved in rural pursuits.

She allowed Maisie to move into a slow canter. This was the fastest she'd ever gone and the fastest she'd ever wanted to go. Galloping would never be her thing. But she was enjoying herself now, and while she didn't feel completely at one with the horse, nor did she feel like a total stranger on its back.

'You have done well,' said Benoit, when she eventually brought Maisie in a slow amble back to the yard. 'You reminded me of Lilou.'

'Don't be silly,' she said. 'I would never remind anyone of Lilou.'

'You two were so alike,' said Benoit. 'Not to look at, perhaps, but in your attitude. But on the horse you were nervous and that made you different. Today, you were not. You were free.'

'You think.' Rua patted Maisie's neck and the horse whinnied gently. 'It was easy not to be nervous on this one. You're right. She's a pet.'

'You are not here to stay?' Benoit repeated his question of earlier.

'No.' She shook her head. 'My life is in Ireland now. But I needed to come back. To remember.'

'I understand,' he said.

'I'll probably sell the house,' she told him. 'It's not that I want to cut my ties with France completely, but I can come back whenever I like for a holiday.'

'There's someone for you in Ireland?' His grey eyes gave her a shrewd look.

'Perhaps,' she said. 'It's something I need to work out.'

'Choose happiness,' said Benoit. 'That's the most important thing.'

'I have happy memories,' Rua told him.

'Happy memories are good, but you also need a happy life,' he said. 'A happy future. I know it's presumptuous to say that it is what Lilou would want, but it is, you know.'

'Thank you.' She leaned towards him and gave him an impulsive kiss on the cheek. 'You were always Lilou's favourite person in Les Hauts Champs.'

'And she was mine,' he said. 'Take care of yourself, Rua. Don't forget us.'

'I won't,' she promised.

She took out her phone to pay him for the ride, but he waved it away and told her it was a gift.

'I didn't come here to guilt you into giving me a free hour on your horse,' she said.

'But it is my pleasure to give it to you,' he said. 'I will be insulted if you insist on paying.'

'In that case, *merci beaucoup*,' she said. 'And . . . well, not *adieu*, Benoit. I'll be back. *À bientôt*.'

'*À bientôt*,' he said, and waved as she walked out of the yard towards the road back to town.

It was the squeak of the front gate that woke Sybil. She blinked a couple of times and then got up from the bed and edged back the curtain. She saw Rua walking briskly down the road, swinging a black riding hat in her hand, her hair glinting copper and red in the light of the rising sun. She hadn't known that Rua was a horsewoman. But she applauded her for getting up early to go for a ride.

Wide awake herself now, she tiptoed downstairs so as not to wake Ailie, then made herself a cup of tea. She scrolled through her phone as she drank it, glancing at the news headlines but not caring about anything other than that she was happy to be away with the women she'd grown so close to. When she finished the tea, she decided to go for a walk herself. She didn't bother with a shower, reckoning she could have one when she returned, but splashed her face with cold water and dressed, like Rua, in a T-shirt and leggings.

She let herself out of the house and walked in the opposite direction to the younger woman, across the square towards the church. There was a certain tranquillity about being alone in the sleepy town. The faint scent of grasses and wild flowers hung in the air, and as the sun rose higher in the sky, it was beginning to warm. Sybil felt a deep sense of well-being and contentment as she pushed open the gate to the churchyard in order to indulge in her habit of studying the gravestones. Theo had laughed at her the first time she confided in him that it was something she liked to do, and then it had become something they enjoyed doing together. Imagining those past lives, wondering about the people left behind, honouring them by saying their names aloud.

The majority of the graves in the churchyard were neatly tended and told the stories of families that had lived in the area for over a hundred years. There were a surprising number of younger people buried there, and an equally surprising number of very old inhabitants. Sybil walked between the graves and wondered what it had been like in Les Hauts Champs a century ago; if it had been a more bustling town than it was now, or if it had always been a quiet rural outpost.

She gained some further insight later, after she'd walked a kilometre or so down a country road that led nowhere in particular, before looping back to the square. She'd noticed the monument earlier but hadn't stopped at it. This time she did, aware that there was a fresh wreath beneath it. There were about thirty names inscribed on the granite, and remembering the French she'd learned at school, she was able to read that they had all been executed here, in the town, during the Second World War. She saw that all of the names were male, and that the youngest was seventeen while the oldest was forty-two. She read each name, saying it under her breath, and imagined the terror that must have taken hold of the town as the young men were rounded up and shot in front of the church. The monument said that they were patriots. Sybil assumed they must have been in the resistance and had been executed by the occupying forces to make an example of them. Some names she recognised from the graveyard. Hector Lamartine had family buried there, as did Georges Auger and Simon Beaumont. Hector had been twenty-one when he died. Georges nineteen. Simon thirty-five.

Sybil had grown up with the knowledge of Second World War memorabilia and mentions on the news and in Hollywood movies, but to her it had been an event that had happened long ago. And yet, she realised, the war had ended less than twenty years before she was born. When she looked at her own life now, twenty years seemed like yesterday.

What is wrong with us as a species that we inflict so much pain and suffering on each other? she wondered. When we all only have one life to live, why would we make it hard on each other? Why would we promote hate instead of love? And it still goes on, she thought. Powerful men and men who wanted to be powerful, to take land that wasn't theirs, destroying lives for no good reason.

Conscious that she was an hour ahead of him in France, Sybil didn't try to FaceTime Fergus for the promised stroll around the town, but she took photos of the memorial to send him later. Then she walked back to the house, a little shaken by the violence that had taken place over eighty years in the past, and resolving to live her own life better, to be kinder, to love more and criticise less in the present.

Ailie woke from the deepest sleep she'd had in months. She recalled Flavia once telling her that sleep was never dreamless, but she remembered nothing since closing her eyes the night before.

She got out of bed and looked out of the window. Her room overlooked the fields at the back of the house, and in the distance she could see a tractor moving slowly across the brown earth. She opened the window and heard birdsong over the engine of the tractor, while the balmy morning air wafted into the bedroom. She opened her door and walked quietly down the stairs, not wanting to wake Rua or Sybil if they were still sleeping.

There was no sign in the kitchen that either of them was up – no breakfast things on the table, or sounds from the living room or garden. She took some fruit from the bowl and a yogurt from the fridge, then put the kettle on for a cup of coffee. That was when she noticed the mug on the draining board. She wondered if one of the others had left it there earlier, but she continued to move as quietly as she could around the kitchen.

She brought her coffee and fruit to the outside table, from where she had a view of both the fields and the road. The farmer was continuing his ploughing while a couple of people walked past the cottage, chatting animatedly.

She relaxed into the chair, casually observing the little that was going on around her. And then she felt a sense of déjà vu, of having been here before. She knew she hadn't, and yet the feeling was so strong that she looked around her to reassure herself that she was in France, a country she hadn't visited since her honeymoon with Josh. They'd gone to Provence. It had been fun, but the cracks were already beginning to show even then.

It came to her in a sudden rush of recollection. Not France, Wexford. A stone cottage. A patio garden. A weekend Airbnb with Giorgio. Sitting outside like this. Enjoying the sunshine, although early afternoon rather than morning. The sound of a tractor in the distance. An occasional burst of laughter from people walking past the cottage. And then the unexpected dark clouds that had scudded across the sky and unleashed a downpour upon them so that they leaped up from the chairs and held the cushions over their heads as they rushed inside again, laughing and shrieking and Ailie saying this was what was wrong with holidaying in Ireland, the weather was so undependable, and Giorgio saying that this was exactly what was right about Ireland because you made the most out of every opportunity; and then he said, 'Let's make the most of this one,' and they were hurrying into the cute little bedroom at the back of the house and their lovemaking had been passionate and exuberant and she'd felt loved and wanted, and known right there and then that Giorgio was the only man she'd ever need.

How could I have forgotten? she wondered, sitting at the bistro table looking out over the street but her mind back on the Irish east coast. How could I have forgotten that day? How could I have forgotten how much I loved him? How could I have gone to Italy without him, and spoken to his family without him, and come here with two women I hardly know without him? How can I keep living without him? What has the last nine months been about? Trying to erase him from my memory? From my life?

She realised that she was crying, hot tears streaming down her face and her shoulders shaking as she suddenly felt the enormity of being on her own. How could she not have fallen apart without the man who'd changed her life forever? And who, even in death, was still changing it? What was wrong with her? Was she an emotional wasteland? Was she incapable of grief, of sorrow, of mourning someone she'd loved so very much.

She looked up at the sound of the gate opening and scrubbed at her eyes as she saw Sybil walking towards her.

'Ailie.' The older woman was beside her, putting her hand on her shoulder. 'Are you all right?'

'I'm fine.' She sniffed and wiped her eyes again. 'I was just . . . Giorgio . . .'

'It's OK,' said Sybil. 'It's not even a year since you lost him. Of course you're crying.'

'I felt guilty,' confessed Ailie. 'That I was living and doing things without him. That I was feeling happy.'

'I understand,' said Sybil.

'I went to Italy. I met his family. All the time we lived together I never met his family, and then, when he's dead, I do. And I kind of held my own with them.'

'You absolutely did,' agreed Sybil.

'And now I'm here without him.' Ailie wiped her eyes. 'Sitting in the sun feeling content without him.'

'It's hard,' said Sybil. 'I know that.'

'I try not to cry.' Ailie sniffed. 'Flavia gets annoyed at me for not crying enough.'

'We cry when it matters to us,' said Sybil. 'If you want to cry now, do. I'll stay here or leave you in peace. Whatever you want.'

'I think I'm cried out,' said Ailie.

'Would you like some tea?' asked Sybil.

'Tea would be perfect, thanks.'

Ailie stayed sitting at the table while Sybil went inside. A few minutes later, she returned with a ceramic pot and two mugs, along with some milk.

'I always feel bad about rummaging around in someone else's kitchen,' she said as she poured the tea.

'Me too.' Ailie took a sip from her mug and gave Sybil a watery smile. 'Sorry,' she said.

'Don't be,' said Sybil. 'I still cry for Theo sometimes.'

'You do?'

'If I'm somewhere I know he'd like. Or revisiting somewhere we went together. It's not the intense grief of the first year, but a sadness that the time we had together is over.'

Ailie nodded.

'As long as we remember them, they're never really gone,' Sybil added. 'I don't believe in an afterlife or anything, but I do believe in holding the memory.'

'Is that what's stopping you having a relationship with someone else?' asked Ailie. 'Holding Theo's memory?'

'Not at all,' replied Sybil. 'Although I could never love anyone the way I loved Theo. We built a whole life together and it was perfect. But I was thinking last night that it might be nice to come to France with Fergus. I have to work out in my own mind what I want. And what he wants too. It's easy when you're very young and you're ready to embark on a journey together. But now I'm a seasoned traveller, I have my quirky ways. I have to think of how I want to adapt.'

'You'll figure it out,' said Ailie.

'Fingers crossed.'

Ailie reached out and held her hand.

'Love hurts,' she said after a while.

'That's why there are so many songs about it.' Sybil sighed. 'You lose someone, you also lose the person you were when you were with them. The dreams you had when you were with them. It's like finishing one book and becoming the sequel to the story.'

'My sequel is like a prologue. Going back to who I was before I met Giorgio. Independent. Strong. I kind of had to be after my divorce, amicable and all though it was. And not that I wasn't strong after I met Giorgio, but I could fall back on him, you know. And now there's no one to fall back on and I'm trying to get used to that again. But there's a whole heap of me that wants to be able to lean my head on his shoulder and let him take care of me. I miss being looked after.'

Sybil squeezed her hand.

They sat together in companionable silence until Rua came home.

'Are you guys OK?' she asked as she sat down beside them. 'I seem to be interrupting something deep and profound here.'

'We're contemplating life,' said Sybil. 'Remembering our husbands. Thinking of the present. Maybe even contemplating our changing futures.'

'I was doing that myself,' Rua said. 'I went to an equestrian centre outside the town, took a horse for a ride.'

'I didn't know you could ride,' said Ailie.

'Lilou and I used to quite a lot when we lived here,' said Rua. 'Brontë too. We'd go out on Sunday mornings. It was excellent for clearing the head.'

'And did it clear your head today?' asked Sybil.

'It's the first time I've been on a horse since she died,' said Rua. 'I wasn't sure I wanted to do it. But it was exhilarating. And yes, it did clear my head.'

'So do you know what you want to do about the house?' asked Ailie.

'I think so.'

The two women looked at her enquiringly.

'Bethany texted,' said Rua. 'Asking how I was. I'm not sure where this might lead, but I do know that she matters to me. There was a real connection between us. Yet whether it works with Bethany or if I eventually meet someone else, I know that as long as I have Les Hauts Champs, I'll always think that I'm connected to Lilou too. I don't want to let her go. And yet . . .'

'And yet?' Sybil raised an eyebrow.

'I can't hold on to her either,' said Rua. 'At least, not by keeping the house. She'll always be in my heart, but I'm not sure I need her to manifest herself in electricity bills and water bills and council taxes for somewhere I'm not going to live any more. And I'm not,' she added. 'Les Hauts Champs is a part of my life that's over. It was idyllic while it lasted, but it's in the past.'

Sybil nodded. 'Moving on doesn't mean forgetting Lilou,' she told Rua. 'It means holding her in a different place.'

'Sybil's been dispensing grief counselling all morning,' Ailie said. 'She had to comfort me earlier.'

'Oh. Are you OK?' asked Rua.

'I'm fine. Doing something the same as you,' Ailie said. 'Moving Giorgio to a different part of my heart. Not that there's anyone likely to occupy the rest of it.'

'You two seem very sure about that,' said Rua. 'But you have Fergus, Sybil. And you're still a young woman, Ailie.'

'Oh, bless you for saying I'm young.' Ailie smiled. 'At best – at very best – I'm middle-aged.'

'Nonsense,' said Sybil. 'You're young enough to have someone else in your life if you want.'

'Thing is,' Ailie looked at her thoughtfully, 'you were right. We do become sequels in our own story. And I'm sticking to this part of me for a while. The one that does it on her own.'

'I was the one who did it all on her own too,' said Rua. 'I stayed home. Worked from home. Didn't socialise – at least, whatever socialising I did was very superficial. I only ever met people in groups. I didn't want to get close to anyone ever again. I didn't expect to. Yet somehow Bethany came into my life and changed how I wanted to live, and no matter what, I'll always be grateful for that.'

'Did you reply to her text?' asked Sybil.

'I said I was doing OK,' said Rua.

'That's all?' Ailie looked disappointed.

'She reacted with a heart.'

'Oh, Rua. That's promising!'

'I thought I'd messed it all up, but maybe I haven't,' said Rua. 'I'll call her later, and who knows, it may be another start for us. But right now, I'm just happy I came here with you guys and happy to be in this house again and to know that there was lots and lots of love here. And that I can love and be loved again. I wouldn't have done it without you.'

'So basically, the Merry Widows group is three women who are happy with where they are in the present,' said Ailie. 'It might not be perfect, but we're OK.'

'And we have the power to shape our own futures,' Sybil said. 'To write our own sequels. We have each other. We have people we love. We have new challenges. We keep going.'

Ailie and Rua nodded slowly.

Sybil went into the house and returned with a bottle.

'I realise that this is like bringing sand to the Sahara,' she said as she placed the Veuve Clicquot on the table in front of them. 'I saw it in the airport shop and thought there might be an appropriate moment.'

'Sybil! It's nine o'clock in the morning,' gasped Ailie. 'It was bad enough quaffing Aperol spritz before noon in Trieste, but nine in the morning is hardly an appropriate moment for champagne.'

'As the inimitable Oscar Wilde once said, "Only the unimaginative can fail to find a reason for drinking champagne."' Sybil began to twist the wire. 'And we are not unimaginative, ladies. We are the Merry Widows, and we can start the morning with bubbles if we choose.'

Rua laughed. 'I have some pretty glasses inside,' she said. She got up and returned with three elegant wine flutes. 'But please give me a minute before you open the bottle, Sybil. I smell of horse and I need to change.'

'You're grand the way you are,' said Sybil.

'Seriously,' Rua said. 'I'll only be five minutes.'

Sybil and Ailie chatted while they waited for Rua. When she returned, they both gasped.

'You look amazing!' cried Ailie. 'Almost a different person. You're fabulous.'

'Stunning,' agreed Sybil. 'Like you're meant to be here.'

'Well, only for a few days.' Rua grinned and then twirled around. She was wearing the bright red top from her wardrobe along with the palest of pink skirts dotted with multicoloured flowers, which still fitted her perfectly. Her hair, falling in a cloud of red-gold curls to her shoulders, shone in the morning sunlight.

'I do love that sound,' she said as Sybil popped the cork and filled the glasses.

'*Sláinte*,' said Sybil. 'Your good health, ladies.'

'*Alla nostra*. To us.' Ailie raised her glass.

'*À la vie*,' said Rua. 'To life.'

They clinked their glasses together, and then Rua noticed Madame Gasquet standing at the wall, looking into the garden.

'Would you like to join us?' she asked.

'Champagne?' The Frenchwoman looked at her in astonishment. 'In the morning?'

'Yes.'

'Well, why not?' Laure Gasquet shrugged cheerfully, then opened the gate. Rua fetched another glass and handed it to her. A short time later, Amelie, the owner of the restaurant, stopped in front of the house too.

'Champagne?' she asked.

'Last drop.' Rua held up the bottle. 'Join us?'

'*Mais oui*. It's champagne after all.'

They took videos. Ailie sent one to Flavia, who pointed out that Ailie herself would have freaked if she'd sent her a reel knocking back champagne for breakfast, but also saying that she was glad she was having a good time and perhaps she might come to Italy again soon. Ailie responded by FaceTiming her and telling her how much she loved her, and Flavia, unable to contain her laughter, had to point out that she was actually working, but that she'd call her later in the day.

Rua sent her video to Bethany, adding that she was going to put the house up for sale later that day and that it had been a joy to hear from her and maybe they could talk later. She also sent the video to Brontë, who wanted to know if she was needed for an intervention because she had never known Rua to drink alcohol in the morning, not even at Christmas. She added that her mother looked awesomely beautiful. And Rua replied that it was a one-off kind of thing but they were having a happy moment. To which Brontë replied with a string of smiling emojis.

Sybil sent her video to Tansy, saying that she was having

a great time even if she hadn't met any sexy French men, only kind and generous French women. Tansy responded by saying that as long as Sybil was happy that was the main thing, but that Liam Walsh, a colleague of Colin's, had finalised his divorce and was back on the market, and that if she was interested, Tansy would organise a dinner party. Sybil laughed but didn't reply. Instead she forwarded her video to Fergus and told him that this was the level of catering she expected when she visited people's houses. He replied that he was pretty sure that was something he could arrange, and she said she looked forward to it.

Afterwards, when Amelie and Madame Gasquet left, Sybil made more tea and the three women sat in the sun and agreed that here and now, they were very happy to be together and very happy too with how the sequels to their lives were unfolding, no matter how many twists and turns the plot might take.

And they agreed that they were looking forward to the future, and whoever they might be then. Because the future was an unwritten book.

Acknowledgements

Possibly the hardest part of writing a novel is the acknowledgements. There are so many people who are either deeply or peripherally involved in turning the spark of an idea into an actual book on a shelf that it's impossible to name them all. So a big thank you to everyone who has been part of *Secrets Between Friends* and has offered words of encouragement along the way.

As always, special thanks to my amazing editor, Marion Donaldson, who always sees what I'm trying to achieve and helps me get there with patience and understanding. Thanks also to Hannah for her support to both of us.

To my agent, Isobel Dixon, who seamlessly combines creativity with commerce so that I can concentrate on being my best writing self, I'm lucky to have you in my corner.

To the Headline and Hachette teams who look after my books with such care and continue to get them onto the shelves, both physical and digital, thank you. And to the translators of my novels who bring my characters to so many people in so many languages, I appreciate everything you do.

Thanks also to my copyeditor, Jane Selley, whose eagle eye spots the not-so-deliberate mistakes every time and who asks the simple questions that leave me staring into space while pondering punctuation and prose.

To Colm, my husband, who has lived through every book with me and has helped me treat triumph and disaster just the same with champagne and chocolates, thank you for everything.

As always, my extended family is the bedrock of my support and I wouldn't have had a career as an author without them. Special thanks to Oisin for the fun social media and to Maureen for giving the thumbs up every time. Also to Hugh who is spreading the word in Germany and to David, James, Fiona and Suzanne for their support in Northern Ireland.

To the booksellers and the librarians who are so supportive of my books but, more importantly, who spread the joy of reading among the community, a million thanks. You are all heroes!

I would be nothing without my wonderful, fabulous readers who support me so much by buying my books and coming to meet me at events. It's always an honour to hear from you and to meet you. Thank you from the bottom of my heart. I do hope you enjoy *Secrets Between Friends*.

RAISING READERS
Books Build Bright Futures

Dear Reader,

We'd love your attention for one more page to tell you about the crisis in children's reading, and what we can all do.

Studies have shown that reading for fun is the **single biggest predictor of a child's future life chances** – more than family circumstance, parents' educational background or income. It improves academic results, mental health, wealth, communication skills, ambition and happiness.[1]

The number of children reading for fun is in rapid decline. Young people have a lot of competition for their time. In 2024, 1 in 10 children and young people in the UK aged 5 to 18 did not own a single book at home.[2]

Hachette works extensively with schools, libraries and literacy charities, but here are some ways we can all raise more readers:

- Reading to children for just 10 minutes a day makes a difference
- Don't give up if children aren't regular readers – there will be books for them!
- Visit bookshops and libraries to get recommendations
- Encourage them to listen to audiobooks
- Support school libraries
- Give books as gifts

There's a lot more information about how to encourage children to read on our website: **www.RaisingReaders.co.uk**

Thank you for reading.

hachette UK

---

[1] OECD, '21st-Century Readers: Developing Literacy Skills in a Digital World', 2021, https://www.oecd.org/en/publications/21st-century-readers_a83d84cb-en.html

[2] National Literacy Trust, 'Book Ownership in 2024', November 2024, https://literacytrust.org.uk/research-services/research-reports/book-ownership-in-2024